"**Magical.**" —*VANITY FAIR*

"**Shimmering**. . . . A wonderful comic satire." —*DENVER POST*

"Funny and poignant. . . . A **refreshing** antidote to all the
negativity currently surrounding Mexico." —*DALLAS MORNING NEWS*

"A **spirited** and enjoyable fable." —*SAN FRANCISCO CHRONICLE*

"A surprising, inventive, and **very funny** novel." —*LIBRARY JOURNAL*

"**Sweet** but serious . . . deliciously composed." —*CHICAGO TRIBUNE*

"Thoroughly **enjoyable.**" —*BOOKPAGE*

Acclaim for Luis Alberto Urrea's

Into the Beautiful North

"A fast-moving and often funny tale.... Urrea captures the affections and conflicts of his Mexican-American heritage. He has produced a powerful narrative and a vivid picture of life in both countries.... With a poet's grace and a storyteller's drive, Urrea tells us about the many ways one man can love two countries."
—Clarke Crutchfield, *Richmond Times-Dispatch*

"Quest novels announce their purpose in a straightforward manner: Colorful, memorable characters prepare for and embark on a journey of immense significance, shot through with peril. They're after the Golden Fleece or the Beast Glatisant. They're off to find the Holy Grail or destroy the Ring of Sauron or find their way back to Kansas, and the reader gets to come along too. *Into the Beautiful North* is just such a novel.... Among the many pleasures of the novel is its big-hearted view of the United States as a foreign country."
—Jincy Willett, *San Diego Union-Tribune*

"No great adventure is told without great characters, and Urrea certainly knows how to create them.... For Nayeli, joy and sadness are intermingled in her journey. So it will be for readers of this uplifting novel.... That Urrea has turned a usually disturbing subject into a book that keeps a smile on your face is a tribute to his storytelling."
—Marta Barber, *Miami Herald*

"Deliciously composed.... Urrea writes in a sweet but serious style."
—Alan Cheuse, *Chicago Tribune*

"A fantastical tale.... In his wonderful comic satire, Urrea stands the cowboy classic *The Magnificent Seven* on its head.... He uses a breathtaking Mexican magical realism to construct a shimmering portrait of the United States."　　　—Dylan Foley, *Denver Post*

"With self-awareness and irony, *Into the Beautiful North* acknowledges its debt to the idealistic quest narrative and the tragic migration story.... There are misfortunes, but this is a comedy, and the suspense, adventure, and resolved hardships are in the service of an exuberant escape and a happy ending. The desperate undocumented immigrants who try to cross for a better life are at the margins of a *bildungsroman*. Urrea simultaneously explicates the seriousness of Mexican-U.S. immigration while drolly narrating a *Wizard of Oz*–like circular fairy tale."　　　—Kati Nolfi, Bookslut.com

"Brightly written, humorous, and insightful."
　　　—Thomas Frisbie, *Chicago Sun-Times*

"Riotously funny.... This wonderfully entertaining novel is starkly different from the heroic magical realism of Urrea's last novel, *The Hummingbird's Daughter*, set one hundred years ago. *Into the Beautiful North* is a picaresque contemporary jape. Imagine John Nichols's *The Milagro Beanfield War*, updated and set in Old rather than New Mexico. *Into the Beautiful North*'s rich cavalcade of infatuating characters is set in motion by Nayeli, a spirited nineteen-year-old.... One of the recurring pleasures in the book is experiencing North American pop culture refracted through an outsider's sensibilities.... In the end, Nayeli's scheme, for better and for worse, doesn't work out the way she envisioned. Not that it matters. The pleasures of *Into the Beautiful North* lie in the journey—and the journeyers."
　　　—David Hiltbrand, *Philadelphia Inquirer*

Other Books by Luis Alberto Urrea

Fiction

The Hummingbird's Daughter

In Search of Snow

Six Kinds of Sky

Nonfiction

The Devil's Highway: A True Story

Across the Wire: Life and Hard Times on the Mexican Border

*By the Lake of Sleeping Children: The Secret Life
of the Mexican Border*

Nobody's Son

Wandering Time

Poetry

The Fever of Being

Ghost Sickness

Vatos

Into the Beautiful North

a novel

Luis Alberto Urrea

BACK BAY BOOKS

LITTLE, BROWN AND COMPANY

New York   Boston   London

Back Bay Books / Little, Brown and Company
Hachette Book Group
1290 Avenue of the Americas, New York, NY 10104
littlebrown.com

Originally published in hardcover by Little, Brown and Company, May 2009
First Back Bay paperback edition, June 2010

Back Bay Books is an imprint of Little, Brown and Company. The Back Bay
Books name and logo are trademarks of Hachette Book Group, Inc.

The characters and events in this book are fictitious. Any similarity to real
persons, living or dead, is coincidental and not intended by the author.

The publisher is not responsible for websites (or their content)
that are not owned by the publisher.

Library of Congress Cataloging-in-Publication Data
Urrea, Luis Alberto.
    Into the beautiful North: a novel / Luis Alberto Urrea. — 1st ed.
        p. cm.
    ISBN 978-0-316-02527-0 (hc) / 978-0-316-02526-3 (pb)
    1. Young women — Mexico — Fiction.   2. City and town life — Mexico — Fiction.
3. Brigands and robbers — Mexico — Fiction.   4. Illegal aliens — United States —
Fiction.   5. Return migration — Mexico — Fiction.   6. Mexico — Emigration
and immigration — Fiction.   I. Title.
    PS3571.R74I56 2009
    813'.54 — dc22   2008039962

17

LSC-C

Printed in the United States of America

for Megan

O friends, I have come searching for you,
I crossed over flowering fields,
And here, at last, I've found you.
Rejoice.
Tell me your stories.
O friends, I am here.

—Xayacamach of Tizatlán

Sur

Chapter One

———————

The bandidos came to the village at the worst possible time. Of course, everyone in Mexico would agree that there is no particularly good time for bad men to come to town. But Tres Camarones was unguarded on that late summer's day when so many things had already changed. And everything that remained was about to change forever.

Nobody in the village liked change. It had taken great civic upheaval to bring electricity to Tres Camarones, for example. Until 1936, ice came in big trucks, and fathers took their sons to observe it when it slid down the ramps in great clear blocks. It took the visionary mayor, García-García the First, to see the potential in electrical power, and he had lobbied for two years to have the wires strung from far Villaunión. Still, there were holdouts a good decade after Tres Camarones had begun to glow with yellow light. Such stalwarts relied on candles, kerosene lamps, and small bonfires in the street. These blazes, though festive, blocked the scant traffic and the trucks bearing beer and sides of beef, and García-García had to resort to the apocalyptic stratagem of banning street fires entirely. Denounced as an Antichrist, he was promptly defeated in the next election. Later, he was reelected: even if his policies had been too modernizing for some, the residents of Tres Camarones realized that a new mayor meant change, and change was the last thing they wanted. Progress might be inevitable, but there was no reason they should knuckle under without a fight.

True, the occasional hurricane devastated the low-lying forest and semitropical jungles and reformed the beaches. Often, parts of the town were washed away or carried out to sea. But the interior clock of evolution in Tres Camarones was set only to these cataclysms of nature.

And then, the peso dropped in value. Suddenly there was no work. All the shrimp were shipped north, tortillas became too expensive to eat, and people started to go hungry. *We told you change was bad,* the old-timers croaked.

Nobody had heard of the term *immigration.* Migration, to them, was when the tuna and the whales cruised up the coast, or when Guacamaya parrots flew up from the south. Traditionalists voted to revoke electricity, but it was far too late for that. No woman in town would give up her refrigerator, her electric fan, or her electric iron. So the men started to go to *el norte.* Nobody knew what to say. Nobody knew what to do. The modern era had somehow passed Tres Camarones by, but this new storm had found a way to siphon its men away, out of their beds and into the next century, into a land far away.

The bandidos came with the sunrise, rolling down the same eastern road that had once brought the ice trucks. There were two of them. They had to drive south from Mazatlán, which was at least an hour and forty minutes away, then creak off the highway and take the cutoff toward the coast. Explosions of parrots, butterflies, and hummingbirds parted before them. They didn't notice.

One of them was an agent of the Policía Estatal, the dreaded Sinaloa State Police. He earned $150 a month as a cop. The drug cartel in the north of the state paid him $2,500 a month as an advisory fee. He got a $15,000 bonus each Christmas.

The other was a bottom-level narco who, nevertheless, was the state cop's boss. What he needed to really get ahead in his game was a territory to call his own, but the cartel had the state sewn up, and there was no room for him in Baja California, Sonora, or Chihuahua. He had hit the drug gangster's glass ceiling and it irked him, because he looked so damned good. The boys called him Scarface. He liked that. In spite of the awful heat and soggy air of the coastal swamplands, he wore a white sport jacket and regarded the world through mirrored sunglasses, sucking on a cinnamon toothpick.

Neither of the two bandidos enjoyed this bucolic trip to the bottomlands. But the one in the jacket had gotten a cell phone call from Culiacán that there were gringo surfos camping on the beach who were in need of some bud. He shook his head as he looked out at the stupid mango trees: all this trouble for marijuana. "It's a job," Scarface said. The cop snorted.

Scarface wore his irritating chrome .45 automatic in a shoulder rig. It made his armpit and ribs into a swamp of perspiration. It was against the law for a Mexican to carry an automatic weapon, though he didn't even think about it. His partner wore a uniform and had a heavy Bulldog .44 in a Sam Browne holster—the narco could smell its leather and was irritated by its squeaking as the car bumped along the bad road.

The holster squeak was the closest they could get to a theme song. There was nothing on the radio out here except the crappy Mexican music on AM.

"Me gusta Kanye West," the narco said, snapping off the radio.

The state cop said, "Diddy es mejor."

"¡Diddy!" cried Scarface.

They argued for a few moments.

Soon, they reverted to silence. The cop turned up the AC. His gun belt squealed.

"Dios mío," Scarface sighed. "I hate the country."

The men kept their windows rolled up, but they could still smell the ripe effluent of mud and clams and pigsties and spawning fish in green water. They wrinkled their noses. "What is that?" the cop asked. "Boiling mangos?" They shook their heads, greatly offended. The other one pointed.

"Outhouses!" he scoffed.

They couldn't believe it! These towns were so backward, Emiliano Zapata and a bunch of revolutionaries could ride through at any moment and fit right in. The bandidos, a generation removed from outhouses, sneered at the skinny dogs and the absurd starving roosters that panicked as the car rolled over oyster shells and brushed aside sugarcane and morning glory vines. The rubes down here had apparently never heard of blacktop. It was all dirt roads and cobblestones. No tourists.

They were slightly pleased, yet jealous, when they noted one of the small houses had a satellite dish.

As in most neighborhoods of most tropical Mexican villages, the walls of the homes in town went right to the edge of the street. Walls were wavery and one block long, and several doors could be found in each. Each door denoted another address. The windows had big iron railings and wooden shutters. Bougainvillea cascaded from several rooflines. Trumpet flowers. Lantana. The bandidos knew that the back of each house was a courtyard with a tree and an open kitchen and some chickens and an iguana or two. Laundry. On the street side, the walls were great splashes of color. One address might be white, and the next might be pale blue and the next vivid red with a purple door. Sometimes, two primary colors were divided by a bright green drainpipe or a vibrating line where the colors clashed and the human eye began to rattle in its socket.

The big police LTD rolled down the streets like a jaguar sniffing for its prey. The two visitors came out of the narrow alleys into the open space of the town plazuela, a tawdry gazebo and a bunch of trees with their trunks whitewashed. On the other side of the square, they spied a restaurant: TAQUERIA E INTERNET "LA MANO CAIDA."

"The Fallen Hand Taco Shop? What kind of name is that?" the cop asked.

"It's an Internet café, too," the narco reminded him.

"Jesus Christ."

"Let's get out of here quick," his partner said. "I want to catch the beisbol game in Mazatlán tonight." He spit out his toothpick.

They creaked to a halt and could hear the music blasting out of the Fallen Hand before they even opened the car's doors.

Chapter Two

———

Here came Nayeli, late for work again, dancing through town on her way to the Fallen Hand. She didn't mean to dance—it was just that everywhere she went, she swung and swayed, and it was all she could do to keep herself from running. She had been the star forward of the Tres Camarones girls' soccer team for four years, and even though she'd been out of high school for a year, she was still in shape. Her dark legs were hard with muscle and she still wore her tiny school uniform skirt, so everybody could admire them. Besides, clothes didn't grow on trees.

Nayeli was dreaming of leaving town again. She wanted to see anything, everything. Wanted to go where lights changed color, where airplanes lumbered overhead and the walls of great buildings were covered in television screens like in that Bill Murray Japanese movie they'd seen at the Cine Pedro Infante the week before. She wanted shimmering lines of traffic in city rain. She was eager to see a concert, ride a train, wear fancy clothes, and sip exotic coffees on a snowy boulevard. She had seen elevators in a thousand movies, and she longed to ride one, though not on the roof of one like Jackie Chan.

Sometimes, she dreamed of going to the United States—"Los Yunaites," as the people of the town called them—to find her father, who had left and never come back. He traded his family for a job, and then he stopped writing or sending money. She didn't like to think about him. People kidded her that she never stopped smiling, and it made her look flirty, but thinking about him made the smile fade. She walked faster.

Nayeli was coming from Aunt Irma's campaign headquarters, located in the stifling kitchen of Irma's house on Avenida Francisco Madero. Irma, sick and tired of the ancient mayor of Tres Camarones ("That smelly old man!" she often complained), was making history by running to replace him in the next election. It would be a first: Irma García Cervantes, the first female Municipal President of Tres Camarones. It had an excellent ring to it. She had leadership experience—Aunt Irma was Sinaloa's retired Lady Bowling Champion—and she was used to celebrity and the heat of the public's attentions. If political power was not her destiny, she reasoned, it could only mean the Good Virgin herself had dictated that Mexico should continue its slide into chaos and ruin.

One of Nayeli's main tasks was to write with fat sidewalk chalk, "¡Aunt Irma for President!" on walls all around Tres Camarones. As campaign manager, she earned twenty pesos a week, proving that Aunt Irma, too, had that affliction detested by Sinaloans yet epidemic in proportion. They called it "el codo duro": the hard elbow, or the unbending elbow—unbending when it came time to spend money.

Twenty pesos! You couldn't even afford corn tortillas anymore on twenty pesos. The Americans were buying up all the maize for fuel, and none of the rancheros could afford to use it for food. What did come down to the people was too expensive to purchase. So Nayeli danced on down the street to her second job, serving tacos and soft drinks at La Mano Caída.

Let's eat," the cop said. They had gotten restless, waiting for the damned Americano surfos to show up. They had a brick of pot in the trunk of their car, and the clock was ticking. He tapped on the bar.

Tacho, the Fallen Hand's taco master, glowered.

"What you got?" the cop asked.

Tacho was tired of the thugs. They glared too much for his taste.

"Food," he said.

The narco smiled.

"You're kind of mouthy for a queer."

Tacho shrugged.

"He's a queer?" the cop said.

"He's wearing eye makeup," said Scarface.

"I thought he was one of those emo kids you hear about." The cop shrugged.

"Emo sucks," Scarface muttered.

"I like Diddy," the cop reminded him.

Tacho had just about had it, but suddenly, Nayeli burst through the doors.

"You're late!" Tacho scolded.

"I'm sorry, Tachito mi amor," she called, automatically falling into her flirting banter with him. "Tachito machito mi angelito."

The gunmen snorted: *Little Tacho, my little macho, my little angel.* That was too rich. They nudged each other.

"You're macho, eh?" the cop said. "A macho angel."

They giggled.

"¿Eres joto?" the narco asked Tacho, because if this hot little girl was talking to him like that, he might not be a queer after all.

Tacho made eyes at Nayeli. She hurried to tie on a white apron. She saw the silver glint of the narco's .45 peeking out from behind his jacket.

"Take a table," Tacho said. "No need for gentlemen like your-selves to sit at the bar."

He smiled at them — it looked as if he were getting a tooth pulled, but anything to get them across the room from him. He didn't want to have them near enough to smell their tacky cologne. One of them was wearing Old Spice!

They sat at one of Tacho's quaking little tin Carta Blanca tables.

"What do you recommend?" the cop asked Nayeli.

"Tacho's fried-oyster tortas are legendary," she replied.

"Sounds good."

She turned away.

He grabbed her hand and pulled her back.

"You," he said. "You're under arrest."

She felt a pure cold bolt of panic.

"Excuse me?"

"You're under suspicion" — he sneered — "of stealing my heart."

He let her go and sent her back across the room on a gale of laughter. Her face was burning. Tacho whispered to her, "Viejo feo." Ugly old man. It was one of his favorite insults.

"Good one," the narco was saying.

They kept laughing, wiping their eyes.

"Hey!" he called. "Girl! Bring us some drinks!"

Tacho sighed. "It's going to be one of those days," he said.

Nayeli fished two beers out of the vat of ice at the end of the bar.

The men scared her. She tried to think about other things when she was tense or afraid, better days, before things had turned so sad, before everyone had become so poor.

She opened the beer bottles, served them, and rushed back to the end of the bar while Tacho started frying up the oysters.

The narco pulled his big pistol out of the shoulder holster and laid it on the table. He held open his jacket and flapped his arm a little. He turned his head and eyed Nayeli. He patted the gun and smiled at her.

"Está caliente, la chaparra," he noted.

The cop glanced over at her to see how hot the shortie really was. They studied her legendary legs. Her bright white teeth against the deep cinnamon brown of her skin made her smile radiate like moonlight on water.

"A little dark," he said. "But she'll do."

He winked at her and sipped his icy beer.

Nobody was quite sure if Tres Camarones was in Sinaloa or Nayarit, since the state line wavered in and out of the mangrove swamps and lagoons thereabouts. There was no major highway going through; there was no local police station, no hotel or tourist trap. No harbor, no television or radio station, no police station, no supermarket. The high school was in Villaunión, a long sweaty bus trip away. The church was small and full of fruit bats. Of course, there was a small Carta Blanca beer distributor, but come to think of it, the office had shut down when the men went north to find work. It was easier to float a boat down the tributaries of the Baluarte River than it was to drive the dirt road spur that angled southwest off the highway to Rosario. At any rate, nobody had ever worried about maps—on the official Pemex highway guides, Tres Camarones didn't even exist.

The American boys who started it all by making a peeved chiba-call to their Mazatlán connection, seeking a key of gold bud, were on spring break from some college in California. They had wandered down the coast, looking for good surfing and party spots, and they'd made the error of picking the sugar-white beaches outside Tres Camarones for their camp. The locals could have told them—but didn't—that the picturesque beaches belied a brutal drop-off, and the waves hammered against a nearly vertical wall of underwater mud. Other hazards abounded. The nearest popular beach was called Caimanero because big alligators lurked in the foul freshwater swamps behind the shore—not a spot for frolic. Portuguese man-of-wars floated onto the beaches all summer, killing everything they could sting. There was a spoiling porpoise carcass on the sand to bear testimony to their powers. The safest salt water in that whole region was in the shallow turquoise lagoons where the women went crabbing with floating straw baskets full of scrabbling *jaibas,* the big crabs taking their last little sea cruise before landing in the cooking pot. But you couldn't surf a tranquil lagoon.

It wasn't like the people hadn't seen Americanos. Tres Camarones had been beset by tides of missionaries from Southern California. But the Jesús Es Mi Fiel Amigo Sunday School and the End Times Templo Evangélico had finally closed down for lack of converts. The "youth center" went back to being a muffler shop that was also closed because its owner had gone to Florida to pick oranges. For a short while, an ashram run by a Wisconsin woman named Chrystal, who was in constant channeling-contact with the Venusian UFO-naut P'taak, rose north of town. Several local workers had made good wages working on Chrystal's pink cement pyramid on her leased forty acres of scrub and pecan trees. But the local water cut short P'taak's mission to the world, and Chrystal rushed back to Sheboygan with typhoid and amebic dysentery. After Chrystal's personal rapture, the Jehovah's Witnesses, known as Los Testigos de Jeová, were forced to leave town when the heroic local bowling champion, Aunt Irma, unleashed her devilish tongue upon them and christened them Los Testículos de Jeová. The Witnesses, deeply offended, packed up their Spanish editions of *The Watchtower* and abandoned the heathens to their grisly fate.

Scarface tossed aside his napkin. The lime juice and Cholula sauce were better when you sucked them off your fingers. The table was a wasteland of empty plates. He stood.

"Where are these pinches gringos!" he shouted.

The state cop checked his watch, put down his beer bottle, and turned to glare at Tacho as if the proprietor were the surfers' secretary.

"We are busy men," he warned.

"I've been here an hour!" Scarface complained.

Tacho shrugged.

"You know how Americans are," he said. "Always late. On their own time."

Scarface kicked back his chair and grabbed his gun. He held it down by his side, as if deciding whether Tacho and Nayeli needed shooting. "If the surfos show up, tell them next time we see them, they each get a bullet in the head. Understand? I don't like to be kept waiting."

"Sí, señor," Nayeli replied.

The bad men strode out and got back into their car. Scarface pulled a fresh cinnamon toothpick out of his breast pocket. He took off the cellophane wrapper, dropped it on the floor, and popped the toothpick in his mouth. It waggled up and down. "Nice town," he said. "No cops."

He adjusted his lapels.

"No men, did you notice?"

He smiled.

"A vato like me could make a real killing here."

He wiped his sunglasses on his shirt and put them back on.

"Watch yourselves," he called out the window.

They drove away without paying.

Chapter Three

———

As the bandidos prowled the town and its outskirts, Tacho and Nayeli went about their day. Mopping the cement floor, sweeping the sidewalk in front, slicing limes, and peeling mangos. But mostly, they did what Mexicans in every small town in Mexico did: they circled their own history.

Nayeli was thinking about the missionaries. Well, she was thinking about one of them. The one saint—Missionary Matt.

All of Nayeli's notorious girlfriends loved Missionary Matt. He was the first blond boy any of them had ever seen in person. They could claim that the vapid white-boy handsomeness of El Brad Pitt or El Estip McQueen at the cinema didn't move them, but up close, it was a different story. A real live blue-eyed white boy was their own romantic freak show. Matt's nose peeled. They had never seen a peeling nose. It was precious.

Matt sneaked away from his pastoral duties every night and crept into the Cine Pedro Infante. Nayeli's girlfriends were not the only ones who sat in restless groups all around him, tittering over his slightest jest. Even mothers and aunties tittered, "¡Ay, Mateo!" whenever he said anything.

That boy was movie crazy.

Matt had endeared himself to the many girls in town by writing their names phonetically on four-by-six-inch cards. When he left, he left behind a hundred broken hearts as he distributed these well-thumbed cards to his sweethearts as farewell gifts, with his address and phone number written on the back of each.

The card was the closest thing to a love letter Nayeli had ever received. She pulled it out for inspection, the ink a little diffuse from her sweat. It read:

nah / YELL / ee

Beneath this, it said:

Love, Matt!

Then an address and a phone number that started with an 858 prefix.

Love, Nayeli thought. She knew enough English to know that. *Love. Was it love-love? Like, LOVE? Or was it just love, like mi-amigo-Mateo-love, like I love my sister or my puppy or peanut butter cups love?*

"Hello?" Tacho said. "Work? Like, sometime today?"

"Oh, you," she said dreamily.

Tacho raised his hands and seemed to beseech the universe.

Nayeli kept Missionary Matt's card tucked in her kneesock along with the sole, tattered postcard her father had sent her from a place called KANKAKEE, ILLINOIS. It showed a wild turkey gazing with deep paranoia out of a row of cornstalks. Before he'd fled to KANKAKEE, Don Pepe had been the only police officer in Tres Camarones. Mostly, he directed traffic and inspected the rare car wreck on the eastern road. Nayeli's father had been gone three years. When it really got hot, and she was sweaty enough to threaten the ink altogether, she reluctantly tucked the two cards into her mirror at home.

She wandered out on the sidewalk and swept listlessly. The scant heavy river breeze stirred her tiny skirt. Boys used to whistle at Nayeli when she went by, but she'd been noticing a silence in the streets. Perhaps nineteen was already too old. Everything was changing for her. There was nowhere for a champion futbolista to go if she was a girl. And it was out of the question for her to head off to Culiacán or somewhere else expensive to attend the university. Her mother took in laundry—but, really, all the old women of Tres Camarones took in laundry. It would take many more dirty and lazy people to sustain the home laundry industry. Fortunately, Nayeli and her mother received some assistance from the formidable Tía Irma—the future Municipal President. Tía Irma's pro bowling winnings had been sufficiently vast that she had actually invested most of her money, and she was further comfortably attended to by monthly retirement checks from her hard years at the canneries. The checks were modest, but she didn't need much more than Domino cigarettes, the occasional bottle of rum, and a steady diet of Tacho's tacos and tortas.

It was Tía Irma, known to the notorious girlfriends as La Osa—the She-Bear—who had pushed Nayeli into fútbol. And it was both Irma and Don Pepe who had enrolled Nayeli in Dr. Matsuo Grey's martial arts dojo when the other girls were taking dance lessons for the various pageants and balls at the Club de Leones. Karate, Tía Irma insisted, was good for the legs. Power on the field. But Nayeli was not fooled. To La Osa, life and love were war, and she expected Nayeli to win as many battles as possible.

Aunt Irma wanted her to beat up men.

Missionary Matt had taught Nayeli a term for Tía Irma: *Es muy hard-core, La Osa.*

¡Ay, Mateo!" Nayeli said out loud. He was on some glorious California beach, and she was at Tacho's.

It was a job, at least. It gave her money for shoes or movie tickets at the cine. Since Matt had donated his Satellite laptop to Tacho when he left, the taquería had been transformed into an Internet café.

Nayeli sashayed in and tossed the broom into the corner.

"I'm going on el Internet," she announced.

"Do you think I pay you to play on the computer all day?" Tacho scolded.

"Yes."

"¡Cabrona!"

Tacho was cranky like this with all the girls. It was part of his routine. A man like Tacho had to learn to survive in Mexico, and he had learned to re-create himself in bright colors, in large attitudes, thus becoming a cherished character. If you wanted to achieve immortality, or at least acceptance, in Tres Camarones, the best thing to do was become an amazing fixture. It was very macho to be a ne'er-do-well, even if you were gay. That's why mewling missionaries didn't stand a chance. Being meek wasn't macho. There was no legend there.

For years, the joke about Tacho's "kind"—los jotos—was that they suffered from the affliction of "la mano caída." The fallen hand, the cartoony limp wrist of the gay man in the common pantomime: just the phrase made people laugh. Except for Tacho. He didn't accept being called "faggot" by anybody (except his girls), and he certainly didn't feel that he was limp-wristed in any way. So he threw it back in their faces by naming his establishment the Fallen Hand. Genius! Even the most macho men in town had embraced him immediately, because he was wittier than they were, and because of this, somehow more macho.

That was years ago. Lately, the Mano Caída mostly attracted bored old ladies with very little money, or Nayeli's troublesome bratty girls—and they never spent a peso. All they wanted to do was look at gringo boys on the Internet. He sighed. What a life.

At least he also sold women's shoes from his back bedroom over on Avenida Benito Juárez. Nayeli wasn't the only one who could work Mateo's computer! Indeed, Tacho had found eBay, and he had begun his second career with the help of Tía Irma's American Express card. Thanks to Tacho, Tres Camarones was now treated to a monthly visit from bright yellow DHL delivery trucks, an exotic touch that made the citizens feel cosmopolitan.

Tacho and Nayeli shared a lust for big cities—any big cities. They used the computer to spy on New York, London, Madrid, Paris. Sometimes, after work, they climbed on the roof of the restaurant to watch the bats. They made believe that clouds were the Manhattan skyline.

Oh no," groaned Tacho, "here come the rest of them."

The notorious girlfriends—what was left of them—were walking up the sidewalk. They were yelling, "¡Adios!" to everybody they knew on the street. People in Tres Camarones didn't say hello, they said good-bye.

Nayeli looked out and grinned. There were only three of them left, but they liked to brag that they were the best of the bunch. Cuquis Cristerna had moved to Culiacán. Sachiko Uzeta Amano had gone to Mexico City to learn how to make movies. María de los Angeles Hernandez Osuna was studying to be a doctor in Guadalajara. Now it was just Nayeli, Yoloxochitl, and Verónica.

Yoloxochitl's phonetic Missionary Matt card read:

YO-low / SO-sheet

He called her "Yo-Yo," which amused him no end. Her parents had been infected with folklore mania, a real danger among liberal Mexicans with college educations. Her father had made it through one year of university, and thus well-connected to his Toltec past, he and Yoloxochitl's mother had decided to christen their offspring with Nahuatl names. Fortunately for everyone, they'd had only two children. Unfortunately for her older brother, they had named him Tlaloc. Young Tlaloc didn't enjoy being known as the Rain God—every time he went to pee, his friends made relentless jokes—so he changed the name to Lalo before he went north with his father to become nameless.

Matt had already known how to say Verónica, but just to make her feel good, he'd made a card out for her, too.

ver-OH! / knee-kah

Lately Yoloxochitl had been working as a pin tender at the three-lane bowling alley down by the statue of Benito Juárez. Verónica worked as a shrimp peeler in the stinking estuaries north of town. Neither one liked her job. Too much sweat. Yoloxochitl wore her faded El Tri rocanrol T-shirt and some gaucho pants Tacho had sold her for half price. Her mother had saved for a year to get her out of glasses; her contact lenses had unleashed the fashion model inside her. She was carrying another one of her paperback books. Yolo—as the girls all called her—was always reading.

As usual, everybody was staring at Verónica, the only goth girl in Sinaloa. She had made her face pale with various ointments and creams, and she had painted her eyelids dark, her lips black, her nails black. She wore a long black skirt that must have been stifling, yet she managed to radiate cool air when she walked by. Verónica ironed her hair so it hung down like a sheet of satin. Her hair was already utterly black, but she also dyed it with Black No. 1 rinse just like her heroes in Type O Negative, whose videos she'd seen with Nayeli on YouTube.

It was much harder for girls to become astounding characters in the fabric of Tres Camarones culture — they were mostly, if they were eccentric, seen as outrageous monsters — but Verónica's every public appearance was a shock.

She had been a goth for three months; before that, she had dreamed of being a pop star in revealing hot pants and see-through blouses of televised Latin American variety shows. She was going to dye her hair that plasticine coppery color that passed for blond among Mexican starlets. Only the notorious girlfriends noted that she'd gone goth after her father and mother had died.

Everyone called her La Vampira.

The girls burst through the door, popping gum and clanking bracelets.

"Tachito, mi flor!" trilled Yolo.

Normally, Tacho would flick anyone who called him a flower with his deadly washcloth.

"Tramp," he replied, not meanly.

"Yolo!" Nayeli called.

"¿Qué onda, morra?" Yolo replied, delighting in street slang. Sounding like a city tough was so rocanrol. She was the best student among them — if she had been able to, she would have studied dentistry in college. She, too, was a soccer star, though Nayeli had overshadowed her on the field.

"Hola, Nayeli," sighed La Vampira.

"Vampi!" Nayeli said. "How is life, Vampi?"

"Sad," said La Vampira. She pulled a rosary from her black

beaded clutch purse (Tacho's fashion emporium, 155 pesos). The beads rattled on the table. "I don't know how much more I can take."

Yolo and Nayeli looked at each other and rolled their eyes. Tacho, a sucker for the goth routine, made up a small bowl of mango and pineapple and orange slices with red chile powder on them, and sat with La Vampira and poked toothpicks into the fruit.

"Eat," he said. "You've got to eat, my angel."

"Oh...Tacho..." she breathed. She squeezed his hand weakly.

"She's an angel?" muttered Nayeli. "Angel of death, maybe."

Yolo snorted.

"You snorted," Nayeli said.

"I so did not snort."

Nayeli clicked the keys and opened a video of a skateboarder getting hit in the crotch by his board on Google Video. She made a face and switched Web sites. Ah! Captain Jack Sparrow. Yolo leaned against Nayeli's shoulder. She turned to La Vampi and said, "Oye, Vampi. La Nayeli is going to marry Johnny Depp."

"Mmm, Capitán Yack Esparrow," Vampi said.

"Oh, yes," Tacho agreed. "Es muy caliente, el Capitán Yack."

Verónica made a face.

"Me encanta," Nayeli said. "I love him."

"Me, too," Tacho said.

"Yack Esparrow," Vampi said, "needs a bath."

She waved her hand dismissively.

"Besides," she added, "I can only marry one man."

"Not again," muttered Nayeli.

She grumbled and went to YouTube. Verónica had never even seen "gothic" people before she had watched Nayeli work Tacho's computer, but as soon as she saw wan boys in mascara, she was lost. Type O Negative was awesome, or "chido," as she put it. The Sisters of Mercy put her way around the bend. And now this. Nayeli huffed, then typed in "The 69 Eyes." Thinking: *Why do I do this?*

"What does that mean?" Tacho asked.

"He must have sixty-nine eyes," Yolo said.

"Who does?"

"Him," said Nayeli, pointing to the goth band on the screen, and at the cadaver sitting in their midst.

"He always wears sunglasses," Vampi marveled. "His name is Jyrki."

"The glasses hide all those eyeballs," Yolo said.

"¿Qué?" asked Tacho.

"Here we go," Nayeli said, mouse clicking to call up Vampi's favorite song, "Gothic Girl."

The girls started to dance. Tacho thought this Jyrki person sounded like he was dead, but he sounded comfortable being a corpse, even happy.

"Dance with me, boy," Nayeli commanded.

Tacho took Nayeli's hand and tried a cumbia to the music. La Vampi went crazy and started jumping up and down, bobbing her head from side to side. In her heavily accented English, she sang, "I love my gothic girl!" Well, what she said was: *"Ay lob myng goddig gorrl."* And everyone laughed.

Nayeli didn't get home until ten o'clock. When she came in the door, her mother said, "What were you doing?"

Nayeli said, "Nothing. Just another day at work, Mami."

"How is Tacho?"

"Fine."

Nayeli ate some calabazas and a glass of milk, then went to bed in front of her ancient electric fan. The geckos chirped on the wall above her bed.

Her mother called, "We're going to the lagoon tomorrow."

"Awesome!" Nayeli called. What she shouted was: "Chido." But her mother did not know what that newfangled word meant. "Night, Mami."

"Good night, m'ijita."

Nayeli rolled her head on the hot pillow. She was asleep before she knew it was happening. She dreamed that she lived in a big white house, surrounded by trees and fountains. There was snow on the distant mountain range. Her horses were white, and the swans in her lake floated serenely as the maids served tea. She had English muffins with strawberry jam on a silver tray. She spoke perfect English. She wore a long gown and ate ice cream when she was done with the muffins. Her husband, Johnny Depp, had gold teeth, black eyeliner, and waist-length hair. "Tomorrow," he said with a metallic grin, "we will go to Kankakee."

Chapter Four

———

Tía Irma headed down the sidewalk like a parade float, and they hurried to keep up with her.

"Crab day!" she called as she motored along on squeaky shoes, thinking the people who smiled at Nayeli were smiling at her.

Crabbing was like going to heaven. A whole day immersed in the clear lagoon, with barrels of ice full of soda and beer, the thatch-roofed huts in the sand swinging with hammocks, the big pots boiling crabs to be eaten on stiff fried tortillas. There was nothing better than crab day.

They boarded the two boats at the sloping little dock. Nayeli had stopped at the graves of her grandparents and pulled a few weeds, shy red-legged tarantulas feeling their way between the monuments.

The river water was deep green and sluggish as it moved by, carrying pollen and leaves. The banks here were dark mud flecked with a scatter of white shells. Fat green frogs, the eternally grinning type destined to be shellacked into bizarre poses while wearing mariachi hats and holding toy trumpets and guitars and then sold in tourist traps all over Mexico, jostled lazily in the dappled shadows. Brilliant egrets and blue herons stalked the reeds on the shore.

La Osa settled into the first boat, tipping it alarmingly but refusing to note the hubbub she caused. She wore a vast straw hat upon her head, and she snapped her 10,000th picture of a tree orchid with her ancient plastic Kodak. "Each flower," she lectured, "as distinct as a snowflake!" Not that any of them had ever seen a snowflake.

Behind Tía Irma sat Nayeli's mother—a well-known hypochondriac since her husband left.

"María," Irma said. "How are you today?"

"Oh," Nayeli's mother said. "Not very well."

Irma snapped, "You've been dying for years. Why don't you get it over with?"

In an hour, they had come to the bend in the river where the boats could be beached and tied to bushes, and the party disembarked and grunted over the slope, breaking suddenly, amazingly, from jungly dark to a dazzling white cove that had at its center a wide oblong lagoon of brightest turquoise. Beyond the far end of the lagoon, the thundering surf of the deadly beach could be seen, dark ocean water exploding in spray and foam with a relentless basso roar. Everything seemed woven of purest sunlight. The coconut palms bobbed with their bright green harvests nestled among the silky-looking fronds. Beyond the coconuts, hibiscus trees stood twenty feet tall, burning with crimson blossoms. Little thatched huts sagged at jaunty angles, and Nayeli wasted no time getting to them, prying open their storage boxes, and unfurling the mesh hammocks stored inside. The breeze never stilled: miraculously, no one could tell how hot it was, or how humid. The faint whiffs of rotting porpoise occasionally spoiled the Edenic effect, but otherwise they had reached the most perfect spot in the world.

Irma said to María, her niece: "Your husband should have

come here before he left. He would have stayed home. ¡En México lindo!"

Nayeli's mother replied, "You cannot eat beauty."

Yolo and Nayeli were in the lagoon. The water only came up to their hips. Tiny fish sniffed and nibbled at their thighs. Nayeli's hair was pulled back in a loose ponytail. Yolo had cut hers for the summer. On the white sand, Tacho had a fire going, and he was boiling seawater with onions and secret sauces. Yolo nudged Nayeli: Tacho was wearing a cloth wrapped around his waist like a sarong. The girls laughed.

They moved deeper into the lagoon. They watched their bellies and hips wobble and distend in the water. The reflected light made Nayeli's skin look white. She regarded it fondly.

Yolo said, "Remember when Mateo the Missionary came here with us?"

"Ay, Matt," Nayeli sighed.

"He was so cute," Yolo said.

"That crab pinched his toe."

"He was screaming."

"I had to bite the crab's claw open."

"Nayeli," Yolo said, "you were always the strong one."

"Do you think he remembers us?"

Yolo gestured at her own body.

"Who could forget this?" she boasted.

But Yolo wasn't blind—she'd seen Matt's eyes as he tried not to look Nayeli over.

"You kissed him," Yolo said, poking Nayeli in the arm.

"I did not!"

"Yes you did."

"No I didn't."

"No seas simple, Nayeli," Yolo scolded. "Everybody knows you kissed Mateo!"

Nayeli smiled.

"So?" she said.

Yolo gasped and splashed her.

"So it's true! You did kiss him!"

Nayeli shrugged with one shoulder.

"Maybe."

The kiss—Matt would remember that, she was certain. His mouth was delicious, with his cherry cola lip balm. Soft lips. Those soft curls, too, smelling like apple juice from that girls' shampoo he used. She liked to think of Matt's mouth as having American lips—labios Americanos. It could be a power ballad by Maná.

La Osa's comadres were across the water, moving toward them. Everyone was hunting for crabs. They each carried a stick. Between each pair of women floated a big straw basket. The notorious girl-friends' open basket already held ten furiously scrabbling crabs. The armored creatures wrestled one another, and when one seemed about to climb out of the basket and make its escape, the others would grab it and haul it back down into the endless battle.

"Look at that," Yolo said. "They never make it out."

"That's us," Nayeli said. "That's Mexico."

"Don't let your aunt hear you say that," Yolo warned.

They shuffled their feet along the bottom, stirring bright white clouds of sand that curled like smoke around their legs. Suddenly, a huge crab burst out of the sand and scuttled along the bottom. The girls yelped and ducked under water. Nayeli got to the crab first, and she pressed her stick to its back, holding it down. She carefully pinched it from behind—keeping well away from its powerful claws—and pulled it out of the water.

She shook her head to get the water out of her eyes and said, "Look at that!"

"Hey!" Yolo said. "¡Es embra!"

A female.

Sure enough, the she-crab had a thick girdle of eggs plastered to her shell. Tacho would be delighted. Crab roe made a paste that moved him to orgasmic delight when he smeared it on a tortilla and soaked it in lemon juice and green salsa. Nayeli tossed her in the basket.

"Don't you feel guilty?" Yolo said. "Taking an expectant mother?"

"What, feel solidarity with a crab?" said Nayeli. Yolo was always simmering with revolutionary theories.

"In a way, she's our sister," Yolo insisted.

This was the trouble with straight-A students: they thought up positions and then thought up a thousand insane defenses for their instant policies.

"This crab is not my sister, Yolo. She is my lunch."

"She's no sister of mine—I'm not pregnant. This crab might be the sister of—" she started to say. Nayeli tried to think of a pregnant woman in Tres Camarones. "No sé quién. Who's pregnant?"

Yolo snorted. She loved her ridiculous debates with Nayeli. They could talk in loops for hours on the merits of rock en español versus regaeton, or on the merits of fútbol versus beisbol. They left poor Vampi suicidal with boredom when they got on their little jags.

"Crab!" Nayeli shouted, pointing.

This time Yolo beat her. She plunged under and worked her stick. It was a small male, but a small crab was still a tasty crab.

"That's a dozen," Nayeli said. "Let's take them to Tacho."

"Let's eat!"

In her atrocious English, Nayeli said, *"Oh yeah, baby!"*

As they waded to shore, she said, "But who's pregnant? Seriously. I can't think of anybody."

Yolo thought.

They came out of the water, each of them holding a handle of the basket.

Yolo shrugged.

"I can't think of anybody, either," she said.

⁓

They squatted and gobbled their crabs, the women and Tacho. The shrimpers and boys sat at the far end of the lagoon, eating beans wrapped in tortillas and minding their own business. Occasionally, Tacho whistled, and one of the boys came running to open beer bottles and bring more crabs from the aromatic pot. La Osa made Tacho surrender three fat crabs to the boys so they could eat some, too. La Osa reminded herself of Benito Juárez at moments like that. She basked in affection for herself.

Nayeli waited for an opportune moment to ask the ladies, "Who's pregnant?"

"Not me," said Tacho.

They threw napkins and crab claws at him.

"Do you mean among us here?" La Osa said, patting her gut. "Because it's a little late for my comadres and me!" The older women chuckled. "You'd better not be trying to tell us anything," she warned. "You'd better not." She shook a crab leg at Nayeli.

La Osa finished another beer. Tacho hustled to fetch a fresh one and fished out a 7 Up for himself.

"Siete Oop," he announced.

"Why do you ask?" Aunt Irma finally said.

"When was Tres Camarones ever without babies?" Nayeli asked. "What an odd thing."

"Excuse me, girlfriends," Tacho interrupted. "You need men to make babies."

The old women nodded.

"What?" Nayeli said.

"Men," said Tacho.

"What are you talking about, machito?"

"Men. Didn't you notice?"

"Notice what?"

"All the men are gone."

"Ridiculous."

"Oh, really."

"Jesus," Irma announced. "Is there anyone sillier than a teenage girl?"

The women and Tacho laughed out loud.

The girlfriends sat there glowering: they couldn't stand being called silly.

"All teenage girls ever notice," Irma said, "is their own little dramas. They're idiots." She used the graphic word *babosadas*, which denoted drool running down their chins but also suggested they were as stupid as *babosos* — slugs.

The girls were outraged.

"Are not!" they cried.

The women shook their heads.

"All gone," Irma said, making a puff with her lips. "Blown away. Off to the beautiful north." She took a swig of beer. "Welcome to the real world, children."

Nayeli stared at Yolo with her mouth hanging open.

All she could think was: *I'll show you who's stupid!*

Irma stood. She smacked the sand off her legs.

"I have one word for the men," she said as she stomped away. "Traitors!"

Nobody wanted to go home after their day at the beach, so they gathered at Tía Irma's house on the corner of 22 de Diciembre and

Madero streets to watch her color television. La Osa set the TV in the window, facing the street, and the guests all hauled chairs out onto the cobbles so they could feel the breeze. They watched a telenovela featuring savage love among hacienda owners in Brazil. Then they watched a telenovela that featured savage love among cattle ranchers in Durango. It grew dark. Cicadas knocked themselves senseless against the television screen. Bats twirled above them like leaves flying in a windstorm. Passersby called, "¡Adios!" and all the watchers politely called back, "¡Adios!"

When a car came down the street, they all rose and moved their chairs up onto the curb so the car could pass. They didn't notice that one of the cars was the big narco LTD. "¡Adios!" they called, then moved their chairs back into the narrow street. Nayeli watched everybody on the curb. She looked very carefully. And she realized Tacho was right. There was nobody left in town but women, old men, and little children.

Adios.

Chapter Five

Although the Mexican government didn't seem to know where Tres Camarones was, its citizens knew in their hearts that they were Sinaloans. They listened to Sinaloan radio from XEHW in Rosario; they did their shopping in Villaunión; and when they went to the big city, as Irma and the girlfriends had done this morning, it was the long jaunt by dirt track and two-lane highway to Mazatlán.

Irma had maneuvered her apocalyptic 1959 Cadillac through the murky verdure surrounding Tres Camarones and hit the main road by 9:00 AM. The notorious girlfriends had snored and snuffled in the big backseat as she drove. Vampi had not been allowed to wear black clothes or black makeup, so she had miserably reported to Irma's house clad in an orange jumper. "¡Así se viste una señorita!" La Osa had enthused, brusquely turning her back and forth, and grabbing her chin to inspect her freshly scrubbed face. She approved: that was the way young ladies dressed.

"You're not even half ugly," she had added.

They'd cut through the great green lowlands—white birds exploded from the fields. The highway to the Durango mountains whipped by, and Irma had told them for the hundredth time that there were waterfalls up there, and one day, when she wasn't so busy, she'd drive them up there for some roasted goat. They'd love the waterfalls—very fresh and chilly. "I went there once," she intoned, "with Chava Chavarín!"

"Who?" Vampi said.

The girlfriends no longer listened to these empty promises. They nodded off to the relentless hum and rattle of the Caddie.

Irma barely saw the oldest cowboy in Mexico trotting along the road on his ancient pony. He lifted his hat to her. She waved with one finger.

Irma lit a cigarette, jabbed on the radio, and heard Agustín Lara. Ah, real music! Not this idiotic ass-twitching noise the girl-friends listened to. Or worse, that norteño crap with the accordi-ons, rube music for cocaine smugglers. La Osa tipped down the rearview mirror and checked her teeth for lipstick and tobacco shreds. She watched the girlfriends leaning against each other's shoulders, sleeping with their mouths open.

"My black-eyed girls," she said.

Tía Irma turned to the vegetable seller in his booth and said, "What the hell is happening to these beans!"

"Excuse me?" he said, pausing in his inventory, holding the stub of a pencil above the wilting pink pages of an order pad. "There is something happening to my beans?"

"How dare you charge so much for beans!"

"Charge?" he said. He looked at the hand-lettered tag he'd magic-markered onto a fragment of manila folder two days ago. "No," he said, "this is the rate."

"*¡Es una infamia!*" she said. "*¡Es un robo!*"

"No, no, señora," he said—not knowing he'd just made her even angrier because she'd never been married and didn't intend to have the slave's moniker of "Mrs." applied to her under any circumstances. "This is the correct price."

"First, tortillas," she complained. "Now this. What's next, water? Will you charge us for water? Ha! What are the poor people supposed to eat?"

He looked at her with wide eyes and shrugged.

"The poor?" he said. The poor did not shop at the fruit market—they sold lizards and birds and corn husk dolls on the highway. They ate armadillos. He didn't have time for the poor.

Beyond the fruit market rose the green Mazatlán hills and the white cliffs of the gringo tourist hotels. They could hear joyous voices and splashing from the hotel pools. They could smell the salt of the sea among the odors of cut sugarcane and fish and crushed mangos and oranges. Music and radios and trumpets and whistling and laughter and shouts and truck engines and some idiot's "La Cucaracha" car horn. Seagulls fighting over pieces of bread. Oyster shells.

"Forget the poor!" Irma shouted. "What about the good working people of Mexico!"

"Go, Tía," Nayeli said.

"We are Mexicans," Irma informed the fruit seller—needlessly, he felt. "Mexicans eat corn and beans. Did you notice? The Aztec culture gave corn to the world, you little man. We invented it! Mexicans grow beans. How is it, then, that Mexicans cannot afford to buy and eat the corn and beans they grow?"

He would have kicked her out of his stall, but he had manners—his mother would have been deeply offended if he had tossed out this old battle-ax.

He smiled falsely.

"Look here," he said, pointing to the burlap sacks full of 100 pounds each of pinto beans. "These beans come from California."

"What!"

He actually flinched away from her.

La Osa took her reading glasses out of her voluminous black purse, and the girls crowded around her. They read the fine print. California, all right. Right there on the bag.

"¡Chinga'o!" she said.

"These beans are grown here in Sinaloa," he said proudly. "The best frijoles in the world! Right near Culiacán. Then they're sold to the United States. Then they sell them back to us." He shrugged at the mysterious ways of the world. "It gets expensive."

Tía Irma took a long time to replace the glasses in the purse.

"That," she finally proclaimed, "is the stupidest thing anyone has ever said to me."

He smiled, hoping she would not strike him with that purse.

"NAFTA," he said.

Irma stormed out of the stall and spied a Guatemalan woman picking through the spoiled fruit.

"What are you doing?" she snapped.

"Provisions. For the journey north," the woman replied. She made the mistake of extending her hand and saying, "I have come so far, but I have so far to go. Alms, señora. Have mercy."

"Go back where you came from!" Irma bellowed. "Mexico is for Mexicans."

The girlfriends were appalled.

"Do you think anyone ever showed mercy to me?"

As the girlfriends followed Aunt Irma, she told them, "These illegals come to Mexico expecting a free ride! Don't tell me you didn't have Salvadorans and Hondurans in your school, getting the best education in the world! They take our jobs, too." She muttered on in her own steamy cloud of indignation. They tuned her out as they marched to the candy seller's. "What we need is a wall on our southern border." At least, she continued, the goopy sweet potato and cactus and guava and dulce de leche Mexican candies were made by Mexicans in Mexico and could still be bought by Mexicans in Mexico!

Irma bought mesh bags full of onions, garlic, potatoes. She bought a kilo of dribbly white goat cheese. She scoffed at the coconut milk sellers with their straws poked into cold coconuts. If she wanted a goddamned coconut, she'd hire Tacho to climb a tree! She purchased some candies and melons and limp bunches of cilantro. To hell with Mazatlán's tortillas—Tía Irma would buy good, hot, fresh tortillas right in Camarones, patted into being by the trusted hands of her comadre Doña Petra. These damned city slickers used machines to press out tortillas, anyway. Ha! Robot food!

"Can I drive?" Nayeli asked when they had reached the car.

"Oh, God," Tía Irma grumbled, but she gave her the keys.

I'm lonely, Tía," Nayeli announced.

Yolo and Vero were asleep again.

The She-Bear scoffed.

"Lonely?" she said. "How can you be lonely with good friends, and . . . and a good book to read!"

"That's Yolo," Nayeli said. "She's the reader." She passed a lopsided Ford truck overloaded with cucumbers.

"Blinker," Irma reminded her. Cucumbers fell from the truck like small green bombs, and the Cadillac slid a little on them as she changed lanes. For a moment, the road smelled like a fresh salad.

"Who will touch my face?" Nayeli asked.

Three children chased white chickens before a small house with an open door.

"Who will bring me flowers?"

"Hmm," Tía Irma responded.

"I want to see the lights of a city at night."

"Mazatlán," La Osa patiently lectured, "is a major city, my dear."

"I've never seen it at night. Only by day. Only to buy groceries."

"Oh," said Irma.

"Did no one sing you a serenade when you were young?" asked Nayeli.

"Of course!" Irma replied. "I was gorgeous as hell!"

"Did no one say dashing things to you on the plazuela on Saturday night?"

Tía Irma smiled.

"Well!" she said. "I suppose. El Guero Astengo was quite dapper. . . . But it was Chavarín, Chava the Magnificent. Well! *That* was the definition of dashing!"

She trailed off. Stared out the window. Nayeli thought she heard the impossible: Irma sighed.

"Who will do that for me?" Nayeli asked. "There are no serenades in Camarones. Who will dance with me?"

Irma could not answer her.

Chapter Six

The election was mere days away. Some of the women, it must be said, had not yet accepted the idea that a woman could be Municipal President. They had been told that they were moody and flighty and illogical and incapable for so long that they believed these things. It took much cajoling and cursing on Irma's part to shock them out of their ruts. Nayeli was a driving force among the young of the village—all twenty of them. Nine of the youngsters could vote, and all of these girls were voting for Irma. Those ineligible signed as best they could a statement pledging moral support for Irma's candidacy, and promised to argue the case to their mothers and grandmothers. As for Irma, she had an argument of her own.

The legendary García-García, owner of the theater, Aunt Irma's distant cousin, and the sole rich man of the town, had spent days on the telephone, fighting bad connections and tropical ennui, calling to far Culiacán and Los Mochis, even all the way to Tecuala, searching for a fresh projectionist, his last one having departed to Michigan to pick apples. Apparently, the trade was a dying concern, and he could find no available takers, so García-García himself was forced to suffer in the sauna-hot booth, tying a rag around his head to keep the sweat out of his eyes and stuffing toilet paper into his ears so the rattling whine of the machines didn't make him deaf.

At the age of sixty-five, García-García was feeling spent. Tired. And he was so worried about money that he had his wife shut off the air-conditioning unit in his cement-block home across the town square from the theater. She was so appalled by this descent into barbarity that she took his Impala and drove herself to Mazatlán to stay with her cousin.

The Cine Pedro Infante took the place of television for most people in town, so it was García-García's endless challenge to maintain a steady flow of double features. He couldn't afford to let a movie run for a week—in two days' time, everyone who could pay to see it would have passed through his doors. The movies were an essential lure so he could collect inflated prices for beer, soda, and ham-and-chile tortas at the little stand behind the screen. So what if it turned out the films were of poor quality, whole reels mysteriously spliced out, Chinese subtitles, cat-scratched frames, and underwater sound tracks—a fresh set of titles on the theater marquee meant a lucrative night at the torta stand.

García-García had a big white house at the end of Avenida Bernal Díaz del Castillo, and its tall metal door—also painted white—boomed like thunder as Irma pounded on it. La Osa fingered a lock of hair behind Nayeli's ear. "Posture," she said. Nayeli stood up straighter. The cinema was visible down the way and across the street, dark and melancholy as a haunted house, its steel shutters down and padlocked.

One of García's five housekeepers answered the door.

"Yes?" she said.

"I am here to see El Señor," said Irma.

"One moment."

She slammed the door.

The door opened.

"He will see you now."

"Gracias." Irma swept in and tipped her head slightly to the young woman, who then looked Nayeli's body up and down, judging her and finding her lacking.

Irma stepped in and Nayeli followed and they were at García-García's desk.

"Ah," he said, putting his cigarette in an ashtray. "My cousin the champion."

"We are tired of this shit," Irma informed him.

Nayeli wasn't sure what was happening; for a moment, she believed Irma was talking about the missing men.

"What shit is that, Irma?" García-García asked. His Spanish made even that inane comment sound elegant. "*¿A cual mierda te refieres, Irma?*"

"Movies," she explained.

"Movies?"

"Movies!"

"Ah, movies."

He spread his hands and leaned back in his chair. Nayeli noticed he had very important looking papers scattered on his desk. Behind his chair, there was a French poster for the movie *Bullitt*, Estip McQueen with a face like a monkey.

"I am here with my campaign manager, Nayeli Cervantes."

His eyebrows went up.

"Campaign manager," he replied, leaning forward and offering his hand. "It is an honor to meet you, Nayeli."

"Sir."

"Am I your uncle?"

"Perhaps."

"Hmm. I must add you to my Christmas list in that case."

She shook his hand and smiled. She was always smiling. His eyes dropped to her chest—fluttered there as nervously as a moth. His eyes sparkled brightly when he looked back up at her. He tugged her hand a little, and for a brief moment, she thought he'd pull her over the desk.

Oh no, she thought, *eso sí que no:* That absolutely won't happen.

"Mucho gusto, señor," she said, getting her hand back.

"Smiley girl," he said to Aunt Irma.

"She is a *karateka,*" La Osa replied. "Nayeli could karate-kick you to death where you sit."

"That's hardly feminine." He sniffed.

"Perhaps," Nayeli suggested, "it is time for a new kind of femininity."

La Osa beamed: that's my girl!

"After the election," Irma warned, "I will expect certain employment opportunities for the women of this town."

"Employment!" He snickered. He laughed out loud. They didn't. "I already hire women," García-García offered lamely.

"Women sell sandwiches and popcorn," Irma said. "Women take tickets and mop out your toilets. But that's not where the real money is."

"Well," García-García explained, "the real money goes to management, to the projectionist—"

Irma nodded, smiling benevolently.

"No, wait," García-García said.

"*You* wait," she replied.

"You must be kidding."

"*You* must be kidding."

"Get out!" he cried.

"*You* get out!"

"This is my house!"

"This is my city!"

Nayeli was thrilled: politics in action!

Irma said, "It could be good for you when I'm in power."

García-García took a meditative puff of his cigarette.

"What does this—this—problem have to do with me?"

"We demand, at the very least, a good job *as projectionist*."

"I am the projectionist!" he said.

"Train a woman!"

He stared at her.

Aunt Irma leaned over the desk and said, "Don't be an idiot."

"Excuse me?" he cried.

"Someday I will be President," Irma said. "It would be wise for you to get with our program and attend to the needs of the women who now rule this municipality."

She audaciously grabbed his pack of cigarettes and shook one out for herself and then posed, waiting for him to light it.

Es la Bette Davis, Nayeli thought, having seen this very scene on Irma's television.

García-García lit the cigarette.

Irma said, "Do you want to make money or not? Do you wish to benefit from good relations with City Hall?"

The Great Man stared over their heads, calculating. He smoked and thought. He slowly nodded.

It was all over in short order. Irma had already spoken to Nayeli's mother, and she was ready to be trained for the job of Projectionist of the Pedro Infante. Nayeli watched, amazed, as the two negotiators shook hands.

"One last thing," Irma said. "As a favor to me."

"Name it, Champion."

"I would like to see the cinema reborn with a film festival of my favorite Mexican superstar."

"Oh, no," García-García said, raising his hands as if to deflect a blow.

"This is nonnegotiable. I need the inspiration in these trying times of seeing Mexico's greatest film star, Yul Brynner!"

"I have told you one hundred times that Yul Brynner is not a Mexican!" García-García cried.

"Are you crazy?" Irma snapped. "I was the bowling champion! I bowled in Mexicali! I bowled in Puerto Vallarta—and I saw his house! Right there in the jungle! On a hill! *¡Es Mexicano, Yul Brynner!*"

"No, no, no—"

"Besides," Irma announced, "I saw *Taras Bulba,* and Yul Brynner spoke perfect Spanish."

García-García shook his head.

"It was dubbed."

"Don't be ridiculous," Irma said. "Come, Nayeli!" she snapped.

García-García stared at Nayeli.

"She's impossible," he said.

"I am counting on you," Irma called.

Nayeli waved her fingers at him and walked out.

Election Day dawned brightly—no clouds in the sky at all. Everyone voted, even García-García—he shoved his ballot marked in favor of Ernesto James, the old mayor, into the box with manly force, then strode out, lit cigar in his mouth, showing his determination before mounting his bike to wobble home. Election monitors from Escuinapa manned the booths in the Secu Carlos Hubbard school assembly hall. Tacho cooked free ham tortas for all voters, and Nayeli busied herself running sodas to all the eaters. Tacho, no fool, put extra chipotle salsa on the ham and charged elevated prices for the cold drinks. The Fallen Hand made a killing.

It was a parade: María, the projectionist-in-training, accepted a round of applause when she swept into the polling place; Sensei Grey wore his fedora; Aunt Irma voted for herself; Tacho took a quick break from his grill to vote, then spelled Nayeli so she could do her civic duty. Yoloxochitl and La Vampira slouched in, acting bored. Tacho kept his eye on two outside agitators, El Guasas and El Pato, who lurked behind the whitewashed trees in the square. The ubiquitous narco LTD oozed past, followed by a black Cherokee with darkened windows.

It was all over by ten o'clock. The ballots were counted in La Mano Caída. As predicted, Aunt Irma won by a landslide.

Outgoing mayor Ernesto James noted darkly to García-García that it was women who counted the ballots, but there were not enough men to force a recount. Despairing, he looked at the female rabble gathered in the square and threw up his hands.

Aunt Irma took the podium in the plaza and announced, "What did I tell you!"

Firecrackers. Bottle rockets. Free burro rides for the children. A ninety-eight-year-old soldier from the last battle of the Revolution broke out a bugle and skronked like a dying elephant. Tacho turned up his stereo really loud and played records by El Tri and Café Tacuba.

Irma, the conquering heroine of Tres Camarones, threw her arm around Nayeli's shoulders. She said, "A new age dawns."

Chapter Seven

———

Night.

Mami was asleep—Nayeli could hear her soft, whistling snores coming from her room.

Poor Vampi, Nayeli thought. She was an orphan—her parents had died in one of those events Nayeli thought of as somehow especially Mexican. They had gone south instead of north, seeking work in Jalisco. Their bus driver had fallen asleep, and the bus had plunged off a cliff, killing all the passengers. The driver had survived.

Vampi's grandmother had raised her. No mother or father in Tres Camarones would have allowed her to get away with her goth outfits, but a tired grandmother could not hope to contain her.

Nayeli wandered through her mother's small house in the dark. The sideboard that held her father's picture was always lit with a few votive candles standing on saucers, Doña María's small altar to Don Pepe.

Nayeli used the hem of her blouse to dust the standing picture frame. Her father looked so handsome in his police uniform, erect and grim—he believed no real man ever smiled in photographs, especially not in uniform. After all, aside from the mayor, Don Pepe was the sole representative of the Revolutionary Government of the Republic. A man's man, but also a leader among men.

He used to take her down to the Baluarte River to shoot his .38. She smiled. He'd set up soda bottles, and she'd shoot six rounds at a time and miss the bottles with every shot. He never said he wished he'd had a son, though she could tell he thought it often. He'd park his police car beside the soccer field, and when she scored a goal, he'd set off the siren, sorely frightening the mothers in the stands.

But he could not make enough money to take care of them. He earned the equivalent of twenty American dollars a week. And he had to buy his own pistol and bullets.

On the day he left, there was wailing and breast-beating. He held Nayeli for a moment — she could smell his aftershave and his shaving cream and his deodorant and his breath mints. And he...

The bus...

The empty street...

She shook her head.

Don Pepe had been philosophical. He had always offered her nuggets of wisdom that he would have given his son if he had only been so blessed. And the short girl he called La Chaparra was a good kid and had listened intently to his insights. So when he told Nayeli, "The more I learn, the less I know," she pondered it. He was a big reader, and he informed her once that all water that ever existed remained in its original form. "You drink the same water that Jesus Christ washed his feet in," Don Pepe lectured. "Cleopatra once took a bath in your ice cube."

His favorite saying, because it was concise, was: "Everything passes." He had written this gnomic prophecy on his postcard from KANKAKEE, ILLINOIS, with its luridly colored picture of a mentally ill wild turkey and cornfield. *"Mi Dear Chaparra — things go well here. Good boys at work. I will send funds soon. I have much luck. But...Everything Passes. Your Father, Pepe."*

Don Pepe was a Mexican man: a fatalist. He meant to impart much more than comfort. He meant that all good things would also end. All joy would crumble. And death would visit each and every one of them. He meant that regimes and ancient orders and cultures would all collapse. The world as we know it becomes a new world overnight.

The announcements were already going out: the Cine Pedro Infante was back in the film festival business. María Cervantes had taken her projectionist exams at the hand of García-García and had passed. He had put in his orders for the first films, and though it felt corrupt, he had caved in to Aunt Irma's City Hall pressure and brought in Yul Brynner movies. Of course, García-García was Mexico's number one Steve McQueen fan. Indeed, he would have shown *Baby, the Rain Must Fall* every week if he could have. Still, was not politics the art of compromise? To be sure, Irma was now mayor and crossing her an extremely unwise strategy. And yet, García-García had some things going for himself, too. He was a cineaste. He knew of Orson Welles and Bela Lugosi and Zeppo Marx, and he knew there were ways to insert Estip McQueen in a Yul Brynner film fest. There was one movie—just one—that featured both of them. "¡Ese cuate sí es todo un hombre!" he announced to his housekeepers as he studied the McQueen poster on his wall. Yes, they agreed, that dude was 100 percent MAN.

For the other film of his planned double feature, García-García was faced with a choice between *The King and I* and *Westworld*. He chose to keep the western theme as pure as possible and went for the killer cowboy-robot thriller. The movie office had promised him that both films were subtitled, not dubbed. They would hear the real voices—well, German-dubbed—of the actors. He would show Aunt Irma once and for all that Yul Brynner was not a Mexican from Puerto Vallarta! The robot movie would play first;

second would come the great team-up, Brynner and McQueen. Second would come *The Magnificent Seven*.

Many of the tropical movie houses had no roofs. Inside, they featured covered galleries along the walls, and when it started to rain, the moviegoers stood under the eaves and kept watching the films until the weather passed. The cheap theater in Culiacán was known as Las Pulgas because it was so filthy you could get fleas from going there. But García-García had put a corrugated-tin roof over his beloved Pedro Infante, leaving open only the last four feet between the tops of the cinder-block walls and the angled roof lest the overwhelming body heat condense on the tin and drop on the audience in a small salty squall. It was true that when the catastrophic summer rains hit every June sixth, the racket was so loud that the sound track couldn't be heard, but those within remained dry. And, really, with subtitles, only the most spoiled moviegoer would claim to have lost the narrative thread.

Inside, the seats were metal, and the joke was that everybody who went to the Pedro Infante was a wetback, because the seat backs made everyone sweat. In fact, the seats were all rusted red from years of back sweat. At either side of the screen stood two huge revolving fans. The blasts of fetid air these fans shot at the crowd occasionally knocked the bats from their roosts on the ceiling, and they fell, fluttering wildly over the heads of the people. Old-timers kept a handy newspaper or cardboard fan at their seats so they could shoo the winged rodents away—which they did without ever taking their eyes off Cantinflas or John Wayne.

The house was filling fast. Nayeli, Tacho on her arm, paid her respects to Father François, as ever in the front row. "When are you coming to church?" he asked Tacho.

"¡Por Dios!" Tacho said. "We would all be hit by lightning."

La Vampi was hanging out with two girls from the Secundaria Carlos Hubbard.

"¿Qué onda, morra?" Vampi called.

"Orale, rucas de la Secu Carlitos," Nayeli shouted back.

Yoloxochitl was with her mother and her grandmother.

There was García-García, sitting with four of his five females. The shrimpers from the crabbing day at the lagoon had come with their wives. Tiki Ledón sat with her mother, one of Chava Chavarín's conquests, the vivacious Doña Laura. Tía Irma studiously ignored her—after forty years, she remained an archrival.

Everybody was there, even Pepino, the town simpleton, who seemed to be selling sodas on a tray. Nayeli and Tacho took a seat behind La Osa, who turned around and warned, "Don't be saying stupid things while I'm watching my movie."

She turned back around and lit a cigarette.

"What's her problem?" Tacho asked.

Irma snapped, without looking back, "What did I tell you, cabrón!"

"The movie didn't even start yet!" Tacho bleated.

Nayeli signaled Pepino and bought each of them a soda.

"Nayeli"—Pepino giggled—"marry Pepino!"

"Maybe tomorrow," she replied.

"¡Ay! ¡Ay-ay-ay!" he enthused, then stumbled down the steps to deliver a Coca to Father François.

Nayeli leaned against Tacho's arm.

"I hate Yul Brynner," she whispered.

"I *know*," Tacho whispered back. "¡Viejo feo!"

The lights went down.

Uproar. Much clapping. Nayeli knew how to stick two fingers in her mouth and blow, unleashing a wail as loud as a passing train whistle.

García-García had a treat for them: cartoons!

He sat back and laughed out loud at the Roadrunner.

The laughter was so loud that the startled bats launched from their perches and did a quick strafing run above the crowd—Aunt Irma simply set her lighter on high and blasted two feet of flame over her head.

Westworld. The title in Spanish was *Robot-Terror of the Psychopathic Bandido*. Nayeli groaned. Tacho whispered, "I've seen this one on TV. They have sex-robots."

Irma turned and glared at him.

"Sorry," he said.

Nayeli and Tacho giggled when Aunt Irma's silhouette clearly fidgeted every time Yul "El Mexicano" Brynner appeared onscreen.

She turned at one point and said, "Do you hear that accent? You can hardly tell he's Mexican!"

Nayeli snorted.

It was over quickly enough. La Osa was obviously displeased that Yul had been shot down and had his face blown away by the gringo bastards in the movie. She was thinking: *I would buy that robot!*

Intermission.

Nayeli abandoned Tacho and made the rounds of all her girlies. They lounged and slumped in the aisles. A cumbia band hired by García-García entered the theater and revved up another mindless vamp about a handsome black-skinned girl whose dancing broke the bones of all the men watching her. The chorus was: "¡Calienete! ¡La Negra está caliente!"

During the intermission, Father François told Nayeli, "Of course you know that *The Magnificent Seven* is based on Kurosawa's classic sword-fighting epic, *The Seven Samurai*."

Hearing "epic"—*epopeya*—Yolo quipped, "Oh! Popeye is in it?"

Angry, Father François continued: "The villagers are beset by bandidos. Overwhelmed and outgunned, they resort to a desperate plan—they go to Los Yunaites—"

"And work at Burger King!" Yolo blurted.

Father François returned to his seat. If he couldn't teach these idiots catechism, what made him think they could be taught about world cinema?

Nayeli followed him.

"I'm listening, Padre. Ignore them."

He huffed.

"As I was saying. They send a group of brave peasants north to Los Yunaites." He cast an evil eye at Yolo and her homegirls.

"What do they do there?" Nayeli asked.

"They find seven gunmen. The magnificent seven, you see? Seven killers that they bring back from the border to fight for them."

In spite of herself, Nayeli felt tingles.

"Chido," she said.

She hurried back to her seat to whisper to Tacho.

When that music started, she got tingles again.

The insanely picturesque color, the gigantic landscapes, even the pathetic Mexican village and the chubby gringo bad guy making believe he was a Mexican bandido, she loved it all.

Tacho yawned. "I want to see a car chase," he said.

Irma: "SHH!"

"I don't like horses," Tacho added.

Irma: "SHHHHH!"

When Yul Brynner strode into the picture, wearing the same

outfit he'd worn as the killer cowboy-robot in *Westworld*, Nayeli nudged Tacho.

"Oh, my God!" he said. "Can't he afford new clothes?"

Aunt Irma growled.

They laughed behind their hands.

Suddenly, there was Steve McQueen.

"He has a stupid little cowboy hat," Tacho noted, marking McQueen a few points down on his mental fashion scorecard.

García-García kept his enthusiasm in check as long as he could, but when Mr. McQueen shot a bunch of bad guys out of windows while Yul Brynner merely drove the wagon they were riding in, he could no longer stay silent. ¡Era más macho, ese pinchi McQueen! That was what Tres Camarones needed! Real men doing manly things like shooting sons of bitches out of windows! He let out a yell:

"¡VIVA ESTIP McQUEEN!"

Irma could not believe this.

"¡VIVA YUL BRYNNER!" she hollered back.

"¡ESTIP!"

"¡YUL!"

All around them, people were shushing them.

Tacho noted, "I thought you wanted quiet."

"Be quiet yourself, you fool. ¡VIVA YUL!"

Someone threw a wadded paper cup at Aunt Irma, and she piped down with some grumbling. She was furious. She could see García-García down there, turning to his seatmates and explaining the many wonders of Estip McQueen. And McQueen wasn't even a Mexican!

Nayeli sat with her mouth open. Tacho was snoring softly beside her. She looked deeper into the theater and saw Yolo and her family calmly watching.

Didn't anybody else feel the electric charge she felt?

She watched the rest of the movie in a daze. She hardly saw what happened on the screen—she had already sunk deep into her own thoughts. When the lights came up and the people clapped and Yolo whistled and Tacho snorted awake and García-García stood and accepted all the kudos, Nayeli remained in her seat.

"M'ija," Tacho said, "I'm tired. I'm going home."

He air-kissed her cheek, but she didn't notice it.

Nayeli pulled her father's postcard from her sock and studied it. A cornfield with an impossibly blue sky, an American sky: she had seen it over and over again in the movie. Only American skies, apparently, were so stunningly blue. She turned the card over. It said: "A TYPICAL CORN CROP IN KANKAKEE, ILLINOIS." She more or less understood the message. *Una cosecha típica,* she told herself. Don Pepe had written, "Everything Passes."

She rose slowly and drifted out the door.

Yolo and La Vampira were waiting outside.

"¿Qué te pasa?" La Vampi asked.

Yolo said, "Are you all right, chica?"

Nayeli waved them off.

"Hey," said Yolo. "We're talking to you."

Nayeli gestured for them to follow her and walked to the town square.

She absentmindedly swept off a bench and sat down. Her home-girls sat on either side of her. She held up a finger for quiet while she thought some more.

She finally said, "The Magnificent Seven."

They stared at her.

"So?" said Yolo.

"Bo-ring," said Vampi.

"The seven," Nayeli repeated.

"What about them?" Yolo said.

"We have to go get them," Nayeli said. "We have to go to Los Yunaites and get the seven."

"¡Qué!" Vampi cried. "¿Estip McQueen?"

"¡No, mensa!" Yolo snapped. "He's dead."

"We have to stop the bandits before they come and destroy the village. Don't you see? They're coming."

"So?" said Vampi.

"Who is going to fight them?" Nayeli asked.

Yolo dug her toe into the ground.

"Cops?" she said.

"What cops?" Nayeli asked.

Yolo shrugged one shoulder.

"I guess...your dad would have."

They sat there.

"We go," Nayeli said. "We find seven men who want to come home. But they have to be—what?"

"Soldiers," Yolo suggested.

"Right! We interview men. Only cops or soldiers can come."

Vampi held up a finger.

"Perdón," she said. "Where are we going, again?"

"Los Yunaites," Yolo said.

"What? Are you kidding?"

"We're not kidding," Nayeli said.

"Oh, great," Vampi complained. "There goes my week!"

"We have a mission," Nayeli said. "We're only going there to bring the men back home."

Vampi said, "Maybe you can find your father."

Nayeli looked at her. She sat back down.

"What about *my* father?" Yolo demanded.

Vampi replied, "He's not a cop."

They sat there, stunned by the enormity of Nayeli's plan.

"We will only be there for as long as it takes to get the men to come," she continued. "The Americanos will be happy we're there! Even if we're caught!"

"You're crazy," Yolo said.

"Dances," Nayeli whispered. "Boyfriends. Husbands. Babies. Police—law and order. No bandidos."

They sat there for ten minutes, looking at the ground.

"Pin tenders, too," Yolo offered. "Because, you know, I am tired of working at the bowling alley."

"Maybe, you know, we could get one gay boy," Nayeli said. "For poor Tacho."

Yolo nodded wisely. "Tacho needs love, too."

"We should take Tacho with us!" Vampi cried.

They turned to her with a bit of awe. It was the first really good idea La Vampi had ever had.

The girlfriends had all seen *Los Hermanos Blues* at the Pedro Infante a few months earlier.

"We're on a mission from God," Nayeli intoned.

La Vampi turned to her and said, "I'm going."

Nayeli cried, "We can repopulate our town. We can save Mexico. It begins with us! It's the new revolution!" She stood up. "Isn't it time we got our men back in our own country?" She was slipping into Aunt Irma campaign mode. She sat back down.

"Oh, my God," said Yolo. "I can't believe I'm agreeing to this."

They slapped hands.

"To the north," Nayeli said.

"Al norte," they replied.

"We have to tell the old woman," Nayeli said.

"¿La Osa?" cried Yolo. "Are you crazy? She'll never allow us to do it."

"I think she will."

"No, she won't. She'll bite our heads off."

"No," Nayeli said. She stood up and brushed off her rear end. "I think she will give us her blessing."

She started to walk away, but stopped and turned back.

"We are going," she said, "to bring home the Magnificent Seven!"

Late that same night, Irma was startled by a knock at her door. When she opened it, she was amazed to discover García-García standing there with a suitcase. His left eye was black, and he had blood trickling from his nose.

"What the hell happened to you?" she demanded.

"They came to my house."

"Who?"

"Bandidos."

"Bastards!"

"They threw me out."

"No!"

"They took my house from me!"

She stood there in her tattered nightgown and curlers.

"Can I sleep here?" he asked.

Irma had only been in charge of the town for scant days, and already the troubles were starting.

"Sleep in the back room," she said.

He trudged in, forlorn and humiliated.

"Hope you don't snore," La Osa added, and slammed her door.

Chapter Eight

Most of them were crammed into Irma's kitchen. The overflow stood in the street, with their faces jammed in Irma's television window. The priest and several concerned grandmothers stood in the living room; the eldest of them took up regal space on the flowered couch. Poor García-García sulked in the backyard, trying to keep Irma's turkey away from him with one foot.

Of course, Tacho had always wanted to go north, but he wasn't going to admit it. What was there for a man like him in Tres Camarones? Less than nothing. Maybe the girls. And there was no way he was going to let the girlfriends face the dangers, or the excitement, of going to el norte without him.

In his mind, they would cross the border under a stack of hay in an old truck, like the heroes in Nazi movies always escaped from occupied France. Some Border Patrol agent might poke the hay with a pitchfork, only to be called away by barking German shepherds just as the tines came perilously close. Maybe Yolo or Vampi would get poked, in a thigh, and would heroically bite back her yelps of pain. Not Nayeli—she was the leader of the commando unit. Tacho saw her in some kind of hot shorts with a red blouse tied under her breasts. There would be a close-up of the blood drops falling on the cobbles, but the impatient Border Patrol agents would wave them through, unseeing—in fact, their own boots would obliterate the telltale blood drops. And then he'd be there: La Jolla and its emerald beaches. Hollywood. Los Beberly Hills. Stars and nightclubs and haute couture. Tacho was ready.

Aunt Irma had to promise to manage the daily operations of the Fallen Hand before Tacho would agree to go with the notorious girlfriends. Then came the tense negotiations between Irma and the mothers, grandmothers, and aunts. No one was willing to let her girl go into the maw of the appalling border. A long journey far from home, predatory men and Mexican police, bandits, injuries, car wrecks, kidnapping, slavers, pimps, drug pushers, illness, jails, *Tijuana!* The word alone speaking volumes about every border-fear they held within them. Coyotes and smugglers. Border Patrol and Minutemen. Rapists, addicts, dogs, robots, demons, ghosts, serial killers, racists, army men, trucks, spotlights. *¡Por Dios!* they cried, these were just girls!

Tacho helpfully informed them: "I am not a girl, thank you very much!"

"If God is with us," Nayeli pontificated, "what harm can befall us?"

Tacho sipped his Nescafé instant and thought: *How about crucifixion? Lions? Burning alive?* He glanced at Irma. She wasn't moved by the religious propaganda, either. But Father François stood at the back of the room and raised his hand over the girls in a benediction and said, "Benditas sean." He looked at Tacho, who was irked that the girls got all the blessings. "And you, too," François amended.

Tacho raised his cup.

"Amen."

"When I was on my master tour of the bowling alleys of the borderlands," Irma said, rising and stubbing her cigarette out in

Tacho's coffee cup, "representing all of you—representing our home—our fine city—I went alone. What horrors did I face? I ask you. What horrors?" She made them jump when she bellowed, "ALL OF THEM!"

She leaned forward on her hands.

"Worse that I was convicted of one crime: being a woman! My efforts for the homeland were disparaged by your men and by you. Admit it! I fought with my bowling ball for all the women—and the useless men—of Camarones. And I did it alone! Yes or no?"

They muttered, "Yes."

"Well, I was an illegal."

Cries of shock. Uproar. Shouting.

She held up her hands.

"I may have a passport now. But then? I had no plans to cross that terrible wire! I was bowling in Mexico! But do you think for a minute that the call of athletics stops at some imaginary political boundary? Eh? What of the Olympics! I was called to bowl in the United States! For the honor of MEXICO!"

Her audience reeled, they rocked in their seats, they thrilled.

"I went into Los Yunaites! By God I did! I was showing them all! Mexican womanhood—I stuck it in their faces! I bowled at the Bowlero! I bowled at the Hillcrest! I bowled at the Aztec Lanes!"

This meant nothing to the gathered witnesses, but it sounded impressive. She could have been saying, "I bowled at the White House!" Maybe she had.

The point was, Aunt Irma had been a champion in Gringolandia, too! "And, like these dear girls, I did it for you, you doubters. You should be ashamed."

Go, Osa! Nayeli smiled at Tacho. She was incredible!

"Do you think I would send these warriors—these brave girls and this fine heroic boy—into the north with no help? No succor? Are you insane! Good God—you ARE insane! First you ladies let yourselves be pushed around by your useless men for a hundred years. Then you let those men escape. Now you deny the future! To bold young women! You are not the new woman! You are shameful!"

She sat back down. She snapped her fingers.

"Get me some more coffee," she told Tacho.

"I'm not your maid," he said.

But he got up and got it.

Irma slurped it loudly and said: "I went there. I bowled Tijuana, you know! How do you think I got into the United States? Hmm? Did I sprout wings and fly? I could have if I'd wanted to, but I didn't want to! No—I used my brain. Do you have brains? These girls have brains. Tacho...well, I don't know about Tacho."

She continued. "Do you think your little husbands, those whore-mongers, were the first to leave Camarones? Do you remember the name...Chavarín?"

Chavarín! He looked like Gilbert Roland or Vicente Fernández! He was their half-Basque fisherman! That mustache! Those two-tone shoes in shades of brown and crème, shoes that allowed him to glide across dance floors like a sweet outpouring of syrup!

Irma chuckled. "I was a mango in my day. Was I or was I not?"

"You were," María agreed.

"I've seen the pictures," Nayeli said.

"That must have been a long time ago, m'ija," Tacho said, "because lately—"

Nayeli kicked him under the table.

Irma glared at him.

"I was the handsomest woman in Sinaloa," she continued, "and Chavarín had the best mustache. He moved to Tijuana in 1963. Did he not? He did! What did I do? I'll tell you what I did. I looked Chavarín up in the phone book. How many Chavaríns do you imagine there are in any phone book? Not many!"

The gathered populace was amazed by Irma's brilliance.

"I called Chavarín! I went to his home! And when the time came, he drove me right across the line in his fine Lincoln Town Car. 'US ceetee-zin,' he said, and I said, 'US citee por sure!' and they let us through! He told them I was his wife!"

Gasps.

The audacity of Chava Chavarín!

"That's it! You need connections to survive and cross that border! I have connections!"

She rose again: all their eyes followed her.

"I," she announced, raising her finger above her head like Fidel Castro, "have sent a telegram to Chavarín in Tijuana! The destiny of these warriors is already assured!"

They clapped for her. They sighed and spoke among themselves. María took Irma's hands in her own.

Irma handed Nayeli a scrap of paper with the outdated telephone number LIB-477.

"Libertad," she noted portentiously.

Ooh, liberty, the aunties thought.

Everything had taken on an air of Revolutionary Mexico.

"You will see," Irma said. "The Americanos are kind. Friendly people. Generous people. They have quaint customs—they aren't really, shall we say, sophisticated like we are. You can't drink the water—it will give you diarrhea. But it's very clean there. Good food. You'll see."

She stopped and pointed at all the girls, one by one.

"Your dead are buried here. You were each born here, and your umbilical cords are buried in this earth. This town has been here since time began! God himself came from Tres Camarones, and don't you ever forget it. When the Apaches rode down the coast, burning all the cities, they stopped here and ate mangos and fresh pineapples! That crazy gringo general Black Jack Pershing came here looking for Pancho Villa! He danced with my aunt Teresa in the plazuela! In the hurricane of 1958, Don Pancho Mena was carried out to sea by the wind, and he rode a dolphin back to shore! And I won't have some rude gangsters, or some exodus of weak-kneed men looking for money, ruin my hometown!"

They were in awe of Aunt Irma, which was the way she liked it.

"Why do you think I run this town?" she asked. There was no need to answer.

Nayeli stuffed her backpack with her change of jeans, her panties, her clean socks, and her blouses. Deodorant. Tampons. She was packing lightly. She wore her best fútbol tennies with white gym socks. García-García had presented her with a paperback copy of *Don Quixote*, but she couldn't make sense of it and would end up leaving it on the bus. Then she pulled out Matt's card and paper-clipped Irma's Tijuana phone number to it and tucked it into her back pocket.

Her weeping mother came into her room.

"Are you taking your father's postcard?" she asked.

"May I?"

"You should."

They stood together looking at the picture of the paranoiac turkey in the cornfield.

"I wish you could go there," María said. "To KANKAKEE. I wish you could bring him back."

Nayeli took her hand.

"If I can," she suddenly heard herself promising, "I will."

"Oh, Nayeli!" Her mother threw her arms around her and sobbed.

Aunt Irma made travel packs for each warrior. In big ziplock bags, she put toothpaste, toothbrushes, small bars of hand soap, small bottles of shampoo, rolls of mint Life Savers, packets of matches, some Band-Aids, small packets of tissues. She gave each of them chocolates, M&Ms with peanuts, in case they got hungry. In Nayeli's bag was a small jar of Vicks VapoRub. "I know you get stuffy," she said.

They were astonished when Tacho arrived at the bivouac. He had chopped his hair into spikes and oiled it up. Even worse, he had dyed it platinum blond. Vampi ran her hands over the spikes. Tacho had a can of pepper spray tucked into his left sock, and his shirt said: QUEEN. He smirked. Nobody in Camarones would ever get that joke.

In spite of the alarming haircut, García-García, not trusting mere girls to accomplish the mission, pressed $500 on Tacho. Tacho added the money to his savings, 600 more US dollars, zipped inside his money belt.

There was more to come. The town had taken up a collection, and they handed their savings over to the girls. The bank converted the pesos and coins into American greenbacks, giving Nayeli $1,256. Yoloxochitl had $150 from her family and $65 in pin-tending money. La Vampi had $35. Tacho handed Nayeli $50 of his own. "It's your tips, m'ija." She split it with Vampi.

Mothers and strangers gathered in front of the Fallen Hand. Irma's Cadillac settled on its springs as the travelers loaded the trunk. Vampi and Yolo hefted small shoulder bags onto their backs. Yolo had clothes and books stuffed in her school backpack. Tacho's duffel was large and heavy, stuffed with discotheque clothes. La Vampi hid a switchblade that El Quemapueblos had once given her in her back pocket. Nayeli carried a tiny gift purse Tacho had given her. Bundles of tortillas were pressed on the travelers. A greasy paper bag of sweet rolls.

Sensei Grey stepped forward and bowed deeply.

He suddenly threw a punch at Nayeli. She blocked it and spun and laid her foot against his jaw. The master smiled and bowed again.

Tears.

Wails of sorrow.

The four warriors waved bravely to the crowd. The girls kissed their mothers and grandmothers. Father François blessed them again. They got into the Cadillac. They slammed the doors. Aunt Irma honked the horn three times, drove around the plazuela a few times waving out the window, and they were gone.

Pepino climbed onto the roof of the Fallen Hand, yelling, "Nayeli! Nayeli! Come back to Pepino, Nayeliii!"

Aunt Irma accompanied them into the Tres Estrellas bus terminal. Poor folks in straw hats shuffled around with paper bags tied with twine. Mothers fed their children beans from plastic containers they were carrying because they couldn't afford the food on the road. Electronic voices echoed off the cement floors.

Irma bought their tickets.

"Four, one-way, to Tijuana."

The ticket taker had seen this before.

He smirked.

"It's not what you think," she snapped at him.

He shrugged.

"I have no opinion," he said.

She distributed the tickets like playing cards to her warriors. She bought them all cold sodas and bottles of water for the road. Vampi cadged a rock-and-roll magazine out of her. Yolo had a paperback book called *Caballo de Troya VI*. The cover announced, "Jesus Christ was a UFO pilot!"

The huge bus loomed outside the window. Their driver was a dark-faced fat man named Chuy. His uniform was crisp, and he wore his bus pilot's cap at a jaunty angle. Chuy oversaw the loading of their bags into the bins under the bus, then he positioned himself at the door to take tickets.

He eyed the girls. And Tacho.

Tacho said, "¿Qué?"

"Nada," Chuy replied. "Aquí nomás."

He took Tacho's ticket.

He looked at Irma, hovering about, fussing with the girls' hair.

"I'll take care of them," he promised her. "No worries."

He gestured for their tickets.

Tacho hopped aboard and never looked back.

"Remember," Irma said. "Call Chavarín immediately. Don't move one step without him."

"All right," Nayeli said, and went to board.

Irma pulled her back.

"Don't forget—former cops. Or soldiers."

"Got it."

"But," Irma said, "don't dawdle. In and out. And call me."

"I will."

"If there's any trouble, I'll fly there and meet you."

Nayeli stared.

"You'll...come to Tijuana?"

"Why not?"

Nayeli was a bit put off by this revelation.

Irma blushed. Fiddled with her hair. "It depends," she said. Her face was bright carmine. Her eyelids fluttered. "It depends, you know, on what Chava says." She laughed a tiny little laugh.

Oh, my God! Nayeli thought. *She's in love!* This was all some kind of bizarre dating service for La Osa!

"You'd better get going," Irma said.

"I intend to go to get my father," Nayeli blurted.

It was a day of revelations.

They stared at each other: stalemate.

"We'll see...." Irma muttered.

Irma would have kissed Nayeli, but couldn't get herself to lay her lips on Nayeli's cheek. She popped an air kiss beside her face and shoved her toward the steps.

Chuy took her ticket.

Irma gave Yolo a brief hug and pushed her toward the bus, too.

Chuy took her ticket.

La Osa smacked Vampi's bottom and said, "Crazy girl."

Chuy took her ticket and smiled.

"Are you crazy?" he said.

"I am a vampire."

"Ay, Dios."

"Make me proud," Irma called, then hurried away before they could answer her.

They found two rows of seats, four across, near the back of the bus. Yolo and Vampi sat on the left side. Nayeli and Tacho fought over the window on the right. They were all amazed that there was a bathroom at the back of the bus. Then they immediately started to flirt when a flushed American boy got on. He was only going as far as Los Mochis, but that didn't stop them from working their magical stares, pouts, and blinks on him. La Vampi sighed a lot. Yolo looked stern yet open to suggestion. Nayeli tried her most enigmatic smiles. Tacho — Tacho ignored him completely.

Chuy boarded and hit the microphone: "We are going to Tijuana, amigos! Via Culiacán, Los Mochis, Guaymas, San Luis, and Mexicali. With a few stops in between. If you think you are going to Guadalajara, get off now!" He laughed. He shut the door. He turned on the air-conditioning, which thrilled them all at first, then froze them until they burrowed under clothing and fell asleep to escape the chill.

He released the brakes.

They rolled into dusk.

Chuy drove for precisely forty-one minutes. He pulled off the highway. The bus tilted in the gloom as he drove it into an alley.

"What the hell!" Tacho demanded.

The American boy was asleep behind them.

Voices were muttering: "Where is he going?"

They brushed between bushes and banana trees. The bus
rocked over potholes and ruts. Then Chuy pulled up behind a small
house.

"I'll be right back," he said.

He opened the doors and hopped out. They craned at the windows to see what he was up to. The back door of the house opened
and a woman appeared. Chuy took off his cap and gave her a rav-
ishing kiss. They went inside and slammed the door.

"Ah!" somebody said. "His wife!"

"Or his girlfriend!" someone else replied.

"He's having supper!" another called out.

"Or his girlfriend!"

They all laughed and waited.

They were already an hour off schedule once Chuy sauntered back
from his layover and bowed when the passengers applauded him.
They drowsed through Culiacán—a rustling stop where peasants traded places with other peasants. They carried tin pots of
hot beans for the road. Tart goat cheese. Then Chuy sped to Los
Mochis, announcing, "Los Mochis, Sinaloa! The most beautiful
city in the world!" The girls awoke and regretfully saw the American boy off the bus. He stepped into the moth-crazy night, bright in

Chuy's lights against the whitewashed trunks of trees on the street. Dog barks and donkey brays entered with the hot air, sounding oddly dull and dusty.

"Now leaving Los Mochis," Chuy said, and slammed the doors shut.

PSSHHT! The brakes hissed.

They rolled.

They were deep asleep when the soldiers stopped the bus. Nayeli was the first to awaken. She sensed the bus braking, the startling lurch as it dropped off the blacktop and stopped. She nudged Tacho awake.

"What?" he said, sitting up. "What?"

Chuy was looking at them in the rearview mirror. He locked eyes with Nayeli and raised his eyebrows, shook his head slightly, made a small calming motion with his palms. Tacho poked Yolo, who snorted awake and elbowed Vampi.

Chuy opened the doors. Everybody on the bus was awake now. A soldier with an M16 slung over his shoulder stepped aboard.

"Lights," he said.

Chuy clicked on the interior lights.

Everybody was blinking, covering their eyes.

A second soldier's head appeared behind the first's back, peering in at them from the steps. Nayeli saw soldiers standing around the bus, looking up at them in the windows.

The first soldier entered, and the second, then a third. They filled the narrow passageway. They looked as young as Nayeli.

They first stared at an old woman alone in the right front row.

"Drugs?" he said.

"¡Ay Dios, no!" she cried.

He nodded, but he was already looking beyond her.

They came down the aisle, poking travelers with the barrels of their weapons.

"¿Mojados?" the first soldier asked a small group of men in front of Nayeli and Tacho.

"Only when we get to the other side," one of the men quipped.

"Oh?" the soldier said.

"We're Mexicans! From Jalisco."

He nodded.

Moved forward.

He paused and looked at Nayeli.

His eyes fell to her chest.

He smiled a fraction of a smile, then turned his eyes to Tacho.

"You," he said. "What the fuck are you supposed to be?"

"Wetback," Tacho said. "When we get to the border."

"Where you from?"

"Tres Camarones."

"Never heard of it."

The soldiers looked at each other and smirked again.

The second soldier said, "This one looks like he's carrying drugs."

"Marijuana?" his partner said to Tacho.

"No."

"Coca?"

"Hell, no."

The soldier laid his rifle across the seat back in front of Tacho's face.

"When you leave Mexico," he said, "don't come back."

"Don't worry," Tacho said. "I'm on my way."

What did he care? He'd never see this piece of crap again. But he knew better than to mouth off.

They looked at Yolo and Vampi, and were about to say something else, when they caught sight of a couple huddled in the rear of the bus.

"¿Y ustedes, qué?" the first soldier demanded.

"Nada," the man said. "Vamos a Tijuana."

"¿Deveras? ¿Para qué van?"

The man spread his hands.

"Trabajo," he said.

The soldiers were jamming in at his seat.

They kicked him.

"¡Ay!" he said.

"You're illegal," the interrogator said.

"No!"

"You snuck into Mexico, cabrón."

"No," the woman cried. "¡Por favor!"

"We're Mexicans," the man said.

"You're foreigners."

"No!"

Nayeli was shaking. Tacho put his hand on her forearm. He looked at the two girls across the aisle and mimicked looking forward with his eyes.

The soldier smacked the man in the mouth.

The two travelers were both crying.

"Where are you from, cabrón?"

"Colombia," he admitted.

Cursing, the soldiers dragged him from his seat. The woman was yelling. The second soldier grabbed her arm and twisted it behind her.

"It'll go better for you if you keep your mouth shut," he said.

The Colombians were dragged and bounced down the aisle and shoved down the steps, and the soldier said, "Get out of here" to Chuy, who made the sign of the cross and shut the doors and started the engine and bounced the bus hard as he got back up on the road.

Nayeli saw the palest ghosts in the night as the Colombians were tossed into a tan Humvee and then were swallowed whole by dust and darkness and were gone, as if it had all been a dream.

Their little bags were still in the overhead bin.

Nayeli caught Chuy's eyes in the mirror again.

He shook his head. He shrugged. He turned off the interior lights.

Gunshots awoke them before dawn.

Tacho dove out of his seat and sprawled in the aisle. Chuy wove across the highway, and the big bus shuddered when he braked. They heard yelling, then three more shots, in rapid succession: POP-POP-POP. Everybody had heard guns go off before—it could have been a rabbit hunt, or a goat's execution for a barbacoa. But it was on the long empty road.

Vampi was on top of Yolo, and she whispered, "Is it bandidos?"

Chuy was rolling slowly, peering out his side window, unsure about how he should respond to this ambush. Stop or speed away? Nayeli moved up to the sideways bench behind his seat.

"Who are they?" she said.

"I don't know."

A pickup wobbled around behind them. POP-POP. Men in cowboy hats, waving their arms in the dark.

Chuy decided: he put it in gear and sped up. The truck followed. Nayeli crouched behind him. Suddenly, the truck sped up and passed them. POP-POP-POP. The men held up banners that read: ¡PAN! They hollered. They waved. They threw beer cans. They sped away.

Chuy exhaled and slowed down.

"Jesus Christ," he said. "A political rally."

Nayeli started to laugh.

So did he.

"Are all your trips like this?" she said.

"Miss," he replied, "if you want to see the damnedest things in life, drive long-haul trips in Mexico."

By the time he had finished telling her stories of flaming car wrecks, armed bandits, UFOs, roadside devils chasing the bus, and the tragic story of Melesio, the driver who sneezed at the wheel and drove off a cliff, killing everyone but himself in the bus, the sun had come up.

Chapter Nine

———

A relief driver boarded the bus in Huila, Sonora. Chuy staggered to a small bunk behind the toilets and fell asleep. The last thing he said before starting to snore was "Thirty-minute break!"

The girls and Tacho stiffly made their way off the bus and stood, overcome by the killing desert light. A melancholy little dog wagged its peg of a tail at them, and Tacho threw a rock at it at the same time that Vampi said, "He's so cute!"

Alkaline dust moved through the flat white land like smoke. Far in the distance, a weak little dust devil whirled up and carried some scraps of paper over the sand to a rattling creosote bush. It dropped its small load of trash there as it fell apart. Immediately upon its demise, another rose and lurched away toward the far mountains that revealed themselves as a black clot of shadows on the horizon.

"Lovely," Tacho noted.

Nayeli clapped her hands together. "Come on! Let's go! Let's have breakfast and freshen up!"

They trotted across the endless black two-lane, standing aside to allow a rusted fuel tanker to bellow past, its driver pulling the air horn chain about twenty times when he saw the girls.

"He could be honking at me, you know," Tacho said.

"Dream on," Nayeli replied, marching forcefully into the tiny bus station and diner.

The toilets were caked in feces. Yolo almost threw up. The girls watched the door as each took her turn peeing in the sink. Tacho, in the men's room, was astonished to find no toilet at all, just a hole in the floor with a ghastly rind of brown stuccoed around its mouth. "Oh, well," he said, and assumed the bombardier position. There was no toilet paper. He was forced to use the newsprint pages of a fan magazine that featured pictures of pop music bands.

Inside the diner, a harried woman was negotiating for bus tickets to Mazatlán. There were three tables on a concrete floor. Passengers from the bus sat outside eating their own beans. They occasionally stepped in to buy a paper cup of coffee or a Coca-Cola. At one table, an immensely overweight boy sat, grunting and wheezing. Nayeli was fascinated by him. Fat welled up off his neck, and his breasts were so huge they ran around his sides and seemed to hold his arms away from his body. His eyes were lost in folds—she thought he might be blind. His hair was so short that she could see his sweaty scalp shining in the neon lights. He had tiny ears that seemed perched on the neck fat, and he turned his head toward the sound of the woman's voice and made little fluty noises at her. She was apparently his mother.

Tacho ordered arroz con pollo. The girls chose simple fried eggs and tortillas. Coffee all around.

The fat boy picked up the sugar dispenser. It was glass, with a slanted chrome top. Nayeli nudged Yolo, who glanced over. The boy tipped the sugar into his fist, put his head back, and poured the white crystals into his mouth. His mother walked over and gently took the sugar from him. He kicked his feet and squirmed. She whispered to him. He got up reluctantly and trudged toward the door.

"Life," the mother said to them as she passed, "does not get simpler."

"Yes, ma'am," Nayeli said.

Their meals came on paper plates.

Tacho's food was watery and gray.

"Yum-yum!" quipped Yolo, whose eggs didn't look too bad. How could you ruin eggs?

Tacho pushed at the rice with his plastic fork. There were two or three little dark blobs in there. He said, "I've never seen raisins in chicken and rice before!"

"Tachito?" Nayeli said. "Those aren't raisins."

"Oh, my God!" Vampi cried. "Tacho's raisins have legs!"

"Arroz con cucarachas," Tacho said. He raised his hands and looked at the cook.

"Qué," she said.

"I give up," Tacho announced. "I really do."

"I'm not that hungry," Nayeli said.

"Me, neither," said Yolo.

Vampi was scooping up eggs with her tortilla.

"Why not?" she said.

When she was done, they threw their plates in the garbage bin and took their coffees outside and stood with the other pilgrims in the shadeless heat.

It felt like the bus was standing still and a dun blanket was being pulled past them, occasionally snagged up with bushes or a battered gas station. Suddenly, there would be an excitement of desiccated mountains, raw peaks exploding out of the hardpan and falling away again. The girls slept. Tacho had startled them all by pulling a radio out of his duffel bag. He was slumped in the seat, chewing gum like a cheerleader, his antenna extended and the tinny voice of a Mexican talk radio host buzzing like a wasp from the speaker:

"What do we do about the Guatemalans? Have you seen the Salvadorans? ¡Por favor! Keep them out! Call me now and offer your opinion...."

Nayeli had made her way up front again, and she sat behind the new driver, looking out at the skeleton of the world.

"Look at that," he said. Green highway patrol vehicles were parked at angles beside the highway; rescuers were prying open a charred vehicle that sat in a wide circle of ashes.

"Look at that." An Indian woman ran along the highway, holding a triangular piece of cardboard over a baby's face to protect it from the sun.

"Look at that." Crumpled wrecks of cars far down ravines.

Nayeli never saw water anywhere. Riverbeds and streambeds looked like long lines of baby powder to her, buzzards circling slowly above them. "Look at that," the driver said.

A raven raced them.

Nayeli watched the cattle become more emaciated and spindly. They stood in the sun as if they'd already been slaughtered, as if they were being barbecued down to charcoal and just didn't know it. They lost their color, went from the reds and creams she knew in Sinaloa to dull brown and dusty black. They hung their heads and nuzzled awful bony weeds and cacti. Their ribs showed—the farther north the bus drove, the more pronounced the cages. Soon the cows looked like old rugs thrown over woodpiles.

"That's sad," she finally said.

"What is?" said the driver over his shoulder.

"How they suffer."

"Who?"

"The cows out here."

"What cows?"

"Those cows."

"Those there?"

"Yes, the cows. They hardly look like they have enough meat on them to eat. They must be too dry for milk."

"What cows?" he said.

"Those cows," she said.

"Where?"

Nayeli pointed.

"There! Everywhere!"

"Oh, those?" He laughed. "Those aren't cows!" he said.

"Excuse me?"

"Things must really be sad down south where you come from," the driver said. "The animals must be midgets."

"What?"

"Darling, those aren't cows. Those are northern rabbits!"

He laughed and slapped the steering wheel and winked at her in the mirror and whistled the opening notes of "Cumbia Lunera."

The aduana station outside of San Luis was squat and ugly in the setting sun. Chuy came back to them. He rubbed his eyes.

"Don't say anything to these cabrones," he told Nayeli. "Tell your girls to shut up. Be invisible. They usually hit people for bribes going south. But they're watching for anything they can get. If you have marijuana, you'd better get rid of it." He slapped the back of her seat twice and bounded down the steps, calling out to a uniformed Mexican customs official, "¡Mi capitán!" He laughed too loud and slapped the captain on the back.

"Great," Yolo said. "It'll be a miracle if we survive traveling through our own country."

Nayeli said, "Did you know it would be like this?"

Tacho completed her thought: "I'm not worried about the Yunaites anymore."

They laughed nervously.

"When we get back," Nayeli said, "we have to tell them what it's like up here."

Yolo was already secretly planning her memoir—perhaps García-García would finance a small first printing.

The aduana officers waved them all off the bus and pointed at the station.

"Single file," the captain said.

Chuy and the relief driver were getting all the bags out from under the bus.

Young Federales in aviator shades and Members Only jackets lounged outside and laughed.

As Nayeli walked inside, one of them murmured, "Buenóta." Its implication was *Very good to have sex with.* She kept her eyes cast down and stepped into the smelly room. It was painted in two faded tones—the bottoms of the walls were green, and the tops were dirty yellow. Desks sat in the corners, and scattered aluminum kitchen chairs lined one wall. A fan turned slowly over their heads.

Two long metal counters cut across the room, and bags stood open upon them.

"¿Drogas?"

"No."

Each traveler went through the same little charade.

"¿Drogas?"

"No."

"¿Contrabando?"

"No, nunca."

"Foreigner?"

"Mexican, señor."

A cop sat in a corner, eating a sandwich. He was laughing into a cell phone. "¡Orale, pues, guey!" he said to his best friend, and snapped the phone shut. He watched Tacho. "Mira nomás," he said. He pointed at Tacho, and several of his cohorts went to his desk and whispered. They laughed. They turned and stared at him.

Tacho could feel the tension in his jawbones. He started to grind his teeth. He didn't mean to, but it just started to happen.

Nayeli dawdled, backing up to him.

He shoved her with his shoulder.

"Move on, m'ija," he said. "I'm all right."

But, of course, he wasn't.

The cop stood, crumpled the wrapper of his sandwich, and tossed a long shot into a trash can. "Three points," he noted. His cohorts laughed and patted him on the back.

"He's the big star," Nayeli whispered to Yolo. "You can tell. He's the Jefe."

"You," the Jefe said.

He was staring right at Tacho.

"Me?" Tacho said.

"Me?" the Jefe repeated.

The other cops laughed.

"You're a drug addict."

"No, I'm not."

"You're on cocaine right now."

"I am not!"

The cop walked over to him. Tacho could smell the Cholula hot sauce and ham on his breath. That and a liberal spritzing of Axe. Nayeli and the girls stood frozen, looking down but watching.

The cop walked around Tacho.

"Where are the drugs?"

"I told you, sir, there are no drugs."

"Oh, really."

He put his hand on Tacho's back.

Tacho jumped like a nervous pony.

"Are you scared of something?" the cop asked.

"No."

"Liar."

He gripped Tacho's upper arm.

"Are you a male prostitute?"

"No."

"But you are a faggot."

Tacho coughed.

Everybody watched him.

"It's all right; we're all amigos here," the cop said. "It's all right with us if you're a faggot. Mexico is a free country." He squeezed. "Faggot."

Then, the most shameful moment in Tacho's life happened, right in front of Nayeli, Yolo, and Vampi.

A single tear rolled down his cheek.

"I—" He cleared his throat. "I am not a—faggot."

"What?"

"I am not."

Nayeli turned around.

"He is my boyfriend."

"Yes," said Yolo. "We're going to Tijuana for their wedding!"

The cop eyed them skeptically. He smiled. She was cute, the little dark one. Too dark for his taste, but she had some ass on her.

"Very good," he said. "Very smart." He tapped his head with one finger.

She flushed.

"What's your name?" he demanded.

"Nayeli," she replied.

He nodded.

"Should I search you, Nayeli?" he said. "Are you carrying some of the good Sinaloan marijuana?"

"No."

He laughed.

"And you?"

He jerked Tacho off balance.

"What is your name, bridegroom?"

"Tacho."

"Tacho?"

"Just — Tacho."

"Tacho no es muy macho," the Jefe called out, and his pals chuckled.

"I've heard that joke before," Tacho said.

"Are you upset?" the Jefe asked him. "You're crying, Tachito. That doesn't seem very macho to me."

He looked at Nayeli.

"I just want a word with the groom," he said.

He dragged Tacho toward the back of the room.

"Tacho!" Nayeli cried.

One of the kinder aduana agents said, "It is better if you stay quiet."

The Jefe murmured in Tacho's ear — "Do you have drugs stuck up your ass, Tachito?"

He slammed Tacho through a door, and they were suddenly in the men's toilet. The Jefe shut the door and locked it. Tacho wiped his eyes and stood firm. The cop smiled at him.

"Faggot."

"No."

The cop bumped into him.

"Oh?" he said. "What was that?"

"What?"

"You bumped into me."

"I did not."

"Oh," the Jefe said, "so I am a liar?"

"No."

"No what?"

"No, sir."

"I am not a liar, then."

"No."

"So you bumped into me."

Tacho stared at the wall. There were ancient hieroglyphs of pudenda and violence drawn on every surface.

"Sí. If you say so."

"You dirty little faggot," the cop said. "Do you think you can work your little tricks on me? Rubbing on me like that?"

"No, sir."

"Apologize."

"I'm sorry."

The cop grabbed Tacho's crotch and squeezed it. Tacho yelped.

"Is this your game?"

Tacho said, "Please."

"Nice big packet. Were you hoping to use it on me, Tacho?"

The cop hit him once, knocking him against the wall. He turned to the sink and washed his hands.

"You make me sick," he said. "Get out of here."

Tacho picked himself up and struggled for a moment with the latch. He hurried out of the bathroom. Everybody stopped what they were doing and stared at him.

"A slight misunderstanding," he said, and rushed to the bus and folded up in the dark and feigned being asleep.

El Jefe stood in the doorway with his hands in his pockets.

"All clear," he said. "Let them go."

The passengers headed for the door.

"Nayeli," the Jefe called, "come back to see me soon."

His men laughed.

Twenty miles outside of Mexicali, the hydraulic system broke on the bus, and they rolled backward to the edge of a precipice but did not go over. After trying to get the doors open for an hour, Chuy kicked out one of the windows and dropped to the ground. He began walking toward civilization in the dark. Cold wind came in the open window. Nayeli cradled Tacho's head in her lap. She could feel his silent tears on her thigh. She could hear coyotes howling outside. All around her, the travelers snored and coughed and cried out in their worried dreams.

Chapter Ten

Chuy did not return. But nine hours later, a second bus pulled up beside theirs. It was full, but the driver got out and told them, "If you're willing to stand, I can take a few of you to Tijuana."

The Tres Camarones group got on the bus and hung on to the overhead racks. Three women followed them and bumped up against Nayeli. Their body odor nauseated her. Then she realized she was also smelling herself. This was a serious faux pas in Camarones. Indeed, she had never been outside her house without sweet scents in her hair and the clean smell of American soap rising from her body. Nayeli tried to hold on to the racks and keep her elbows down so her underarms weren't exposed. She was ashamed and felt filthy. When the bus started, the woman standing in front of her fell back against her and stayed there. Nayeli could feel the woman's hard buttocks against her belly. She couldn't move away.

Tacho seemed to be asleep on his feet. His eyes were swollen and red. Nayeli noticed Yolo watching her over Tacho's shoulder. Her eyes were dark as the highway itself, and she simply stared at Nayeli. Neither of them could believe the world they had entered.

Somehow, La Vampi managed to swoon into the lap of a sixty-year-old cowboy with a straw hat and a mesh bag full of onions.

He cautiously put his arm around her and sat erect, never looking at her once all the hours of their long drive to Tijuana. She knocked his hat askew, and he stoically let it ride sideways on his head.

In a vast flat of sagebrush and far dirty hills, their driver turned on his microphone and announced, "To your right, the fabled American border."

They craned and stared.

They looked for fences and helicopters and trucks and dogs. Nothing. There was nothing there at all.

Tacho noted, "It just looks like more Mexico," before he closed his eyes again and sank into his misery.

Nayeli tried to do one of Sensei Grey's meditations, seeking Buddha in the illusion of the moment. She tried to make the lake in her mind still as a black mirror. Someone stepped on her foot. She meditated on the pain instead.

They came down out of the mountains. They saw the Rodríguez Dam standing above the city. They could see sedimentary rings on the cliffs where the shore had receded.

"Empty," the driver said. "I saw it in 1965, full to the top. But there's no water left."

Down, into the hard dirt of Tijuana. Shacks and huts and scattered little cow farms gave way to small colonias and clutches of houses around gas stations and stores, and the roads got bigger and fuller, and there were newer cars, and more of them. Trucks everywhere. They saw canals, and now the fences appeared as all trees vanished. They saw their first bridges. A prison. They plunged into the maw of the city—shantytowns surrounded the dusty center. Cars everywhere. Everyone stirred and craned, and Tacho nudged Nayeli and pointed, and she looked up at a dead hill across a tall fence where white trucks sat watching and a helicopter circled.

The USA didn't look as nice over there as it did on television.

They lurched and turned a hundred corners and pulled into the battered new bus station on the far side of Tijuana.

They fell off the bus, dizzy and exhausted and thirsty. But they laughed. They danced. They were in Tijuana! The first leg of the journey was over!

They watched the driver unloading bags and suitcases.

"Let's get a motel," Tacho said.

"We have to save our money," said Nayeli.

"I want a bath," Vampi said.

"You need a bath, girl," said Yolo.

"I wouldn't talk, cabrona."

"Where's the bags?" Tacho said.

"I'll call Chavarín," Nayeli promised. "I'm sure we can take showers at his house!"

"Together?" said Tacho.

"¡Ay, tú!" Yolo cried.

"I want to see you all naked," Tacho announced. "I want to see what all the fuss is about."

"If you see me naked, boy," Nayeli promised, "you're going to change your ways!"

"Or throw up," Tacho retorted.

La Vampi sighed, "I want my bag."

But there were no bags.

The bin was empty. The driver slammed the doors down.

Nayeli stepped up to him and said, "¿Señor? Disculpe, pero ¿donde están nuestras maletas?"

He stared at her.

"¿Qué?" he said.

"Our bags."

"What bags?"

"Our bags from the last bus."

"You don't have any bags."

"He loaded our bags."

The driver shook his head.

"No bags," he repeated.

He lit a cigarette and walked away.

The girls cried out. Tacho cursed. Nayeli yelled, "Wait!" but the driver never looked back. They stood there between the big buses and watched him leave.

"Now what do we do?" cried Vampi.

Nayeli looked at Tacho, and they both turned and stared out at the alien city surrounding them. Even Yolo was starting to cry.

"I'll think of something," Nayeli said.

Nayeli could not find a phone booth. She hunted all around the bus station. There were no pay phones anywhere.

She stopped a man in an old checkered sport coat and said, "Señor—could you direct me to a pay phone?"

When he ascertained to his satisfaction that she wasn't begging for alms, he said, "Use your cell phone," and rushed away.

They pulled together and stood in a tight group, looking around. The norteño accents were a bit off-putting, but at least it was still Spanish. They told themselves it wasn't like they had suddenly landed in Shanghai or Beirut. This was still Mexico.

"Let's go downtown," Tacho said. "Let's get some food and a Coke and find civilization."

"Good idea," Nayeli said.

"There must be a phone booth downtown," Yolo said.

"Must be," said Vampi.

"I'll pay the taxi," Tacho said.

"Our benefactor," Yolo said.

They were scared out of their minds.

Vampi tugged on Nayeli's shirttail.

"Nayeli?" she whispered. "Do you have any Kotex?"

"What?"

"I started my period."

"Now?"

"On the bus. My Kotex is in my bag. I used toilet paper."

Nayeli still had her small purse—it had a tampon in it.

"I've got this."

"What's that?" Vampi said.

"It's a tampon," Nayeli said. "No seas simple."

Vampi stared at it.

"How's it work?"

"You don't use these?"

"My grandmother would never let me use that."

"It's all I have."

"It's kind of small, isn't it?" La Vampi asked.

Nayeli whispered, "It goes inside."

The other two were now staring at her.

"I can't do that!"

"I'm not going to do it, girl, so you better figure it out," Tacho said.

Vampi made a face.

"We'll help," Yolo said.

"You go right ahead, girls," Tacho said. "I'll stay right here."

Vampi started to cry.

"I'm sorry," she said.

"It's all right," Nayeli said. She put her arm around her. "You'll get used to it."

They hustled to the women's toilet.

Tacho wondered if he was the only one who knew they were in serious trouble.

Apparently, taxicabs in Tijuana carried as many human bodies as possible. The four of them piled into the backseat of a middle-aged Chevy and were astounded when two more people shoved in on top of them while an old woman with a cane and a bag of groceries got in the front.

"Welcome aboard!" the driver quipped, and they were off on a bone-rattling journey through the unbelievably crowded streets. The driver turned on the radio, and they were amazed to hear a Mexican techno song announce, "Tijuana makes me happy" in English.

"Does Tijuana make you happy?" Tacho asked the driver.

The driver looked at him in the mirror.

"Sure," he said. "It's the happiest city on earth."

He dropped them off outside the jai alai frontón.

As they got out, the old woman in front handed Nayeli an orange.

"Eat fruit," she advised.

They walked with the restless throngs. The tide of American bodies dragged them down Revolución, the central party artery of Tijuana. Techno and Van Halen boomed from shops and bars and eateries. It was only afternoon, but lurid lights were already blinking and sizzling outside the bars. Hawkers stood in the street, calling to passersby: "Hey, amigo! C'mon, c'mon, amigos! Tequila buena! I got good prices on shoes! For you, two-for-one special! C'mon!" Nayeli almost laughed. Tacho began to strut again. Maybe Tijuana was his kind of city. That made him feel better. He almost forced the Jefe and the bathroom out of his mind; he forced himself to forget the missing bags.

A boy with blue eye makeup called him "guapo."

"Oh, my God!" Tacho said.

"That boy had eye shadow," Vampi said. "I like that."

Donkeys in the street stood stoically before madly painted carts decorated with Aztec and rural scenes in vivid colors. The donkeys were spray-painted white and black to look like zebras. Americanos sat on the carts and giggled with huge sombreros on their heads as bored Mexicans snapped their pictures. Mexican cops kept an eye on the crowd. Tacho noticed soldiers in black body armor on several corners, their evil black machine guns slung low.

Children shined shoes, walked up and down the sidewalks with boxes of Chiclets, or carried poles hung with bracelets and woven chokers. Vampi bought a black cross made of shiny thread. It had a red bead in the center that looked like a drop of blood.

"Gothic Catholics unite," Tacho said.

They paused in front of an upstairs eatery, and before they knew it, they were swept up into it and seated at a table.

"What can I get you?" the waiter said.

"I'm dying for a cold beer," Tacho announced.

The waiter nodded.

"Four?"

Yolo and Vampi started to giggle. They had not yet drunk beer. Nayeli smiled up at him. He was quite handsome.

"Sí, por favor," she said.

"Bring limes," Tacho said.

"Claro."

They were fascinated by the passing tourists on the street below. Cholos and surfos cruised by, pickups and low-riders, old work vans and bicycles. They watched cops pull over and shove a drunk American sailor into their car and inch back into traffic. Flocks of schoolgirls in their uniforms hustled along, chattering and laughing. Fat Suburbans with black windows carried cocaine cowboys on their rounds.

"We can buy new clothes, can't we, Nayeli?" Vampi asked.

"Don't worry, morra. I'll take care of you."

She looked at Tacho. His face was without expression.

The waiter put the sweating bottles of Corona in front of them.

"That's urine," Tacho noted.

Nayeli kicked him under the table.

"I'll have shrimp, please," she said.

"We'll share an order of spaghetti," Yolo said, leaning on Vampi's shoulder.

"We're on a diet," Vampi announced.

"Do you want garlic bread?" the waiter asked.

Vampi stared at him for a moment.

"It's good," he promised.

"Yes, please."

She beamed at him.

Tacho said, "Carne asada, amigo. Lots of salsa."

"Corn tortillas or flour?"

"Corn, of course! Who eats flour tortillas?"

The waiter studied them.

"You're from the south."

"So?" said Tacho.

"So be careful," the waiter said.

He walked away.

"What's his problem?" Tacho groused.

The girls took long pulls from their beers. Yolo felt the bubbles burn up into her nose and sneezed. Vampi was dizzy immediately. She looked at all of them, opened her mouth, and belched noisily.

"Piglet!" Tacho scolded.

When the waiter came back and started to set their plates down, Nayeli said, "Is there a pay phone here?"

"By the bathroom."

"Gracias."

"Don't be calling your coyotes here."

"Coyotes?"

"You won't make it across without a coyote, chica. But the management doesn't like them coming around here. They give the gringos the creeps."

"How do you know we want to go across?" Tacho asked.

"Everyone in Tijuana will know what you want as soon as they see you," the waiter said. He was more than bored with pilgrims. "They have seen you a thousand times a week, brother."

"Oh."

"Can I bring you anything else?"

Nayeli shook her head and got up to find the phone.

"Your food will get cold," the waiter said.

"I'll be right back."

Tacho said, "Do you have any advice for us?"

"Get a passport," the waiter said.

***

Nayeli asked the cashier to give her some coins for the phone.

"Mexican or American?" he asked.

"What's the difference?"

He shrugged.

"American money is boring. All the same color, and the coins are dull. But it's actually worth something. Keep your pesos—give me dólares any day."

Nayeli suddenly remembered Aunt Irma telling her that's where *gringo* came from—from the English word for *green*.

"It's for the phone," she said, handing over a few limp Mexican bills.

He dug out fat Mexican coins for her.

"Over there."

She stepped into the hall between the bathrooms. American women were laughing and chatting in the doorway. They looked so tall. So glamorous. They smelled good, unlike her, smelled of vanilla and fruit and white musk and shampoo.

She turned her back on these giantesses and dug out her card. Chavarín's number was a little streaked but still legible. She had the coins on the metal shelf in front of her. She fed a few into the phone, until she heard a dial tone. She studied the number and punched the LIB digits in. The phone made a weird noise, an ascending scale of derision, and a robot voice told her there had been an error. The phone clicked, and she heard her coins drop into the coin box. She dug through the coins and found enough to get the dial tone again. Again, she was kicked off and lost her coins. The third time, she dialed O and told the operator the number. The woman sounded offended. "There is no such number, miss," she said. Nayeli repeated it. "I'm sorry. There is an error on your part, miss." Nayeli tried to argue with her, but the operator informed her there hadn't been a phone number like that in Tijuana since 1964. And there was no listing for a Chavarín. Not in Tijuana, Tecate, Ensenada, or Mexicali.

Her stomach was tight. It started to hurt. She pressed her hands to her face and breathed. She had to keep her wits about her.

She went back to her seat and stared at her food.

Tacho was eating a carne taco and swallowing his second beer. Yolo and Vampi were laughing helplessly. They each had two bottles in front of them.

"We are so drunk," Vampi noted, and they both snorted and fell on each other.

"They're weak," Tacho said.

Nayeli picked at her shrimp.

She looked at Tacho.

He raised his eyebrows at her.

She shook her head.

He closed his eyes, just for a moment.

He turned away from her and watched the bodies moving down the street.

Chapter Eleven

They stood on the street in the dark. The sound was relentless yet somehow flat. There were no echoes in Tijuana. Car horns were sour brays. Cops blew whistles, and they fell dull and bitter on the ear.

Nayeli went into a botica and bought Vampi some pads. She had a hairbrush, four toothbrushes, and a tube of toothpaste in her shoulder bag. Tacho apologized for his vanity and bought hair gel. He worked on his spikes as they stood there, pressed to a wall. His little radio hung from his belt loop by its strap.

"Call Aunt Irma," Yolo said.

"And tell her what?" said Nayeli.

"I want to go home!" Vampi cried.

"We will go home," Nayeli said. "When we have completed our mission."

"This was all a big mistake," Vampi said.

"I think we have failed," Yolo added.

"No," Nayeli replied. "We haven't even started."

I am going to Kankakee, she thought. There was no way this mess was going to work, she decided. Not without Don Pepe.

The other girls gasped and slumped and threw their hands around.

Tacho said, "Ladies, ladies. We have to get off the street. That's first. There is no Chavarín. All right. Then we have to use our own initiative. Am I right, m'ija?"

Nayeli nodded.

"We'll get eaten alive if we spend the night out here."

Happy tourists went by in colorful gangs, but among them were hustlers and sailors and marines and street kids and police and dogs. Men made kissing sounds at them—they couldn't tell if the kisses were come-ons to the girls or mockery of Tacho. One slim boy in a black T-shirt paused and hissed: "Want to cross? Los Angeles? Safe?" He frightened them. They turned their faces from him until he walked away.

"We'll find a hotel," Tacho said. "Things will look better in the morning."

They didn't know which way to walk to find a hotel. They mistakenly thought that if they walked north—toward the US border—things would be of a better quality. They got off the main drag and headed down feeder streets and dark sidewalks in front of third-run movie theaters. Nayeli moved fast. She thought speed would keep them out of trouble. Some cementeros came out of an alley—tattered street kids fried on glue and reeking of chemicals. They tugged at Nayeli's shirt and shoved Tacho and one grabbed at Vampi's breast before they faded into the dark like a pack of hunting cats, the only thing left behind them, their laughter. Nobody noticed they'd stolen Tacho's radio.

Shaken, Nayeli stopped at a taco cart on a corner ripe with smashed fruit rinds and peanut shells. The cook stood in a cloud of beef and charcoal smoke, his radio bobbing on a wire by his head, rocking to the distorted cumbia music. Two guys in cowboy boots ate tripe tacos in the glow of a streetlight on a crooked pole. The cook and the men looked Nayeli over, then took in the delicious sight of Yolo and Vampi. Tacho had slipped his pepper spray out of his sock and had it in his pocket with one hand wrapped around it and his finger on the nozzle.

"You lost?" the taco chef asked.

"Yes," Nayeli replied.

The three men looked at one another and smiled.

"You don't want to be lost down here, prieta."

Nayeli was taken aback by that. Nobody had ever called her "dark-faced girl" in her life. Maybe morena—brown girl. That was almost romantic. But prieta was considered rude in Tres Camarones.

"Can you direct us to a hotel?" she asked.

One of the men laughed out loud.

"I'll give you fifty pesos," he said.

"Excuse me?"

"I'll give you fifty pesos each, and I'll even pay for the room."

The other man, who wore a bright yellow sport jacket, said, "No seas guey" to him. "These fine young ladies aren't hookers."

"We just need to get off the street," Tacho said.

"Oh?" the man replied. He finished his taco and wiped his fingers on a napkin. "Come here," he said.

He led them into the red-light district.

"It ain't pretty, but it's cheap," he said, directing them to Hotel Guadalajara, a small cement-block hotel beside the scariest bar they had ever seen.

"Don't go in there," the man said, pointing at the bar.

"Don't worry," Nayeli said.

They got a room with two beds on the second floor. The stairs were on the outside, and there was a walkway that ran the length of the floor. A woman asked Tacho if he wanted to get his rocks off for cheap, right there on the steps where it was dark, then called him a queer when he shook his head.

"I smell marijuana," Vampi said.

"That's a shocker," Tacho replied.

The door was cheap plywood, and the lock wouldn't latch properly. Tacho put the chain on the door. The room had a cement floor with no rug. The beds were narrow and stiff as cardboard boxes. They could hear the endless thump of Kid Rock songs coming from next door; shrieks and laughs; a breaking bottle. The room would never be dark, so much street light came in the one window that they could have read magazines, even with their lights out.

They had two towels in the bathroom. Vampi went first, and she stayed in the shower too long, and there was no hot water for the rest of them. Tacho yelled curses. Then he cursed again when he had to dry himself on the wet towels and get back in the same dirty clothes. They looked like street urchins. But their hair was clean.

Yolo and Vampi snuffled and cried in their bed. Tacho kept his back turned to Nayeli in theirs. She found him inscrutable. She lay on her back, listening to the insanity next door. Then feet passed outside their room, and the voices of a woman and a man. It was the same woman from before—Tacho's girlfriend. Nayeli started to hear sounds she recognized immediately, though she had not heard them before. The man was actually grunting. She scrunched her eyes, as if that would shut out the walkway copulation. The man let out a long moan.

Tacho called, "Somebody milk that cow! It's starting to moo!"

"Oh, my God!" Yolo said.

They buried their faces in their pillows, laughing.

Just when they thought they were falling asleep, one of them would say, "Moo!" and it would start again.

The men came for them at about three in the morning.

Nayeli heard the whispers first and came awake immediately. The faulty latch on their door began to rattle. She held her breath, thinking it might just be ambient sound or perhaps the remnants of some dream. She squinted at the door, and she saw the knob turning back and forth. Then, a bolt of fear when the latch popped and the door cracked open. She stiffened in the bed. The door swung open slowly, reaching the end of the chain. Hisses. A low man's voice.

She shook Tacho. He snorted. She punched his arm. He buried his head under his pillow.

She looked around for a weapon. There was a small chair by the bed—she could club them with it when they broke in. She rose silently and stared. An arm was trying to reach into the room, the hand scrabbling like a spider, reaching around for the thin chain to get it off the hook. Nayeli squinted: a yellow sleeve. That bastard! The man from the taco stand.

"Almost," the yellow man was saying to his associates. She could see their shadows through the window shade, backlit by the neon and streetlights.

She stood in the center of the room, in her panties and her T-shirt, watching the hand clutch at the chain.

Her girls were deep asleep in their bed. Tachito was snoring. Nayeli stretched. She shook out her arms and raised each leg once. She rotated her neck and felt it pop. She grabbed Tacho's pepper spray can from the bedside table and positioned herself in front of the door.

The yellow man's hand grabbed the chain and began to work it free.

"Got it," he said.

Nayeli kicked the door closed on his arm. He screamed. She held the door against his wrist and threw her weight against it three times. He yelled curses. She grabbed his little finger and bent it back until it snapped. He made a terrible sound of shock and agony. But he let go of the chain. She pulled the door toward her and leaned into the gap and fired the pepper spray directly into his eyes. She slammed the door on his bloody arm again.

He jumped and howled and thumped against the wood as if he were being killed. His partners ran away and thundered down the stairs like bison. Tacho was beside her now, yelling, "Kill the bastards! Kill them!" Yolo and Vampi were yowling like air raid sirens. Nayeli fired another round into the yellow man's face and released the door. He fell on his back and writhed. She stepped out and stomped him once.

"Oh, my," Tacho noted. "Right in the balls."

"You," Nayeli growled, "stay away from me and my friends or I will kill you."

The man was trying to crawl to the steps.

Tacho kicked him in the ass.

"Dog!" he said.

They slammed their door and fastened the chain again and locked the worthless latch and braced the chair beneath the knob. The girls stared at Nayeli with awe. Tacho was so jazzed that he couldn't stop dancing and talking. Nayeli sat on the bed and shook.

She trembled until morning came and they went back to the street.

Chapter Twelve

I want to go home," Vampi said.

"All I ever wanted was a boyfriend," Yolo complained. "A nice little house, a quiet life."

"Me, too," said Tacho.

"I wanted Missionary Matt," said Yolo.

"Me, too," Tacho said.

"But Nayeli got him."

"¡Cabrona!" Tacho cried.

Nayeli kept walking. It was morning. Tijuana was silent. The sun was buttery, and doves cooed all around them. Dry palm trees made soft oceanic sounds in the breeze. Where was the Sodom of last night? They trudged between small yellow houses with falling fences. Little dogs wagged their tails. Alley cats swirled between their legs. Nayeli led them north, toward the Tijuana River.

An old woman in a small yard poured water from a coffee can onto clumps of geraniums.

"Buenos días," she said.

"Good morning," said Nayeli.

"Good morning, señora," said Tacho.

"Nice flowers," Yolo said.

"¡Adios!" Vampi called.

They came to a big street, and across it stood a rusting wall of metal. It rose high on a bluff and seemed to run forever. It was covered in bright paint—an American flag, coffins full of skeletons, words, poems, a white dove. They stared at it, reading the graffiti.

"Somebody doesn't like George Bush," Tacho noted.

"They don't like Calderón, either," Nayeli said.

"The new revolution," Yolo announced, "will be the war of the media!"

They cast jaundiced eyes upon her.

"Don't start with your Zapatista crap because, right now, I am not in any mood!" Tacho scolded.

"Who's Calderón?" Vampi asked.

They stared at her, aghast.

"Calderón, Verónica?" said Nayeli. "Your president?"

Vampi said, "Oh. I didn't see the news."

Looks were traded.

Vampi stared at a melancholy skull that seemed to be weeping naked bodies out of its eye sockets.

"It's beautiful," she said.

Tacho made a rude noise with his lips.

"*¡Ahora tú vas a empezar con tus babosadas!*" He moved down the street. "*Parece que ando con una bola de pendejas. Ay, sí. Todo el día con chingaderas. Pos, ¡estoy harto con esta mierda! ¿Me oyeron? HARTO. Hasta la chingada. Hasta la madre. Con esta MIERDA.*"

All the girlfriends noted that Tacho was venting his profound disquiet over their recent spate of bad luck and trouble.

"Wow," Yolo said. "What's his problem?"

"Look at Mister Snotty," said Vampi.

An ice cream man walked toward them, tinkling his little bell as he pushed his cart down the street.

"Early for ice cream," Nayeli said.

"It is never early for ice cream, amiga," the man replied.

Tacho was steaming, with his arms crossed and his spikes drooping.

"Your boyfriend needs some breakfast," the ice cream man noted.

"He's in a bad mood."

"I see that. He has a bad haircut, too. If you don't mind my saying it."

Nayeli made a command decision—her troops needed a morale boost.

"Four paletas, please," she said.

The ice cream man opened the lid, and the Camarones crew looked for their favorite flavors. Even Tacho slunk over and angrily grabbed a strawberry bar and gobbled it in big bites.

"What is that?" Nayeli asked, gesturing at the barrier with her frozen treat.

"Are you kidding?" the man asked.

She shook her head.

"Where are you from?" he asked.

"Sinaloa."

"Ah."

He nodded.

"That," he said, "is the legendary border fence."

Everyone stared up at it.

The man dropped his lid and accepted Nayeli's coins.

"Ugly, don't you think?" he said, and walked on, tinkling, tinkling, tinkling.

They went east along the fence. They picked that direction because west veered sharply uphill, and they were tired. East was flat.

It was already hot from the sun. The fence smelled like rust. Yolo ran her hand along the metal. Her fingers came away tainted orange.

They got to the barbed-wire edges of the fence.

"It stops!" Tacho noted.

They climbed up a steep bank and found themselves on the edge of a concrete flood control channel. Kids sat in groups and watched the other side. Masses of cars were already twinkling in the border lines at the international crossing. Below them, the Tijuana River was a narrow green smear of water. Clumps of grass and weeds rose from islands of deposited sewage and runoff mud. Nayeli saw a tattered pair of corduroy pants and one running shoe in the muck. They filled her with dread.

They could see a huge American freeway ahead, and beyond it, dead hills covered in rough trails. Boxcars stood on tracks along the base of these mounds, and a red trolley moved away from the borderline like a model train. All over the hills, they glimpsed white vehicles. They were close enough to the US to see burger joints and discount shopping strips.

Yolo said, "The Mexican border is the only major border on earth where huge cities sit across the fences from each other. It's true! Look on a map. All the countries in the world keep their big cities far from the border. Not here."

"She's so smart," Vampi said.

"San Diego and Tijuana. ¿Qué no? Look at a map. El Paso and Juárez. Brownsville and . . . whatever. And Nuevo Laredo, too."

"She got all A's," Nayeli said.

"Show-off," Tacho said.

"That's why it's such a big problem. Nowhere to hide. Capitalism has to do its work in the light, instead of in the shadows."

"Thank you, Fidel Castro," said Tacho.

"I'm not wrong," Yolo replied.

On the opposite slope of the channel, Nayeli saw a Border Patrol SUV. The agent was standing outside his truck in his green uniform. He was watching her. She nudged Tacho and pointed. The Border Patrol agent raised his hand and waved at her with a cutesy fingers-only gesture. She waved back.

"Don't be stupid," Tacho said.

"Really!" scolded Yolo.

But Nayeli couldn't help it—she started to smile at the agent.

He lifted a pair of binoculars and looked at her. She could see his mouth under the lenses. He was smiling back.

She pointed at herself and pointed to the USA.

He shook his head.

She put her hands before her face as if in prayer and pantomimed begging.

He laughed loud enough that they could hear his voice.

Then he shook his head again and got into his truck.

"He wants to date you," Vampi said.

"If we follow the fence west," Tacho suggested, "won't it run into the ocean?"

"Are we going to the beach?" Vampi asked.

"Don't be dumb," Tacho said. "The ocean—like, the fence stops here. Won't it stop there? We could swim around it and walk up the beach into Los Yunaites."

The poor boys sitting on the slope started to laugh.

They spoke in a bizarre code that took several moments to decipher:

"Nel, socio, la frontera 'sta gacha, guey, hasta las playas, guey, orale, pos la onda es que la wall esta se avienta al agua, guey! Me entiendes, yes or no? Tienes que echarte, vato! Swim, loco! Swimeando pero la wall no se acaba!" The one talking had tattoos and a fedora. He rose and dusted off his butt. "Ahi te wacho, homeboy!" He rocked and rolled on down the road.

"What," Tacho asked the universe, "in the hell," he raised his hands in entreaty to the Almighty, "did that boy say?"

"¡Agarra la onda, guey!" Vampi suddenly spouted. "Don't you speak cholo, vato? ¡La mera neta! I speakin' the cholo! ¡Bien de aquellas, de aquellitas! Rifamos, ¿sí o no?"

Tacho let out a small cry of despair.

"He said," Vampi explained, reverting to a human dialect, "that the wall extends into the sea. You can't swim around it."

"Oh."

"Ahi te wacho."

"Whatever."

Tacho raised his hand to his brow as if looking a great distance and turned in a small circle.

"So this is the border," he said. "I don't get it."

They trudged, lost. Vampi and Tacho had never walked so far in their lives. Even Nayeli and Yolo, the soccer stars, were tired. They kept veering north, as if there would be some magical gap in the fences. As if there would be some way into the USA that nobody had ever tried, or that the Border Patrol had overlooked. They made their way into the Río de Tijuana corridor, an area of nicer hotels, shopping malls, nightclubs with volcanos that erupted all night on their dance floors. They saw an IMAX theater in the shape of a white sphere.

"The Death Star," announced Jedi Master Yolo.

They finally collapsed in the hot shade of the city fruit market. It was a warren of sheds and shops, and the smell of cooking, fruit, rot, diesel, fish, onions, and cigarette smoke filled the air. It reminded Nayeli of Aunt Irma's trips to the Mazatlán market. She looked into the glass cases holding stacked Mexican candies and saw the same drunk bees staggering around, wiped out by the same fermented sugar.

Yolo found a small chapel in the parking lot dedicated to some local saint. She dragged Tacho in there to pray and light candles. Vampi somehow latched onto a gringo missionary group that was buying beans and potatoes for an orphanage run. She followed them around, trying to make small talk with the blond boys in her strange pidgin English.

One of the burly men working the fruit trucks stopped beside Nayeli.

"Tired?" he said.

She glowered at him. After last night, she was not about to talk to strange men.

He smiled.

He handed her a mango.

"It gets better," he said, and walked down the line of trucks. She watched him shoulder a hundred-pound bag of rice and stagger away.

The mango rained juice down her front, but she didn't care. She ate it with her eyes closed. It tasted like home.

The beggars were having a bad day. Doña Araceli was dressed the way the mestizos expected her to dress—in indigenous clothing. She was a Mixtec Indian, one of the main tribal groups working the Tijuana area. She and her husband, Porfirio, had come north—not to cross the line, but to earn money in Tijuana. They didn't know that it was the most visited tourist city on earth, but they did know there was a great flow of money to be had if you worked hard. The worst insult they could think of was: *That man doesn't want to work*. Work was everything to them, even though they had no work left to do. Their small farm plot in Michoacán had died out in a drought, and their two cattle had been sold, then their one pig, and finally their ten chickens. They left their plot of land to

Porfirio's parents and rode freight trains to the border, looking for a new life.

Don Porfirio had worked the trash at the Fausto Gonzalez dump, while Doña Araceli dressed as a "María," one of the indigenous alms-seekers, and walked the long streets of the city looking for coins. Don Porfirio used to say, "At least in Tijuana they have garbage," because even the dumps of their homeland were barren and picked clean. But then the city of Tijuana closed down the Fausto dump, started trucking the trash to Tecate, and three hundred garbage-picking families had to find new ways to survive. Some followed the trash to Tecate. Some crossed into the US. Most struggled along like he did. Don Porfirio washed windshields. He didn't beg—begging was for women, children, and the infirm. No, even if it was for two dollars a day, swiping a filthy rag on American windshields, breathing in exhaust fumes on the borderline, a man worked.

Don Porfirio and Doña Araceli were on their way home to the dompe. They met at the fruit market and counted out their money. Not great: four American dollars. They bought some cheese, stale sweet rolls, and three potatoes. They saved enough to take the bus back to their small house in Fausto. Baptist missionaries had built their home out of old garage doors smuggled in from San Diego.

It was Doña Araceli who saw the bedraggled group sitting on a folded rice bag made of burlap. They were so exhausted and filthy that nobody even yelled at them to get out of the way, and trucks pulled around them in the crowded lot. She pointed them out to Porfirio, and he laughed. He didn't often see mestizos like these so beaten down.

"They look worse than we do, vieja!" he said.

She liked it when he called her "old woman." In turn, she liked to call him "gordo," though he was anything but fat. He would like to be fat. That would be nice. He would like to weigh three hundred pounds when he died, so it would take ten cabrones to carry his coffin.

They ambled over to Nayeli's group.

"Are you all right?" Araceli asked.

They looked up at her.

"Indians," said Tacho.

"Yes," said Porfirio.

"We are in some trouble, I think," said Nayeli. "But I'll get us out of it."

Don Porfirio looked around, wiped his brow, sighed.

"How?" he said.

The four friends looked at one another and shrugged.

"I want to go home," Vampi told Don Porfirio.

He nodded.

Araceli said, "You are far from home?"

Vampi nodded.

"You are going over there?"

Araceli nodded to the north.

Vampi nodded again.

"Are you?" Yolo asked.

Porfirio laughed.

"Me? Over there?" He waved his hand before his chest.

"That's not for us," said Araceli.

"We lost our things," Nayeli said. She didn't know why she was talking to these strangers, but they seemed kind. And she was tired. And she wanted to go home, too. She didn't dare spend the rest of their money on hotels. Not yet.

Porfirio and Araceli spoke softly in their own tongue. It was a melodic sound, full of vowels. Their hands moved slowly in the air as they spoke.

"It will be night soon," Araceli said.

"Yes," said Porfirio.

"You do not want to be here at night."

"No, you don't!" he agreed.

"We are going home."

"Home for the night," he said.

"You should come home with us," she said.

"Why not," he said.

"It is humble."

"It is." He nodded.

"But God has been good to us."

"Amen," he said.

Nayeli looked in their battered dark faces. Porfirio had two yellow teeth in front. Araceli wore a bright red-and-yellow shirt. She extended her hand.

"Come," she said. "We will give you a bed tonight."

Nayeli let herself be pulled up. She didn't know if she should trust them or not, but she didn't know what else to do—she could think of no options. As soon as she was up, the others rose slowly. They stood in a loose bunch, looking at their feet.

Don Porfirio said to Tacho, "I like your hair."

They mounted the ancient Chevrolet bus painted two-toned, in blue and white. The driver had hung baubles from the ceiling—he had brocade strung along the top of the windshield, and saints and skulls dangled from the loops of yarn. Nayeli insisted on paying the fare for Porfirio and Araceli. They let the doña sit, and the rest of them stood as the bus snorted through downtown and out the road toward Ensenada. Araceli held her bag on her lap. They made their way along crumbling dirt cliffs, and Nayeli looked up arroyos at paper-and-scrap shacks growing like toadstools in all the gulleys. They approached an army battalion's base, and the bus mounted the periférico, the peripheral highway that cut around Tijuana from east to west. They drove a couple of miles until they came to a big flea market set up on the left side of the road. The signs said: SEGUNDA. The bus went down a ramp to the right and made a sharp left turn at some abandoned maquiladora warehouses, passing under the periférico through a tunnel covered with political signs: PRI, PAN, PRD. It began a slow trudge up a rough street that was mostly dirt and rocks.

At the top of the long rise, Don Porfirio said, "Here."

The bus pulled over, and they hopped down on a slope of tan soil pocked with bits of glass and can lids. Five dogs danced and gamboled around them. Tattered paper kites rattled in the phone lines. Down the slope, car tires, car wrecks, and shacks crowded the arroyo. Nayeli could hear children yelling and playing.

"This way," said Porfirio, and walked across the dirt street and up a hill.

They were too tired to be afraid or worried as they followed him. Araceli walked beside Nayeli, patting her back softly. The soil turned gray, then black. "We will fry potatoes," Araceli said.

Nayeli smelled smoke, and a tart, ugly stink.

She saw gulls in great clouds above them, circling, whirling, so many gulls they looked like fog, like some strange tatters of white clouds blown by a hurricane rolling up the coast of Nayarit.

They topped the rise, and Nayeli ran into the backs of her girls. They were standing there staring. She peeked around Yolo's back and opened her mouth but said nothing.

Tacho looked at her, and for once she thought she saw real awe in his face.

"Home," Don Porfirio said.

Before them, a malodorous volcano of garbage rose two hundred feet or more. It was dark gray, ashen, black, and it was covered in flecks of white paper as if small snowdrifts were on its slopes. Gulls swirled and shrieked, and packs of feral dogs trotted downslope. The black mountain was stark. A road cut across its face, and far above, they could see and hear orange tractors moving soil over the trash. The sky above the hill was gray and heavy with clouds. Occasionally, smoke broke from the slope and curled away, blue and thin, in the wind. It made Nayeli feel cold.

"From up there," Don Porfirio said, pointing, "you can see America."

Chapter Thirteen

Huddled at the foot of the hill, dark brown men bent to small fires. They were burning electrical wires—the acrid chemical stink of the smoke wafted across to the friends. The men melted the plastic sheaths off the wires and sold the copper strands to the recyclers. Nayeli saw them poking at the small fires with sticks and small poles, hunched, cavemen in a wasteland. The sky peeled back for a moment, and a weak ray of sunset spilled over the scene like the diseased eye of some forgetful god—the light bearing with it cold in place of heat.

A gust of wind came from the ocean. They were astounded to see a bright vista of the Pacific to their right. Copper sun fell upon the water. The wind had shattered the clouds there and spilled rainfalls of illumination. Fat oil tankers lounged in the glow, and beyond, islands could be seen on the horizon. It looked warm.

"Is that Hawaii?" Vampi asked, but they all told her not to be an idiot.

The ocean breeze lifted white plastic bags from the slopes of the black hill. They rose like ghosts. It was quite beautiful. The bags floated silently in waves, soaring and falling, and drifting, too—pale balloons full of unwanted wind. They drifted off the

slopes and settled slowly upon the foreground, a dry empty cres-
cent of graves and rough holes in the ashen soil. All before them, a
crude cemetery sprawled. Uphill, to the east, a squat crematorium
waited in a fenced enclosure. Its chimney was not spewing smoke,
and its door hung open, but the chain-link gate was sealed with
a great combination lock. Sweeping past them, at the foot of the
garbage volcano, were graves. Some were cement slabs. Some were
bare mounds of trash and pebbles. Nayeli saw many handmade
crosses—blue wood, red and white wood. A rusted tractor sat at
the edge of the boneyard, a backhoe. Its rear claw was raised and
frozen in place, caked with old, hard mud. It was posed like a huge
scorpion, forgotten there. Before it, seven open holes.

To the west, set against the vista of the sea and the islands, was
a low hill covered in a hundred small plots. Cribs and playpens
stood guard over these rectangles. Some cribs were painted. Wild
mustard and dandelions sprouted among them.

"The children," Tacho said.

And he was right. As they moved down the slope, following
Doña Araceli, they saw names painted on the baby furniture. Old
glass jars with wax flowers. A doll propped against a baby's crib,
all of it muddy and collapsing in the ashes. Huge truck tires lay at
the foot of the children's hill. Collapsed graves festered in the mud,
small crosses tumbled. The smell of human feces rose from the centers of the tires.

Beside this long, sad place, there were many houses. Porfirio
stood in the doorway of a square blue shack and waved at them.
"Come!" he was calling. "Welcome!"

The four friends reached out for one another as they walked,
and they held one another's hands.

Life is good!" Don Porfirio hollered.

Tacho had made the mistake of walking down to the bodega of the barrio to buy eggs, and he spied a bottle of rum and bought it as a gift. Now Don Porfirio guzzled rum from a peanut butter jar and danced in place, raising dust from the floor of the shack. The girls sat on an ancient bunk bed jammed in a corner—salvaged, though they didn't know it, from the trash. On the other side of the bare room, Porfirio and Araceli's sagging bed. The shack smelled of smoke and spoiled lard. Tacho sat on a wooden kitchen chair as Porfirio danced. Nayeli wondered if he was doing a Mixtec dance or an alcoholic shuffle. She did not know.

Araceli had a stove, set halfway between the bunk beds and the other bed. It was really the shell of a stove, and Araceli was stuffing paper wads into the oven and lighting them. Fire came out of the burner holes on top. She fed twigs in, then a few chunks of two-by-four, and slammed the oven door closed. She put a big pan on a burner and amazed the friends by lifting a hinged flap in the wooden wall so the smoke could go outside. She fastened the wooden shutter to a hook screwed into the wall.

"I invented that!" Porfirio shouted. "I am a genius!"

"Bravo," Tacho said. He sipped some rum from a plastic Hamburglar cup.

The girls just stared. They were appalled by the filth. They were scared of the dump and the dirt. Yolo could almost see tides of lice awakening and creeping toward her. Her scalp crawled with imagined vermin. She began picking at herself, sure that little creatures with many legs were piercing her scalp and depositing disease in her flesh.

Doña Araceli sliced her potatoes with a huge knife. They sizzled in the melting lard. Nayeli's stomach growled as soon as the heady odor hit her. Vampi moaned. Araceli deftly diced an onion and dropped it in with the thin slices of potato. She poked at it with her knife. When this part of their supper was done, she slid it onto a cracked plate and immediately broke Tacho's half-dozen eggs into the skillet and fried them. The girls had never smelled anything so delicious in their lives.

Porfirio stopped dancing long enough to pull a small table in from the yard and set plates all around.

"Six plates," he noted. "It is a feast. God is great! Isn't God great, vieja?" he called to Araceli.

"God is great," she replied, putting a little food on each plate.

Porfirio followed her, placing two stale rolls on each plate.

He produced a huge can of jalapeño peppers.

"Missionaries!" he crowed. "God loves chile!"

He handed each of them a fork.

"Let us pray," he said.

They gathered at the table and held hands. Porfirio was listing to port. Nayeli thought he'd fall over. But he smiled and tipped back his head and said, "Thank you, God!"

Two tears rolled down his face.

"Amen!"

Tacho sat, then noticed that none of the rest of them had chairs, so he stood back up. They stood eating together, and when the main meal was gone, they wiped the grease off the plates with pieces of sweet roll. Porfirio laughed all the way through the meal, patting Tacho's spiky hair.

"Do my hair like that!" he kept repeating.

They all laughed.

After a while, a baby pig wandered in, followed by a yellow duckling. Porfirio tossed them bits of his rolls. He laughed again when the animals vanished under his bed for a good night's sleep.

The outhouse was noxious, and nobody wanted to use it.

It was very hard to get comfortable on the narrow mattresses of the bunk beds, and Tacho gallantly insisted on sleeping at the foot of the bed, on a folded blanket. It broke Nayeli's heart to see him lying in the dirt, but he was so rummed up he fell asleep quickly. He snored, but so did Porfirio and Araceli. They had hung a blanket between the two halves of the room to give the friends some privacy. Everyone slept in their clothes.

Yolo took the top bunk and refused to share it, so Vampi lay across Nayeli, on the bottom, whimpering and muttering in her sleep, sticking her foot in Nayeli's back, laying her arm over her neck. No wonder Yolo was sick of sharing a bed with the Vampire.

At dawn, Nayeli rose and slipped her shoes on and stepped outside.

The dump was still. The light was the color of a winter ocean, and a thin pall of smoke lay over the village. Chickens clucked softly around her. She could hear snoring coming from the shacks on either side. Suddenly, a rooster down the block let loose his call. Pigs snorted and fretted.

The yard was a small patch of gray soil. Doña Araceli had planted roses. Nayeli was startled by them. The fence was apparently made of bedsprings, tied together. The pig next door shoved its snout into the fence and wiggled its nostrils, trying to catch a whiff of Nayeli. All along the fence, rosebushes bloomed. Red roses, pink roses, yellow.

She stepped out into the dirt alley. A dog with peeling fur stood and wagged its tail at her. She waved her hand at it to try to make it back off. It trotted to her and put its filthy head against her leg.

Nayeli backed away from the dog and wandered down the alley to the edge of the cemetery. She was startled to see smoke rising from one of the graves. The crosses and painted furniture were stark in the morning light. Etched like charcoal drawings. Somewhere, a radio was playing—she recognized the song. Dave

Matthews. She always liked that rola, the one where he asked the woman to crash into him, though now it seemed like the loneliest thing she'd ever heard.

It shook her, this place. It was awful. Tragic. Yet...yet it moved her. The sorrow she felt. It was profound. It was moving, somehow. The sorrow of the terrible abandoned garbage dump and the sad graves and the lonesome shacks made her feel something so far inside herself that she could not define it or place it. She was so disturbed that it gave her the strangest comfort, as though something she had suspected about life all along was being confirmed, and the sorrow she felt in her bed at night was reflected by this soil.

She stepped toward the graves. She had to touch them. She had to see the names painted on the crosses. She smiled. She was acting like Vampi—Nayeli, the Goth.

There was no one in sight as she passed among the graves. She picked a few blue flowers from the weeds and put them on the mounds. She picked trash off the cement slab of Uvaldo Borrego. She straightened the tilted cross of María Zepeda and braced it with stones.

She stood among the graves and looked back at the huts and shacks of the village. If she squinted, it almost seemed rustic—a sweet little town painted in all the Mexican primary colors. Somewhere, Tacho had found a store. She wondered if there might be a telephone there. She had Irma's number memorized. And she had Matt's card in her pocket. Should she call?

She heard a voice behind her say, "Psst!"

She glanced.

An awful young man was standing on a garbage mound above her. She turned her back on him.

"¡Oye, morra!"

She moved away and stood by a fresh grave.

Nayeli had just about had it with badly behaved border men.

"¿No me oyes?" he called. "I'm talking to you."

"No," she said. "I hear you. I am just not listening to you."

He stared down at her.

"Your mistake, sweetheart," he said.

Chapter Fourteen

There he stood, surveying his realm, the warrior Atómiko. King of the Hill. Baddest of the trash pickers. The master of the dompe, known by all, feared by many. He wore baggy suit trousers cinched tight at his narrow waist, a sleeveless white undershirt. His tattoos were exposed: Zapata on his right biceps, the yin-yang symbol on his left shoulder. Ever since he'd seen the movie *Yojimbo* on San Diego public television when he was stationed at the Mexican army's dismal Seventh Battalion down the periférico, he knew he was a warrior. He'd formed a judo club in the barracks. He'd declared himself a samurai. And that's what he was — his head was shaved and his brow was covered with an Apache red bandanna folded tight and tied just above his brows. His mustache drooped at the corners of his mouth, and his chin whiskers were getting thick, hiding the smallpox scars on his cheeks. Across his chest, a tight sash made from curtains he'd found before the dump was closed down. And beside him, his long samurai sword. Well, it was a staff. But it was noble and powerful in his hands.

Every garbage picker worth his salt had a staff of some sort. Most of them just had broom handles with a nail or two in the end. They had no vision. No pride. You had to have something to move the trash and fish for goodies; you had to kill the rats and chase off the dogs. For most of them, any pole would do. But not for Atómiko. He was a ronin—his staff was his pride and his weapon. It was an extension of himself. And there it was, beside him in the dawn light. Gripped in his right fist and forming a fulcrum upon which he leaned, like a Masai warrior (National Geographic special, Tijuana's Channel 12), with his right foot propped against his left knee.

It was his second staff. The first had splintered when a tractor drove over it. This one was a wrist-thick six-foot length of bamboo. It had taken him years to find it. It was pliant but firm. He had discovered tubes of epoxy glue in the dump, and he'd carefully filled the hollow center of the shaft with it, allowing it to harden. But that wasn't all he'd done. He'd inserted the knob from a broken-off Hurst power shifter into the end of the staff, and after the epoxy had glued it in place, he had carefully and fastidiously wrapped copper wires in overlapping patterns to bolster the bamboo around the stick shift. At the other end of the staff, he had poured in marbles and ball bearings before the last epoxy drooled in. He capped the open end with a hammered can lid, superglue, and more of his elaborate copper wire work. In the middle, he had wrapped the smooth bamboo with friction tape. All things found in the endless bounty of the garbage dump. It was a thing of beauty, his staff. Frankly, it was a bit heavy for dump work, but it was also lethal. Nobody ever messed with Atómiko—not when he was carrying his weapon.

He looked down upon this mysterious dark girl and scratched his whiskers.

"Hurt me, girlie!" he called. "I want to be wounded by you!"

She made a dismissive sound and walked farther from him.

Atómiko watched her. She was short, just like he liked them. He could see the muscles in her legs. And she smiled even when she frowned. He was a fool for that. That right there made him crazy.

He put his foot down, spun the staff once like a great baton, and inserted it under the sash at his back. He put his hands on his hips and called:

"I am Atómiko!"

He hopped down off his mound and paced along behind her.

"Who are you?" he demanded.

"None of your business."

"Ooh. Saucy."

She walked three rows away from him.

"Go away," she said.

"Never."

"I'm busy."

"I am here to serve you."

"Oh, please." She had heard better lines than that.

Atómiko was the kind of man given to visions and illuminations. Since they'd closed the dump, he had wondered what the Buddha had in store for him. Would he follow the trash to Tecate? Hell, no—he wasn't some country boy. He was a city dog! Perhaps he could mine the old garbage, like the old-timers who were now digging in the sides of the hill. But the trash mafia that the owners had hired to police the slopes would beat the miners if they caught them. Atómiko had entered into several fights already, defending the peasants from the hired guns. But, nah—climbing in stinking dark holes wasn't for him. He was in need of a quest.

"You're not from here," he noted.

"No."

"Where, then?"

"You're so rude," she snapped.

"I'm ugly, too," he said. He scratched his whiskers. She could hear his nails scritching in them. God! "So?"

"I'm—we're from Sinaloa."

"We?" he said.

"They're asleep right now," she said. "But they'll hear me if I call, so don't do anything funny."

He said, "I am Atómiko, esa! I don't do anything funny!"

She thought that was funny.

"We came from a place," she said, "that is under threat."

"What kind of threat?"

"Narcos," she said. "Bandidos."

It sounded dramatic. Silly. She blushed.

"So," she continued, "we came seeking soldiers."

He stood taller and smiled. He pounded his own chest.

"I am a sergeant in the Mexican army! Well, I was, until I ran away."

"Wonderful," she said. "You ran away." She shook her head and moved away from him again.

"I am a great warrior."

"Shoo," she said. "Go on your way."

People in the dump had no money for cocaine or pot or pills. But they were fools for tweak. The lost young ones smoked cheap meth as fast as they could get it. These hopeless ice zombies were so racked with chemical poisons and dry rot that they didn't even have shacks—they tipped sheets of plywood against headstones in the boneyard and slept and twitched right there in the dirt. It was the curse of the dump—a shocking thing that the self-respecting trash pickers rejected out of hand. These terrible tweakers stole everything, even the meager cans of orange juice and broken toys the garbage miners managed to dig out of the black hill. They never made it all the way to the top, so they never saw the view. Besides, they were too skinny and broken to battle the mafiosos up there. So they stuck to the graves and the sad wire burners, and they shuffled out to the streets and mugged women coming home from work in the dark.

Two of the ice zombies watched Nayeli as she walked away

from Atómiko. She had clearly said something severe to him, and he'd waved his hand at her in anger and turned his back. Now she was coming down the hill toward the big tires and the mud bog.

They could jump her fast, they thought. They could get her on the ground before she cried out. She looked good, looked like she had a watch, at least. The meth made them crazy for sex when they were fired up, but now they were in the gray dregs, their teeth hurt, their guts churned, and all they wanted was money for more smoke. They could steal her shoes.

The zombies rose in front of her and behind her, ragged and stinking. They put their hands out to block her escape. She looked back and forth at them. Nayeli planted her feet. She feinted to the right, but the tall tweaker in front of her smiled and blocked her. His teeth were black.

Thinking it would be impressive, the zombie said, "How about a kiss?"

Atómiko's staff whistled slightly as it came down. The noise the shifter knob made connecting with the tweaker's head was truly shocking, and Nayeli flinched. The addict dropped like a wet towel. Atómiko leaped behind Nayeli and spun the staff slowly in both hands. The other tweaker stared at the propeller, hypnotized. Atómiko moved slowly in a circle, and the ice zombie tried to back away.

"Oh no, my son," Atómiko said. "There is no escape from Atómiko!"

Nayeli was noticing that Atómiko needed to announce his idiotic name at every opportunity.

He grabbed the staff in both hands and made three lunges, swinging the bamboo savagely with each forward stomp of his foot. The tweaker, whipped, battered, and flipped over in three seconds. Both his shoulders were smashed, and his head was cracked open. Flat on his back, he saw the gulls double and triple before he passed out.

Atómiko spun around to face Nayeli and whirled the staff and caught it under his arm, holding it extended before him. He looked all around them and grinned, then inserted his weapon back in his sash, where it rose at a jaunty angle above his shoulder.

"I am Atómiko," he said.

"How do you do," Nayeli replied.

I like the maricón," Atómiko said.

Tacho said, "Thank God for small blessings."

Atómiko punched him on the shoulder. They were great friends, in his opinion. Tacho looked at him for an extended moment.

"Ow," he said.

They were sitting around, enjoying the sun, on benches Don Porfirio had hammered together out of scrap wood. Tacho was putting gel in Porfirio's hair and working it up into spikes. Porfirio, still buzzing from last night, sipped more rum from his jar, only he had put milk and sugar in it. Tacho held up a mirror, and Porfirio laughed at his own hair.

Nayeli said, "I didn't need you to save me."

Atómiko sneered.

"I did my duty," he said. "I defended you."

She shook her head. He had followed her through the alleys of the little workers' village. He'd stood aside as she called Aunt Irma, collect, from a battered pay phone on a crooked pole outside a small bodega that gave up the smell of fried pork rinds and sheets of beef jerky. As the phone rang, Atómiko cast evil glares at passersby, holding his pole before him in a threatening manner.

The phone rang and rang.

Tía Irma was apparently out, running the town or working the counter at the Fallen Hand.

Nayeli could imagine the sound of the phone, echoing in the

empty house. She had heard it a hundred times before. She could see the table, the chairs, the yellow walls, the old refrigerator. It almost made her swoon. She could smell Irma's house. She could see the insane tom turkey strutting in the courtyard, inflated and threatening the phone, rattling his feathers as he made mindless noises in his throat.

"Miss?" the operator said. "No one is answering."

"Let it ring."

Three more rings.

"Miss?"

"Wait."

Five more rings.

"Really, miss."

Three more rings.

The operator cut her off.

Nayeli had tears in her eyes.

"Don't be sad," Atómiko said. "I am here."

Chapter Fifteen

Vampi was with Doña Araceli, watering the roses. Yolo was sitting with Don Porfirio, and she took a sip of his rum-and-milk cocktail and liked it. Nayeli was trying to ignore Atómiko as Tacho told him their story. At certain cardinal points of the epic, the intensely irritating Warrior of the Garbage Dump snapped his fingers and exulted some hipster phrase like "Orale" or "Chido" or "¡No chingues, guey!"

Eventually, he stopped Tacho to clarify the narrative: "Wait. You're going across illegally to collect vatos to take home?"

"Correct."

"You're collecting men."

"Seven men."

"And you'll smuggle them out of the Yunaites."

"Yes."

"Back to Mexico."

"Exactly."

"But you have to sneak."

"Sí."

"Because it's illegal to transport illegals."

"Correct."

"Even if they're going south."

"Right."

"Holy Christ, I love this story!"

It was his kind of yarn: a quest. He slapped hands with Yolo, who kept sipping the rum milk shake and was feeling warm toward everyone. He was thinking: ¡*Ronin!*

Yolo, growing impatient with all this talk, said, "I don't know why you don't simply recruit seven of these men right here, and let's go home."

"Recruit me!" said Porfirio. He and Yolo took swigs from the jar. "I want to go!"

Vampi cried, "Take Atómiko!"

Tacho said, "I'm going north. I want to see Hollywood, and that's that."

"We have a mission," Nayeli reminded them.

Atómiko patted his belly like the Buddha and smiled upon his poor, benighted children.

"Get seven of these muchachos right here," Yolo advised. "Get on the bus. Go home."

"No fuss!" Vampi said.

"No Border Patrol."

"No border."

"No money spent," Yolo said. "We can go home and give them back their money!"

Porfirio tipped the jar at her and gulped some more rum-milk.

Doña Araceli appeared and pried the jar from his hand and took it away.

"Hey!" he said, but he couldn't focus on her.

Atómiko cleared his throat.

"No," he said.

He shook his head.

"No, you can't do it that way."

"Do what? Which way?" Nayeli said.

Tacho said, "I know where he's going. Listen to him."

"You can't recruit vatos from the dompe," Atómiko said. "It's not what you set out to do. You have to accomplish your quest. To el norte. Besides, these warriors are not worthy."

"What is this," Yolo complained, "a fairy tale? Y tú, ¿Qué eres? King Arthur?"

He smiled at her.

"I am Atómiko," he reminded her.

"As if we haven't heard that," she said.

"Look—these men here, they came from there!" The Warrior pointed south with his staff. "They came from the lands you left! And they ran out of steam right here. You need the men who made it through the border. You need the warriors who have passed their challenge. Men worthy of the honor."

The girls had not heard this kind of talk outside the movies, and it was kind of stirring.

"We, here, have our lives," Atómiko said. "Some of us failed to make it across; some of us just wanted to pick the trash. Some of us, like me, were born right here! But this is home. We have houses and families, ¿Qué no, Porfirio?"

"Right!" Porfirio yelled.

Atómiko swung his staff north.

"The warriors are before you," he intoned.

Everyone stared at him: he liked it that way.

"You must go across the line to retrieve them."

Yolo shook her head and looked bored.

Tacho nodded at Nayeli.

"We have to go," he said. "Besides, there will be men there who miss Mexico."

Nayeli looked into all their faces.

"Still..." Atómiko drawled.

He poked at the gray soil with his shifter knob.

"You need a man like me," he said. "On your journey."

"They would run you out of Tres Camarones on a rail," Nayeli replied.

"I don't care about your stupid town! I live on the border, esa! This is where it's all happening! Did I say I wanted to go to your sad little town? What I said was, you need a man like me on your mission."

Nayeli laughed dismissively.

"I can get you across," he said.

"You?" Nayeli scoffed.

He drew himself as tall as he could, tightened his sash, and ruined the noble pose by scratching his whiskers again.

"Sure," he said.

"Have you ever been across?" she asked.

"Me? Why would I go across?"

"Oh, yes—your life is so elegant here," she said. "Why would you leave?"

Atómiko turned to Tacho and said, "My life? What is wrong with my life?"

"Nada," Tacho said. He gave Nayeli one of his Looks, that Tacho eyebrow and tip of the chin. It said: *M'ija, you're being rude.*

"In fact, pinchi Nayeli"—Atómiko sniffed—"I used to go to the other side all the time. Me and my soldiers used to run across the fence and buy soda at McDonald's." He spit. "So there."

"Wait—illegal-alien soldiers?" Nayeli said.

He shrugged.

"Until we got caught," he muttered.

He planted the end of his staff in the soil and looked implacable and, in his own opinion, formidable. "You want to go or not?"

Nayeli crossed her arms.

Tacho said, "Yes. I want to go."

"Orale pues," Atómiko said. "We boys are going. What about you girls? You have cojones or what?"

Yolo said, "Where did this creature come from?"

"I want to go after my father," Nayeli said.

"There you go!" Atómiko enthused.

He stepped out of Porfirio and Araceli's small yard. He looked back toward the bulk of the village, and he put his fingers to his lips and whistled louder than anyone Nayeli had ever heard. She opened her mouth in shock. He was whistling a ditty, what people in Los Yunaites might have recognized as "shave-and-a-haircut." But, of course, there was no such phrase in Mexico. That same rhythm was bad-boy code for the ultimate obscenity, "chinga tu madre." No self-respecting gentleman in Tres Camarones would whistle *that* in front of three fine young ladies!

Before she could comment, a decrepit and slouching white Olds 88 crept out of an alley and made its rough way over the rocks and broken glass. Its muffler was gone, and it made a loud glubba-glubba noise as it came, leaking curtains of blue fumes. It eased to a halt and seemed to list a little farther to the left. A driver as ugly as Atómiko leaped out. His hair was slicked back with oil, and he had a mustache that looked like he'd stolen it from a pimp downtown.

"Was he just sitting there, waiting to hear from you?" Nayeli said.

"I have powers," Atómiko boasted. "I summon the wind and the stars."

"You are such a loser," she said.

The new cholo snapped his fingers and pointed at Nayali. In badly accented English, he barked, "Jou! Show me jou papers!"

He and Atómiko knocked knuckles and laughed.

The cholo turned to Tacho.

"¿Tiene papeles?" he demanded. "Jou wetback?"

Again, gales of laughter from these rude idiots.

Nayeli walked away from them.

"Loca," the driver said. "You need me."

"That's like saying I need cancer."

"¡Ay!" he said. He put his hand over his heart and staggered backward. "Badass! She's hard, brother!"

He and Atómiko slapped palms.

"Está firme, la morra," Atómiko announced. "She's so fierce, my little brown girl."

Nayeli hung her mouth open at Tacho in disbelief that Atómiko would say so many stupid things.

"I can take you, no problem," the driver said.

"I doubt it," Nayeli snapped.

Tacho, the goodwill ambassador of Tres Camarones, stepped in.

"How?" he asked. "What do we do?"

The driver looked at him.

"¿Y este?" he asked.

"He's cool," Atómiko said.

The driver said, "I'll take you to Libertad. You know Colonia Libertad?"

Tacho shook his head. Nayeli thought of the nonexistent Chavarín's phone number. Yolo and Vampi stared at the ground in their despair.

"It's rough; I'm not going to lie," the driver said. "But I'll set you up with a good guide, and you'll go under the fence and into the canyons. They'll get you up to Otay."

"What's Otay?"

Atómiko smiled, spun his staff in front of him.

"That," he said, "is the United States."

Tacho and Nayeli looked at each other.

"When?" she said.

"Right now."

"How much?" Tacho asked.

Atómiko and the driver muttered.

"My socio here wants me to give you a good deal," the driver said. "I'll take you for one hundred and fifty. Each."

Tacho and Nayeli got together and acted as if they were discussing the proposal, but they didn't know if the price was good or bad, or what they were doing.

"I guess so," Nayeli said.

"Good!" Atómiko crowed. "Wait here!"

"Why?"

"I'm going to get my stuff!" he cried, and ran off.

Don Porfirio had sneaked out and swiped his jar of rum and milk and sugar from Araceli, and he'd poured the rest of the rum in and had it shaken up into a sweet foam, and he and Yolo powered down the whole thing.

Yolo, feeling no pain at all, said, "That Atómiko, he is definitely not Yul Brynner!"

"Mexico's greatest movie star," Nayeli said, with deep nostalgia for Irma and Tres Camarones.

Nayeli was deeply opposed to Atómiko's presence, but Tacho and the girls voted her down. They felt they could use another warrior for the crossing, and frankly, now that Yolo was drunk, she thought Atómiko was handsome and dashing. Nayeli couldn't believe her ears—but she also knew the crossing was supposed to be deadly, and maybe Atómiko's pole would be of use should they meet any bad men. He also carried a tiny Hello Kitty backpack. Maybe he had weapons in there. Vampi, to be helpful, gave him her switchblade.

They said their farewells to Araceli and Porfirio. The couple absolutely refused any money for their hospitality, but Nayeli sneaked into their house as they were hugging and patting Vampi and left a twenty-dollar bill on their little table. Vampi cried disconsolately when she said good-bye to their hosts, and Araceli gave her a rose.

Nayeli and Tacho and Atómiko crammed into the backseat, the staff out the window.

"Why are you coming, again?" Nayeli asked him.

"I'm bored. Nothing on TV," Atómiko replied.

Yolo laughed and threw him a wide drunken wink over the front seat.

"Nayeli and Atómiko are going to get married," she said to Vampi.

"Really?" said Vampi.

"We should go to Las Vegas," Yolo said.

"Oh, yes!" Vampi enthused. "Elvis!"

"Enough," Nayeli warned.

"Want to hold my hand?" Atómiko asked.

"Are you crazy?" Nayeli shouted.

He looked out the window mildly.

"Sweetheart," he said.

The driver's name was Wino. The Camarones crew didn't speak any version of Spanglish, so they didn't know how dashing and bad it was to be called Wino. To them, it sounded like "*¡Ay, no!*" which was a cry of dread.

He was an excellent tour guide — they realized to their shock that he loved Tijuana. On the way to Libertad, he veered off the road and drove up the tormented streets of a hillside colonia. "You have to see this," Wino declared. They pulled into a dirt gulley and beheld a three-story house built in the shape of a nude woman. She was painted in flesh tones, and her nipples were large red ovals. There was a door in her pubis.

"That," Atómiko announced, "is great art."

"Oh," Yolo said, "my God."

Tacho said, "If she gets pregnant, does she give birth to a garage?"

Atómiko chuckled.

"One point," he said, "for the maricón."

Onward! Down the narrow and clogged road that accessed the free road to Ensenada but for them would be passage to the Centro! On to the center of town, past the back end of the Palacio Azteca hotel! A quick detour into the edge of Colonia Cacho, for a restorative stop at taco row! Eighteen-cent carne asada tacos at Tacos El Paisano! A brief gawk at the municipal bullring! And on—down to the traffic circles and pedestrian bridges and Mexican department stores! Conasupo and Pemex on every side! See that statue there of the Aztec king? Holding his sword by his side? He starts out every morning holding it over his head—but he gets tired and the sword droops! Across the boulevard and to the right, up the hill! Onward—Wino and Atómiko singing out the varied delights of Fair Tijuana, the planes coming in above them at Tijuana International Airport, the street dogs, the hot women in their impossible heels, the taxis, the multicolored buses, and into the labyrinth of Libertad.

Onward, to the Crossing!

Colonia Libertad was the notorious launching pad for a million border crossings. The United States had foiled the massive incursions of the 1970s and '80s with the beefed-up new border fences and stadium lights and plowed-under acres of roadway on the other side, where white Border Patrol trucks cruised like sharks in a lagoon. Dirt streets and alleys piled up and down steep ravines.

Houses went right up to the line. You could climb on a chicken coop and look into the windshield of a migra truck. People played soccer. Young men sat on the slopes and watched the fences, waiting for their moment. They were still going across, in spite of the heightened security. Now they weren't gathered in hundreds but in dozens, and many of them would be caught. They'd be back tomorrow to try it again.

All around, music blared from speakers in shop doorways and on the roofs of cars. Children ran through the scene, impervious to the plots and plans making their way among the groups of adventurers and their shady guides. The fence here was old and battered and patched. Taco carts blew smoke on corners and in empty lots, the fence runners having last meals in Mexico—cheap tripe and chicken tacos. Rabbit tacos were supposedly for sale over by the drugstore where the bottles of water were double the usual price. Coyotes, hanging cigarettes off their lips and demonstrating their tattoos and Slayer baseball caps, liked to quip, "Those rabbit tacos—I saw a guy unloading a truck by the cart, and those rabbits had long tails!" Ha-ha! The walkers got queasy every time!

Christian do-gooders rolled through in vans. Their blond locks and shiny white faces shone in the sun like headlights. Nayeli watched to see if Matt's face was among them.

Atómiko and Wino negotiated with a vato with a deep slouch and a black porkpie hat. This character wore fingerless gloves and chain-smoked. The three girls would not admit it, but they were afraid of him. Afraid of the entire colonia, and the fence, and the border. Afraid of Tijuana. They hid behind Tacho, who threw out his chest and looked fierce and tried to hide his own fear.

Wino kissed Vampi's hand and pinched Yolo's butt and decided not to touch Nayeli. They watched him drive away, honking his horn in that awful shave-and-a-haircut rhythm. Nayeli never imagined she would miss Wino, but there it was.

Suddenly, people were jumping up and yelling and trotting along the fence. Nayeli craned to look. The white roof of a Border Patrol truck showed over the top of the rusted metal wall as it cruised the other side. Boys threw rocks over the fence, and some of the rocks clanged off the sheet metal roof of the truck. It stopped. People cursed and laughed and hurried away. Nayeli saw the top of the agent's head as he got out.

The coyote sidled up to them.

Nayeli asked, "Is he going to shoot at us?"

The guy flicked his cigarette away.

"Nel," he said, which was his cholo way of saying no.

The agent vanished behind the top of the fence as he walked around to the near side of the truck. In a moment, Nayeli saw his arm rise. His fist came up and he shot the finger to the Mexicans. They laughed and whistled insults back at him. She watched him walk back around the truck to his door. She caught a quick flash of his face—he was laughing. The truck moved on, kicking up dust that drifted over the fence and settled on their heads.

"That dust," said the coyote, "is the United States invading Mexico."

"It's an act of war," Atómiko proclaimed.

Far to the east, the hills were still black from the last great California fires.

The coyote said, "There was burned-up Mexicans all over those hills."

It seemed to amuse him.

Yolo was almost sober. She nudged Nayeli with her elbow. "Girl," she said, "there is still time to go home."

"Yeah," Vampi agreed. "We are making a terrible mistake."

"We don't know this man," Yolo said.

"Don't worry, I'm here," Atómiko said.

"We don't know you, either!"

Tacho ran his fingers along his money belt. He was this close. He wasn't turning back.

"I'm going," he said.

Nayeli said nothing, just stared over the fence as the dark spread and the noise behind them changed to the heavy breath of Tijuana at night.

"Nayeli, what are we going to do when we get there?" asked Yolo.

"I don't know," Nayeli admitted. "Call Matt?"

"Oh." Yolo started to smile. "All right."

And the coyote spoke.

Orale. Gather around, gather around. You, what's your name? Nayeli? You're the leader? Good, listen up. My socio Atómiko here speaks highly of you, so I am going to take you quick, right in. No chingaderas, all right? Move fast, don't cry, don't give me any shit, understand? We're going under the fence right there. The metal's cut—we hit it with acetylene torches when the migra isn't look-ing. There's a doorway right there behind the bushes. I go first—if it's clear, I'll whistle. You haul ass. Girls first, the boy—what's your name?—Tacho last. Atómiko will slide the door shut. He says he'll follow. I think he's in love with Nayeli—though it could be Tacho. Ha! I got my eye on the vampire. Hot. In another life, right, morra? Come see me when you get rich in Gringolandia! Orale. Run straight across the migra road. Straight! And fast, cabrones! Do you hear? Keep low and run fast. Right across the road, through the bushes, is an arroyo. I'll be down there. Don't jump on my head. But get down in there with me. We'll haul ass to the north—that's to the right, for you little girlies who don't know what direction you're going. Right. Pay attention. I don't have time to repeat this shit. To the right, run fifty yards, and we cut sharp left. Keep close enough to see the person in front, because if you get separated, you stay behind. There's junkies and monsters and rateros in there that'll cut off your legs and fuck you as you die. I'm not kidding you. Stay close to me. Nayeli, you're the leader, be right behind me. Atómiko will cover the end of the line. Single file. Hustle. Can you hustle? You better fuckin' hustle like you never hustled before. If the migra catches you, they'll crack your heads. If it looks like they're going to catch us, you don't know me. I'm not a coyote, just a guy from Sonora looking for work at the racetrack tending horses. You got that? You rat me out, and my socios will hunt you down and cut your throats. If we get separated, you girlies, you run for the road and hope the migra comes along before the rateros get you. Don't be out there alone. If you get lost, I'm not going to come looking for you. Mama's far away. Stay behind me or you're on your own, and there's no negotiating. All right. Straight, arroyo, right for fifty yards, hard left. We'll be going down a canyon for a mile, and then we'll get to a bridge. We can rest under that bridge. If the rateros jump us, and they've got guns or knives, I ain't dying for you. No way. I'm gone. Good luck, cabrones. Give them what they want, and that includes your money. If you want to live. You, Tacho. Maybe you'll be lucky. Maybe there's faggots in the canyons, too, and they won't cut your legs. Maybe you can blow them. What? Have I offended you? ¡Ay, ay, ay! ¡Qué lástima! I'll tell you what will offend you worse—having the tendons sliced in your legs so you flop like a fish, having ten filthy junkies or gang-bangers or white gangsters rape you and take your money. How's that for offensive? God damn it, you're wetbacks now! Nobody gives a shit about you! So stick to me like ticks, and I'll get you through. When I tell you we're there, we're there, and I'm heading home. No whining, no complaining. I will take you far enough so you can figure it out for yourselves. You ain't paying me real money. You want the deluxe *crossing, you pay for it. Put you in the trunk of a car. But we're not those coyotes in Libertad. I'll get you in, but you have to take it from there. If you get caught and deported, I ain't giving you your money back. Me vale madre. Tough shit—life is hard. But if you want to pay me again, orale, I'll take you in again. Got it? Any questions? No? Good. Are we ready? Next stop, San Diego, Califas, los pinchis Yunaites!*

When the next Border Patrol vehicle came down the dusty trail across the fence, the gathered runners pelted it with stones. Suddenly, three other trucks appeared, and the agents leaned across their roofs and fired teargas grenades over the fence. The coyote took off running, and before Nayeli could ask what was going on, Atómiko had them up and running, too. Clouds of choking smoke swirled across the hill, stinking and choking. People ran from the border and charged between the small houses, as if walls and fences could protect them from the fumes. Boys with rags tied over their mouths and noses laughed and danced, taunting the agents, throwing more stones and bottles. The coyote stood with his fists raised, shouting, "Act of war! Act of war!"

Atómiko was laughing. He'd gotten them to a perch far enough away from the gas that only Tacho's eyes were watering.

"Welcome to Palestine!" he yelled.

"I've never seen anything like this," Nayeli said.

"I love it," Atómiko replied.

Tacho hawked and spit.

"You don't see this on TV," he said.

"*Sábado Gigante,*" said Nayeli. "Today, we feature Chinese jugglers, the song stylings of Ricardo Arjona and Juanes, and border war!"

The girls laughed, sort of, more nervous than amused. They had stepped into the apocalypse and wanted nothing more than to be bored in Tres Camarones.

It took about a half hour for the gas to fade and drift away. The runners, wiping their eyes, moved back to the fence. The coyote signaled them and walked back to his spot.

It was as dark as Nayeli had ever seen it. Far to the west, she could see the eerie hazy glow of searchlights on their tall poles. She coughed, dust clogging her throat, small tendrils of the gas still lingering in the air. They huddled on their haunches behind the coyote, hands on one another's backs like monkeys. She clutched the coyote's shirttail. He slapped her hand away. "Don't mess up my clothes," he said. There was no whispering. She'd thought there would be whispering.

Behind Tacho, Atómiko squatted with his staff across his knees.

"If we get separated and you get caught," he said, "I'll meet you where they drop off the deportees in Tijuana."

"What do you mean, meet us?"

"Nobody's catching Atómiko," Atómiko proclaimed. "I'm not going in a Border Patrol cage! Never been in a cage, and will never go in a cage!"

Nayeli was suddenly scared to face the border without the Warrior.

"I will be there," he said. "Come back to me, brown girl."

"Where will you be?" Nayeli said.

"Don't worry—they all get left in the same spot. I'll wait for you there. Nobody will touch you."

"Our hero," said Yolo, perhaps not completely sober yet, but so scared that her buzz was evaporating through her pores.

"Listen," the coyote said.

They heard an engine approach. Headlights made pinholes in the wall light up like stars. The engine receded. The truck moved on.

"Let's go. We have about fifteen minutes," the coyote said.

He squat-walked to the fence and knocked the dry bushes aside and yanked a section of fence loose. It squealed loudly.

He popped through and was gone.

Nayeli followed, trying to make herself small, but she caught her scalp on the edge of the metal and cut a small wound in her forehead. Blood ran into her right eye, and though she wiped it away, it looked like she was weeping blood.

Vampi went through on her hands and knees. "My rose!" she cried. "I dropped my rose!" Yolo shoved her. She followed. Tacho crawled through and panicked for a moment when he saw no one on the dirt road. Then he remembered the arroyo across the way, and he ran and plunged through the creosote bushes and came flying down upon the group like a cat falling off a roof. "Hey, idiot!" the coyote cried as he crashed into them.

Atómiko stepped through the gap, bent back to the doorway, and kicked the metal back into place. He might as well have rung a bell, it was so loud. He raised his staff over his head and yelled, "Atómiko is in the house!" in trash dump English. He swung his staff all around, then laid it across his shoulders and strolled across the road.

"So much for secrecy," the coyote said.

And he was off.

Nayeli had to run to keep up. She clutched a tattered wad of tissue to her forehead with one hand and knocked branches out of her face with the other. Vampi yelped and trotted after her, and Yolo grabbed the back of Vampi's shirt to hang on. Vampi took the brunt of the whipping branches Nayeli charged through. She cried out a hundred times as she got smacked. She was alarmed to see a pregnant woman running beside her. Where did she come from? The woman held her belly up with both hands and charged ahead. Tacho was a few paces behind them all, watching the pale ghosts of the running girls. They seemed to vanish. He knew they'd found the left turn. He passed it, fumbled back, and heard them breaking through the brush in the dark. He never saw any gap. It was all just more shadows. Headlights suddenly cut across the valley from the road along the fence. Tacho plunged into the darkest clump of shadow and prayed he didn't step on a rattlesnake or fall into some pit full of tarantulas. Atómiko had completely vanished.

Vampi was out of breath. "¡Ay, ay, ay!" she gasped as she ran. The ground was rough. They tripped, twisted their ankles. The pregnant woman suddenly grabbed Vampi and held her up. Vampi was startled at first, then leaned on the stronger, older woman. She might have been an angel. She might have been the wraith of a murdered paisana come from the shadows to save them. Vampi surrendered to her fate and ran.

Nayeli had to slow down for the coyote—he was a smoker, and he wasn't really in shape. She could hear him wheezing. If she'd known the way, she would have pushed him aside. Her legs were like steel springs—she could run cross-country all night. She was pretty sure Yolo could keep up. But she was trapped behind this slow, malodorous, coughing male.

"Hurry up," she said.

He rounded a curve, Nayeli right on his back—the moon made the sandy path glow a faint violet gray. They came in sight of the bridge the coyote had told them about. It was low, and the coyote dove under it and clutched his chest and gasped as if he were dying. Nayeli crawled in beside him, then received Vampi and the mystery woman. Yolo dove in next. After about a minute, Tacho was heard announcing, "Oh, God!" outside as he staggered in and fell in the sand.

"Are we all right?" Nayeli said.

Yolo made a muscle and gave her a double thumbs-up.

Vampi sighed and lay back in the sand.

Tacho said, "Oh yes, m'ija, I am just wonderful."

The mystery woman said, "I am fine."

"Who are you?" the coyote demanded.

The pregnant woman said, "Candelaria."

"You owe me money," he said.

"I have no money."

"What, do you think this is a Christian charity, morra? You think I do this for fun?"

"What are you going to do," Candelaria asked, "walk me back to the fence?"

"Shit!" he said.

Before they could argue more, engines sounded above them. A truck went by, then a big bus. The bridge groaned.

"They're transporting prisoners," the coyote said.

A third engine came along. They listened as it came over the bridge. The coyote put his finger to his lips. "Shh!" he said. The engine stopped. "¡Chingado!" he said. They heard the radio. They heard the door of the SUV open and slam. The coyote was gone like a tatter of fog. He didn't even make a sound—just vanished.

"Hey!" Nayeli whispered.

A walkie-talkie muttered above them. She heard a gringo voice say, "Arroyo Seco overpass, over."

A bright flashlight beam hit the gulleys around them like a ray from a spaceship. Yolo and Vampi and Tacho held hands so hard they thought they'd break their fingers. Vampi was trembling. The light clicked off.

Silence.

A stream of water came off the bridge and hit the ground before them.

The migra was peeing!

They stifled their giggles. They couldn't believe it. His stream arced over them and formed a puddle. They moved back so they wouldn't have to touch it. The stream died out. Then: spritz-spritz-spritz. They laughed into their hands.

"Clear," he said into his radio and slammed the door and drove away.

Tacho fell on the ground and laughed with his feet in the air.

"Welcome," he gasped, "to America!"

Chapter Sixteen

They stood in the wash beneath the bridge in a loose group. The coyote was gone.

"Now what?" Tacho asked.

Nayeli had to take charge; she knew that. But how? Take charge of what?

"That way is east," she said. "I think that's all desert and mountains and stuff."

"And stuff," Candelaria said.

"So we should go west. Right?"

"Right, Nayeli," said Yolo. "We need to go toward the city."

"Right."

They stood some more, frozen to the spot. Tacho, for one, recognized they were not heading anywhere. They had used up their momentum.

"We're going to an American hotel," he announced.

"Oh, yes!" cried Vampi.

"We're going to get hot showers and nice American beds."

"And MTV!" Vampi enthused.

"I can't believe this chick," Nayeli said to nobody in particular.

"In the United States," Candelaria said, "you can flush the toilet paper down the toilet."

They eyed her skeptically. Everybody in Mexico knew that toilet paper went in a basket by the sink. The plumbing couldn't deal with paper.

Candelaria shrugged. "What can I say?" she said. "They are advanced here."

"Well, then," Tacho announced, "I will flush the toilets, too!"

"Vámonos," Nayeli ordered.

She climbed the slope and started to walk along the dark road.

"Watch for lights," Candelaria said.

They trudged along, and their fantasies started to come out into the air. The mixed gabble of voices forming a tapestry of sound:

"Ice cream. Hamburgers. Bubble baths. American beer. The Sixty-nine Eyes. Disneylandia!"

An ersatz owl began to hoot in the distance.

Nayeli shook her head and laughed in spite of herself: that crazy Atómiko, signaling from the bushes.

⁓

Cantinflas is the greatest movie star in the world."

"Yolo, you're crazy! Everybody knows Johnny Depp is the greatest movie star."

"Ay, Nayeli. There you go with your damned Johnny Depp."

"What about Banderas?"

"Vampi, when did you decide you liked Antonio Banderas?"

"Oye, Vampi—Banderas could be your father."

"No way. Did you see Banderas in *Interview with the Vampire*?"

"Oh no, morra. Not that vampire stuff now!"

"Oh, really, Mister Smarty-Pants? So who, in your fine opinion, is the best, Tacho?"

"M'ija. Don't embarrass yourself. Es la Streep."

"And you, Candelaria?"

"This is stupid. You should be quiet. You're not strolling in the park, you know."

They dashed to the bushes and hid when a helicopter flew over.

It made a terrible racket, its rotors thwacking the air as it slid sideways across the sky above them and turned slowly in midair. A hard beam shot out of it and raked the distant hills. The dark that hit when the beam snapped off was almost as strong as silence. They blinked. The helicopter angled away and churned farther down the line.

"Like a giant dragonfly," Vampi intoned, as if they all hadn't thought that very thing.

They walked a quarter mile and rounded a bend and were illuminated by the brutal glare of two headlights and a spotlight that switched on and blinded them. The truck was parked right in the middle of the road. If the lights hadn't come on, they would have walked into it.

"Hello, amigos!" a voice called from behind the lights. "This is the US Border Patrol! You are in the United States of America illegally! You are under arrest! Everybody come on over and keep your hands on your heads. Slowly, now. Stay calm. If you have papeles, now's the time to break 'em out!"

He got on his radio, spoke some numerical coordinates.

Said: "I've acquired five clients, over."

The helicopter came back and hovered above them. Its prop wash knocked Nayeli into Yolo. She squinted up into the light it shot down at them. They were caught in light. They couldn't move. The copter moved off and scanned the scrub around them. Its deafening noise receded until she could hear voices again.

Agent Anderson was shining his light in Tacho's face, and he had one hand on Vampi's arm. Another SUV was bouncing at them from the north. Good old Agent Smith was over there. He and Anderson went to the same Bible study when they weren't out in the bush, collecting bodies.

"Yanqui bastards!" came a wail from the south.

They all looked.

"¡Cabrones!"

"What the heck?" said Anderson.

The helicopter was lighting up Atómiko.

He stood at the edge of an arroyo near the fence. Nayeli could not believe they'd walked so much and were still right by the fence. How was that possible? In the dark, she'd imagined they were already halfway to Los Angeles.

Atómiko swung his pole at the copter.

"Come down here and get me, puto!" he was yelling.

The Camarones crew started to giggle.

The migra agent stared over there and shook his head.

"What's wrong with that guy?" he asked Tacho in Spanish.

"He's an idiot," Tacho said.

"You know that knucklehead?" asked Smith.

"He's our guardian angel," Vampi said. "I'm a vampire. We're on a mission from God."

"Great," Anderson said.

Smith looked the friends over, looked back at Atómiko, shook his head, and said to his cohort, "This ain't a full moon, is it? 'Cause the crazies are out tonight."

He put his handcuffs back on his belt.

"Behave," he told Tacho, wagging his finger.

"I will. It's that one out there you have to watch out for."

They all watched Atómiko do some daring staff moves on his

little hill. He danced backward, holding his staff across his chest. The two Border Patrol guys seemed to really be enjoying the show.

"Sweet moves," Smith commented to his friend.

"I am Atómiko!" the Warrior shouted to them.

He struck his chest. He raised his staff. He cried, "!Nayeli rifa!" They were all impressed. *Nayeli rules*. She blushed a little.

The agents looked at her and raised their eyebrows in appreciation.

"You Nayeli?" Smith asked.

She nodded.

"A love story," said Anderson.

"We are just friends."

Atómiko turned, and he ran, and he greatly pleased all the gathered watchers when he stuck the end of his staff in the dirt and pole-vaulted over the fence and vanished back into Mexico.

"I'll be darned," both Border Patrol agents said.

They were herded into the back of the migra Expedition. Smith helped Candelaria up. "Watch your head," he said. "Hey. Didn't I see you last week?" Nayeli didn't know the agents spoke Spanish. Candelaria nodded. "I bet you were happy to see me again," he quipped.

"Don't you ever take a day off?" she asked.

"I always take Sunday off. Try coming back on Sunday."

He closed the back door and climbed in. Candelaria had her face against the metal grille.

"I will try on Sunday," she called.

"Oh, good!" he replied.

He muttered into his microphone. Nayeli heard "five bodies" and "clear" and "over."

The truck pulled out.

"I will send you a postcard!" Candelaria shouted over the engine noise.

The agent laughed.

They pulled a brush-clearing U-turn and got back on the road and chased their headlight beams down the dark valley.

They stopped and watched two migra agents beat the holy hell out of a boy in a checkered shirt. "Well," Smith said. "He must have done something bad." He seemed embarrassed. Yolo and Vampi started to cry. They were terrified and mortified—it was not in their life plans to be arrested and dragged around in the back of a wagon like criminals. Kenny jumped out and helped the two in the road subdue their client. He put his knee in the small of the kid's back and pinned him to the dirt while they yanked his arms behind him and cuffed him. They got him back up. Blood was running from his nose. He tried to kick the nearest agent: the agent theatrically shook his finger in the boy's face and hauled him into the gloom.

Smith returned to the truck and said, "It's not an easy job, you know. Why don't you folks stay home and make my life easier?"

Tacho laughed.

Smith liked Tacho.

"I wish I had stayed home," Tacho said. "I can't keep my hair combed up here."

They watched the vehicle with the bloodied boy drive off.

"That right there," Smith announced, "was your typical bad boy."

"We are not bad, señor," Nayeli said.

"Oh, I know!" he said. "You are Nayeli, right? The one the

Olympic pole-vaulter was hollering about." He turned and winked at Tacho. "Nayeli," he said. "You rifa!"

⁓

He off-loaded them at a big school bus lit by spotlights. Tacho jumped down by himself. He helped Yolo and Vampi, who seemed to be collapsing in fear. Nayeli jumped down, pushing Tacho's helping hand away. The Border Patrol agents helped Candelaria down.

Anderson was there.

"Mother," he said to the pregnant woman.

"Señor," she replied.

He supervised the handover, and armed men herded them onto the bus, where they took seats among tired men who smelled of smoke and dirt and sweat. Candelaria ended up several seats behind them, and they lost sight of her and did not find her again. There was a sick man slumped in the front seat, wheezing and groaning. A migra agent gave him water and shone a light in his face. There was a commotion near the front door, and suddenly agents pulled their sidearms and backed a Libertad bad boy down to his knees. He was hauled away. Coughing in the bus. Nayeli was amazed to hear snoring. Some of the men were dead asleep! Young guys joked and called insults to one another, cursed the migra. They made kissing sounds at Yolo and Vampi. Nayeli got up and walked to their seat and stood there, facing the boys, looking like an Aztec warrior priestess. Before the bus could roll, though, the migra matron who was driving with an armed cohort told her she had to sit down. But someone had taken her seat, so she sat on Tacho's lap.

"Everybody," the guard with the big shotgun announced, "we are going in to register you. A quick interview. And you will all be going home. Stay calm."

Tacho said nothing.

Nayeli couldn't tell if he was angry or depressed.

Vampi was so scared she could not stop crying.

Yolo was so mad, she wanted to slap Nayeli's face and go back home.

Tacho was thinking: *The United States is a little disappointing so far.*

ICE agents, customs agents, soldiers in camouflage, Border Patrol agents, agents with DEA on their windbreakers, EMS ambulance techs, dogs, white men in slacks and black ties, a San Diego city cop, men in red T-shirts, frightening men in black outfits. It looked to Nayeli like one of those boring old James Bond movies where 007 dropped inside a big plastic volcano to blow up the communists' spaceship. But this place was more scary because they were in it. The guns were real. The lights were too bright.

The gates of the holding pens slammed loudly. All the young Mexican guys were yelling. Suddenly, Nayeli was separated from her friends as the tide of bodies split and sent them into two different groups. Vampi looked as if she was drowning, turning once in the tide and going under. Yolo caught Nayeli's eye and stared at her, sending venomous lightning through the air. Nayeli had known her long enough to read the look: *You did this to us!* she was saying. Someone put his hand on Nayeli's rear and squeezed; she spun around, but he was gone; she looked back, and Yolo had vanished. A hand brushed her breast.

Signs in Spanish asked them to follow requests, to report any violations to the agent in charge, to report any criminal activity in the pen, to make a free phone call if they had representation or needed to report human rights violations to the Mexican consulate. Many of those in the cage just stared at the floor. Most of the people herded into the pens were like them. Just...people.

Small, brown, tired people. Nayeli was stunned to see mothers with children—the kids weeping and snot faced. She heard indigenous tongues in the pen—shamanic-sounding utterances that felt a million years old to her, sounds of jungle and temple and human sacrifice.

Nayeli looked at the migra agents through the iron mesh. Big men. Happy, bright-faced men. Shiny and crisp. Green uniforms. Short hair. Mustaches.

What made them different from her?

She could not tell.

They moved around with real efficiency, she noted. Sensei Grey would have appreciated their economy of motion, their obvious ease with their strength. And—a woman! A woman migra agent! Nayeli was fascinated by her. She had a big fat gun on her hip, and she was as short as Nayeli herself, but she was also stout and moved like a little tractor. A black man! Nayeli had never seen a black man outside of Irma's porch television or the Pedro Infante on movie night. She was amazed by his hair, gray and white, tight to his skull. His skin shone and, she was astounded to realize, he had the same skin tone as hers, just a shade darker. She knew she was a sweet tanned color, but she had always imagined herself as white.

He saw her looking at him.

He stopped by the gate and peered in at her.

"You eyeballing me?" he said.

"¿Perdón?"

"¿Usted me está mirando?" he said, in Spanish.

"Sí."

"¿Porqué?"

She looked at her feet.

"It is . . . your skin," she said. "It is . . . beautiful."

He laughed out loud.

Just then, Smith came along.

"Hey, Arnie," he called to the black agent. "That's Nayeli. She rules."

"Nayeli, huh," said Arnie. He opened the gate. "Let's get you processed, Nayeli. You can get back to invading the United States in an expeditious manner. Get to you in a minute."

"¿Qué?" she said.

Chapter Seventeen

Agent Arnold Davis had seen it all. After twenty-seven years in government service, he was close enough to retirement that he was bulletproof as far as the bureaucracy went. He had so much retirement built up that if they were to fire him tomorrow, he'd get close to a full salary anyway. It was what he called "f-you money."

He had sore feet and a bad back. He'd been in counseling twice. He had hemorrhoids. Insomnia. His prostate was probably the size of a Krispy Kreme doughnut—he peed five times a night, and it ruined what little sleep he got. And his left knee was shot. Join the Border Patrol—taste the glamorous life.

His wife had left him in 1992, and she'd taken his kids. They didn't talk to him, but they did accept his monthly checks. He drove a Ford pickup, but the gas bill was getting crazy, and he was actually thinking of trading it in. But . . . a USBP senior supervisory agent just didn't belong in a Hyundai. Maybe they'd come up with a hybrid Mustang.

He looked around the station and tried to block his sense of smell so he didn't have to breathe in all the sweat, panic, despair, piss. He tried to ignore the ugly lighting that, the older he got, felt more and more like a personal insult to his eyes. As he walked around the floor, holding his limp to the barest minimum so nobody could see it, he was secretly looking into the back of his brain, at retirement and escape and Colorado mountains and trout streams. Elk. He wasn't going to shoot them—just watch them walk on by.

Even now, there were not a lot of black agents in the Border Patrol. Hell, there were barely any agents at all. Oh, there were bodies, all right. There were more people in uniform than ever before. Homeland Security had flooded the Border Patrol with gung-ho new Terminators. But they didn't know squat about the border, not really. How could they? It took a guy ten years to really get it.

Arnie had served at Wellton Station in Arizona. It had been a tight little unit of almost thirty guys. Then DHS had started pumping in the fresh bods, and the station swelled to three hundred people jammed into the crumbling building. They had to tear it down and build a bigger station, not to hold more wets but to hold the overflow of agents.

Arnie had relocated to Calexico, and now he was on loan to San Diego. He put on his reading glasses to study the papers on his clipboard. He glanced into the cage.

The little smiley Mexican girl was looking at him.

My black skin, he said to himself, *is beautiful.*

He laughed out loud and moved on.

The government knew a secret that the American public didn't: the numbers of border crossers were down, across the board. Maybe the fence, maybe the harsh new atmosphere in the US, maybe everybody had already fled Mex, like the old guys occasionally joked. But all these new agents were here, pumped, eager for action. The DHS paranoia and training had them searching for terrorists under every desk, Arnie shook his head. They actually believed an atomic bomb would be discovered in one of these backpacks, tucked under the underpants.

So they had to do something, now that talk radio and cable TV were so fascinated with every bit of border enforcement—until the next election season, anyway. The suits and the big dogs came up with a great assignment for the new Terminators—they were being sent out to arrest wets who were *leaving* the United States for Mexico. Hey, if you can't catch 'em coming in anymore, bust 'em when they're doing you a favor and trying to get back out.

Arnie thought a lot about that "f-you money."

Elk, man, elk.

He came back for Nayeli. Crooked a finger at her. Opened the gate for her.

"Gracias," she said, shyly grinning.

"We're not going on a date," he replied.

Photographs. Fingerprints. They sat at a table surrounded by other tables with worried paisanos and bored immigration agents. Arnie made some notes on a form. He wanted to know why she was carrying American money. Drugs? She shook her head. Hooker? No! When Nayeli started to tell him her story, he stopped writing. His mouth hung halfway open.

"Hey," he said to the guy at the next table, "you gotta hear this."

Nayeli told her story again. The agents shook their heads. It was the dumbest thing they'd heard all night. But they handed her all due respect: Nayeli had the most original wet story they'd heard in a week.

"You're taking them back," Arnie said.

She nodded. "I am here as a service to both our countries."

He laughed. He looked around. He dropped his hands on the table.

"Well, well, well," he said.

He laughed again, wiped his eyes.

"Do you not believe me?" she asked.

"Not really. But it's a great story, I'll give you that. Extra points for originality."

She crossed her arms and frowned.

"I am not a liar," she said.

"No. Just an illegal immigrant. That makes you so reliable!"

"I am not illegal!" she insisted. "I am on a mission. I am a patriot."

He put his hand to his brow.

"Okay," he said. "Whatever."

He was thinking: the last time he'd seen his daughter, she was wearing a Kangol beret and mouthing hip noises and saying, *Whatevs, dawg.* Dawg? Who really said *dawg*, anyway? He shook his head. Nayeli was her size and close to her age. Almost her color.

"What am I gonna do with you kids?" he asked no one in particular.

He patted his own arm.

"Thanks for the compliment, by the way," he said.

He got up, gestured for her to rise. The place was loud and awful. He wanted to be in the high country. Snow and ravens standing on the crowns of lightning-struck lodgepoles. He had a hold of her arm, but he didn't go to the holding pen. He didn't know what he was doing. He was going on instinct. Who could fire him? Who could write him up? He'd go fishing.

Arnie bought Nayeli a cold Coke from a battered machine. He bought some Zagnut bars and M&M's from the agents' machine for her friends. Then he locked her in the holding pen.

He stared in at her.

She smiled back.

"Don't let me catch your ass again," he warned.

A dog began barking savagely at a small group of young men.

More terrorists, Arnie thought as he walked away, ignoring the whole thing.

Nayeli burned with shame.

She had thought the Americanos would be happy to see her.

~

We're going back to Tijuana?" Yolo snapped.

They had found one another in the big pen. They never spotted Candelaria. Tacho was feeling his money belt, amazed that nobody had discovered it.

"We're starting all over?" Yolo yelled.

"Would you rather be in jail?" Nayeli snapped back.

"I would rather be in Tres Camarones!" Yolo said. "I would rather be home!"

She shoved Nayeli.

One of the migra agents waded into the crowd.

"Hey!" he said. "¡Calma!"

"Sorry," said Yolo.

"Do I have to separate you?"

"No."

"I'm watching."

"Sorry."

He signaled another agent, and they stayed close enough to the friends to intervene, should trouble erupt.

"Great," Nayeli said. "Thanks."

"Don't get smart with me, girl," Yolo replied. "Thanks for what? I didn't get us arrested! I didn't get us deported!"

"Come on, now," Tacho said. He was stroking poor Vampi's tangled vampire hair. "Let's not fight."

Tacho thought sadly about La Mano Caída. He was missing the counter and the drink cooler, the cement floor and the stinking evil iguana in the window that snuck in every day to steal his mango and pineapple slices. He was suddenly worried that Aunt Irma wasn't taking proper care of the lizard.

"I can't believe this!" Yolo said.

"I know," Tacho said. His voice could be soothing when he wanted it to be. "I know."

Yolo crossed her arms around her stomach and huffed. She had tears in her eyes. The people jammed in with her bumped into her and pushed against her. She had never hated people as much as she did right then. One tear escaped her eye and ran down her cheek.

Nayeli reached out for her, to give her a hug. She resisted, then gave in.

"I'm sorry," Nayeli whispered.

Tacho said, "Just think of home. That's what I do when I feel bad. I think of home."

It was so noisy. Fences were clanking. People shuffled, muttered. The buses pulled up and the agents were yelling and the pneumatic doors were pulling open and the chain link was rattling. Migra agents moved through, telling them it was time to go home. The friends had to yell to be heard.

"What?" Yolo shouted.

"Home!" Tacho yelled. It was so absurd, he started to grin. He yelled as loud as he could: "Think about home!"

"What about home?" Vampi clled.

"I think about La Mano Caída!" Tacho yelled.

"¿Qué?"

"¡LA MANO CAIDA!"

Instantly, the Border Patrol agents froze.

"Al Qaeda?" the nearest one said.

"What?" said Tacho.

"Did you say Al Qaeda?"

"¡No! ¡Dije 'La Mano Caída'!" Tacho shouted a little too loud.

The agents jumped on him, wrestling him to the ground.

"This guy's Al Qaeda!"

People shouted and surged away. The gate stood open and the bus loading began. The three girls were forced from Tacho, who was under a pile of ICE agents. People shoved. The girls shrieked. A man's voice yelled, "Get them out of here!" They were borne onto the bus.

Agents were wading into the crowd from all sides, heading for Tacho.

The bus doors slammed.

The bus lurched away, and the girls were trapped inside, watching them manhandle Tacho.

They sobbed and banged on the glass.

But the bus did not stop.

Norte

Chapter Eighteen

Morning.

Tijuana street toughs with nothing better to do entertained themselves by jeering at deportees as they came back to Mexico, tired and dirty and downtrodden. Old hands among the returnees knew the border game and faded away and vanished among the tough guys and headed back to the fences. But the fresh meat, the crying ones, the hunched and scuttling guilty-looking ones, they were the source of sport and derision.

The barracudas could smell helplessness on them, and the bad guys laughed and flicked cigarettes and called insults and offered to relieve the women of any sexual tension they might be feeling. It was better than TV, better than drinking in the cantina, to watch the weeping and broken stumble and look about themselves, lost. Anything could happen. Who would know? Do-gooders? Missionaries? The Red Cross? Everyone was tired of these wanderers—everyone who mattered, anyway.

These men said dreadful things, and boys joined in because that is what boys do. Some of the women had lost track of their children and come back sobbing and frantic, and if they hoped for help or compassion back in border zone Tijuana, they were mistaken. The street toughs merely pointed and laughed.

Beyond the few nasty bastards at the fences, there were worse men waiting—coyotes selling the immediate return. Bottom-feeders. How much could a deportee pay? Chances were, not much. But they found ways. After all, they had nowhere to go—this homecoming reminded them that they had no home. Nobody but Nayeli's gang was on a quest to protect and repopulate their villages. They were there for food, to send money home. These invaders, so infamous on American talk radio, were hopeless and frantic with starving compulsion. So they would make whatever desperate deals their guides suggested, or they would borrow money or dig hidden rolls of cash from their own orifices and gamble their last stores to try again. And the agents of despair were there for them, offering an immediate return. They didn't care where the money or the promises or the barter of the bodies came from. It could all be washed off. All they offered was the simple promise: I can take you back, back to Libertad—or beyond, east into the mountain or desert wasteland, where the legendary fence merely stopped. There was nothing out there but a few traffic barriers and fires and rattlesnakes and cowboys. And among these hustlers, there milled taxi drivers heading nowhere. On some days, a pimp might try to recruit a young woman or a boy with promises of quick money, short service, and protection, mostly lies.

The good people of Tijuana went about their business, looking away from the returnees, hurrying on into their days. Most citizens of Tijuana had never seen a pimp and wouldn't give him the time of day if they did. Outside the borderlands, Mexicans seemed to believe that every young man in Tijuana was a hustler or a coyote, but most of the citizens of Tijuana had never seen a coyote and wouldn't know one if they saw him. They didn't think about the border—they had no time for it. The border was an abstraction to

them at best. Many citizens of Tijuana crossed it every day to shop
for a better cut of meat in San Ysidro, or to buy polyester underwear and stretch pants in the secondhand shops and factory outlet
stores. Hundred of women walked through the Immigration turn-
stiles and boarded the red trolleys that fed them into the hills and
valleys of San Diego, where they vacuumed and dusted and wiped
out toilets and cooked grilled-cheese sandwiches in the homes of
other women who could afford to hire people to do their household
chores for them.

And many hundreds of others never went to San Diego at all,
never even really looked across the river. They did not have time for
returnees. They didn't like all these newcomers who crowded their
streets and brought dirt and panic into Tijuana. They suspected all
crimes were inspired by these people. All drugs came with them.
Old people remembered a day when you could leave your doors
unlocked in Tijuana. When you knew all of your neighbors, and
everyone kept an eye out for one another. Not now, not with these
tides of aliens pouring in from everywhere. So Nayeli and Yolo and
Vampi came into the hard sun, crying and wiping their noses, dirt-
ier than they had ever been, afraid and lonesome and homesick,
and nobody cared at all.

They walked in a huddle, hugging one another, holding hands.

"¿Taxi?" a chubby man called. "¿Centro?"

They shook their heads.

"Mamacita," a laughing smoking boy cooed. "Come here."

They walked on—Indian women in clothes like Doña Araceli's
sold trinkets and chewing gum and held out dark brown palms,
making small mewling begging sounds. Big, hearty Americanos in
madras shorts and straw hats and baseball caps and bowling shirts
jostled them and marched on, laughing like they always laughed,
owning the earth and secure in their mastery. Nayeli wanted what
they had, but she did not know what that was. Loudness. No

cares at all. Nothing slowed the Americans, nothing made them silent. Americans did not cower. When cholos insulted them, they walked through the clouds of anger and hatred as if deaf, as if they didn't have time to hear such foolishness, and if they did hear it, they raised a middle finger or laughed or said something tart and marched, marched, marched into the laughing world. There were so many Americans in Tijuana that she didn't understand what the border was supposed to be. People in the holding pens had told her that it was the same in el otro lado, that there were so many Mexicans milling around San Ysidro and Chula Vista that it looked like Mazatlán. There were more Mexicans in Los Angeles than there were in Culiacán. She spun in a circle and saw nothing but barbed wire and guards. The whole border was the same dirt scrub dust stinking desert blankness. With helicopters.

"¿Taxi?"

"No, gracias."

The girls were despondent. Nayeli did not know what to do now. How would she keep her troops going? Had they lost Tacho forever? She could not imagine how she would find him again. How could they go ahead without him?

She looked up.

Standing at the end of the cracked and upthrust sidewalk, leaning on the staff, one foot planted against the opposite knee, red bandanna now gone, and shaved head gleaming in the sun, was the Warrior.

"I am Atómiko," he called.

He leads them through the hot streets, his pole over his right shoulder. Nobody looks at him. They have seen men with poles before. They have seen stranger things than him. And the girls follow in a cluster. Nobody looks at them, either. They have seen men with poles leading groups of women. They have seen everything.

He stops at a food stand carved out of the side of a white-and-blue building with cursive writing in red slanting over the opening that promises SEAFOOD! SHRIMP! OYSTERS! FRESH WATERS! By *waters*, of course, they mean fruit juices and rice water and hibiscus tea. Atómiko knows the girls are dehydrated. He plants his staff and points at the counter and says, "Buy juice."

Nayeli is so relieved to see any friendly face, even his jackal's countenance, she meekly goes to the counter and digs out money and buys them tall glasses of iced fruit juice. She can't believe how delicious it is. They gulp like people lost in the desert. Atómiko sips at a glass of agua de Jamaica, red as blood and tart. He thinks he would rather be drinking Mexican beer, the best beer in the world. Yolo guzzles tamarind juice, Vampi drinks horchata sweet rice water, and Nayeli is chewing chunks of strawberries floating in her glass.

Atómiko points down the street with his staff, and they follow. He leads them to a small motor court. A motel, white with blue trim. Three cars are parked in its sloping blacktop lot. A Mixtec woman sweeps the sidewalk in front of the rooms. A sputtering neon sign sizzles orange against the morning light. The cardboard sign taped in the window lists a reasonable price for rooms. Atómiko points, scratches his chest, and grunts.

"Sí," Nayeli says.

"Two rooms," says the Warrior.

She complies. She doesn't care. She can end up with no money at all. She just wants to bathe. To sleep.

The girls share room 101. They cry out, they weep, they fall on the beds, they fight for the shower and the toilet. They turn on the air-conditioning. Atómiko has the key to 102.

"I am next door," he says.

He belches.

He says, "Wash your panties."

He slams the door.

In a minute, they hear the television in his room turned up very loud, and strange thwacking sounds and thumps. Shouts. They listen. Finally, Nayeli smiles.

She says: "He is practicing."

~

They slept till five o'clock, the girls scattered across the two beds like dolls, insensate and snoring in their exhaustion. Their panties and blouses dried in the bathroom, hung over the shower rod. All their socks drooped from the edges of the sink and the top of the toilet tank. Vampi's nose whistled in three distinct notes as she breathed, descending in pitch as each exhalation waned.

Nayeli was the first to awaken. She lay there for a while, listening to Vampi snuffle. She still had the tiny purse that Tacho had given her. She picked it up off the floor and dug out her KANKA-KEE postcard. She read her father's message again. "Everything Passes." A better day would come.

She slipped it back into the purse and pulled out her Missionary Matt card. She looked at his phone number on the back. She sat up and saw Yolo, propped against her headboard. She was holding her own Missionary Matt card. They stared at each other.

"He used to call you Yo-Yo," Nayeli noted.

"Call him," Yolo said.

"Yes."

"What do you think he is like now?"

"He is rich."

"I think he's a movie actor."

"He is a famous surfer and rock star."

"I hope he's not married."

"Me, too."

Nayeli got up to put on her clothes so she could go find a phone.

Her shirt and her underwear were damp, but she pulled them on anyway and quietly opened the door. That irritating Atómiko stood there talking to Wino. Wino was smoking, and he looked up at her and ducked his head. "¿Qué hubo?" he muttered.

Nayeli stepped outside.

"How did you get him to come?" she asked Atómiko.

"I have powers," he said.

"Yes," she replied. "We noticed the other night that you could fly."

"Oh?" said Wino. "¿La mera neta? This vato can fly?"

There was a pay phone on the wall outside the motel office. Somebody had written "Octavio Slept With My Wife" on the metal. Nayeli punched O and got another polite Tijuana operator and placed her collect call to Tres Camarones.

It rang twice, and Aunt Irma grabbed it off the hook.

"What the hell do you want?" she barked.

"Collect call for Doña Irma García Cervantes from Nayeli."

"Yes, yes, of course. Hurry up—I don't have all day."

The phone clicked and clacked a few times, and Nayeli could barely speak, her throat was so tight.

"¿Tía?" she said.

Aunt Irma was yelling at the turkey: "General! Leave that chicken alone, you mindless idiot!"

"¿Tía?" Nayeli repeated.

"My girl!" Irma cried. "How goes the epic journey?"

Nayeli started to cry.

"Ay, Tía," she said. "It has taken us forever."

"It's only been a week!" Irma said.

"A week?"

"Six days, actually. Are you in San Diego yet? Have you seen Chava?"

"Chava?" Nayeli said.

"Chava Chavarín," Aunt Irma snapped. "Don't tell me you forgot to call Chava Chavarín! He was the finest bowler I ever saw."

Nayeli sniffled. How could it have been only a week? Surely they had been on the road for weeks. Nayeli tried to remember anything Aunt Irma might have said in the past about Chavarín.

"Where do I begin?" Nayeli said.

"Tell me everything."

"Everything? Well…"

It all poured out. The whole long story of the bus and the dump and the crossing and the migra. Irma interrupted often.

"Chavarín?"

"No Chavarín."

"He didn't help you? That bastard! Or"—a tone of dread and disbelief seeped into La Osa's hectoring voice—"is he, uh, dead?"

"No, Tía. I don't think so."

A tiny gasp of relief.

"Is it possible—did he—did he not…remember me?"

"No, Tía. Nothing like that. There was no Chavarín. He is not here."

"That is absolutely incorrect," Irma insisted.

"I'm sorry."

"He cannot be gone. He married a damned—a gringa. They live in Colonia Independencia."

"No."

Silence.

"He went across," Irma decided. "Call him when you get across."

"Is this why we're here?" Nayeli asked. "To find Chavarín?"

"Don't be silly. Goddamnit."

Then:

"You were saying you are involved with a criminal named Atomic?"

Nayeli thought: *A change of gears.*

And:

"Did you also say Tacho is a terrorist?"

There was far too much to explain, so Nayeli forged ahead:

"We are going back across," she said. "I don't know how, but we will try again. People here go back over and over, and so will we. I have Mateo's phone number."

"Mateo who?"

"The missionary."

"Jesus Christ, you're calling the Christian."

"Yes. What else can I do?"

"That simp."

"Yes, Tía."

Irma sighed.

"All right. Fine. Good. Keep the project rolling."

"We will go to him for help."

"You are there to collect Mexicans," Irma reminded her. "Don't fall in love with that missionary!"

"I won't."

"And don't screw him, either. If you give him the milk for free, why would he buy the cow?"

"¡Tía!"

"Don't bring me any damned American surfers. And don't bring me any American babies. Bring me Mexicans."

"That's what I wanted to tell you," Nayeli said. "I . . . I think I want to go get my father."

Uncharacteristic silence from La Osa.

"To Kankakee," Nayeli continued. "I want my father to come home."

Irma sighed.

"Well," she said. She knew there were one hundred things to tell her black-eyed girl, but to what avail? Nayeli was listening to her own heart. She was going to do what she was going to do.

"Very well," La Osa finally said. "Good luck. Bring that good-for-nothing father back if you have to. I will kick his ass when he comes home."

Wino said, "The gay boy—they thought he was a terrorist?" He whistled. "They'll send him to Guantánamo." He and Atómiko shook their heads. "That's rough."

"At least he gets to see Cuba," Atómiko said.

"No, thanks."

They looked like two ancient crows to Nayeli, all ruffled and hunch shouldered, looking at the ground and smoking. The door opened behind them, and the girls came out, rubbing their eyes and trying to wrestle their hair into shape with their fingers.

Atómiko looked at Yolo and growled in the back of his throat.

"What are you looking at?" she said.

"I'm looking at you."

"I thought you loved Nayeli."

"She will not have me."

Yolo shrugged him off and turned away as Nayeli reported on her telephone call. All three girls agreed that Mateo's house was a fine destination. Mostly because it was the only place they could imagine finding safe haven in Los Yunaites. But they did not want to cross the border again. No way.

The two men stood listening, and Atómiko nudged Wino, who cleared his throat to get their attention.

"Listen," he said. "I feel bad you got caught. My socio here has been making me feel bad. So I'm going to do you a favor. It's my first favor ever. So you'd better appreciate it."

"He is Wino!" Atómiko announced, showing that he had diversified his usual train of thought.

"I'm going to take you to the hole."

"The hole?" Nayeli said.

"The hole, esa. That's what I said." Wino nodded. "The hole. I had to call in some favors, you understand. This is big-money stuff, going to the hole. Homeboy says you'll pay me one day, when you get money."

"The hole?"

"Trust me," Wino said, which made all three girls doubt him. "You'll see," he insisted. "It's guaranteed."

Atómiko held out his staff and tapped Nayeli with it.

"Guaranteed," he repeated.

"Just remember one thing," Wino said. "You will forget you ever saw the hole. ¿Comprenden? Once you go through it, you were never there." He sucked down the last of his cig. He studied the cherry at the tip. "Most people? They stumble into the hole? They don't live to see another day."

He flicked his cigarette away, and it bounced across the parking lot, unleashing showers of burning sparks.

"Bang, bang," he said.

The cigarette butt smoked in the street.

Chapter Nineteen

They were out beyond the Tijuana airport. Fences and walls and the usual border boneyard vistas. They pulled up at a scruffy cluster of gas stations and bodegas and auto shops and warehouses. The building where they parked had a tin man welded together out of mufflers in front. His hat was a steel funnel. The sign above the closed door said MOFLES. It all stank of burning taco meat and dogs, spilled car oil and exhaust, trash fire smoke.

"What's a mofle?" Yolo asked. She was always the scholar. She liked words. But she had never really heard Spanglish before.

"A mofle is a mofle, damn," said Wino. "It's, like—what do you call the pinchi thing in back of your car?"

"Silenciador," Atómiko said.

"A muffler!" Yolo said.

"What the hell have I been telling you?" Wino snapped.

Vampi got out of the car and pointed at the tin man.

"He'so cute!" she cried.

Nayeli was tense. The girls apparently hadn't taken note of the isolated nature of this nasty little clot of ruin. They could be on their way to being raped and killed. They could be kidnapped and forced into sexual slavery. They could be filmed being killed; she had seen stories about that in *¡Alarma!*

A Tijuana cop in a bulletproof vest stood on the corner, a matte black assault rifle pointing at the ground; his bottomless shades turned their way, and he regarded them coolly, then turned away.

She was jittery and angry—angry at the day and the border and the very buildings where they stood. But it was the presence of Atómiko that calmed her. She did not like him, but she did not believe he would allow them to be harmed. She looked at him. He had abandoned his campaign to woo Yolo and turned his attentions to Vampi. He was actually wiggling his eyebrows at her. Nayeli stifled a laugh.

She made a fleeting sign of the cross and muttered, "Ave María purísima."

"Come on," said Wino.

He banged on the steel-shuttered door of the muffler shop, and it clanged and rolled up. Smoke and rocanrol billowed out.

"Let's go," said a kid inside.

Wino hunched over and went in, so the girls followed. Atómiko held his staff across his chest and stooped through. The door slammed back down behind them.

Black Glocks in belts, small machine guns in hands.

"This is them, huh?" said a man in a running suit.

"That's it," said Wino.

"Who am I talking to?" the man asked.

"Excuse me?" said Nayeli.

"Who am I talking to?" the man repeated. He pointed at Atómiko. "You?"

Atómiko shook his head.

"Her," he said.

The man turned to Nayeli.

"You! You're the boss?" He smiled, not warmly. "This short girl?" He barked out one laugh. "All right." He took her arm and led her to the back of the room—it was much bigger than it looked from the outside. "You were never here," he said. "You don't know anything about this shop. Right?"

"Right."

"The vato with the pole led you across. Not us."

"Yes."

"We will not help you again. We do this only once. All right?"

"All right."

She was confused and was answering the way she thought he wanted her to answer.

Wino gestured with his chin.

"Mota," he said.

"¿Marijuana?" Vampi cried.

Bales lined the walls.

The boys in the mofle shop stared at her.

"Big-time!" Wino said.

"¿Coca?" Atómiko asked.

The man in the running suit said, "I knew a curious monkey that got his nose cut off."

Atómiko shrugged.

"I was asking for a Coca-Cola," he lied.

Wino sneered.

The man in the running suit said, "If Wino wasn't my nephew, you'd be lying out in the street right now. We move product in the hole, not bodies!"

He threw back a trapdoor. He reached into the shadows and flicked on a light switch.

"Welcome," he said.

Wino winked and started down the ladder.

~~~

The girls recognized it at once. They had seen this in the Cine Pedro Infante, during one of García-García's endless Steve McQueen film festivals. It was the dirt tunnel from *The Great Escape;* it was strung with electric lights on drooping power lines, and the floor was flat and well trampled.

Atómiko whistled.

"Sweet!" he said. "I could make a million dollars with a tunnel like this!"

The man in the running suit came down behind them and said, "That's all? A million?"

He laughed.

"It runs for over half a mile. Right across the border. Right under the noses of the migra. It comes up in a curtain-and-drapery-stitching company on the other side. The workers in there don't even know. When night comes, my associates will slide two big sewing machines out of the way and open the door."

Nayeli had never heard of such a thing. Vampi and Yolo had eyes as big as doughnuts. This was truly a thing of awe.

"What if you're caught?" Nayeli asked. "What if they're found out?"

"We have a burglar alarm." The man in the running suit laughed. "And we blow the tunnel on this end and drive away."

Atómiko whistled again.

"But, you know," the man said, "it's a lot of money. ¿Me entiendes? There's people who know about us over there. God willing, our little donations are enough for them to protect us."

He wore a gold crucifix on a chain.

"...God willing," Nayeli said, sounding skeptical.

The man smiled.

"God loves us all," he said.

The girls looked at one another; Vampi was smiling sweetly, and Yolo was very serious. Nayeli set her jaw, hoping she looked fierce.

"Go," the man said. "It's straight. You can't get lost."

"Are there bats?" Vampi asked.

He laughed.

"No, no bats. Go."

"Rats?"

"No! No rats! There's nothing there but dirt. Go!"

"¡Adios!" Wino said. "Good luck!"

They had to duck their heads as they entered the hole, but it was fairly comfortable. Nobody had to crawl. It was well lit, and hard to believe. Nayeli imagined the Border Patrol trucks driving above her head as she walked. Their feet raised dust as they shuffled: she sneezed.

Wino's voice came down the tunnel behind them: "Send me a postcard," he called.

"He turned out to be a good boy," Yolo said.

Nayeli had to concede the point.

"He treated us well."

The Warrior, bringing up the rear, reminded them: "But he is not me."

Vampi said, "Thank God!" and the girls laughed at him.

They saw one vast brown spider in the hole, but the rest of the walk was a dullness of dirt walls and wooden support beams.

"I could use some of that cocaine," Atómiko noted.

The girls had never known a real drug user, and they regarded

him with new eyes. He was so gangster. The mota-heads in Camarones kept their marijuana to themselves.

They got to the end of the tunnel, and there it was, another
ladder. Three small boxes stood in the tunnel, and the girls sat on
them. Atómiko squatted in his baboon fashion.

"Hey, look at that!" said Vampi.

A clamshell was stuck in the tan soil of the tunnel wall.

"That came from Noah's flood," Atómiko said.

"Don't be ridiculous," Yolo scolded.

They argued about evolution for a few minutes, then fell into a
sullen silence.

"Now what?" Yolo said.

"We wait," Nayeli replied.

After a long time, Vampi said, "I'm bored."

Yolo stretched.

Nayeli said, "I want to go to Kankakee."

"Ah," said Yolo. "Your father."

"Where is it?" asked Vampi.

"It's around Chicago someplace," Nayeli said.

"What about us?" Vampi asked.

"We," said Yolo, "will visit Mateo."

Atómiko amazed them by starting to snore.

They heard loud scraping above them, and the roof popped
open and a gruff male voice said, "Hurry up."

They came up into a storeroom full of carpet rolls and tables covered with bolts of material. The two sewing machines that covered
the opening were slid aside on rollers, and the rug pulled up and laid
over so the trapdoor could open. The room was muffled, insulated
by all the curtains and rugs. The man pointed to an open door.

"In the garage," he said.

They shuffled into the garage and found a delivery van standing
there with its back door open. They were startled to see, through

the one small window in the garage's side door, that it was dark outside.

"In," the man said.

They climbed up.

They made themselves comfortable among rolls of carpet. He reached up, grabbed a leather strap, and slid the door down with a loud crash. They were thrown into darkness. The girls reached for one another. Atómiko clutched his staff firmly, though it didn't seem likely that he could break the van's cargo doors open with it. They heard the door latch click into place. The driver got in the front—the springs squeaked. He started the engine. They heard an electric door opener lift the garage's big door, and they rolled. Down the slope of the driveway, then settling onto a smooth flat street. They made several turns, fell over when he stopped at red lights. They could hear traffic sounds from outside. He was listening to Mexican radio in the cab. Suddenly, they could feel acceleration, and they were on a freeway. They drove and drove, and they merged to the right and swooped.

None of them could tell how long they'd been driving when the van rolled down a ramp and made an abrupt stop. The driver honked his horn, shouted something rude, made a left turn and a right turn, drove for a few minutes, and made another, more abrupt, right. They heard gravel crunching. He stopped but left the engine running. The door latch rattled and the door shot up. Cold night air rushed in.

"Out," he said.

They jumped down from the back of the van, and before they could say anything to the driver, he was back in the cab and driving out of the big dirt lot.

They stood in the darkness, looking around. They could see, at a distance, a lit Spanish mission on a hillside on their right. Before them, a wall of oleanders and scraggly trees, and on the other side of that, rushing traffic. If they craned to the left, they could see some hills. One of them had a lit cross on the top. Behind them, they sensed a void—it was pitch-black and smelly. But that seemed to be the way out of the lot, so they walked in that direction. A street cut across their path; they turned right, toward the hill with the cross and away from the old church on the other hill. San Diego seemed to be offering them lit beacons, each one promising that Jesus was watching over them.

They came to a small low bridge, and as they crossed it, they saw the turgid dark water of a slough beneath them, and they smelled the heavy odor of old seawater. On their left, they saw an expanse of lawn and water—they were walking along a great bay. It was lit by streetlamps on tall poles. When Vampi saw a playground across the street, she ran to it and jumped on the swings and started to push herself back and forth. Yolo and Nayeli felt old and serious—far too old to play on swings. But Atómiko surprised them by joining Vampi. He actually put down his staff so he could swing.

Nayeli followed.

"Children," she muttered.

Yolo walked beside her.

"Look," she said. "The United States has grass."

When the sprinklers came on with a loud PFFFT and began their automated *spit-spit-spit-glide, spit-spit-spit-gliiide,* they ran.

Giddy with the Good Old USA, everybody laughed. The air smelled great, smelled of salt water and jacaranda trees. The air was cool—too cool for the girls, but running had heated them a bit.

Clean little sidewalks wandered among small green hills with strange little barbecue stands and even more playgrounds. Vampi had to swing at every one. Atómiko climbed a monkey bar igloo and stood atop it, holding his staff over his head and bellowing.

"Es King Kong," Yolo noted.

They were delighted to find well-lit public bathrooms. Clean, too. The girls took up three stalls and chattered as they did their business. Atómiko entered his bathroom with his staff extended before him, ready to smite muggers. But there was no one there. He availed himself of the urinal, then surprised himself by washing his hands. He could not believe he could wash his hands in steaming-hot water. He had some trouble managing the blow-dryer, and finally simply wiped his hands on his pants and stood guard outside the girls' door. Their laughter and gossip echoed inside. They could be heard all over the bay. He felt it was a terrible security problem, but you couldn't dampen high spirits at a moment like this. Their happiness would get them far on their journey before despair slowed them again. So he planted his staff and struck an ominous pose.

The notorious girlfriends exited the bathroom and set off at a brisk pace. They looked at the stars. They watched the bright white cross atop the hill. They looked around them at the many house lights on the slopes of Clairemont.

A man walking three pugs on leashes came along and said, "Good evening."

"¡Adios!" Vampi chirped.

Nayeli nudged her.

At the visitors' center, they gathered and stared into the soda machines. More lights. Moths battered themselves on the neon tubes. Two policemen in shorts and bike helmets pedaled by on their mountain bikes. One waved. Vampi waved back.

"¡Adios!" she called.

"Shh!" Yolo scolded. "You want to be deported again?"

Atómiko laughed.

"Those are city cops!" he said. "¡La Placa, esa! They don't care if you have papers or not!"

Vampi crossed her arms and said, "See?"

"I love America," Nayeli sighed. "The policemen ride bikes and wear shorts."

"This was a good idea," Yolo said. "I didn't think so, but now I do. It is so clean!"

"It's too damned clean," Atómiko complained. "Where are the bonfires? How can you party with no bonfires?"

Vampi pointed across the water. Bonfires burned on a low island. They could see fat men in lawn chairs drinking from cans.

"I stand corrected," Atómiko announced. He raised his staff and called, "Party!"

"Maybe we can find some dead dogs, too, so you'll feel at home," Yolo said.

"You are very humorous," the Warrior replied.

A VW Bug circled the round driveway. It was full of American girls. The bass was bumpin', and the girls laughed as the car circled. Nayeli could smell them from this far away—shampoo and perfume and cigarettes.

"Eminem!" Vampi shouted.

The girls waved and sped off into the night.

"It is the sisterhood of music," Vampi intoned.

Yolo and Nayeli shook their heads.

"This chick is too much," Yolo complained.

Vampi was so happy, she threw her arms around Atómiko.

"Do you love it here?" she asked.

"It's peachy," he said.

"Ooh, you're so tough!"

"I love you, though," he offered.

"Me and every other hot girl."

"You are hot," he agreed. "Muy, muy caliente, mi chiquita."

"All right, buster," she said.

She let him go.

"*¡Morras!*" she shouted. "What do you want to do now that we're in Los Yunaites?"

Nayeli: "Find my father."

Yolo: "Find Mateo."

Nayeli: "That, too."

Yolo: "Find Tacho."

Tacho! They all started crying again. Darling Tacho!

Atómiko hawked up some phlegm and spit.

"I want to go to Disneyland," he said.

They goggled at him—everyone expected he'd say something like *I want to go to a strip club and see hardbodies,* or something like *I want to get into a gang fight and kill a hundred men with my bare hands.* He felt self-conscious, the way they were staring at him and sniffling, wiping their eyes and noses on their sleeves.

"What!" he demanded.

They giggled.

"Disneyland, Atómiko?" Nayeli said.

"Hey," he said. "I just want to whack Mickey Mouse with my pole!"

The girls burst out laughing.

"Your pole!" Yolo cried.

"You could have whacked Tacho with your pole if you were lonesome!" Vampi said.

Then they thought about Tacho and felt weepy all over again.

Nayeli banged on the phone one time.

"Tachito," she said.

"Food," Atómiko proclaimed, saving face.

He pointed with his pole at a Jack in the Box across the freeway.

"Did you bring money?" Nayeli asked.

"Nel."

"I suppose I'm buying you a meal?"

"I am earning my keep, guarding you on your journey. I am—"

"We KNOW who you are!" Yolo blurted.

The girls all crowed: "You are Atómiko!"

He shrugged, looked away inscrutably.

Nayeli pulled out her Missionary Matt card.

She and Yolo stared at each other.

"Should I?" Nayeli said.

"You have to."

"I'm nervous."

"Just do it."

Nayeli picked up the phone, then laughed and hung it up.

"You coward," Yolo said.

"No!" Nayeli replied. "I don't have any American coins left! We spent it all. I have pesos, and it won't take pesos!"

Atómiko coughed, spit.

"Food," he repeated.

They walked over the bridge.

Chapter Twenty

———

The girls had never eaten tacos made with hamburger meat.

"American food," said Yolo.

Vampi slurped a Dr Pepper.

"Doctor Pimienta," she translated. "But I don't taste any pepper."

"Let me taste it," said Nayeli.

She scrunched her nose.

"I think that's prune juice," she said.

"Let me taste! Let me taste!" demanded Yolo. She took a pull.

"Cherries," she said.

They had been lucky. All the employees in the burger stand were undocumented Mexicans except for one Guatemalan. They exchanged pesos for dollars at a bad rate, but at least Nayeli could buy food and get change for the pay phone.

Atómiko had acted out a violent attack of nausea and retching when they ordered tacos. He wasn't falling for that. He ordered two Jumbo Jacks with cheese and large fries and a chocolate milk shake. And a piece of apple pie.

"Enjoy your diabetes," Yolo muttered.

"You're in America now, cabronas," he noted. "Apple pie!" He pronounced it *appo pize!* "That's what they eat!"

"If we keep you here very long," Nayeli noted, "you will spark a famine all by yourself."

"All the paisanos will come home on their own," Vampi said, "just so you don't force them to die of hunger."

They slapped her high fives, always eager to reward her for saying something witty or pithy.

"Let's get some onion rings," Atómiko recommended.

Ma Johnston was one of those good, invisible, hard-luck women who lived along the tougher low-rent sections of Clairemont Drive. Her duplex was in a line of duplexes that were set face-to-face across small yellow strips of lawn. They turned their sides to the main street, and their large living room windows had peered at one another for forty years. The occasional palm tree shot into the sky like a frozen firework and seemed to be caught as the trajectory of its ascension started to decay, curving a bit before it fell back to the ground. Pigeons and palm rats rattled the dry fronds. Ma's place was the rear unit, back off the street, beside the alley that ran between Clairemont and Apache. She had two bedrooms and a small kitchenette and a bathroom with a fiberglass tub. She liked to keep her plants on a table by the living room window. Matt used to sleep in the back room, separated from her by the bathroom.

She was the first mom of any of the boys from the high school to have HBO, and though she knew they were coming over to see naked girls, she liked their company when they piled in on Friday nights. She didn't even mind it if they smoked or snuck a beer, though if they smoked dope, they had to go out to the alley, and she'd pretend she didn't know.

Matt's crazy surfer friends always brought her presents — sand dollars or starfish, a bag of doughnuts or some beer. The ZZ Twins were wild-haired long-boarders of the old school — so old-school they still wore Hang Ten shorts, though everybody else was wearing high-tech neon-colored threads. Zemaski and Zaragosa. When they became born-again, they brought her Bibles and CDs of Christian singers. She still had her Rick Elias and the Confessions CD in her little stereo beside the TV.

The ZZs were her favorites, and even when Matt had gone missionary on her, run off to Mexico to save the Mexicans, the ZZ Twins had hung around her house, keeping her company in his absence, keeping the bad guys at bay. They spoke that weird surfer talk she had never quite translated. Once, when she'd asked Zemaski how he was feeling, he said, "I'm creachin' the bouf."

She had laughed for weeks about that one.

Two years later, she'd been hunting through the library's cast-off $1.00 sale table when she glanced at their computers and ventured to access the Internet. The librarian helped her search the phrase "creachin' the bouf." The best translation they could come up with was "I am a fool for the light comedic opera." She liked to think that's what Zemaski meant, though she knew it wasn't.

It had been rough since Matt had returned from his missionary days, unsure of his faith. He had questions. Well, she was never happy with his Bible-thumping phase. He had come home from Mexico and lost his friendship with the ZZs when he'd fought with them about the Rapture. Matt was of the opinion that there was not going to be a rapture, and nobody would be "left behind" to battle evil demonic hordes because nobody was going anywhere, no matter what the Twins' favorite books said. The ZZs might have forgiven this theological breakup, but Matt had also become, heretically, disinterested in surfing. The boys could not believe it. To abandon the waves was truly abandoning the Lord. "Dude," Zaragosa had warned, "Satan's whispering in your ear!"

Oh, well. It was a crisis of conscience for poor Matthew. Ma Johnston knew how thoughtful he was. She knew he was given to liberal ideas. She was a Reagan Republican all the way. But she knew that young people had to search. Hadn't she searched? It had brought her from Virginia to San Diego and Matthew's father. Ah! She tossed her coffee. Ancient history.

Ever since she'd retired, things had been tighter than usual. Being a low-level secretary for the school district had not provided them with lots of money. She had to admit that Matt's missionary phase almost broke her. But between her retirement and her late husband's Social Security, she had done all right. The rent was low and she could manage, even though Matt had gone to San Francisco to work in some store, selling "art pins," whatever they were. They sold a ceramic nipple pin that you apparently wore on your breast. Ha ha. He sent her fifty dollars, sometimes hundred-dollar checks, stuck inside funny greeting cards. The kind that had kittens hanging on to the ends of ropes and said, "Hang In There!" Matt...he was a good boy.

She maintained his room for him, at least for the few times he came home to visit. All his Steve Miller albums were stacked up in there, in order, the way he liked them. His black Jimi Hendrix banner hung above the bed. Matt liked the old stuff—he said new music didn't speak to him.

Instant coffee, Rice-A-Roni, dry cat food for the alley cats she fed, strawberry jam. She walked out of the little shopping center and thought about buying some doughnuts at the Winchell's, then remembered they'd torn it down. Why did everything good have to be destroyed?

It was a little over a half mile to her house. The next day was trash day. She put away her things and was seen by skinny Carla who hung out in the alley hoping to score some ice off the bikers that lived next door to Ma. Carla was sweet. She always waved at Ma Johnston.

That was a Thursday.

By Saturday, Ma hadn't come out to collect her empty garbage cans. Carla wandered across the alley to see if she was okay. And she found Ma Johnston, dead on the kitchen floor, a broken jar of jam beside her.

Matt was through crying, really.

His mother's sad last effects—used books, little doilies and figurines. Albums of photographs of people he did not recognize. He had given her clothes to Goodwill and had thrown out her bras and underwear. Carla was majorly stoked to get the nipple pin. She laughed out loud when she saw it. The Mongols who lived next door came over with beer and sat with him for a while. They scared the hell out of him, but they were decent and spoke highly of his mom.

Carla ventured over and spent the night with him, their sleep asexual and melancholy. Even naked, he felt nothing for her—she was all ribs and butterfly tattoos. It was mostly about body heat.

She fancied his Hendrix banner, so he gave it to her.

How was he hanging with bikers and naked dope fiends? In San Francisco, he was learning to eat sushi and dating a ballet dancer. He went to art museums. But who was he kidding? The ballet dancer was over before Ma passed away. Driving home had been almost easy.

He kept the windows open to air the place out. This stinking duplex was as depressing as anything he could imagine. He'd choked on its hot air all through junior high and high school. He was going to get out of here, wasn't that the plan? Some kind of success story. Anywhere but San Diego. San Die Go. Sandy Eggo. He'd played that Hendrix song over and over to his red-haired high school girlfriend, Rockie Lee. "Come back and buy this town," Jimi sang, "and put it all in my shoe." He hadn't seen her in ten years.

Matt thought he'd get Ma out of this place somehow, before it was too late. He used to tell Rockie Lee that Hell was located in Clairemont. You died and drove into Ma's neighborhood and just went in circles, from cul-de-sac to cul-de-sac, with those dead palm trees above your head, and you never found your way out. Another mission aborted.

He sat on the couch, staring at the TV.

Now what?

He drank another beer — Tecate.

He'd left his job in San Fran to get her cremated and her "cremains" scattered in the ocean. The man at the funeral home made human ashes sound like breakfast cereal.

He had driven down in his '67 Mustang fastback, now parked beside Ma's wasted minivan in the alley. He was too frozen to think. He was afraid — he was trapped in a bad story, where the Venus flytrap of Ma's duplex somehow reached out and consumed him. Rod Serling stuff.

He ate Ma's macaroni and drank her instant coffee and Tecate and slept on the couch. He just couldn't bear to lie in his bed unless Carla was there with him. But in the morning, it was worse to wake up beside her.

When Ma's phone started to ring, the cards he had handed out those years ago in Tres Camarones were the furthest thing from his thoughts.

He pulled into the parking lot in Ma's minivan. This had to be the weirdest thing that had happened to him. Ever.

He got out of the van and said, "Nayeli?" but didn't manage to get much more said because the three girls flew at him and threw their arms around him, crying out and squeezing and dragging him back and forth. He fell over against the van, but they didn't let go as they rubbed him and hugged him.

He wasn't all that thrilled with the grunge merchant with the big stick, but he was delighted to see the girls again. He thought: *They are short.*

He didn't know what to do, so he took them home.

He couldn't believe they still had his number! How unlikely was that? In his mind, they had remained gawky and silly teenyboppers. And now. Now! He looked at Nayeli, perched beside him. He glanced back at Yolo and Vampi. They were not gawksters anymore.

"Wow," he kept saying. "Wow!"

"Ay, Mateo," Nayeli sighed, shaking her head.

"But, like, wow!"

"Mateo, Mateo. ¡Eres tremendo, Mateo!"

To Atómiko, the whole thing sounded demented and silly — he busied himself during the drive looking at the nice houses, the cars, and the shining 7-Eleven atop the hill. A man could steal a fortune around here. He was amazed that all the cars looked new. Maybe he'd boost one and drive back to the dump in style.

Matt prepared to apologize for how sad his ma's place looked, but when they walked in, Atómiko whistled. He plopped on the couch and said, "Hey! You've got a remote!" He switched on the TV and said, "Got any beer?"

"Uh," said Matt.

Nayeli cried, "Mateo! You house! Is a palace!"

"Beer in the fridge," Matt said.

Atómiko pointed at Vampi.

"Get me a beer, will you, morra?"

She dutifully went to the kitchen and fetched him a can.

"What a pimp," Yolo said.

She and Nayeli hugged Matt from either side. He put his arms across their shoulders. Their breasts pressed against his ribs. Whoa. Their heads smelled a little oily, though. That was semignarly, right there.

"Would you like a shower?" he asked.

"Bubble bath!" Vampi said.

He had to go across the alley and get Mr. Bubble from Carla. She followed him back over to stare at the illegals. Vampi got into the bathroom and soaked for about an hour.

When she was done, Matt pulled a chair out of the kitchen and sat quietly, watching them watch MTV. Nayeli and Yolo kept casting glances his way and smiling. Vampi seemed mesmerized by the television. Atómiko had laid his pole on the floor in front of the couch.

He said, "I want pancakes."

Nayeli winked.

Matt just watched.

Chapter Twenty-one

—————

Tacho sat at a nasty little plywood table in a dull green room. The tabletop was splintery and gouged with initials and half words. It was charred in various places from cigarettes left burning. The walls of the room were cement blocks, and the floor was old lino-leum. He noted the ugly industrial green of the tiles—they looked like they had skinny little off-white clouds swirling in them. His captors were not only stupid, they had bad taste.

His left eye was black, and his lip was swollen. He held a wet cloth to it and winced. He prodded at a tooth with the tip of his tongue. He thought it might be loose. His hair spikes were all plas-tered down flat, and if he could have looked in a mirror, he would have been appalled to see he looked like Julius Caesar, with his tiny blond bangs sticking to his forehead.

Tacho put his hands on his belly and surreptitiously felt his money belt. He couldn't believe these morons hadn't taken it and discovered his dollars. Good for him, though—they would have really thought he was a terrorist with all that cash. As it was, they had given him a good tune-up, bouncing his body on the floor and "accidentally" running his head into the wall.

An American in a badly fitting black suit came into the room and set a manila folder on the table and smiled as he sat.

"Mr. Lora," he said.

"Hmm," said Tacho, looking away angrily.

"Do you understand English?"

"Chure. I espik good Englitch."

"Fine."

The fellow opened the file, moved three papers around, cleared his throat. Tacho sneered: the guy was wearing musk cologne. That was for thirteen-year-old boys. Tacho would have recommended Aramis. And a serious haircut.

"Yes, ahem, well. There was certainly a misunderstanding here."

"Yes."

"You understand that the heightened security demands of the post-Nine-Eleven world..." blah blah blah.

"An' mine ass get kick pooty good by gringos," Tacho interrupted.

"I—cannot agree with your assessment. Perhaps there was involuntary roughness in your apprehension."

"Is not soccer game, guey!"

"No. It is not. However, you were already guilty of entering the country illegally. And when you blurted the name of a terrorist organization..."

"¡Mierda!' Tacho cried. "Is name of my restaurant!"

"Ahem."

They had actually called around Sinaloa and found that La Mano Caída was indeed a cantina of some sort, owned and operated by Mr. Lora. The information on his Mexican driver's license corresponded to his official domicile. So now they had to make sure the forms were in order. These days, even illegals were litigious.

"Although you will be returned to Mexico, we would like to extend our apologies for any harm you might have accidentally suffered when resisting arrest."

Tacho smiled. The bastard. He nodded.

The man rose and walked briskly from the room.

A migra agent stepped in and crooked a finger. Tacho followed him.

"Are you going to lodge a complaint?" the agent asked in Spanish.

"No."

"Are you going to cross again?"

"Yes."

They got to the bus.

"All right," the Border Patrol man said. "See you next week."

"See you," Tacho called as he boarded the bus.

Back in Tijuana, in the dark. He called Aunt Irma.

"Nayeli's gone to Matt's house," Irma told him.

"Really?" Tacho said.

"That is the plan."

"So they made it?"

"I don't know."

"What is Matt's phone number?"

"I don't know."

"Well, m'ija, what *do* you know, because I am calling you to find out, and you aren't telling me anything!"

"Now, now."

"Don't now-now me!"

"Tacho! Get a grip on yourself! You tell me. What will you do?"

"I don't know."

La Osa spit a small curse.

"I will go to San Diego," he said. "Somehow. I can't let my girls do their business alone."

"Good boy," said Irma.

Tacho rubbed his face. Cross the border again. That was just great. Just what he wanted to do. Tacho sighed. He had a little crust of blood around the rim of his nostril. He flicked it away with a fingernail.

"Has my restaurant gone out of business yet?" he said.

"Not yet, but it currently lacks your feminine touch," Irma replied.

"Look! Don't start with me, Doña! I am in no mood for your pendejadas! I been arrested, I been beat up, I been deported! And I'm not going to listen to your homophobic comments. Oh, no! Eso sí que no. Not tonight!"

But Irma, of course, had already hung up.

The taxi driver did not bat an eyelash when Tacho told him, "Take me to a gay bar."

How he had longed to visit a gay bar. To drop his guard for just an hour. To laugh with men who did not laugh at him. He was afraid, for an instant, that the taxi driver would tell him there weren't any gay bars in Tijuana. But the driver merely mentioned two, and Tacho sat back, closed his eyes, and said, "Take me to the nicest one."

It wasn't far from the Palacio Azteca hotel. The front had a kind of Mediterranean motif. Neon tubes ran up the sides of the building, causing the crenellations in the salmon stucco to glow like hot sheets of glass. He was terribly underdressed, and dirty, but he didn't care. He could hear the music coming out the door. He could hear laughter. Smell cigars and cigarettes.

Inside, he let the dark and the lights and the heavy bass wash over him. They were playing Justice and Kid606. A bar gleamed invitingly under amber lights at the far end of the room. He let it pull him through the crowd. He had earned a drink. *Several* drinks.

He met Rigoberto at the far end of the rosewood bar, as he leaned over a green-apple martini and swayed to the comforting music. The men around him smelled good—Hugo and Versace. People who understood him. Someplace that felt safe. He'd downed the first martini and resisted the approach of a sad sack in very bad makeup and false eyelashes. The guy actually had a beauty mark blotted above his lip with eyebrow pencil.

"Not tonight," Tacho said.

A handsome middle-aged man nodded to him as he pushed into the bar.

"Hello, señorita," the man said to the makeup queen, who went away unhappily.

Tacho accepted his second martini from the bartender.

"Do you smoke?" The man offered him a black cigarette.

Tacho shook his head.

"It's a Sherman," the man said. "Chocolate."

"Chocolate?"

"The best cigarette ever."

Tacho took it.

"I shouldn't," he said.

"But you will."

The man fired up Tacho's smoke with a lapis lighter and lit his own and dropped the lighter into his jacket pocket.

"Muy rico," Tacho said.

"I told you so."

The man gestured at the bartender—he didn't have to order; the barkeep nodded.

"Who are you?" the man asked.

"Tacho."

"A wanderer."

Tacho nodded.

"Yes. I'm a stranger here."

The man laughed.

"Brother," he said, "this is Tijuana. Everybody's a stranger."

He put his hand out.

"Rigoberto," he said. "Call me Rigo."

Tacho shook his hand.

"Pleased," he said, swoony—the martinis and the exhaustion were just about knocking him over.

Rigo sat on the stool next to him and stared at his face.

"What?" Tacho said.

"Your face," said Rigo. He received a Johnny Walker Blue, one rock. Tacho raised his eyebrows. He had good taste, this Rigoberto. He didn't approve of the ice, though—a waste of space in the glass, in his opinion.

"I've looked better," Tacho said.

"Oh, you look good," Rigo answered. "Just beat up."

"The Border Patrol."

"Oh," Rigoberto said, a bit of distaste in his voice. "You're a border crosser."

Tacho laughed.

"You wouldn't believe me if I told you."

"Try me."

So he told. Rigo listened with his head cocked to one side. He kept a small smile on his face the whole time. He sipped his whiskey and crunched the ice cube.

"You're kidding," he said when Tacho was done.

Tacho shook his head.

"Look at this trash I'm wearing," he said. "I look good in the real world. Would I go out looking like this if I hadn't just escaped with my life?"

Rigoberto laughed.

Everybody around Tacho was dressed well. The men danced and chatted. Tacho felt the sweet liquor move out his arms, down his legs, relaxing him almost as much as the men's laughter. Rigoberto gestured at them.

"Professors. Lawyers. Office managers. The cream of Tijuana." He ordered another drink. "You're the only criminal in here." He grinned. "Very exotic."

Tacho didn't think a third green-apple martini was a good idea, but Rigoberto pointed at his glass and nodded at the barkeep, and it was refilled.

"It's boring tonight," Rigo said. "So slow. If you want to have fun anymore, you have to go to San Diego."

"Tell me about it."

Rigoberto regarded this mysterious stranger with the crazy dye job. He *liked* Tacho. There was a certain aplomb about him. But he'd have to get him in some better clothes.

"God," Tacho said.

"What?"

"I feel like . . . like I'm home."

"Home?"

"We don't—" Tacho smiled ruefully. "We don't gather where I come from. We don't have clubs."

"Ah."

"It's nice."

Tacho felt his eyes sting a little—he was more tired than he thought, he told himself.

Rigoberto raised his glass to Tacho.

"Salud," he said.

Tacho tapped his glass to Rigoberto's.

"By the way," Rigo said, "I'm a doctor. I could look at that eye. And that big fat lip." He smiled.

What a sly one, Tacho thought.

"You want to do something about my lip," he said.

"I could. It's a bit...swollen."

Smiling.

"You're devilish," Tacho said. "Aren't you, Rigo?"

"Devilish? I am indeed. Incarnate."

They bumped knees.

Tacho could not believe that in his state, as tired as he was, as sad and fed up and physically sore, Rigo was getting him turned on.

"Let's go," Rigo said.

"Where?"

"We can go to your place," Rigo said.

Tacho snorted.

"I'd have to take you to Sinaloa."

"Oh, right."

"Or back to the Border Patrol station."

"Por Dios."

Rigoberto gave the barkeep a credit card and pointed at both their glasses.

"Allow me," he said.

He signed the chit and stood.

"I suppose," he said, "we will have to go to my house. You know. To attend to your lip."

Good Lord.

Tacho followed Rigo and was deeply gratified to settle into the leather seat of his fat BMW. Chet Baker came on the CD changer. Tacho closed his eyes. He was snoring before they'd left downtown and headed into the posh hills to the southeast.

When Rigoberto woke him, he thought for a moment he'd gone home. They were surrounded by hibiscus, bougainvillea, birds-of-paradise, lantana, sego palms, and small pine trees. The whole lush jungle was backlit by red and blue spotlights.

"Welcome," Rigoberto said.

Tacho asked, "May I take a shower?"

Rigoberto replied, "Thank you. I was about to say, 'Would you please take a shower?'"

They walked into his house, laughing.

Chapter Twenty-two

———

Nayeli, she's hot," Atómiko whispered.

"So is Yolo!" Matt replied.

Atómiko had never given up the couch. Matt had dragged his mattress out of his room, and Nayeli was in there, sleeping on the box spring and a mattress pad. Yolo and Vampi had pulled apart Ma's bed and were jammed in the other bedroom. The two men were drunk and giggling like Boy Scouts. Matt couldn't believe his Spanish had returned so easily, though his accent was atrocious. Atómiko didn't care. He was enjoying his own mastery of English. They were speaking some conglomerate pidgin. He'd downed eight Tecates, and Matt could have been speaking Chinese. They found a bottle of Ma's tequila, and Matt was veering toward cactus juice visions.

"Chingado," Atómiko sighed as he gulped a shot of Cuervo.

"Thank you, Jesus," said Matt.

This struck them as hilarious, and they buried their faces in their pillows and guffawed.

A door opened in the dark.

"Uh-oh," said Matt.

Yolo came out, wearing one of Matt's T-shirts. It barely covered her nether regions. They could see her in the streetlight glow, luminescent in the hallway.

"Morra," Atómiko growled. "Hurt me. Damage me. Put me in the hospital."

"Would you," Yolo said, "please—I am being nice—please—be quiet so we can get some sleep!"

"I'll help you sleep," Atómiko said.

She went back and shut the door decisively.

"Oh, my God," Matt noted.

They snorted into their pillows some more.

"Hey, gringo," Atómiko said, "don't you got any shorter T-shirts?"

They screamed into their pillows for a minute.

The door opened.

"I mean it!"

That was even funnier than whatever they'd found funny a minute ago.

"You are such idiots!" Yolo said.

The door slammed.

"One time," Atómiko said, "there was this chick named Alma Rosa. She was hanging out at the dompe when the missionaries came around. I used to help the gringos give out beans and, uh, potatoes. Alma Rosa took me back by her father's pigsty and showed me her chi-chis. Can you believe that? I guess she wanted more beans."

Matt lay on his back, staring into the dark.

"I'm lost," he announced.

"Huh," Atómiko replied. "You're drunk."

"No. Yeah. I know I'm drunk. But it's deeper, dude. It's like, I'm lost."

"Ah."

They listened to the muffled and sparse traffic going down Clairemont Drive. The Mongols were in residence next door — they could hear the TV going. Atómiko farted explosively.

"Did you hear a duck quack?" he said.

There was thump on the bedroom wall.

"Yolo threw a shoe," Matt noted.

"The world," Atómiko proclaimed, moved to alcoholic profundity, "is lost! Not just you, Mateo. Look at it, vato. Look! At the ice caps! At the pinchis Arabs! Look at, uh, the border and shit like that!"

Matt could not drink any more. He put the bottle down and gave up trying to find the cap in the dark.

"Grf," he said.

"Me?" Atómiko continued. "I was a soldier! That's right! I was in the Mexican army! I was a sergeant! But so what — everybody in the Mexican army is a sergeant! My real name is Kiko. My mother call me that. But that was me! Soldier! How you think I became a warrior! You think I can't kill everybody? I can kill everybody! I can kill the pinchis Mongols right now! I'll go over there and do it!" He struggled symbolically to rise from the couch, then lay back down. "In a minute," he said.

"So how'd you end up in the garbage dump?" Matt asked.

"I got caught stealing a chicken."

This struck them both as hilarious.

After a while, Atómiko said, "Is not big deal. Everybody in the Mexican army steals chickens! But I was illegal in San Ysidro."

"Wow."

"Mexicano army don't like that!"

"Yeah. No."

"You steal chickens?"

"Not so much."

"The Mexican army, they teach us English. Why I speak so good? Army! And they no pay in pesos, Mateo! They pay in gringo dollars!"

"The Mexican army pays in dollars?" Matt managed to say, though his lips were completely numb.

"Hell, yes. In Tijuana is all English and dollars. They know where everybody's going when they get out!"

"I'm going to sleep."

"Me, too."

"But first, I'm going to think about Yolo in that T-shirt."

"Me, too."

They chuckled and sputtered themselves to sleep.

The girls crept around in the morning, doing their laundry in Ma Johnston's little washer-dryer in the alcove by the back door. Nayeli and Yolo wore Matt's T-shirts and nothing else. They were quiet because they couldn't bear the boys looking under their hems. Vampi had found Ma Johnston's tatty bathrobe. She was a sight—goth eyed and raven haired in an unraveling quilted puce wrap. The dryer banged and rattled, but it didn't wake the guys. The girls nudged one another and laughed: Atómiko slept like he'd been shot in the head, and he had his right hand stuffed into his boxers. Matt was a lump on the floor. He had his head buried under his pillow. One-fourth of his bum-cleavage protruded whitely from his blue checkered boxers.

The girls were dressed and drinking instant coffee before the guys even moved.

Atómiko snorted, sat up and glared at them, rubbed his shaved head. He rose like a zombie and kicked Matt. "Pancakes," he said. He staggered toward the bathroom, scratching his ass. He stood peeing with the door open. Nayeli went over and shut it. She shook her head. "What a pig," she muttered.

Matt sat up.

His blond hair stood up all over his head. His eyes were puffy. He smiled like sunrise. Nayeli wanted to kiss him and climb under his blankets with him.

"Good morning, beautiful," he said.

She thrilled.

"Hi, gorgeous," he said to Yolo, who still acted angry with him over last night but secretly smiled. Nayeli studied this stratagem. How did she do that? How did she scowl and smile at the same time? How did she know what angle worked best when she glanced sideways like that? Nayeli's face just broke into her crazy smile and made her look like a clown.

"Buenos dias, you goddess," he said to Vampi.

Vampi didn't waste time worrying about how to deal with Matt. She walked over and plopped down beside him and pulled the covers over herself. She looked up at him and smiled.

"Hello, handsome," she said.

Damn, Nayeli thought. *Just like a puppy!*

Atómiko yelled from the bathroom: "Pancakes!"

~~~

¿Qué son pancakes?" Vampi asked.

They were in the minivan, tooling down the street.

"Son jo-keks," Yolo said.

"¿Jo-keks? ¿Qué es eso?"

They passed the Von's market where Ma used to shop, and the library where she got her books, and they swung around a wide bend and were delighted to see the sweep of Mission Bay before them. It looked like Mazatlán.

Atómiko said, "¡Los jo-keks son panquéquis!"

"¡Qué!"

Nayeli said, "It's like a tortilla, Vampi."

Matt was laughing.

"You put syrup on them. Butter. You know?"

"No."

"They put blueberries in them. Or chocolate chips."

"Blueberries and syrup on a tortilla? Guácala. I will have huevos rancheros."

They pulled into the little strip mall at the bottom of the hill. There was the Jack in the Box they'd eaten at ten hours ago.

"I been there," Atómiko said.

"You're a local," Matt said. "Leave your pole here, though."

They walked into the American Eagle diner. It was full of fat and happy Americans. Old duffers with white baseball caps cracked wise with the waitresses. The waitresses had stiffly sprayed hairdos and frilly skirts. Paintings of rampant stags and soaring eagles graced the walls. The Camarones crew goggled. It was still 1965 in the restaurant, but they didn't know that.

"Hi, doll!" a waitress whose bosom proclaimed *Velma!* said to Matt. "Haven't seen you for a while."

"You know," Matt said. "My mom and all."

"Hey—we were so sorry to hear about that. It was real sad."

"Thanks."

"Five?" she said.

"Yup."

She snagged five plastic-covered menus out of a slot in the counter and whisked them to a corner booth.

"Booth all right?"

"Great, thanks."

"Who's your friends?" she said as they sat.

"They're old friends from the mission field."

"Oh! Missionaries!"

It was too hard to explain, so Matt just smiled up at her.

"Mexicans?"

Matt nodded.

"Welcome to the United States," *Velma!* shouted at them as if they were deaf.

Everyone smiled warmly, wondering if she was mad at them.

"You'll have to meet El Brujo. He's around here someplace."

Vampi looked up: El Brujo? There was someone here named the Wizard?

"Get you some coffee?" *Velma!* asked.

Everyone nodded.

"Please," Matt said.

"Five coffees. Coming right up, doll."

They stared out the big window at the spotless USA. People lined up across the street for five-dollar gas. No dogs anywhere. Skateboarders zoomed by on their way downhill.

El Brujo appeared, carrying five waters. Vampi turned and froze. He wore an apron. He was as short as she was. His black hair was pulled back and hung in a heavy ponytail. She saw a dragon in the swirl of ink on his arms. But his T-shirt, his T-shirt! Nayeli nudged Yolo. They stared at the man as he put the glasses down, then went to retrieve five silverware setups from his cart. The shirt was black, THE 69 EYES in red across the chest.

"Oh, no," Yolo said.

"Vampi," warned Nayeli.

But Vampi was deaf to them. Vampi was turned in her seat. Vampi's mouth hung open.

El Brujo put down the napkin-wrapped forks and knives and glanced at Vampi. At the apartment, she had done her eyes in fresh death makeup. He smiled a little at her. He looked like an Aztec warrior.

214 • Luis Alberto Urrea

"Soy una vampira," she whispered.

El Brujo did a double take.

"¡Ah, cabrón!" he said.

～

The other girls were out of practice. They didn't remember how fast Mexican romances moved. By that evening, El Brujo had arrived at Matt's duplex and swept Vampi off on a date. He drove a '71 Chevy pickup that had a Héroes del Silencio decal in the back window. The girls were stunned and jealous. "Just like that?" they kept saying. "Just like that?"

"We didn't come here to get boyfriends!" Nayeli said.

"We are not here to go on dates," Yolo agreed.

"We're on a mission!"

"We can't fool around with boys—we came to save Tres Camarones!"

Matt came into the kitchen.

"Hola, Mateo," Nayeli cooed.

"¡Ay, Matt!" sang Yolo.

"How are you?" Nayeli asked in English. *Fou va jou?*

"Matt!" Yolo cried.

He looked at them and smiled and got some water and went back out to watch wrestling with Atómiko.

"Vampi," Nayeli said, "is out of control."

"She'd better get her priorities right," Yolo agreed.

～

They sat in the pickup truck on Mount Soledad. The lights of San Diego were scattered before them. Rivers of high beams and tail-lights beneath them on I-5. The bizarre hair-thin beacon of a laser kept shooting over the mountain, some sort of urban art project.

In the distance, the icy-looking white spires of a Mormon temple.
And above them, the shining white cross Vampi had first seen when
she'd jumped out of the smuggler's truck. Had it been yesterday?
Was that all? Every day seemed a week long to her. She watched the
lights of a jet as it descended in the distance.

"It's magic, isn't it," El Brujo said.

"It's the prettiest thing I ever saw," she replied.

"You must not have looked in the mirror this morning," he
said.

Oh, Brujo!

Lovers were parked all around them. Music and smoke snaked
out of cracked, foggy windows. El Brujo—his real name was Ale-
jandro, but everybody called him Alex—kept the radio tuned to
the Mighty 690, and he sang along softly when a good song came
on. Vampi sat beside him with her fingers laced through his, rubbing his knuckles with her thumb. She looked at his ferocious
profile, his luxuriant hair—he had let it down for her. His hoop
earring made him look like a pirate. *Sometimes*, she was thinking,
you just know. Did he know, too?

"People don't believe it because of the way I look," he said, "but
I don't take drugs, and I don't drink."

"Me, neither."

"I don't smoke."

"Me, neither!"

He leaned over and smelled her hair.

"You are my drug, Vampira."

"Oh, Alex!"

She furiously buffed his knuckles with her thumb.

"This hill," he said, "this is where all the rich bastards live."

"Oh?"

"Part of the hill fell down, on the other side. It swallowed a bunch of their mansions." He smiled. "God reminded them to be humble."

Vampi sighed. She scooted closer and put her head on his shoulder.

"Besides," he continued, "they'll hire a bunch of Mexicans to fix it for them."

She raised his knuckles to her lips and rubbed them against her mouth.

"We'll live up here one day," he added.

She felt a jolt.

"We will?"

She fell upon his chest.

He was quiet for a moment.

"Probably not," he admitted.

"But we can make it magic wherever we are . . . right?"

She was speaking into his collarbone. She wanted to nibble it.

He put his arm around her.

"I must have done something right," he said. "For you to come into my life."

And he won her heart forever, in that instant, for he broke into song. His voice was deep, a rich baritone. And he sang it! He sang: "'Just like a gothic girl, lost in the darken world.'"

Vampi started to cry.

Alex knew!

He knew.

He had come north from León, Guanajuato. He was a guitarist for a darkwave metal band in Mexico known as Cuernos de Hielo. But there was no money in Guanajuato for a darkwave band. And Alex's family was hurting—his dad had retired, and his mom was caring for him with little money. So Alex had sought his fortune in Los Yunaites. Wasn't that where all the big metal bands came from? Black Sabbath, for example. No, wait—Sabbath was from England. Cradle of Filth, maybe? England again. He gestured at his shirt, but Vampi just smiled sweetly. The 69 Eyes were from Helsinki, maybe, some pagan, Viking nosferatu place.

"I think they worship Odin," she noted.

To his astonishment, Alex found out that there was not much market for an undocumented Aztec death shredder without a guitar and without any English at all. He thought anybody could become a rock star in the USA. He thought you got on MTV and got rich. He thought he'd be opening for Motley Crüe on a world tour. He didn't think you hid from authorities and felt the Americans' eyes pass right through you in the supermarket. If nobody could even see him, how was he going to get famous?

It took him a year or two to admit that he never would get famous. He might never play in a band again. He fell into the slums in Logan Heights, southeast of the city, then worked his way up to a Taco Bell in Pacific Beach. He shared an apartment with five other chavalos from Chiapas and Guerrero. They were gardeners. They ate lunch at the pancake house one day and saw the cardboard sign in the window seeking busboys. They told Alex, and he found himself in the happy family of *Velma!* and her duffers.

He'd been at the pancake house now for six years. His dad was dead. ("May he rest in peace," Vampi said—Alex turned and looked into her eyes and kissed her savagely, unable to contain himself.) He had some money put away, but he was afraid to go to the funeral, so he'd sent it all to his mom via La Western Union.

"Now what?" she asked.

"I don't know. I've got this truck. I guess I'll work six more years."

She nuzzled him. He smiled down at her. This sweet-smelling girl. She was so soft, so warm. She was better than a million bucks, right there in his truck. Alex hadn't been with a woman in—well, it had been a long time. He wasn't sure what to do.

"Are you my girl?" he asked.

"Is it crazy?" she said. "Is it too soon?"

"You might as well ask the moon," he said. "You might as well ask the stars."

In Vampi's opinion, Alex spoke in song lyrics.

The La Jolla laser came back on and shot a vivid emerald beam over their heads.

It seemed like a sign.

Everything seemed like a sign to Vampi.

"My real name is Verónica," she confessed.

She climbed into his lap and kissed his mouth. She sat on the horn and startled all the lovers—the honk echoed down the hill. She grabbed two handfuls of hair and gazed into his eyes.

"You could come back home with me," she said.

And she told him her story.

Matt and Yolo looked in the phone book.

"S. Chavarín," he called out.

"S.," Yolo said. "Must stand for Salvador, you think?" *Jou teen?*

"Sí," Nayeli said. "Salvador-Chava. That must be him."

"La Osa's boyfriend," said Yolo.

"No! You think so?"

"Yeah."

Matt and Atómiko didn't know what the fuss was all about.

"You do it," Nayeli said.

Yolo smiled nervously and punched the numbers. It rang three times; she scrunched her nose at Nayeli. A man answered.

"Hello?"

"¿Señor Chavarín?" Yolo asked.

"Yes?"

"We are from Tres Camarones," she said.

"¿Qué?"

"Tres Camarones. We have come from there, and we represent Irma García Cervantes."

"Dios mío."

"She is the Mayor of Camarones," Yolo reported.

He gasped.

"Mayor? Irma?"

"She asked us to call you."

He said: "I have to sit down."

Don Chava worked the night shift at the Hillcrest Bowl. He didn't want them to go there. Yolo could hear the tone in his voice. She thought it was embarrassment. What was there to be embarrassed about? She herself worked in the Camarones bowling alley. She promised to call him in the morning. She hung up.

"What's he like?" Nayeli asked.

"Sad," Yolo replied. "Old. Nice."

She twisted the phone cord around her fingers.

"He told me where he works. But he doesn't want us to come."

Nayeli said, "Do you really think he's Aunt Irma's boyfriend?"

Yolo smiled.

"Once upon a time. God, Nayeli—he almost had a heart attack when I mentioned her name."

"Really?"

"Yeah."

They grinned at each other.

"Let's go see him," Nayeli said.

"Let's."

They turned to the guys.

"Mateo?" they sang in their sweetest voices. "Are you busy?"

Chapter Twenty-three

Salvador "Chava" Chavarín owned the first clear bowling ball in Sinaloa.

It was pale orange, and it could have been a jewel. Nobody could roll the ball like Chava. He released the ball like a dancer, his arm rising and cutting across his face and holding there as his slim hips seemed to steer the ball to yet another strike. Oh yes, Chava Chavarín was Irma's guru. She followed him to the lanes in Mazatlán, Acaponeta, and Los Mochis. When he had a bowling shirt stitched Americano-style, she saved up her money and sent away for real American shirts from Los Angeles. His shirt had orange piping on a blue-and-white two-tone placket with his name over his heart. Hers was silver and black and featured a lurid 15,000-thread stitching of a ball smashing pins against a white inset.

It was Chava who introduced Irma to the cinema. When she was a girl, she was a tomboy—she was always busy swimming in the river, or crabbing, or climbing the mango and date trees to get fruit. Things like music and movies didn't catch her eye at all. Until she saw Chava squiring puff-skirted young ladies to the movies. He was exquisite! His mustache was a thin line of inexpressible suggestiveness over his sharp yet tender upper lip! He smoked

222 • LUIS ALBERTO URREA

cigarettes in holders that jutted from his mouth like an old-time
Yanqui president's—he had FDR in mind. He saved every cent he
earned and spent it on finery—his bowling winnings making him
increasingly dapper. And since he lived with his mother, he had
money to burn, plus she kept his clothes washed and ironed. He
even wore a white dinner jacket! He carried a flask of rum and a
silver cigarette case, and he tapped his cigarettes on the case three
times—¡sas! ¡sas! ¡sas!—before he inserted them in the holder.
He lit the ladies' smokes with a gold Zippo that appeared with a
Fred Astaire flick of the hand that revealed a faux Cartier watch,
glittering with paste diamonds, on his wrist. He was always laughing, and everybody in town called him "That Chava!" As in, "Oh,
that Chava—he's too much!"

Sometimes, when he walked down the street, he was so deep
into his own rhythm that he snapped his fingers and shuffled a tiny
sideways dance, keeping the beat.

Irma, feeling fat and awkward, slunk into the cinema and
watched Chava more than the movies. She writhed with envy, the
way he put his arm around whatever tramp he was escorting. He
would cool them both with a paper fan on a stick, the fans (distributed by the beer dealer) featuring blurry black-and-white photographs of great stars like Lola Beltrán. It was so gallant.

Of course, in those days, nobody dared kiss in public. But was
there any doubt, when Chava got his fan going, that he was going
to reap great kisses from his various concubines? Everyone assumed
he was a devil with the lights out. It made Irma feverish just thinking about it.

Her moment of glory came in a rush, in a twelve-lane bowling
alley with a layer of cigar smoke hovering two feet below the ceiling and the sound of a brass band punching the tuba and trumpet
cacophony as sweat poured down her back.

It was on the epochal night of the mixed men's and women's

state bowling finals in Culiacán. Chava had gone down in flames to an upstart from El Rosario. There was no catching the blond bomber, Beto Murray, damn him! So Chava nursed his disgrace and was free to sit in the Camarones section, among the women who had gathered to cheer Irma. And she was magnificent. Just the hot sensation of his stare burning—finally—into her rump sent her hurtling down the lane. His gaze tingled her bottom and lifted her onto her tiptoes. Her throws were devastating. The pins seemed to shatter into toothpicks as she scored strike after strike after strike. Magnificent Irma! Chava rose. He cheered. He shouted. When she won, he leaped over the rail between them and lifted her off the floor in a wild embrace. Irma had not believed a man could lift her: it was disconcerting yet thrilling.

They made love for the first time in Chava's car, pulled off the road in a huge bean field. Cicadas bombed the car, and worried Brahman bulls sniffed the windows. He was Irma's first, and only. Frankly, it didn't feel all that great, and it left a mess. Chava, stylish even with his white skivvies around his ankles, produced a silk hankie and cleaned Irma with it, an act of tenderness she would never forget. But more than the feeling of Chava's hands carefully blotting her with the cool silk, Irma would always remember the hazy half-moon out the back window. Ever after, when she saw the full moon wane, she grew melancholy. If she'd had any musical gifts, she would have sung ballads to the sky.

Chava ran a small shrimp boat out of the estuaries. In the off-season, he fished for tuna and flounder and occasionally drove a truck. It was on a long-haul mango and banana run that he lost his head and broke Irma's heart. He drove the ancient Dodge stake bed to Tijuana. He'd been to Tijuana before. What touring bowler hadn't? But he startled them all by not returning. Perhaps they should have seen it as a harbinger of their future migratory fate. That Chava was always ahead of the curve. There it was, 1963, and he was already gone north.

He sent word that he'd found work. He'd found a cheap house and a good-paying job, and he was going to apply for a green card and work in the tuna canneries of San Diego. His letters and telegrams to Irma were full of innocence and joy—amazing tales of bright American days and clean American beaches. Shining American bowling alleys! When he went on a small tour, he showered her with postcards of bowling alleys in Tucumcari, New Mexico; El Paso, Texas; Benson, Arizona. When it came time for her to bowl in the north of Mexico, the year of 1965, she went to Chava on a Mexicana flight, clutching a shiny black purse and wearing high heels for the first time in her life. She was expecting a wedding.

But Chava had stayed in el norte for other reasons. True, the cannery had paid him well. His little yellow house in the bucolic hills of Colonia Independencia was cute. His sly smuggling of Irma into the United States for her San Diego bowling premiere was memorable. But he'd been oddly chaste with her. Even distant. And in the end, he had sent her home with a mere peck on the cheek.

Only when she was back in Tres Camarones did Irma hear from Chava's mother that he had impregnated an American woman. A blonde, no less. A cocktail waitress from the Aztec Lanes in San Diego. Chava was marrying her.

That was the end of Irma, that day.

La Osa, her alter ego, appeared in all her relentless glory to inspire chagrin and penance in the homeland.

⁓

Matt drove them to Hillcrest. Yolo had nabbed the shotgun seat, and Nayeli beamed smiles at him from the back. Their overwhelming girlscents filled the minivan. He was baffled by the whole visitation. What did they want? It was what the ZZs would have called "a for sure blow-mind."

Atómiko was sprawled in the third row, snoring again.

Matt had the address on a scrap of paper. They took I-5 south to Washington and cut up the hill. The Hillcrest Bowl was across the street from a shabby little medical tower. They pulled into the lot. It was mostly empty. Atómiko stayed asleep in the backseat. A drunk street person addressed them in some ancient Babylonian tongue. Matt handed him a dollar, and they moved away from him.

Nayeli put her arm through Matt's as they walked into the bowling alley. She had this way of looking up at him from under her brows that made him happy. The old sound of bowling washed over them like a tide, the rumble/*crash* of balls and pins. Matt heard Patsy Cline playing on the jukebox. It must have been a law in America that every bowling alley installed "Crazy," "Walkin' After Midnight," and "I Fall to Pieces" on their jukes.

At the front desk, they asked after Chava.

"Who?" the guy said.

"Señor Chava," Nayeli repeated.

The guy looked at her.

He turned and yelled, "Hey, Sal! You know anybody named Chávez?"

"Chava," Nayeli corrected.

"Whatever."

They looked over at "Sal." He was carrying a rubber bucket and a mop out of the women's toilet. He wore blue rubber kitchen gloves that reached almost to his elbows. He wore thick-soled work shoes, and his gray trousers were pressed. His white shirt was buttoned up to his neck. Without the pomade, his hair had gone back to its tight curls. Except it had become white, as had his little mustache.

He looked at them with a frozen half-smile on his face.

Nayeli stepped forward.

"¿Don Chava?" she asked. "¿Chava Chavarín?"

───

Yolo and Matt were bowling. Atómiko wandered in and nodded to Nayeli and Chava. "¡Orale, guey!" he said. He settled in the booth at Matt's lane and started insulting the bowlers.

"That boy just called me a water buffalo," Chava noted.

He and Nayeli sat at a small table, sipping sodas.

"He is a funny boy," Nayeli said.

"Funny. Yes."

Chava fidgeted. He seemed to have trouble meeting her eyes. He unwrapped her straw for her.

"Gracias."

"Root beer is good," he said.

"What was it you said to that rude man?" she asked.

"Which one? There are so many rude men. Oh. My boss? That was what they say here—'*Take five.*' It means I am taking a break. They have all these phrases you need to know. Like '*easy ice.*'"

"Easy ice," she repeated.

"Yes. When you order a drink. They always put too much ice in it. It saves them money. But you want your money's worth, you see. So you tell them not to put so much ice in the drink."

"Easy ice."

"Easy ice. Take five. See you later."

Nayeli did her smile for him and sipped her soda.

"So. Tres Camarones," Chava said, as if it had just come up in conversation. "How—is it back there?"

"Hot."

They laughed.

He rubbed his face.

He said, "You will think I am a bad man."

And he told her the story of how he betrayed Aunt Irma so many years ago. Nayeli listened carefully, hiding her smile when he admitted to making love to La Osa.

"We were young!" he said when he saw her grin. "Well, she was young."

His face was tragic as he told her about the blonde. He hung his head, turned his glass of soda around and around on the ring of water it left on the table.

"Sal!" the guy at the desk called.

"In a minute, boss!" Chava called. He glanced up at Nayeli. "Pendejo," he muttered.

They laughed.

He cleared his throat.

"And—Irma? What can you tell me about Irma?"

"She is alone," Nayeli said.

Chava Chavarín might have jumped a little.

"She never married."

Chava let out a small puff of air.

"I think I mentioned that she has won the election for mayor."

Chava laughed.

"That's my girl," he sighed. "That's my Irma."

"But Don Chava," Nayeli said. "What of the blonde waitress? What of the baby?"

"Sal!"

"Hol' your horses, boss!"

He put his palms flat on the table. Studied the backs of his hands.

"I have to go," he said.

Then he settled back in his seat.

"I am not going to go."

Atómiko walked past, on his way to the toilet. He flipped Nayeli's hair. Chava watched him.

"She left," he said. "The blonde. Of course. She left with a sailor. Who wants a poor Mexican cannery worker? She took a bus to Texas. I never saw her again. I never saw the baby."

He closed his eyes. Nayeli fell back. He was crying.

"I could not go home. I was so ashamed!"

He banged his fist on the table.

Atómiko reappeared.

"Cheer up, pops!" he said.

Chava looked away from Nayeli and collected himself by watching Atómiko try to cadge a bowling lesson from Yolo so he could feel her arms around him. Chava wiped his eyes. "I don't know if I like that fellow," he noted. His face was the saddest thing Nayeli had ever seen.

"Off your butt, Sal!"

"On Mexican time here, boss!"

Nayeli reached across the table and put her hand on his.

"Now it's my turn," she said. "Let me tell you a story."

When Chava Chavarín volunteered to join them on their journey, it was only after Nayeli assured him that everyone in Camarones would be thrilled to see him again. Everything would be forgiven—they needed him. Even Irma needed him. He wrung his hands. *Irma,* he mouthed. He nodded once and shook her hand and went back to work. Nayeli looked across the rail at Yolo and held up one finger. Yolo hurried over to her.

"Isn't he old?"

"He's wise."

"I thought we wanted young men."

Nayeli said, "He knows all the words the Americanos use. It's a very complicated language."

Yolo thought about it.

"He's not a soldier. Or a cop."

"But Irma asked for him."

Yolo nodded slowly. She grinned.

"That's one," she said. "For Tía Irma!"

They slapped hands.

Matt and Atómiko were rolling appalling gutter balls. When the girls were able to pull them away, Nayeli made her full report. Matt drove home. He had to admit, he was loving this whole story. It was like falling into one of the books he'd been reading before he dropped out of college to go to Mex. It was crazy.

They got home to the doors of the duplex standing open, and the lights all on. Vampi was out on the lawn with Carla the tweaker. They had a hibachi fired up. Apparently, nobody cared that they were cooking hot dogs at midnight. Next door, Sundog the Mongol and Alex El Brujo were engaged in a furious bilingual game of Guitar Hero III.

Yolo nodded at Vampi and held up one finger.

"We got one," she said.

Vampi smiled and looked into Sundog's door.

She raised her hand and showed them two fingers.

"Two," she said.

Chapter Twenty-four

Rigoberto wouldn't let Tacho spend any money. Tacho felt guilty, but Rigo seemed to get a thrill out of helping him. He had prisms hung in his kitchen windows, and they shot rainbows all around the walls. In his bathroom, he kept tall brown bottles of almond oil shampoo and conditioner. Tacho smelled edible. Rigo's housekeeper and cook were laughing girls from Playas de Tijuana, and they recolored Tacho's hair and made great omelets that they ate with sourdough English muffins. Tacho had never eaten English muffins, and he had never heard of sourdough.

"Let's have some tea," Rigo said.

The girls placed a clear glass pot on the table. They dropped in a green puck of crushed leaves.

"Watch this," Rigo said.

They poured in steaming water. The puck unfolded into blossoms and leaves, a small garden in the pot. Tacho had never seen the like—his mouth fell slightly open and he sat there smiling.

"I love that," Rigo noted.

His lover, Wilivaldo, was in Mexico City shooting a commercial for Pan Bimbo. It turned out that Wili was also bleached blond, and his clothes fit Tacho, more or less. Rigoberto decked Tacho out in fresh black Jordache jeans and a black silk T-shirt. He put a pair of Italian shades on Tacho's face and smiled. "What do you think?" he asked his cook. She nodded.

"Exactly," she said.

"Exactly what?" Tacho asked.

"Keep the sunglasses on," Rigoberto said.

He left the kitchen and returned in a minute with a picture in a gold frame. "Wili," he announced. Wili looked like Tacho, or enough like Tacho with the shades that you would look twice. The spiky blond hair, the skin color. Tacho looked like Wili after Wili had slacked off at the gym for a year. The same sunglasses. They could have been mistaken for brothers.

"Audacity is the only solution," Rigo said.

He reached into his back pocket and produced Wilivaldo's passport.

He smiled. The girls smiled. Tacho smiled.

"Who wants to go to San Diego?" Rigo cried.

"I do! I do!" said Tacho.

It's different in a BMW," Rigo said.

They were in the slow simmering lanes of traffic waiting to enter Los Yunaites. The windows were up: the world was silent. The inside of the car was cool and dark. It had the scent of leather and Tacho's sweet almond hair. Rigo had dabbed on the slightest hint of XX, and the cologne sweetened the smell imperceptibly. The CD changer was murmuring Manu Chao. Tacho held a go-cup with cinnamon coffee.

"No kidding," he said.

The many gates of the border crossing were open. Agents in booths asked questions. Tacho watched them walk around cars, sometimes inspect trunks. On the big bridge over the booths, he could see cameras mounted every few feet, watching the traffic. Mexican curio sellers in blue smocks walked between cars, selling an amazing array of kitsch: plaster skulls, blown-glass pirate ships, brightly painted flowerpots, shawls, sombreros, Mexican blankets, statues of Bart Simpson, bulls' horns, paper flowers, plaster Yodas, churros. The ubiquitous Indio kids wandered among the cars with their sad cardboard trays of Chiclets. Fake Red Cross volunteers with cans asked for change. A man with no legs wheeled his chair up and down the line, looking in car windows. He gestured at Tacho. Tacho hit the button and was hit by the wave of sound and exhaust as the glass slid away like melting ice. He gave the man his Mexican coins. The man said nothing, simply turned his chair away and rolled to the next car.

"Tacho," Rigoberto said. "Don't encourage them."

The window re-formed and shut out the sound and the light.

"Don't say anything when we get to the booth."

"No problem."

Rigoberto grinned and reached over to squeeze Tacho's knee.

"I'll miss you, you criminal."

Tacho laughed.

"I owe you."

"Not at all."

"More than I can say."

"Don't be silly."

They moved forward a car length.

"This is a good day," Rigo said. "It takes three hours to get across these days. We're really moving. Everybody's hunting for Iranians. Nobody cares about us."

Tacho looked up at the dead dirt-clod hills above the border and saw the trucks watching. He watched a team of US agents walk down the line with an agitated German shepherd. It sniffed at the cars. It strained on its leash, wagging its tail.

"You think it's hunting for drugs?" Rigoberto asked. "Or bombs?"

"Or us," Tacho said.

Another car length.

"Look relaxed," Rigo said. "But bitchy. You'd be amazed how far a BMW and some attitude gets you. Let me do the talking."

Tacho slumped in his seat and put on his best bitch face.

"That's hot," Rigo said. "Keep the shades on."

He rolled up to the booth and opened his window. He took off his own sunglasses. Smiled up at the suspicious woman sitting on a tall stool within. She stood, adjusted her gun belt, was already looking beyond them to the next car as she held out her hand for their papers. She typed in the license plate information of the next car with one hand and reluctantly turned her eyes to Rigoberto.

"Nationality?" she said.

"Mexican, of course!" Rigo replied.

He handed over both passports, flaring them out like a small hand of cards.

She plucked them out of his hand and bent down to the window.

"You're Rigoberto?" she said.

"Correct."

"And you?"

Tacho ignored her.

"You!" she repeated.

Rigoberto smacked his arm.

"¡Oye, cabrón!" he scolded.

Tacho turned to her.

"What!" he said.

Rigoberto turned to her and blushed deeply.

"Please forgive Wilivaldo," he said. "We're having a bit of a spat."

"A spat."

"I thought a weekend of shopping, a nice stay in a hotel ... You know. I am trying to bring love back into the relationship."

She had a look on her face that almost made Tacho laugh.

"Love."

"If not love," Rigoberto confided softly, "*sex.*"

She stared at him, her face a complete blank.

"I am hoping what they say about hotel sex is true!"

She handed him the passports and said, "You two have a real nice day," and backed into her booth.

Rigo put up his window and sped into California as they laughed and turned the stereo up very loud.

Tacho had never seen such a huge freeway. It was so clean. No dogs or donkeys anywhere. No trash. He smiled when they passed a white Border Patrol truck and the agent inside didn't even look at them.

"You will like it here," Rigo said. "Los Yunaites is our kind of place."

They parked in the Gaslamp Quarter downtown, and Rigo took him to Croce's for some jambalaya and corn bread. They sipped Heinekens and ate in peace. Tacho was trying to make the moment last, so he wouldn't have to face the inevitable farewell. Rigo understood. He knew Tacho had to get on with it, though. It wasn't like they'd gotten engaged to be married. He checked his watch. He slid his cell phone across the table and nodded.

Tacho took the phone and called Aunt Irma. She had gotten Matt's phone number from Nayeli's mom. "Tell them not to go anywhere until I talk to them," she ordered.

Tacho punched in Matt's number.

A gruff male voice answered.

"¿Qué onda?" it said.

"Uh ... Matt?" asked Tacho.

"He gone out, ese. Bye."

"No! Wait!" Tacho shouted. "Is Nayeli there?"

"Nayeli? Who jou think Matt go out with, pendejo?"

"Oh."

"Hey, is this the maricón?"

"Oh, no," Tacho said. "Not you."

"I am Atómiko."

"God hates me after all," Tacho replied.

Rigoberto dropped Tacho off at the visitors' center on Mission Bay. He wasn't into teary good-byes or big kisses. They slugged each other on the arms, and they pushed each other a couple of times, and they threw a wide back-slapping abrazo. They could have been celebrating a football win.

Rigoberto leaped into the BMW and jauntily sped to the freeway ramp. Tacho strutted around happily, in case Rigo was watching in the mirror. When the big black land-shark had vanished in the traffic, Tacho sat on a bench and held his head in his hands. He wasn't going to cry. He wasn't a teenage girl; he wasn't Vampi or anything. Damn! He wiped his eyes. He walked down to the water, then he walked back.

He called Matt's house on the pay phone.

The girls erupted in screams and bellows and shrieks and sobs.

Tacho had to smile.

In about fifteen minutes, a battered old pickup truck pulled into the lot. A terrifying Aztec covered in devil tattoos got out and glared at him. His T-shirt bore a dreadful occult symbol and the inscrutable words FIELDS OF THE NEPHILIM. Whatever that was, it couldn't be good.

Tacho wasn't sure what was going on. Was he going to get bashed? Oh, shit. He wasn't as good a fighter as Nayeli.

The heavy-metal monster slouched toward him. The girls had given El Brujo a password. He didn't understand it, but they said Tacho would. They said to find a boy with blond spikes. Mostly, it was old ladies and moms with strollers. Just this one guy.

El Brujo walked up to Tacho's bench.

He looked around, not making eye contact. He crossed his arms.

He said: "Yul Brynner."

Chapter Twenty-five

Poor Matt Johnston. He had never heard such shrieking, seen so many girlie tears. You'd have thought some freaking movie star had arrived in the duplex. Or the Queen of England. Ha! The Queen! He rubbed his gut. They actually butted him out of the way to get at the dude. And who wore spikes in their hair anymore? What was up with that?

He was stretched out on Carla's rattan couch.

"They run you out?" she said.

"There's too many of 'em," he replied. "Like, where was I gonna sleep, right? There's three chicks and two dudes in there! Where's ol' Matt going to crash?"

He toked deeply out of the Phish bong she had set on the wooden spool table.

"Baked goods," she said.

They snorked and horked as they laughed.

"Jes' like Grandma used to make!"

Matt answered his own question: "Ol' Matt's gonna sleep with Carla."

She glommed on to the bong and baked for a full minute.

"You. Know. It. Babe," she choked.

238 • LUIS ALBERTO URREA

"I mean, *dude!*" He gestured to the heavens. "Illegal aliens!"

"Whoa."

"Am I right?"

"Build a fence."

"Right?" He reached out. "Pass it, man! Don't hog it! Damn."

Gurgle-gurgle-gurgle.

The smoke filled the house with a blue haze. It smelled like a fire in a rope factory. Carla held up a pink stuffed pig and made it dance on the table. This reduced her to snorts of hilarity. Matt's puzzled face only made her laugh harder.

"Whatever, Carla," he said. "I'm spilling my guts here."

"You Grinch," she scolded.

He apparently didn't hear her. "Fly Like an Eagle" was cranking on her lil' bookshelf stereo.

"I oughta call the freakin' Border Patrol on 'em!"

He laughed. She laughed.

"Oh, wow!" she noted.

"The trouble with illegals," Matt announced, "is that they get in and settle like they own the place. Then, like, you never get rid of 'em."

"Like, Spanish an' shit."

"You got that right." He nodded. "Red, white, and blue, right? These colors, uh, don't...run."

Pause.

"That's deep, Matt. Deep shit."

Long pause.

"This here is some deep shit," he said, waggling the bong at her.

She beamed. Good ol' Carla. She could still get the righteous bud. She still had what it took, even if her teeth were starting to fall out.

Matt staggered over to her kitchenette and peered out her tiny window at his mom's duplex across the alley.

"I gotta admit, though, I'm totally swooping on that chick."

"Which chick?"

"The cute one."

"Huh," said Carla.

She had to hit the bong with her lighter again. Fumed up and coughed and wrinkled her nose and got her smoke on.

"I can't even tell 'em apart," she confided.

⁓

They were dancing in there. Alex the Brujo had come up from work and was frying up meat and beans. Tacho had some kind of disco radio blaring. Atómiko wasn't into that. He was happy the maricón was free from jail and all—but disco dancing? He shook his head. He sat on the front porch and smoked a cigarette, nursing a tepid Tecate. The sky was overcast. Atómiko could see the faintly pastel lights of the city glowing in the bellies of the clouds. He wondered if his jefito and jefita could see clouds in Heaven. They were long gone, of course. It hurt him to think he sometimes could not recall his mother's voice. What did it sound like? Sometimes, he caught a tiny wisp of her laughter in his memory. He shook his head to clear it. He drained the beer and tossed the can on the lawn. He took up his staff and prodded the dead grass.

He liked the United States. Like the gringos said: *So far, so good*. The air was cool and clear up here. The cars looked good. The women were nothing but fine! He could get into some of these ten-foot-tall American women! ¡Ay, caray!

But he was missing his little hut beside the dump. He'd made it himself. Wooden pallets for floors. Wooden garage doors for two of the walls. He'd managed to cobble together some sheets of plywood and a classroom blackboard for the third wall. Most of the fourth wall was a chicken wire fence he'd attached cardboard to with little wire ties. He covered the fence with plastic bags that he insulated with newspaper duct-taped to the inside. That cabrón was tight—waterproof and snug. He'd cleverly hung a faux

Persian rug off the top for a door. Inside, he had a fine plastic jug for water, a small stove fashioned out of a heater—the chimney was hammered cans. He had old magazines in there—death rags and a few moisture-swollen porno beauties—his favorite a hilarious black-and-white bondage magazine from the 1950s. For a bed, he had stuffed a cardboard shipping box with wadded papers and laid a slightly soiled Boy Scout sleeping bag over it. *Un pleeping bek,* he called it. Two rough wool blankets kept him warm enough—when it turned cold, he wore all his clothes and laid a few plastic bags over the lot, and if he didn't want to be comfortable, he could get in the bag or even under it. Warmth outweighed a soft bed any day.

The roof of his shack was slats, bits of pallets, and tar paper that he'd bought with the money he'd earned recycling bottles. One hundred fifty pounds of glass got him one US dollar. Copper usually paid much better, and aluminum was about the same as the glass. What did he care? It was all work, and all money! A dollar for glass was as good as a dollar for Pepsi cans. It bought the same tortilla. It bought the same beer.

Like everybody else in the dompe, he had burned old mattresses and collected their inner springs and frames. They made fences, and Atómiko had a sweet fence that ran from the back of his hut to about twenty feet in front of it. To come in off the street, you had to unbind barbed wire holding his gate shut. He often nursed abandoned dump puppies back to health, so there were usually guard dogs loyal to Atómiko in the yard. Nobody was going to mess with him.

He lay back on the duplex's cement slab of a porch. Felt the heat of the day radiate into his back.

"What can I say?" he muttered aloud. "It's a good life."

Chava Chavarín had the night off. It was a rare treat for him, to actually have somewhere to go where he could forget his sorrows. The girls had invited him to meet their friend, recently released from the clutches of the migra.

They delighted him. He realized there was no one in Los Yunaites who could transport him so easily to Tres Camarones, the Camarones that throbbed in his mind every night, the old world that would not let him sleep, that would not allow him to read a book or watch a movie. Every hamburger tasted like cardboard to him when he thought of the red chile–soaked shrimp of his homeland! His tidy little apartment in Kensington felt like a tomb when he recalled the narrow cobbled alleys of his boyhood! Those alleys hung with red blossoms and wooden gates! Those alleys that ran with floods every June—where chickens and car tires and tree branches and girdles sped down the flood to the river! In Camarones, he had never been cold—not once! In Camarones, he had been a fire on two legs, he had been a human waltz and a walking tango, he had brought music and cologne into the plazuela on each humid mysterious love-scented Saturday night! Talking to Nayeli brought it all back, rich and sweet.

He steered his sensible little used car along the slow lane, thinking of his fat-bottomed Irma! How her ankle-high white socks had inflamed his passion! How they had danced to "Begin the Beguine" at the Club de Leones New Year's Eve Ball! He in a pearl dinner jacket with a small black rose pinned to his chest, and she in a puffy skirt resplendent with tiny white polka dots and her feet in saddle shoes!

Who could understand such things? The grace and magic of such things? The unbearable erotic promise of those small ankle socks! He was ashamed to acknowledge that in his lonely room, he gave in to sexual urges remembering the socks coming off Irma's paper-white feet! Who in Los Yunaites could know the secret these

Tres Camarones warrior girls knew deep in their bones? The smile of Nayeli! The toss of Yolo's hair! The hand gestures of Vampi! They were all like occult rites that transported him back to the holy years of his youth! To the lost religion of Mexican womanhood!

He veered into the passing lane and cut off a small Toyota truck. The driver honked and sped past, making rude gestures. Chava Chavarín was blind to him. He was seeing the river, the movie theater, the whitewashed tree trunks, and the bobbing Christmas lights of his sacred homeland. He was fretting, too. Worried that now, in his ruined state, along with his long-standing shame, his Irma would look upon him with revulsion ... or worse, pity.

As if driving itself, the car left the freeway and started up the hill, an ascension.

¿Qué onda, guey?" Atómiko shouted when Chava Chavarín walked up to the door.

Inside, Chava said to Nayeli, "That boy keeps calling me a buffalo."

He enjoyed a brief dance with Nayeli—he kept her at a decent arm's length—and he was surprised that he also enjoyed El Brujo's cooking. Tacho seemed like a pleasant young man. All in all, it was a fine evening for Chava, and he was sad to realize he had so few nice evenings—if he wasn't working, he went alone to the movies at the Ken theater or he read books in a booth at the Golden Dragon restaurant; he was partial to the poems of Ali Chumacero. Sometimes, he bought flowers for his apartment. Little Nayeli and her silly friends made him understand how alone he was.

In a break from the music and eating, Chava pulled Nayeli aside.

"There is something I want to show you," he said.

"¿Sí?"

He nodded.

"I know a young man—a boy, really. He's a good boy. He works as a migrant harvester. Lives in a camp. I don't know, but I think, perhaps..." He smiled self-consciously. "He could handle your bandidos. He was in the Mexican navy, you see. I believe he knows judo."

"We have a navy?" she said.

"Yes, we do. I think we have one ship."

They laughed.

"If you don't mind my saying so," Chava continued, "he might be a little more suited to your needs than myself or... the Wizard."

Nayeli glanced in the kitchen. El Brujo was showing the devil's horns to Vampi with both hands. She jumped into his arms. His left wrist had 666 tattooed on it.

"I am old, and probably not even wise. But Angel is young, strong, and a good boy."

"I would love to meet him."

"Tomorrow?" Chava asked. "I can come for you."

"Yes, sir," Nayeli said. "I would like that."

"You won't be sorry," he said.

Atómiko walked by.

"Famous last words," he said.

The Battle of Camp Guadalupe started simply enough. Chava Chavarín knocked on Matt's door at eight the next morning. Nayeli was ready for him, freshly showered, perfumed, brushed out, wearing Carla's Depeche Mode T-shirt. She wore Tacho's tiny purse over her shoulder. She gave Chava his morning abrazo and delighted him with a chaste kiss on the cheek. Oh, paragon of Mexican girlhood! Oh, product of good breeding and traditional manners!

"Ready?" he said.

"Ready," she replied.

They stepped off the porch.

"Wait a minute!" called Tacho.

"Oh?" said Chava.

"Tacho wants to come, if you don't mind," Nayeli explained.

"Oh! Not at all!"

Tacho came out in tight white jeans and checkerboard Vans slip-ons from the Rigo Boutique.

Chava was going to say, *That's quite an outfit for going to a migrant camp* but held his tongue. These kids did things their own way.

They had started toward the car when the heinous croak of Atómiko arrested them midstride: "Hey, guey! You ain't going without me!"

Chava cast a slightly irritated look at Nayeli. Gentlemanly yet firm. She shrugged and hit him with that hopeless smile of hers.

"You're bringing the stick?" Chava complained.

"La mera neta, socio," proclaimed the Grand Cholo.

"What did this fellow say?" Chava asked.

"He said yes," Tacho translated.

They got into the car.

"Hey, Grandpa," Atómiko said. "Buy us some pancakes."

Chava was driving north. "You don't want to go too far north," he said. "The Border Patrol has checkpoints on the freeway. We'd most certainly be stopped. I would go to jail!" This seemed to amaze him; he hadn't thought about it before.

Nayeli turned in her seat and traded looks with Tacho. Atómiko was snoring.

"I met Angel," Chava continued, "when my car broke down. I was on the side of the road, and this old van jammed with men came along. When they stopped and the doors opened, I thought I was going to be robbed. But out jumped this young fellow from Michoacán. I hate to admit to you that I am not very good at automobiles. Repairs?" He shrugged. "But young Angel had my car running in a few minutes, and he would not let me pay him. He has come to visit me at the bowling alley. I arrange with the counter girls to slip him free meals." He tapped Nayeli's knee. "He's handsome, too."

From the backseat, Tacho piped up: "Oh, good!"

Chava looked at him in the rearview mirror with a bemused half-smile on his face.

They were in Del Mar, on the far side of La Jolla. The ocean was insanely blue — Nayeli thought she could see porpoises in the surf, cruising north. Surfers rode the sultry little waves toward shore. Hang gliders like giant multicolored kites drifted in the sky.

Suddenly, Nayeli said, "I still want to find my father."

Idly, Tacho said, "Why would he want to go back?"

"Me," she replied.

"Ay, m'ija," he sighed. "All they need is a few hot-air balloons to make it perfect here." Ahead of them, a hot-air balloon rose. "Oh," he said. "America wins every time."

Chava cleared his throat.

They turned their attention to him.

"I have only been to the camp a few times," Chava told Nayeli. "I make it my habit to stop at the store to buy them supplies. It is..." He thought for a moment. "It is very hard where they live."

They got off the freeway and entered the town. All green: palm trees, ice plant, ferns on patios, pine trees, gardens, lawns. Big haciendas everywhere — or the red-roof-tile versions of haciendas. Fine cars. All shiny. Tacho felt he could definitely live in Del Mar. Atómiko awoke and looked out at rich ladies in hats. "Nice," he noted. They pulled into the lot at the big supermarket. Atómiko stayed in the car, and the other two followed Chava Chavarín into the store.

Glories of food. The yellowest peppers. The reddest apples. The crispest asparagus. Small cartons with mushrooms piled inside like snowballs. The vegetable bins periodically sang "Singin' in the Rain" and started to sprinkle water on the coddled produce. Nayeli ran her hands through the mist and laughed.

In the meat section: no blood, clean cuts set out neatly like books in a library. Fish lay in mounds of ice, no stink. Tacho was thrilled that refried beans came in different flavors in Los Yun-aites: they sold traditional beans and vegetarian beans (which was kind of odd, in his opinion—weren't beans already vegetables?), hot 'n' spicy jalapeño refried beans, and chorizo-flavored beans. They also had low-fat beans. Nayeli lost interest in the Mexican section and found herself studying the breakfast cereals. This was truly astounding to her. Who was Count Chocula? What was a Boo-Berry?

Two young white men with shaved heads were standing at each end of the aisle, watching them.

Tacho insisted the Quaker Oats guy was gay. "Look at him!" Tacho said, pointing to the oatmeal box. "He's like the old queen who does an Elizabeth Taylor drag show!" Nayeli laughed and pushed him away.

"¡Ay, Tacho!" she gasped.

He made her laugh so much she couldn't even breathe. She was so *happy*. Tacho was back!

They turned to head up to the coffee aisle. A boy was there, blocking the way. Sully.

"Hey, Jimbo," he called,

"Yeah, Sully."

They turned. Jimbo was behind them. His stubbly scalp bore

an 88 tattoo. He was as tall as the top of the highest cereal shelf. They turned back to Sully. He wore a military jacket. He had heavy black work boots with bright red laces.

"Check out the wetbacks," Sully said.

"I can smell 'em from here," Jimbo said. They snickered.

Nayeli and Tacho stood in place, looking up at Sully. He was smiling at them. Why were they so afraid of him?

"You illegals?" Sully asked. "Are you, amigos? Wets?"

"Jesus," Jimbo said. "They's mute, too."

Sully shook his head.

"We have *standards*," he said. "We have *laws*. ¿Comprende?"

"Sí," Nayeli said, taking Tacho's hand and trying to move past Sully.

"Hey," he said softly. He moved in front of her. "Don't you want an American baby? Huh? You came here for an American baby, right? So you can stay forever?"

"Mud people," Jimbo offered.

"I'd do you," Sully said. "But, you know, I don't want the AIDS."

Jimbo barked out a single laugh.

"Check out the homo," Sully said.

He reached out to touch Tacho when Chava Chavarín ran into the back of his heel with his shopping cart.

"Ow!" Sully yelled.

"Oh!" Chava cried. "So sorry! Sorry, boys! Stupid Mexican! My fault!"

He had Nayeli and Tacho in tow and was out of the aisle and in line at the checker before Sully and Jimbo could regroup.

"Who are they?" Nayeli asked.

Chava shook his head.

"Don't look at them."

The two boys appeared and hovered, glaring and looming but

unable to do anything with so many witnesses around. Before they slammed out the electric doors, Jimbo pointed at them.

"Catch you later!" he called.

"Some people," Chava noted mildly, "don't like us here."

~

Nayeli had no idea where she was. They crossed the freeway on a small bridge, heading away from the beaches and the magnificent buildings. The hills were dry, yellow. Valleys and small canyons fell into shadow. In the distance, the fields and hills were crimson, pink, yellow, baby blue.

"Flowers," Chava said.

"Duh," said Atómiko.

Chava pulled off the road and parked against a steel barrier. They got out and each took a bag of groceries. Atómiko held his bag in one arm and his staff over his right shoulder with the other.

Chava said, "This is the richest country in the world." He looked at each of them. "This is the richest state of that rich country." They watched him. "And this is probably the richest city of the richest state of the richest country. Let's go."

He stepped over the barrier and started downslope, into one of the dry canyons. The friends looked at one another and shrugged. They followed him down. It wasn't far. At bottom, they found a small creek running with green water. Atómiko was delighted to see tiny fish scattering from under his shadow. They walked upstream, toward a stand of salt cedar and bamboo. They could smell the camp before they saw it: smoke, trash, human waste. Atómiko perked right up: home!

Chava called out, "¡Hola! ¡Somos amigos!" He made it a habit of letting the paisanos know he was a friend before he trudged into their camp—seeing them flinch or run simply broke his heart. He hated it. So he announced himself. Still, they would be tense until he revealed himself. "¡Amigos Mexicanos!" he called.

He pushed through the bamboo, and they followed him. They stopped and stared. A dog ran at them, barking, and Atómiko immediately crouched and growled a few friendly curses at the dog, and it wagged its tail and bumped into him with its chest.

Dark, thin men stood staring at them. Smoke. The ground was muddy, darker than the men. Improvised tents were gathered in a rough U shape. Splintery poles propped up sheets of plastic. The fires in the small clearing held coffeepots on stones, frying pans. The men nodded—a few looked at Nayeli and dropped their eyes shyly. They had managed to hammer together a little wooden shrine. It was lifted off the ground by a stout wooden pole. In it, covered by a shingle roof, standing on a small shelf, was a statue of the Blessed Mother.

Tacho's shoes and pants were ruined. He didn't care. He said, "We brought groceries."

"Are you missionaries?" a man with terrible teeth asked. Tacho and Nayeli blinked—he could have been Don Porfirio at the Tijuana garbage dump. When was that? A year ago?

"No, paisa'," Chava said. "Just friends. I am a friend of Angel's."

"Ah!" The man's face creased in a deep smile. "I remember you! Don Salvador!" He stepped forward and shook Chava's hand.

Chava said to the friends, "This is the jefe of the camp. Don Arturo."

Don Arturo shook all their hands.

"Welcome to Camp Guadalupe," he said. "Have some coffee."

Atómiko went right to the nearest pot. One of the paisanos handed him a battered cup. "Orale, carnal," he said. He poured himself a stout shot and drank it. The paisanos were checking out his staff. "I've only killed about twenty cabrones with it," he noted.

"Angel is washing up," Don Arturo said. "He will be here in a minute. Sit, sit."

They squatted on crates around the fire. Chava handed Don Arturo a box of doughnuts.

"¡Ah, caray!" the old man said. "Donas."

He handed doughnuts out to his men. They all said gracias almost silently, nodding their heads and keeping their eyes downcast.

"You live here?" Nayeli said.

"Yes."

"What do you do?"

"We pick flowers."

The boys nodded. *Sí, sí,* they murmured.

"We pick chiles and tomatoes. When the season changes, we go north and pick strawberries and apples."

That's right, the paisanos said.

"Is it hard work?" she asked.

He laughed.

"How does it look to you, señorita?"

"Hard."

They all laughed.

"If you were born to be a ten-penny nail," Don Arturo said, "you cannot curse the hammer."

The paisanos all nodded.

"Forty brothers camp here and work the farms. We share costs—food, things like that."

"Beer," one paisano called out. The men laughed.

"Sometimes," Don Arturo admitted. "Better poor and happy than rich and miserable."

Atómiko said, "Better still rich and happy."

"That's a fact," agreed Don Arturo.

Atómiko poured himself some more coffee.

"We boil water from the stream so we can drink," Don Arturo explained. "Churches donate clothes. Sometimes, it is too hard to wash the pants, and we throw them away."

Nayeli noted a muddy pile of old clothing strewn in the reeds.

"It's a shame," Don Arturo said. "We don't make enough money to rent motel rooms or houses."

Then the bamboo parted and a very handsome young man stepped through.

"Angel," Chava Chavarín said.

And behind him came Sully and Jimbo and four companions.

Sully had a chain hanging from his right fist. Jimbo carried a bat. The other four were unarmed. Sully swung the chain like a pendulum.

"What do we have here?" he asked. "What do we have here?"

Chava had never been in a fight in his life. He held up his hands placatingly, and he hated himself for it.

"Immigration rally?" Sully asked.

The paisanos backed away.

"They found me at the water," Angel said. "I'm sorry."

Jimbo pushed Angel, hard.

He fell to his knees.

"Stay down, doggie-doggie," Jimbo said.

His homeboys laughed.

"Beanertown," Sully said. "Christ, you people. See what the mud people do to America? It's Calcutta down here." He spit at Chava's feet. "You people stink."

Jimbo lectured his associates: "They come in here, turn our country into the third world. Am I right, Sully?"

"Right-o."

Atómiko lowered his coffee cup and belched loudly.

"Did you hear a bullfrog?" he quipped.

These border jumpers, Atómiko thought, how subservient could you get? They all hung their heads and acted like they were wringing their hats in fear of these gringo thugs. They ought to come on down to Tijuana and face the cops if they wanted to be scared. Too bad there were no women here; it would have been fun to show off for a sweet little brown girl. Oh well, he had Nayeli, even if she was blind to his charms.

Atómiko stood up and tossed the dregs of his coffee into the fire. He hung the cup on a nail. They all studied him carefully. He scratched his crotch, stared at the thugs and chuckled.

"You boys want to help me scratch this? Got a bad itch!" he hollered.

Angel started laughing and turned and looked up at the skinheads. You would have thought that Sully and his boys were the most amusing monkeys in the zoo.

"What are you looking at, José?" Sully demanded.

Nayeli turned to Tacho and asked, "¿Qué dijo?"

Atómiko relocated his scratching to his beard. He kept his other hand dangling loosely over the butt end of his staff. It hung across his shoulders like a barely noticed tool for the harvest.

He replied, in his Tijuana English: "I dunno what I look at. But I figure it out pooty soon!" He laughed. He squinted at Angel. "What are they, brother?" he asked.

"I don't know," Angel replied. "I never saw anything like them."

"You want to dance with me?" Sully asked, playing to the boys now.

He showed Atómiko his chain. Atómiko made an *Ooooh!* face.

"I no wan' dance with you," Atómiko said. "I wan' break

you neck. And then I go to your house an' make babies with you madre."

"¿Qué?" said Nayeli.

"We're in serious trouble," Tacho whispered.

"Oh."

She rose.

"Sit down, bitch!" Sully snapped.

"Ay." Atómiko winced. "You made a mistake, pendejo."

Nayeli turned back to Tacho.

"Did he call me a bad name?" she asked.

"Sorry, m'ija," Tacho replied.

She held up a finger at Sully and waggled it, scolding him.

"Nayeli," Chava warned.

"Morra," said Tacho, "don't start anything crazy."

"They started it."

"What's your name?" Angel asked, still kneeling.

"Nayeli."

"What?" Sully demanded. "Speak English, greaser."

"¿Qué?" Atómiko demanded.

"Goddamned beaner."

"Te voy a chingar."

"What?"

Nayeli said, "Watch his chain."

"Shut it!" Sully barked.

"I see it, I see it."

"I put greasers in the hospital, man," Sully said.

"OK," Atómiko said.

Sully was a little confused. The script dictated that at this point, the greasers begged or tried to flee. Fear. These two were just standing there. Then Angel stood up.

Atómiko pulled the staff off his shoulders and started to spin it languidly in front of his face.

"What are you, a cheerleader?" Sully said. His boys guffawed.

"Baton twirler." Jimbo laughed.

"No," Atómiko said. "Samurai."

He cracked the pole across Sully's face so fast it looked like a cloud had passed in front of him; his nose smashed loud as a small firecracker, blood exploding from his face. Angel grabbed Sully and launched him through the reeds and into the creek. Nayeli knee-kicked Jimbo, and he went down clutching his leg and howling. His baseball bat fell on the ground. He tried to sit up, and she spun once and kicked him in the jaw. His head bounced off the mud and he wet his pants. Sully came out of the creek, swung the chain blindly, the blood and tears ruining his eyesight. His homeboys spread out with their arms open. They were closing on Nayeli.

Atómiko stood still, wide-legged, holding his staff perfectly erect before his face. He screamed and lunged four times, smack-smack-smack-smack. Sully's scalp parted over his eyebrows and more blood covered his face. He fell to his knees as Atómiko's blows cracked on his shoulders.

Angel was moving around like a crab, and he seemed to be bowing to everybody, but when he bowed, the white boys flew through the air.

"Yeah!" Tacho shouted, jumping to his feet. One of the thugs decked him with one punch. Nayeli was on the boy in an instant, jabbing him in the neck and around the eyes with her nails, striking like a bobcat. He staggered around with her on his back, on his front, up on one shoulder. "Get her off! Get her off!" He tried to bear-hug her, but she head-butted him.

Angel stood in front of Chava and Don Arturo, defending the elders.

"You all right?" he called.

"We've got it," Nayeli replied.

One of his boys turned to help get Nayeli off the kid's back, and Atómiko swept the staff across the backs of his knees and dropped him into a campfire. He screamed. "My hair! Fire! I'm burning!" His head smoking like a torch, he broke through the bushes and fell sobbing into the creek. Nayeli hopped down.

The remaining thugs circled her and Atómiko. Jimbo had lurched to his feet and limped toward them, gripping his thigh above his ruined knee. The two friends stood back-to-back. Atómiko made patterns with his staff, swinging it around and around, covering Nayeli's left, then her right. As the three thugs closed in, Tacho and Angel attacked from behind with a frying pan and Jimbo's abandoned baseball bat. The bat made a horrid flat clang when it hit the nearest fighter's head. Poor ol' Jimbo. He dropped like a bag of frijoles.

"Aluminum," Atómiko noted. "I prefer wood."

Whap! His staff stung the boy in front of him in the throat. The boy fell to his knees, choking. Atómiko jammed the end of the pole into his solar plexus, then smacked him on each ear so he'd remember the day.

Nayeli jumped in front of the last one standing. She was breathing heavily, covered in sweat. It dripped off her hair. But she was smiling. That was what scared the boy the worst: the crazy beaner chick was *smiling*. She licked her lips. She raised her fists.

"Hello, baby," she said.

The boy plunged through the bamboo stand and ran all the way up and out of the canyon.

Nayeli turned to Angel and said, "Do you want a job?"

～

Chava dropped them off near midnight. Angel was going home with him to shower and buy some clothes. Nayeli couldn't wait to hold up three fingers to Yolo to see her smile. But her arms were so sore from the battle that she didn't think she could raise them. Her legs were trembling.

Tacho got out of the car and limped as if he'd been the one fighting everybody.

"M'ija," he noted, "I am just too old for this. And too pretty."

She laughed.

Atómiko said, "I am more pretty than you are."

They walked up the little lawn and found Carla. Somebody had set up a huge inflatable pool on the grass, and Carla was lounging in the water. Atómiko pulled off his filthy shirt and kicked off his shoes and fell into the pool, sending a big wave out onto the grass.

"That there's the only water that grass has seen this year," Carla told them.

"¿Y la Vampi?" Nayeli asked.

"Gone with that Satan dude," Carla replied.

Atómiko was blowing bubbles under water.

"Yolo?"

"Inside with the Matt-ster."

"Gracias," Nayeli said.

"No prob."

Atómiko surfaced.

"Pretty thing," he said to Carla as he moved her way like a crocodile.

Tacho stood there watching Atómiko and Carla as if they were a National Geographic special.

Nayeli stepped into the duplex.

"Yolo?" she said.

She heard it before the screen door had closed: *Oh-oh-oh-oh-oh!*

She could smell incense. Most of the lights were out. *Oh-oh-oh!*

She should have backed out, left right away, but she could not.

She moved forward, toward the sound.

The bed was making thumping, squeaking noises. In Matt's room. The door stood half open.

Nayeli looked in at them. She watched him atop Yolo. She could *smell* them. His bottom was pale blue in the window light. Yolo's thighs were dark, like shadows. Her feet crossed over Matt's back.

"Sí, sí, sí," she cried. "¡Mateo!"

Nayeli backed out. She tiptoed to the living room. She stepped out onto the porch. She had her hand over her stomach. She put her other hand over her mouth. Yolo? Matt and *Yolo?*

"Hey," Carla shouted. "You got a call."

Nayeli just looked at her.

"El phone-o? While you were out? Una call-o?"

Carla helpfully held her hand up to her face, thumb and pinky extended to form a phone.

"Ring-ring?" Carla said.

"Hurt me," Atómiko breathed. "Break my bones, devil-woman!"

"Huh?" Carla said.

Nayeli gulped and stepped off the porch. She had tears in her eyes. But really—they weren't children. They were all grown up. They were outlaws! She hadn't staked a claim on Mateo. Still...

"Some lady?" Carla continued, fending Atómiko off with one hand. "Your tía?"

"My tía?" Nayeli said.

"Right—Irma? Is that the one?"

"What did she say?" Tacho asked.

"She was lookin' for Nayeli. Said she'd call back. She's down at some hotel."

Atómiko splashed Carla.

"Te amo," he said.

"Excuse please?" said Nayeli.

"Yeah. She's in a hotel. I wrote the number down. She's here. In town. Flew in today."

"Here?" cried Tacho.

"Yeah, mon. She's got the hots for that Chava dude, if you ask me."

Atómiko clutched her and they sank beneath the waves.

Inside, Yolo let out a long cry.

Tacho's eyebrows rose.

Nayeli covered her eyes with her hand. She walked down to the alley to be alone.

"I see," Tacho said.

His shoes were black with mud. The bottoms of his white jeans were a hideous brown. His shirt was torn. Tía Irma had arrived. Yolo had stolen the boy.

Tacho said to no one in particular, "What a day."

Chapter Twenty-six

Carla's bikini almost cut Nayeli in pieces, it was so tight on her. She sank into the water of the inflatable pool. It was late and the sky was hazy — she could barely see any stars. Few cars passed by on Clairemont Drive. She thought: *None of them know I'm here.*

Yolo, her betrayer, was asleep in Matt's arms in his bedroom. Vampi was gone with El Brujo, so Tacho was asleep in her bed. Atómiko snored like a tractor on the couch. All very domestic. All very peaceful.

She was the only one who couldn't sleep.

How could she?

She submerged, felt her hair lift, the cold water shrinking her scalp. She came up staring at the vague smear of moon in the haze. The palm tree fronds made awful skeletal sounds. She watched a battered cat saunter by. He paused to back up to the pool and spray it before vanishing into the alley.

"Perfect," Nayeli said. "Just perfect."

She could not comprehend where she'd been, what she'd seen, who she'd met, or what she'd lost. Now that La Osa was here, she was reminded that she was far from her home, and even farther from her true mission. She had lost Yolo, and she had lost Matt. Vampi? Well, in some ways, she never had Vampi. Not even Vampi had a real relationship with Vampi. But even she was gone with that Satanic busboy. She pondered Chava, too. Now that she had found him, would she lose Aunt Irma? To love? Was this whole absurd experience an elaborate dating service for La Osa? Of all the threats of the journey, Nayeli had never imagined romance would be the most ruinous.

With Aunt Irma here, would she lose the entire project? There was no way La Osa was going to allow anyone but herself to recruit the warriors, Nayeli realized. She was being demoted, even if Irma didn't mean to demote her.

She slapped the water.

Her world was coming apart.

Pretty soon, it would just be her and Tacho.

KANKAKEE, she told herself.

What else remained but KANKAKEE?

When Nayeli, Tacho, Vampi, and that tramp Yolo walked into the Bahia Hotel on Mission Bay, they found Aunt Irma sitting on a couch in the lobby, talking bowling with a retired couple from El Paso. She was resplendent in black slacks, a bright yellow top, and tight pin curls in her hair. Her socks were silver.

"Oh, my God," muttered Vampi. "She dyed her hair."

"Shh," said Nayeli.

"My girls!" Irma cried, struggling out of the couch. She hugged and patted and kissed them and lifted Nayeli off the floor. She turned to Tacho. "And you." She smacked his arm.

She spied Atómiko and Alex the Wizard slouching outside the glass doors.

"Good God," she said, "what is that?"

"Well..." said Nayeli.

La Osa gave them a withering look.

"This is what you managed to find?" she said. "In all of the United States, you came up with two drug addicts?"

Before Vampi could speak up to defend El Brujo, Tía Irma screwed a cigarette into her mouth and marched to the doors. They gasped open before her, and she stomped out to the lurking males. She looked them up and down.

"¿Y ustedes?" she demanded. "¿Qué?"

"I am Atómiko!" the Warrior announced.

Alex glowered at her and didn't say anything.

"Hey, you jerk," Atómiko scolded. "Light the lady's cigarette."

"No mames, buey," Alex muttered. He lit Irma's cigarette. They stood there glaring at each other.

"So," Irma said. "You two degenerates got hold of my girls."

Angel, the mechanic from Camp Guadalupe, stepped up.

"Ma'am?" he said. "I am not a degenerate."

The other two snorted.

"I haven't touched the young ladies."

"Yeah," said Atómiko. "He's after Tacho."

He and El Brujo laughed and slapped hands.

She inspected Angel. A nice, clean boy. Muscles like cantaloupes.

"You're not much," she said. "What's your name?"

"Angel."

"That's a pimp's name," she said. She blew smoke at him. "Have you even reached puberty yet?" she asked mildly.

Frightened by La Osa, Angel retreated and lurked in the shadows.

Irma smoked her cigarette.

"I am Alex."

"Do tell."

"I am Vampi's man."

Irma barked out a laugh that turned into coughs. She spit.

"At the wedding," she cooed, "will you both dye your hair purple?"

El Brujo fired up a cigarette and squinted at her through the smoke.

"That's not a bad idea, Auntie," he replied.

"Good Christ in Heaven," she said. "And what about you, stick man?"

Atómiko showed her his staff.

"I am your protector."

"Are you marrying someone, too?"

"Nel, esa."

"What?"

"He said no," Alex explained.

"Why didn't he just say it, then?"

"La mera neta," Atómiko blurted, meaning absolutely nothing to Irma. "Baby," he said, "I'm only married to freedom."

"I'd better get back inside," she said. "Before you degenerates give me a heart attack."

Nayeli knocked on Chava's door again.

"¿Don Chava?" she cried.

"Go away!"

"It's me, Nayeli!"

"I know who it is."

"Let me in."

"I'm not home!"

"Open the door, Don Chava!"

"Are you alone?"

"El Brujo is waiting downstairs."

"But She—is She with you?"

"No. But she has sent me."

After a moment, she heard him rattling the chain and throwing the bolt. He cracked the door open and peered out at her.

"She did?"

"I'm afraid so."

"But," he stammered, "I-I-I am so old!"

Nayeli was startled to see he was wearing flannel pajamas. His face was unshaven. His hair stood straight up on his head.

"She is older, too," she assured him.

"What am I going to do?" he asked.

Nayeli said, "You are going to have to buck up, Don Chava."

He let her in.

"You must shower," she said. "Get a clean shirt and comb your hair. Shave!"

"Yes, Nayeli."

She sat on his plastic-covered couch and idly flipped through his Mexican *Reader's Digest*s, called *Selecciones*.

After his shower and shave, he appeared in gray slacks and an undershirt. He wore black socks and had his feet shoved into slippers.

"That's better," she said, sitting now at his little table.

He sat across from her, looking as miserable as any man she'd ever seen.

"I know you are worried," she said. "I understand the romantic tragedies that have separated you. But La Osa is on a mission. You must help her now and worry about the past later."

"Help her? Me? How?"

"I must go to find my father. You must help her recruit the rest of the seven."

She wrote down the name of the hotel, Irma's room number, her telephone number. Chava Chavarín simply stared at the paper.

In a small voice, he said, "I will try."

"There is no trying," Nayeli said, sounding like her aunt and liking it. "There is only doing."

Before Nayeli left, he handed her his gas card and three hundred dollars he retrieved from under his bed.

"¡Gracias!" she cried.

"Go with God," he said, kissing her forehead.

"You, too. You'll need God more than I will," she said.

Irma was deeply appalled to learn that La Vampi had promised Alex full control of the Cine Pedro Infante for one night each week.

"Heavy-metal concerts?" she gasped. "In Tres Camarones? Are you crazy?"

Her idiot girls had come to San Diego and handed over the world to these refugees. That Goody Two-shoes Angel believed she could get him a mechanic's shop. No doubt Chava Chavarín would expect a dance studio to run. Oddly enough, she took a shine to Atómiko. He had immediately become her bodyguard, and he scowled in the corner of every room over which she presided.

Irma invested in a conference room on the ground floor of the Bahia, ordering a pair of long tables and several chairs. Here, she, Chava Chavarín—if he ever showed some spine and revealed himself—and Yolo and Vampi would interview applicants for the remaining four openings. Just like a business—as it should have been handled from the start! All this romantic twaddle! Ha! That was no way to run a government operation.

La Osa could not convince Atómiko to come to Sinaloa. He was adamant. Too bad. If she washed him and bought him clothes, he could be the town's first new policeman.

She provided Nayeli with a Bank of America debit card for her foolish jaunt to Kankakee.

"Do you think," she bellowed, "that I am simply a provincial rube? You don't think I have resources?"

And:

"Men are no good."

"My father is good."

"Your father is a dog like all the other dogs."

"I will prove you wrong."

"You will prove what you prove."

"What does that mean?"

"It means what it means."

"¡Ay!"

Matt had laid out his road atlas on the kitchen table at the duplex.

"You can't go up I-5," he told them. "The Border Patrol checkpoint will nab you for sure."

"Ay, Mateo," Yolo marveled—he was so wise! She rubbed his arm. When her hand rose to his shoulder, he laid his cheek against it.

Yolo's face announced: *I win!*

Nayeli sneered.

"Kankakee—man, that's pretty far," Matt said.

Angel and El Brujo were outside, tuning up the minivan, putting in fresh oil, adding coolant to the radiator.

"But you go up Fifteen. See here? You've gotta go to Vegas."

"Vegas!" Carla crowed from the couch. "Oh, for sure!"

"Right?" said Matt.

"'S awesome!" she enthused.

"After Vegas, you keep heading north, dude—the Virgin Gorge is awesome. Then watch for Saint George, Utah. All right?"

Tacho was taking notes.

"It's totally easy. Up past Saint George, you hit I-70 east. Bro—just keep on truckin'."

"Truckin'," Tacho said.

"Tee-ruckin'!" Carla chirped.

Tee-ruckin'? Tacho mouthed to Nayeli.

"Trip out," Carla said.

"Trip," said Tacho. Of course it was a trip. What did they think it was?

"Es un viaje," Nayeli said to him. "Like opium."

Tacho looked at the map again.

"Oh," he said. "That kind of trip."

"Totally," Carla added.

I-70: they'd ride that sucker all the way across the Colorado Rockies and the Midwest plains to Illinois. But they had to promise, swear to God, they'd zoom up to Estes Park in Colorado and check out Rocky Mountain National Park.

"What's there?" Nayeli asked.

Carla got up and stretched—Nayeli could hear her back popping.

"Mountains," she said.

"God's country," Matt promised.

When Tacho and Nayeli pulled out the next morning, everybody was still asleep.

Chapter Twenty-seven

The morning light was red. Interstate 15. Only the two of them in all that distance.

Their drive to Las Vegas through the American desert was vividly dull. Dead gas stations. Outposts of I-Don't-Want-to-Live-Here sat in ruin beside the road. Border Patrol trucks puttered ignored around the off-ramps as Mexicans in wasted cars passed them in reeking oil smoke. The dense brown cloud of Los Angeles exhalations felt its way out across abandoned drive-ins and peeling ice cream stands. White men in pickups with ear-flapping big dogs in the back. Old trailers faded to white. Industrial buildings and dying palm trees, alkaline flats and military bases. Vast blacktop lots of abandoned RVs, the pale boxes arrayed like iron cows in a feed lot. Small triangular flags in vivid plastic colors rattled in the endless wind. And rocks, rocks piled upon rocks, whole hillsides of nothing but rocks.

Brown birds lined up on telephone wires like beads on a cheap Tijuana necklace.

Nayeli had Matt's old Spanish-English dictionary. *Bañera/bathtub,* she studied. *Barbecho/fallow land.* The Spanish word was new to her, she was embarrassed to admit. She gestured out the window and proclaimed, "Barbecho."

The air conditioner cut their engine power till they climbed at a crawl, so they sweltered on the way up hills and punched it back on when they dropped. The minivan rattled and groaned on the grades—both up and down. On the radio, they heard many angry Americans with loud voices saying Mexicans were unwanted, and immigrants carried disease and harbored terrorists. English only, the AM shouters boomed; English was the official language of America.

"What did he say?" asked Nayeli.

"Nada," said Tacho.

On the next station, a woman doctor thought her caller should dress in skimpy black lace to seduce her husband instead of the hairdresser she had a secret crush on.

"What?" said Nayeli.

Tacho shrugged, hit the radio buttons.

Country music. Talk radio. El Rushbo. JEE-sus.
Country music. Sports talk. Hannity. JEE-sus.
Country music. Norteño. News talk. JEE-sus.

Tacho turned off the radio.

Nayeli observed the land in its splendor.

7-Eleven. Subway. Motel 6.
7-Eleven. 24 Hr Adult Superstore. 65 MPH.
7-Eleven. 29 Palms. Carl's Jr.
70 MPH. Super 8. 7-Eleven.

Numerology reigned in Los Yunaites.

The desert," Nayeli said after an hour of silent staring, "is so harsh."

Tacho shrugged with one shoulder. He was shrugging a lot lately. He was thinking about Tijuana, about Rigoberto's magic teapot.

"The deserts of Mexico," he boasted, "are more brutal."

She stared out her window. She thought she could see a concrete dinosaur in the distance. Bikers screamed around them and flew down the road, laughing skulls on their backs. Crows bent to flattened animal carcasses in the road. They seemed to be bowing to the tatters of rabbit fur, the skunk tails. The midday's light was white.

Matt had told them to get off the road at Baker, California. They'd find it, he promised, right before they crossed into Nevada and really began their cross-country jaunt. They'd know it, he said with a laugh, by the World's Biggest Thermometer. "Don't worry," he told them. "There's a sign if you don't see the actual thermometer."

Tacho could not comprehend what was so funny about it. He hadn't been in the United States long enough to have seen the Jolly Green Giant statues, the jackalopes, or the giant Indian arrows sticking out of the sides of highways. He did not know that Matt was proud of the World's Biggest Thermometer in a way that equaled patriotism. Who could have understood that, say, a cement statute of Babe the Blue Ox with a garden hose running through his penis so he peed a constant stream outside a roadside diner was sacredly American? In Mexico, such things would have been shot to pieces, or stolen, or a family of beggars would have moved into the hollow centers of these attractions and made room for their pigs as well. He pulled off the road at Baker.

Graffiti on a pink stucco wall: CAPTAIN BEEFHEART SLEPT HERE.

"¿Qué es eso?" Nayeli asked.

"It is a mystery," Tacho muttered.

He was bored with the USA.

No, the giant thermometer did not impress Tacho. He had to admit, though, the running fat man on the Bun Boy sign was pretty funny. Matt had told them to stop at the Mad Greek's for the best milk shakes in California. Nayeli had a date shake, Tacho eggnog. Matt had told him it would taste like rompope, but it did not taste like rompope. Maybe if you poured four or five shots of rum into it.

Ma Johnston's minivan offered more than enough room for just the two of them, but Nayeli had plans to fill the extra space. She would, she still believed, not only find her father in far KANKA-KEE, but convince him to return to Tres Camarones, and they'd need the room for his luggage, maybe some of his smaller furniture. A color television would be nice. And though Tacho had his doubts about the project, she was his girl. What could he do? Just drive. Drive. Drive some more. Then, when he got tired, relieve that by driving for a spell.

And there would always be driving to do. One thing was obvious: Los Yunaites was much too big. He was crossing a distance the size of a small Central American country just to get to pinchi Las Vegas!

No wonder Americans seemed crazy to everybody else — they were utterly alone in the vastness of this ridiculously immense land. They all skittered about, alighting and flying off again like frantic butterflies. Looking for — what? What were they looking for? What was in Las Vegas? And, really, what was the big deal? Why couldn't they just sleep at the Bun Boy? But no! Matt had insisted they plow through to Las Vegas. First off, what a joke! The place was called Vegas? "Fertile plains"? Nothing outside but dead lizards and black highways glittering with a million busted beer bottles!

Nayeli had been moody ever since Yolo rode the pony at Matt's.

Tacho sighed. Not easy to strike up a conversation with Miss Heartbreak. He tossed his milk shake into the trash. She daintily got out, minced to the barrel, and gently dropped her half-full cup into the garbage can. He hated it when she played the girlie-girl. And now she was watching her weight, too. She got back in without a word, and he got back on the road.

It was already late afternoon. Tacho was amazed and delighted to see an RV ahead, pulled off the side of the road and going up in flames. Massive billows of black smoke roiled above the burning machine. A small group of Americans stood about forty feet away and stared intently. They seemed to believe a revelation was at hand. Tacho passed them slowly, gawking like all Mexicans are compelled to do when a catastrophe ruins someone else's day more than their own. Nayeli seemed to be reciting a prayer. Tacho felt guilty that he wasn't more spiritual, but he still craned his neck to see.

They flowed into some crazy glittering Nevada border town that seemed to have a roller coaster going over the highway. Parched sand.

"Nevada?" Nayeli said. "They call this place snowy?"

They laughed.

Tacho said, "Maybe it melted."

TONITE! GALLAGHER!

Casinos.

LOO$E LOT!

The largest building looked like some kind of big boat.

BONNIE AND CLYDE'S DEATH CAR!

"We saw that movie," Nayeli said.

She noted a prison on the desert slope above the electric town.

"How odd it must be," she said, "to lie in your bunk and stare across the miles of sand at all the free people having fun."

"Yeah. Like the people in Tijuana looking over the fence."

Tacho: Zapatista provocateur!

They stopped for gas and paid with Chava Chavarín's gas card. It was a family project, no doubt about it.

It rained for about an hour as they headed deeper into the desert. As dark fell, they saw the vast, flat hardpan on either side turning purple with a thin layer of water running to either horizon. They could have been on the causeway at Guaymas that they'd crossed on the Tres Estrellas bus heading north.

The evening light was violet.

And then —

LAS VEGAS.

Nayeli would always remember it like this. In capital letters. It exploded out of the dark plain, a twisted nest of neon and lightning. Black pyramids shooting beams at the moon. "There's your bright lights, girl," Tacho said. At first, she couldn't stop laughing. It was as absurd as her childhood fantasies of dream cities — it only lacked flying carpets and gassy airships. Baffling, winding streets through glitter canyons were interrupted by whole blocks with ceilings of light. She pointed at an eye-aching electric sign that cried CÉLINE DION!

Hundreds of fun-seekers wandered in the night, grimly hilarious. When they stopped at a red light, a man came by and handed Nayeli a flyer with color pictures of writhing naked women and an 800 phone number. She showed it to Tacho.

"Viejas feas," he opined.

They parked behind a giant sphinx and were shoved along the street with their heads rotating and their mouths open. A plaster Elvis stood on a sidewalk: chubby women in glittering clothes clutched it as their husbands in plaid shorts and golf hats snapped pictures. Nayeli took Tacho's hand. Down the street from Elvis, a white gorilla statue, apropos of nothing they could see. Tacho bought a cardboard camera and made Nayeli take pictures of him being carried off like Fay Wray. They skipped. They ran. They stumbled through glass doors and into caverns of billions of ringing bells and tolling electric bongs. Old ladies bent to the one-armed bandits. Coins dropping everywhere, ka-link, ka-link, ka-link, into cardboard buckets.

They found out how to get coins, and they immediately lost seventy-five dollars.

Tacho—inflamed with slots fever something awful—peeled open his money belt. Nayeli almost fell over when she discovered his hidden stash. He marched her to a change-making cage and placed a stack of quarters in her hand. She won thirty-five dollars on a Slingo game. He fed quarters into a machine until he caught a break: three cherries! Bong bong bong! Lights flashed! Coins fell out of the machine!

"I won! I won!" he shouted. "I won fifty dollars!"

"For which," Nayeli reminded him, "you paid a hundred and twenty-five."

"I'm on a streak."

"Let's go."

"But I'm hot right now."

"Vámonos."

Out! Into the street! Into a bizarre little curio shop that sold cactus planters in the shape of clowns with droopy trousers, and the cactuses thrust up rudely from their open flies. Tacho was astonished to see they also sold small wind-up mechanical penises on feet that hopped around on the table. "Popping Peckers," the sign said.

"Don't worry," Tacho advised Nayeli. "The real ones are bigger than that. Though they don't have wind-up keys...."

Nayeli dragged him out.

"We could get one for Yolo," Tacho suggested.

She did not find it funny.

They retrieved their minivan and wandered around until

they found the tawdry little plasterboard-walled motel Matt had reserved for them on the wrong side of the freeway. Even here, slot machines blinked in the forlorn corners of the lobby. They signed in as Shakira and Ricky Martin. The spangled woman behind the counter didn't get the joke. Cardboard holders beside the front desk were stacked with flyers and pamphlets, the colorful headlines of which read, in progression:

FREE!! *FREE!!!* **FREE!!!!** <u>*FREE!!!!!*</u>

In the all-you-can-eat diner next door, short, chunky Mexican men and downtrodden Vegas retirees slumped over their plates of mashed potatoes drowned in gray gravy. Straw cowboy hats and big gimme caps were greatly in evidence. Nobody talked. After supper, up in their room, they opened the curtains and stared at the insanity for a while, then collapsed into their beds. The cable television featured a Latino news program with disturbing videos of gang violence, seminaked women, and burning human bodies. Tacho switched around until he found an American show featuring a vampire detective. He reminded himself to tell Vampi about it.

Nayeli pulled the blankets up to her chin.

She said, "Tacho? Are we ever going back home?"

He was quiet. He turned off the TV with the remote. He lay back.

"I don't know," he confessed.

When Nayeli fell asleep, he sneaked down to the lobby and pulled the handle on a slot for an hour, but he didn't win anything.

~

The morning sun was a vicious ocherous blast. They bought cheap sunglasses and could not believe that in the light of day the electric wonderland of the night before was just a big pile of ghastly cement and cracked sidewalks. Fortified with McDonald's coffee and hot cinnamon rolls, they left Las Vegas, headed northeast, buzzed by snarling jet fighters on strafing runs, bombed by strung-out long-haul truckers on their way to Denver or Salt Lake. As soon as you escaped the island of neon and cement, the whole world was charred ruins, hoodoos and spires, dust devils and drooping power lines. Shreds of truck tires like fat black lizards. Smears of fur and brown blood upon the blacktop. Quivering heat waves suggesting spills of mercury on the distant horizon. They crashed into tumbleweeds, puzzled over signs that said HIGH WINDS MAY EXIST and later, EAGLES ON ROADWAY. Thinking about Tía Irma in San Diego. Speeding on to greater America.

Chapter Twenty-eight

Tacho found a station on FM playing oldies. Donovan sang, "First there is a mountain, then there is no mountain, then there is." Nayeli understood every word of the song. She loved it. It reminded her of the strange Zen sayings of Sensei Grey back home. She found herself missing his dojo, missing the smell of the morning, the iguanas, and crazy little Pepino and his rusty bike.

"I miss mangos," she said.

"I miss hair gel," Tacho replied. "Do you have any?"

She shook her head and ignored him.

Mountains loomed beyond Saint George, the golf courses below insanely verdant in the violent desert morning. Nayeli bought chocolate doughnuts at the gas station. She asked Tacho, "¿Quién es Saint George?"

"Quién sabe," he replied. "George Clooney?" He was enjoying pumping gas. It was so butch. He wore a black tank top, and he felt that his muscles looked chiseled this morning. "Didn't he kill a dragon or something?"

Nayeli looked it up: *dragón/dragon.*

"We are more alike than we think," she lectured.

Utah.

Beside a cemetery, a sign that read TAXIDERMY. Nayeli translated it with Matt's dictionary. They laughed for twenty miles.

They drove toward a crumbled vista of landscape. The horizon made it look as if the ground were rising before them. They were on the port side of the Markagunt Plateau but didn't know what it was. They passed Washington, Leeds, Cedar City. They were soon into strange place names: Enoch, Parowan, Paragonah. "They sound like Star Wars planets," Tacho noted. The Sevier Plateau loomed in the distance. They had never seen such big trucks—eighteen-wheelers pulled double and triple trailers. They hit Beaver. "What is a beaver?" Tacho asked. Nayeli worked her dictionary.

"Es un castor," she explained.

"¿Un castor? ¿Un castor? Out here? In this desert?" Tacho was lodging complaints with the cosmos.

Thirty or so miles north of the legendary Beaver, they came upon the I-70 turnoff. Salina, Utah, had dire warnings: LAST SERVICES FOR SEVENTY MILES. And: LAST GAS HERE! Tacho said it in Spanish to the attendant: Sal-EE-nah. And the attendant corrected him: Sal-EYE-nah.

"This is America, bud," he offered wisely.

They filled up. They ate ham sandwiches. Tacho tried a Mountain Dew and spit it out. Nayeli took the moral high road and drank orange juice—her every sip scolding Tacho with health. They plunged over the end of the Wasatch Plateau, dropped into the heat, surged across the bottom end of Castle Valley, over the San Rafael Swell, along the flank of the San Rafael Desert.

Ahead, nothing but sun.

Rolling in for more gas and relief from the seemingly endless emptiness of the freeway, they made a tactical error in Green River.

The Green itself flowed silently east of town, cutting jade and cool between junkyards and old buildings. Nayeli gawked at a yellow raft full of red, muscular Americans as it made its stately way toward Moab, the craft passing under I-70 and then consumed by sparkles and reeds and short bluffs in the light. The air was so dry the inside of her nose stung.

Nobody laughed in the gas station. It made her nervous. She had been noticing that America was a country where everybody was a comedian. The Americanos had this way of saying sardonic or even outrageous things to one another, and they tipped their heads or raised an eyebrow and great rolling chortles overtook the crowd. She had seen strangers in lines yell some absurd phrase at other strangers, and the grannies in their vivid Mickey Mouse shirts would shriek in delight and men would guffaw and adjust their beanie caps. But in Green River, she saw stringy men in faded shorts; she saw dusty 4WD trucks and Jeeps. Crows. But no laughter. The station attendant just looked at them and said nothing. ZZ Top coming out of the radio, falling flat on the dry soil.

They made their way to a Mexican restaurant. They were so nostalgic and homesick that the thought of chorizo or chilaquiles or tacos made them swoon. They banged in through the door and were greatly relieved to smell Mexican steam. Frijoles and garlic and tomatillos and rice. Onions and chicken and lime and salsa.

"We're home!" Nayeli said to Tacho.

They took a seat, and the cook, a Mexican man peering out from the kitchen, called, "Welcome, amigos!"

"Hola," said Nayeli.

"Buenas tardes," Tacho called.

The waitress came to their table with two menus and two glasses of water.

"Ay, gracias, señora," Nayeli sighed.

The woman looked at her and walked away. Nayeli assumed, correctly, that she was the chef's wife. She returned in a moment with a plastic basket of tortilla chips and a plastic bowl of salsa.

"Gracias, señora," she said.

The woman said, "We speak English here."

Nayeli blinked at her. She watched her go to the kitchen and talk to the chef. He looked at them over the serving counter.

"¿Qué dijo?" asked Tacho, gobbling chips and salsa like a starving prisoner.

"She told me to speak English."

"Vieja fea," Tacho said.

The woman returned.

"Can I take your order?"

"Number three, please," Nayeli enunciated in her best English.

"Red chile or green chile?"

"Red?"

"And you?"

Tacho leaned back in his seat.

"Pos, se me antoja pura machaca. Con frijoles caseros."

The woman didn't seem amused by his insolent tone.

She wrote on her pad. Walked away.

Tacho called: "Una Coca, por favor."

She brought a can of Coke and put it down with a straw.

"Where are you from, por favor?" Nayeli asked.

"Colorado," she replied.

"But...qué es la palabra...original?"

"Colorado."

They all looked at one another.

"My folks come from Durango," she finally said. "My husband's from Chihuahua."

Nayeli launched one of her famous smiles at the chef—he nodded at her and grinned back.

The food came quickly. Nayeli's #3 was chiles rellenos and beans. Tacho's machaca was watery, the eggs undercooked. The chef came out, wiping his hands on a white towel.

"OK, amigos?"

"Yes," said Nayeli. "Gracias."

"Muy sabroso," Tacho lied to be polite.

"Speak English," the chef corrected.

"OK," Tacho replied. "Buddy."

He smiled to himself: this was a comedic masterpiece, in his opinion.

"Vacation?" the chef asked.

"Not really," replied Nayeli.

"Not really? What, then?"

"Work?" Nayeli offered. Not sure of what she was saying, wishing she had brought the dictionary with her.

The chef put down the towel.

"Work," he said.

He turned his bloodshot eyes to his wife.

"Work," he repeated.

"We came from Sinaloa," Tacho offered, exhausting his English for the day. It sounded like: *Gwee kayne fronng Sinaloa.*

"Came? How?"

Nayeli, thinking she was among paisanos, thinking she was part of a great story and an adventure, made the mistake of winking at the chef.

"You know."

"I know? What do I know?"

She tipped her head charmingly.

"We…came…*across.*"

The chef glared at her.

"You're illegals."

"Pues..." Tacho started to say, but the chef cut him off.

"No!" he said. "No, not here. You get out."

"¿Perdón?" Nayeli asked.

"Wha—?" said Tacho.

"You get out of here. Illegals. What about the rest of us? What about us, cabrones? I came here LEGALLY! You hear that, LEGAL. You criminals come in here, make me look bad? I'm sorry, but you have to leave. Get out!"

He was trembling with rage. He waved his hands.

His wife called, "You better go now."

"It's hard enough!" he was shouting. "I kill myself! And you! You! Get out!"

They hung their heads and rushed out the door, their faces burning with shame. They ran as fast as they could to the van and slammed the doors and locked them and trembled inside and both of them cried because they were so lost and confused. The river never slowed.

They were not amused by Fruita. Nayeli kept trying to pronounce it in Spanish: *Frooweetah!* Parachute failed to intrigue them. The Book Cliffs, the Roan Cliffs, and mighty Battlement Mesa tried to amaze them, but Tacho and Nayeli were blind with shock and embarrassment. The land itself seemed to rebuke them. Every car that passed, they were sure, was dense with curses and accusations.

Wisely, Tacho pulled off at Rifle for Eskimo Pies and a visit to the trading post. Nayeli, caught up in patriotic guilt, bought a silver plastic rendering of the twin towers and mounted it on the dashboard. She attached an American flag decal to the windshield. Tacho bought a T-shirt with a picture of armed Apache warriors on it. It said: HOMELAND SECURITY SINCE 1492. It never crossed his mind that Geronimo and his warriors would have killed him in a second.

Chapter Twenty-nine

———————

Chava Chavarín polished his best loafers for the fifth time. He spit on the leather and took a chamois to the uppers. He uncapped a shoe polish roller and carefully colored the edges of the soles. He made the heels look like new. He placed his shoes on folded newspapers on the table and let them dry. He tipped Quinsana foot powder into them so his feet would smell fresh. He chose white briefs fresh out of the package, and he pulled on long black nylon socks that rose well above his calves. He tugged on a snug white undershirt that helped control his small paunch, tucking the undershirt into his skivvies before putting on a peach-colored cotton shirt with slight cream stripes. He had dry-cleaned a handsome pair of pleated pearl gray slacks and added a brown belt with a faux gold coin buckle. His pocket handkerchief was also peach. Behind it, snug to his thigh, he inserted a gold money clip with seven crisp twenties, two tens, three fives, and ten new ones. His slimmest leather wallet went in his left back pocket. He had bought an Invicta Dragon Lupa watch from a television shopping network. It was massive, a watch Ronald Colman himself might have worn, its magnifying crystal face making the thing look even more massive. His tie was off-white and picked up the thin stripes of his shirt. He at first rejected a tie clasp as too flashy, then decided a free-flying tie was simply too risqué, debauched even. He clipped the tie with a fine gold scroll that spelled out CHAVA, a small shining zirconium tucked in each *A*. Chava added a pale turquoise breast pocket hankie to the ensemble and regarded himself in the mirror. "Nice," he whispered. "Very nice." He spritzed himself with Aqua Velva. "There." He was as ready as he would ever be. He combed his tiny mustache one last time. He made moochie lips at himself in the mirror: the mustache squirmed on his face like a caterpillar, as if it were 1961 again! He grabbed his keys and whistled some old sentimental favorites to build up his spirits. He locked the door and started downstairs and only realized when his feet hit the grass outside that he'd forgotten to put on his shoes.

He was all right driving to the hotel. It was another blue San Diego day, the glittering bay and the white sand and the gulls and the kites and the girls and the breeze in the palm trees. One white cloud hung above it all like some sort of angel. Why, it was almost like Mazatlán! Only better! ¡VIVA LOS YUNAITES ESTAITES NORTE AMERICANOS!

He felt a little shaky pulling into the Bahia Hotel's lot, imagining his Mighty Irma watching him from a window. His lost Irma. Queen of Strikes! Empress of the 7-10 Split!

Which room was hers? He parked and tried to rise from the car in one fluid motion, as if he were still dancing like he'd danced on those tropical nights so long ago, as if the years had not piled on him and tired him, as if his hairline were not thin and gray and flashing bright spots of light where the sun hit his scalp. He squared his shoulders and set his jacket and strode toward the doors, all the while feeling eyes, phantom eyes, burning into him from every direction. He maintained his splendid stride and positioned one flat hand before his belly like a blade, thus emphasizing the excellence of his slim physique.

There was no one in the lobby. He boldly stepped to the desk and announced her name. The young man called her room and murmured to her. It was like a Humphrey Bogart mystery!

"Yes, ma'am," the young fellow said. He hung up the phone. "Room two twenty-seven," he intoned.

Chava Chavarín slapped his fingers on the counter and grinned with less verve than he would have preferred. He turned in sheer terror and lurched toward the elevator.

He tiptoed down the hall. There was still time, he promised himself, to leave. He could clear out his apartment in a matter of hours and head up the freeway to San Francisco. 219. 221. He smoothed his mustache. 223. He coughed. 225. He needed to pee. 227.

He stood there and shook himself, got ready to knock.

The door burst open.

Atómiko bopped out.

"¿Qué onda, guey?" he said and went on down the hall.

Irma called from within:

"Chava? Is that you?"

He stepped away from the door. He turned right, turned left, headed back toward the elevator. Atómiko was standing there. He shooed Chava back toward the room with his hands.

"I'd hit that nookie if I was you, pops!" Atómiko yawped. The elevator pinged. He got in. "Good luck," he said. The doors closed.

"CHAVA CHAVARIN," Irma's voice boomed, "YOU COME HERE THIS INSTANT!"

He turned.

She stood in the doorway. Forty pounds heavier. Dyed. In tight black stretch pants and a large loose red satin top. Magnificent.

He smiled. .

Took a step.

She blushed.

Oh, my!

She giggled.

Oh, you've still got it, Chava!

His step lightened. He rolled up and bobbed down. He glided. When he got close enough to smell her lilac eau de toilette, he said, "Hello, my love."

She rushed back into her room.

He followed.

Quietly, he closed the door.

Chapter Thirty

The next day, Nayeli and Tacho left Grand Junction and rose to Glenwood Springs. The mountains had teased them, stepping close and jumping away, until suddenly there they were, in all their dread and mass: the great Storm King brooding over the steaming hot springs while a small wildfire worked the canyons behind the Burger King. Nayeli and Tacho sat on a cement table and watched helicopters drop buckets of water on the thin line of flames. A group of metal chicks in black T's and wallet chains slurped milk shakes and smoked. They all looked upslope at the copters.

"Hey," one of them called. "You guys Pakistani?"

Tacho shook his tail feather and said, "Mexican! Queer, too!"

"Wow," she replied, flicking some ash. "Don't tell my dad that."

The helicopters whopped in the sky, their blades flickering silver in the sunlight.

"How you likin' that burger?"

"Is like God cook it!" he enthused.

"Dude, you're a riot."

Everyone basked in cross-cultural bonhomie.

"Later," the chicks called as they hove to their feet and shambled away.

Tacho drove into Glenwood Canyon, along the cantilevered freeway; to their right, the Colorado River surged green and cold, and across the water, a yellow locomotive pulled a train into the side of a cliff and vanished.

Nayeli said, "Why do they call the river 'red' when it's green?"

"It's the USA, morra," he said. "They do whatever they want."

Rafters bobbed along. Apparently, an avalanche had recently destroyed part of the elevated roadway. A road crew stopped the traffic. Tractors and trucks beeped and huffed. Far uphill, a guide vehicle began to lead the oncoming line of traffic along the single open lane. To their left, as they sat in the ticking traffic jam, Storm King and his minions formed a solid wall of rock. Aspens flounced all around them, peeking their heads above the sides of the highway. Their little yellow leaves, in the light, flashed like soft coins.

Suddenly, a mayfly hatch burst out of the gorge. Millions of mayflies. Gold, shimmering, they rose from the water of the Colorado in swirls, wafting like metallic snow blowing up into the sky, silent.

Nayeli could not stop laughing.

"Look how beautiful!" she cried. "This is some kind of sign. No? God making a miracle for us."

A Native American in a hard hat waved them ahead. Tacho slowed and showed him his Apache Homeland Security T-shirt. The man gave him a thumbs-up. "Yes!" Tacho enthused.

They drove on, higher and higher. Nayeli could not breathe. They were too high. She had never been so high. It gave her a headache. Her lungs could not pull enough dry air into her body. It made her dizzy. Tacho grimly clutched the wheel and leaned into the climb, as if he could force the straining minivan up the increasingly impossible slope.

But they hadn't seen anything yet. Ravens, hawks, eagles. Deer beside the road. Evergreens took over from cottonwoods and aspens: great lodgepole pines stood straight as spears. They topped off one of the many rises and beheld before them huge saffron valleys and ranges of mountains with vivid snowcaps on their points marching to infinity. The sky was fractured in great blocks of cloud—chunks of white, blue, orange, violet. Nayeli gasped. She began to cry upon sight of it.

"Is it always like this?" she asked no one in particular.

Suddenly, Tacho shrieked: "Oh, my God! Mountain goats!"

There they were, three cranky little mountain goats, off-white and dirty, their beards bobbing as they munched roadside flowers and pondered the passing cars.

At the Frisco rest area, they peed madly and were ambushed by marmots. Nayeli thought they were beavers. She opened a packet of Twinkies and was about to eat one when a camp robber bird dive-bombed her and stole the treat and flew away. The thief was immediately chased by two immense magpies, looking like black-and-white cows in the sky.

"What is this," Tacho said, "the garden of Eden?"

The Eisenhower Tunnel waited for them at 11,015 feet. The Continental Divide. TURN LIGHTS ON IN TUNNEL.

"¿Un túnel?" Nayeli asked.

Tacho pulled on the lights, and they plunged in. But it was well-lit, tiled as handsomely as a restroom.

"Ooh," he said. "Scary."

Idiots in front of them and behind them started honking their horns to hear the echo. So did Tacho. Nayeli powered down her window and hollered. "¡Ajúa!" she cried.

They burst out and were hit by sun as heavy as a bomb.

"Holy crap," Tacho noted.

Watered vales of cottonwoods and aspens and houses with

colorful wooden trim. Down, down; Tacho had to put it in low so he didn't fry the brakes.

BUFFALO OVERLOOK.

"Look at that sign!" Nayeli cried.

BUFFALO BILL'S GRAVE.

"¿Quién?" Tacho asked.

Nayeli shrugged.

"Buffalo! Buffalo!" she shouted.

Tacho sighed—dad had to keep the kids happy—and pulled over. They parked and got out, and there it was—the Buffalo Bill Buffalo Herd. Monsters, all. Wise looking with their great beards and foul, stinking humps. Nayeli hung on the chain link. The beasts ignored Tacho's kissy noises and moved along the grassy hillside like languid tugboats in a harbor.

A blue jay scolded Nayeli as she collected pinecones from the gravel.

Tacho noted: "Here, even the birds hate Mexicans."

It was dusk before they knew it, and cold. Indeed, Nayeli could not believe how cold it was. "I'm shivering!" she said. It was a first. Tacho fiddled with the knobs until hot air jetted out of the dashboard. "Look!" Her arms were covered with goose bumps. Frankly, Tacho could not see what Nayeli found so charming about freezing your ass off.

They found a motel on a dark purple defile in the mountain foothills near Golden, and they booked themselves as "Mr. and Mrs. Vicente Fox." The friendly woman at the desk offered them each an orange. The office was in the living room of her unit. Behind her, they could see an old man with an oxygen tank, staring at the flickering light of a television set. The office smelled like tuna casserole. A small hand-lettered sign on the wall said: IF YOU DIED TONIGHT, DO YOU KNOW WHERE YOU'D GO?

"Where you kids headed?" the woman asked.

"Estes," said Nayeli. "Is right? Estes?"

The woman smiled.

"I bet you never saw nothin' like Estes Park in Iraq!" she bellowed. "Paw Paw," she called to her old man. "These Iraqi kids is going up to Estes Park!"

"That right," he muttered.

He waved one white hand.

"Bless your hearts," he said.

"He's real sweet," the lady confided.

They went down the road and filled the tank at a BP station. Nayeli bought sandwiches, cookies, Fritos, and Cokes in the foodmart. Tacho was miserable and freezing and tired. He drove back to the motel in a sulk and rushed into room 113 and ran himself a hot bath. Nayeli ate her sub and watched Captain Jack Sparrow on HBO.

Her father was still a million miles away.

Thank you for driving me," Nayeli said.

"Don't mention it," Tacho replied.

They followed Matt's directions. They skirted the Front Range of the Rocky Mountains without knowing the name of what they were seeing. Nayeli thought of it as the Sierra Madre. Tacho thought of it as the Mountains. They didn't care for Boulder—too much traffic, too many skinny people jogging in ridiculous clothes. At Lyons, they turned up the mountains and again found themselves climbing, among vast spikes of pines, dark, nearly black. Bright pale granite upthrusts. Butterflies burst from the weeds beside the precipitous highway like little scraps of paper. Everywhere, relentlessly, crows. Nayeli had never seen glaciers. Again, her head ached, and she had trouble breathing, as if she had just run up a staircase. "Waterfall!" she cried over and over. The Rockies, apparently, never ran out of little waterfalls.

Just when they thought they would never get there, they swooped down a great curve to the left: before and below them, a valley rimmed by brilliantly snowy peaks. In the heart of the valley, a turquoise lake. Nayeli caught what breath she had left. Yolo had once made her read a translation of *Heidi,* and this big valley in the mountains looked like the paintings in that tattered old book. Just for a moment, she thought what almost all travelers on that road think when they break through the pines and behold the great vista before them: *I will live here.*

In the valley, the lawns along the edges of the lake were crowded with great shaggy animals that looked like horses with antlers.

"Can we pull over?" Nayeli the Nature Girl asked. "What are they?" she wondered.

Tacho's butt hurt. He was bored. Mountains, he thought. Motels. Big ugly deer. Gringos. He wondered who was running his restaurant, now that Irma was in San Diego. He wondered if the giant iguana was lurking inside his shelves.

"They're robots," he said. "Put there to lure suckers into town."

He was delighted to say to himself: *Bitch!*

Nayeli jumped out and instantly regretted it. She was *freezing.* The icy wind dropped off the snowy peaks and raced over the choppy water of the lake. The big animals ate grass — she could hear their teeth working. They were magnificent.

A sole fisherman stood on the edge of the water, ignoring her and the beasts. He wore a big army coat and had a gnarly beard and a nose burned a few thousand times by the sun. He turned his head.

"Hello," she called.

He eyed her.

"How do," he grunted.

Reeled in some line and cast again.

"Please?" she called. "What is? What . . . are?"

She pointed at the beasties.

"Ain't you cold, sweetheart?" the man replied. He pantomimed a shiver.

"Yes."

There went that smile. She pulled it down, but it sprang back up. He smiled. That was some cute señorita, he told himself. He set his pole against rocks, walked to his truck, and fished out a hoodie sweatshirt.

"C'mere," he said. "I won't bite ya."

She glanced at the minivan. Tacho seemed to be asleep. She cautiously came to the big man.

"Here," he said. "Put that on 'fore you die of cold."

He tossed it to her.

She pulled it on. It said STEAMBOAT SPRINGS on the chest. SEARCH AND RESCUE. There was a picture of a Saint Bernard on the front of it. The hoodie's hem fell to her knees. She had to bunch up the cuffs. To the fisherman, she looked like some kind of elf.

"Gracias," she said.

"De nada," he surprised her by saying. "And don't say I never gave ya nothin'."

This seemed to amuse him.

She pointed at the animals.

"Please?"

"Them's elk."

"Elk?"

"Uh-huh."

She rushed to the van and checked her book: alce. She had never heard of an alce, even in Spanish.

"Son magníficos," she said to the fisherman when she came back.

"Good eatin'," he said. "Marinate you an elk steak in wild blueberries for a night, then grill it. Oh, yes."

In less than ten minutes, he was teaching her how to fish. He showed her where the eagles came down to the water from the cliffs. He told her that condors had been seen there, too—that they'd probably sneaked through the Rockies all the way from California. Somehow, she understood what he was saying. When it was time to go, he gave her a hug and she kissed his cheek and realized halfway across the big valley that she didn't even know his name.

They drove to the main gate of Rocky Mountain National Park. The female ranger in the booth took Tacho's money. He just held out a sheaf of bills and said, "Please?" She counted out the proper amount and handed him his change and a nifty map. Neither of them was ready for what they found inside the park. Insane peaks, more glaciers, more elk, eagles, deer. Tacho, nature hater that he was, shrieked when he saw a bobcat sitting primly on top of a tall rock beside rushing water.

"It's a robot," Nayeli reminded him.

Rivers. Waterfalls. They walked around Bear Lake. It was cold—there was nobody there. On the far side, under the peak of a bizarre boxy mountain, white flakes began to wobble out of the clouds.

"Where did these feathers come from?" Tacho asked.

Nayeli let out a cry: "Tacho! It's *snow!*"

He said, "No, it isn't."

But it was.

They licked it out of the air, ran and screamed and jumped.

Nayeli had never heard the world go so silent. Jays and magpies and camp robber birds muttered fretfully. She could hear the soft swish as the snow landed on the ground. Tacho had flakes on his long eyelashes. Nayeli took them off his eyes with her lips. They held hands as they walked back to the minivan.

As they drove down the mountains, she pulled the fisherman's hood up over her face and pretended to nap so Tacho wouldn't see her crying again.

They plunged. They hit the flats. Denver—scary and confused: they didn't know if they were seeing roller coasters or factories. The minivan's engine started to make a faint clacking sound. Out into yellow and brown lands. Into the lonely wind. Across the emptiness of the high plains. To a courtyard motel on the Kansas border. The men in the next room pounded on the wall if they talked too loud or laughed. Nayeli found a praying mantis outside their door, studying the moths coming to the light. They were afraid of the neighbors, so they whispered and decided not to turn on the television.

In the morning, they were blinded by wind. Grit stung their eyes. They swerved and rocked as Tacho tried to navigate the buffeting gusts. A semi trailer rig had blown over on a cloverleaf onto I-70. It lay on its side. No one was visible for miles.

They pulled off for gas at a place called Kanorado. Nayeli kept the fisherman's hood up, but the wind sliced through her clothes like scissors. A state trooper pulled up to the pumps just as a siren on a pole started to howl. "Come on!" he shouted. "Tornado warning!" They trotted into the small food shop behind him and everybody hunkered down and drank burned coffee.

"She's blowin' up a whistler," somebody said.

The cop said, "Driving somewhere?"

"KANKAKEE, ILLINOIS," Nayeli explained.

"Huh, how 'bout that." The cup turned to the woman who worked in the shop. "Vicki—how 'bout that? A working American can't afford to gas up his rig, but the illegals can just drive cross-country all they want."

When nothing tornadic happened, they paid for their gas and drove away.

Chapter Thirty-one

It was 9:00 AM.

In Conference Room 1A of the Bahia Hotel, the "Pelican Room," Tía Irma's tribunal sat at the wide folding banquet table. The hotel workers—two guys from Tamaulipas who had entered the United States just south of Ajo, Arizona, on a cloudy night in 1998—set white paper tablecloths on the tribunal's table, and they brought La Osa plastic pitchers of water and a cauldron of coffee. Atómiko could have just attached his mouth to the spigot, he guzzled so much of it.

"Oye, Tía," he said. "Can't you order some doughnuts? Maybe some pastry? Damn! Don't be cheap!"

To everyone's astonishment, she had the Tamaulipas boys bring in a tray of pastries and muffins. Atómiko nearly gagged when he bit into a bran muffin.

"Bird food!" he yowled.

However, when he discovered the exotic sublimity of cheese-filled Danish, he fell silent.

Irma herself sat at the center of the table, a yellow legal pad before her and an array of Bahia Hotel complimentary pens fanned out precisely on the cloth. To her right, the gleaming and suave Chava Chavarín—now Deputy Mayor of Tres Camarones, Sinaloa. He had gotten a shave at a barbershop, and his skin was tight and shiny. To her left, Yoloxochitl. On the other side of Chava, La Vampi slumped in her seat and played with her hair. She was distracted—Atómiko and El Brujo were the tribunal's security guards, and every time Vampi caught El Brujo's eye, she giggled and blushed. She wore a short skirt and brazenly flashed her panties at him. He scowled and shook his head.

Atómiko did not notice. He was licking frosting off his fingers so his mighty staff did not get sticky.

In the corner, like bad boys in a sixth-grade class, Matt and Angel sat on folding chairs. Matt got himself a cup of coffee and wondered how Nayeli was doing on her trip. Good old Nayeli. Yolo, exercising her frightening Mexican woman's psychic love powers, turned and glared at him.

"Whoa, dude," Matt whispered to Angel. "She knows what I'm thinking."

"Stop thinking," Angel advised.

Chava had put ads in several newspapers. Atómiko and the boys had spread the news at taco shops and barrio stores. Nobody knew what would happen.

Hipólito, one of the Tamaulipas boys, peeked into the room.

"Applicants," he said.

"Send them in," Tía Irma proclaimed.

Chava felt a thrill. This was a moment for the history books! He nudged her knee under the table with his own. Irma smiled.

A small line of nervous men straggled in. Five, six, ten. Some had hats. Atómiko pointed at them with his staff and growled. They pulled off their caps. Grinned sheepishly.

Twelve. The door opened again. Thirteen. It was getting crowded in the Pelican Room.

"We seek seven!" Irma intoned. "Soldiers or policemen!"

The men murmured *yes* and *sí*.

"We have three. Of you standing before me, I can only take four more."

The door opened. Fourteen, fifteen, sixteen.

Hipólito looked in and shook his head.

"What is it?" Irma called.

"Men." He shrugged.

"How many men?"

He looked out.

"Many."

Irma signaled Atómiko.

"Yeah, boss!" he said and marched out to the lobby.

A line of men snaked out the door. The people at the front desk were perturbed.

"Brother," one of the men said, "take us back to Mexico."

"Please," said another.

The voices rose.

"It is too hard. We want to go home."

"We just need jobs."

"Can they promise us jobs?"

"Maybe a house?"

"Are there girls?"

"I want a wife. Are there women I can marry?"

"Can I bring my family?"

"I want to move my mamá from Durango. Will they let me bring her?"

"Ask the boss-lady inside, muchachos," Atómiko announced. "She's the chingona here!"

"I hear they got fishing down there. Is that right?"

"I miss dancing in the street, man! I miss bullfights!"

"Did you ever do fireworks on independence day?"

Some of them started laughing.

"You guys got rodeos down there?"

"How about bars?"

"What kind of work? Is there work for a meat cutter?"

"I'll drive the bus!"

"You mean you'll ride a donkey!"

They were all laughing now, jostling and slapping one another's backs.

"What can you do, pendejo?"

"I don't know how to do a goddamned thing. Why do you think I came to Los Yunaites?"

"¡Ay, buey!"

The people at the front desk were on the phone, checking with management. Men were streaming in, flooding the hotel, clotting its passageways, crowding its corners.

"Slow down, muchachos!" Atómiko said. "Slow down!" He held his staff up as if to guide them through a dangerous cleft in the rocks. "Calma," he said. "Soldiers and cops. Soldiers and cops. Everybody else can go home."

He went back through the doors. Behind him, their voices rumbled and hummed.

He grabbed a blueberry muffin and sniffed it. "What's this blue shit?" he muttered to El Brujo. He peeled off the paper and looked at La Osa.

"Auntie," he said, "the revolution has begun."

Chapter Thirty-two

———

They didn't know the history of the plains and prairies, and they didn't care. The world looked to them like a great roll of butcher paper unfurled on a table. The land here was so vast and so empty that a bomb could have exploded and there wouldn't have been any echo. Gas stations had canopies two stories high. Trucks wobbled and grunted in the wind, their miniature puffs of diesel smoke rushing north. Nayeli felt as if they had stopped moving at all, that they were floating and that the ground had started to roll, passing under them as they stood still.

Unknown to them, a Mexican wind had blown up from Durango and it battered them now as it rushed to Canada; Sinaloan rain pattered on Nayeli's window, smearing the taste of Tres Camarones down the glass in long worms as they sped.

"I don't like the sound of this engine," Tacho managed to say.

It was hard to talk. They felt tiny and exhausted. Nayeli started to say something, but her mouth didn't want to open. She couldn't stop fretting about her father. Other thoughts were crowded out of her mind.

The road from Kanorado to the Brewster exit was only about forty miles, but it felt like a thousand. Nayeli was feeling that old slide in her belly, that heavy, slow alarm. And she was bloated, crampy.

They passed Mingo. Signs appeared: SIX-LEGGED CALF.

COW WITH TWO HEADS.

6,000-POUND PRAIRIE DOG.

"¿Qué es un prairie dog?" Tacho asked.

Nayeli worked her dictionary.

"Not in here," she said. "A dog? Of la pradera?"

He drove.

"But six thousand pounds?" he said.

She felt the bite of a fresh cramp.

"Tachito?" she said. "Papito?"

"Yes?"

"I need to stop, Tachito."

"Stop for what?"

"I have my little problem coming."

She patted her abdomen.

"Ah. That." He shook his head. "Again."

"Don't be mean to me. I'm delicate."

"I'm not mean, girl. And you're as delicate as a brick."

She looked out the window.

"Maybe sometimes I want to be delicate, Tacho."

He looked sideways at her. He reached over and squeezed her hand.

BULL WITH SIX LEGS, OAKLEY, KANSAS!

"Let's stop at the gas station, my sweet little apple pie," he crooned. Oddly, he was too embarrassed to make a joke. "They'll have . . . it. You know."

She smiled.

"Gracias," she said.

In the gas station's food mart, he discovered Corn Nuts while she took her purchases to the bathroom. He bought four bags of Corn Nuts and a violently pink-and-purple glob of pureed ice called a Slushee. He was overjoyed to be alive.

"Where is," he asked the silent woman behind the counter, "giant pradera dog?"

"What."

"Six-thousand-pound dog of the pradera."

"What dog."

"Please? The sign say six thousand pounds of dog. Of the pradera!"

The woman said, "Oh. The big giant prairie dog." She leaned forward. "It's a lie. It's made of cement."

Tacho stood there slurping his Slushee. Suddenly he put it down.

"Ay," he said. "My head!"

"Brain freeze," a trucker explained.

The woman nodded.

"Honey, you got brain freeze."

"It's the Slushee, pardner." The trucker nodded.

"¡Ay!"

Tacho went out to the minivan and massaged his forehead.

Nayeli jumped in and said, "Just in time."

She was baffled when he announced, "It is all a cruel illusion."

Still, he drove down to the Prairie Dog Village. Old cars were parked in the lot, so he figured it was a popular stop. When he stopped, he noticed grass growing around their tires. They were derelicts.

"Interesting," Nayeli said.

"Lures!" Tacho realized. "They use empty cars to fool tourists!"

"Like it's a really busy place," Nayeli noted, trying to crack a Corn Nut with her teeth.

"Maybe they eat people who come inside," Tacho said.

"Oh, boy. I can't wait."

They walked in. The shop was chock-full of mementos and gewgaws. A man sat at the far end of the room. He smiled at them, waved, and took up a stick.

"Wanna hear the rattlesnakes?" he asked.

"Excuse?" said Nayeli.

He reached over to his right and banged on a big wooden box. Sizzling rattles rose from its mesh top.

"Fifty rattlesnakes in there!" the man confided.

Tacho crept to the box and looked in.

"Guáu," he offered.

The man said, "Hey. You know what the cows do for fun on Saturday night?"

"Excuse?" It was Tacho's turn.

"I say cows, son. What do cows do on Saturday night. For fun."

Tacho shrugged.

"They go to the moo-vies!" the man shouted. He laughed and sipped some coffee from a chipped mug. "Good one, right?"

"Right!"

Nayeli was amazed to discover that one shelf of souvenirs featured shellacked chunks of horse feces with little google eyes stuck on them. They stood on wire legs with plastic feet. Some of them were playing golf with wire clubs; one strummed a guitar. The handmade sign said: ORIGINAL "TURDY-BIRDIES."

Tacho pulled back onto the freeway and rolled into the brown glare of the flat horizon.

Quinter, Voda, Ogallah, Hays. They were weeping with boredom and despair. Grain elevators looked like 170-story science fiction towers from ten miles away. Salina.

"Otra vez Salina," Tacho complained. "Weren't we just in Salina?"

Before them, a vast smear of smoke. Not smoke. Birds. Aloft. Suddenly, as one, they turned, vanishing in the air like the louvers of God's own opening window blinds. Appeared. Vanished. Appeared. Swept away to stubbled fields.

They clattered to a stop in Topeka. They felt like they had sandpaper in their shorts, old glue in their mouths. They rented a room in a motel run by a Punjabi family. They signed in as Mr. P. Villa and Mrs. S. Hayek. They avoided the eyes of strangers. They sat next to a black family at an early showing of a three-dollar movie about a woman named Madea. They walked back to the motel, and Tacho went next door to buy a sack of tacos. Nayeli found crumpled soiled tissues under her bed.

"Another day in paradise," Tacho said.

They passed through Kansas City, crossed the state line, and were alarmed to find themselves in Kansas City. Tacho thought he'd driven in a circle.

They shot out the far side and banged along, heading east. Missouri, at least, offered some hills.

The car's engine was now whining as well as clanging. Tacho felt queasy. "This trip," Tacho said. "Forgive me, but it's torture."

"I'm sorry."

Nayeli felt weepy.

Oh, spare me the waterworks, Tacho thought, surreptitiously wiping a tear from his own eye. They were far from anything they knew. They were far from any world they could understand. They were naked. *You did this to me.*

They came in view of Saint Louis. The arch terrified them. It looked like an alien force, a terrible metal presence looming over the panicked mortals.

Tacho stared at it as they approached.

Finally, he said, "Wow. Look at the size of that arch. That must be McDonald's World Headquarters."

He had to stop for the Mississippi. They walked around the base of the arch, frightened of it as if it were a giant robot from a bad monster movie. Rangers in their Smokey Bear hats looked like Border Patrol agents. Families ate funnel cakes. "Fat churros?" Nayeli asked.

They stood at the edge of the Mississippi and beheld its deceptively slow-looking brown water, the scaly old boat across the river, the stained cement walls of the banks, the grinding train on the far side. A single duck muscled futilely against the current, gave up with a squawk, turned around, and shot downstream.

Tacho felt sharp pinpricks in his gut, said nothing. But he told Nayeli, when she bent down to a drinking fountain, "Don't drink the water."

He could already tell he was in for a bout of Washington's Revenge.

Pepto-Bismol, 7 Up, Subway sandwiches, and yogurt in a motel somewhere near Vandalia, Illinois. The Subway guy had alarmed Tacho by confiding in him, "We got black UFOs down here a mile wide."

"Tomorrow's the day," Tacho told Nayeli as they went to bed.

He threw up his sandwich at midnight.

Chapter Thirty-three

Tacho had a fever by the time they got to 57 North. His fingers felt like sausages, and his head felt swollen. He shivered. He stopped at gas station toilets and rest areas and was amazed he still had anything left in him. Ma Johnston's minivan, too, was sick. It screeched, banged, and clacked as they drove. When he shut off the engine, it fumed. And when he went to start it again, it coughed and groaned. "I wish you had a license," he said.

"Almost there, Tachito," Nayeli cooed. "Almost there. I'll put you in bed as soon as we get there. Don't worry. My father will take care of everything."

She kept up a stream of heroic and uplifting chatter, but all he did was moan. Tacho didn't believe any of it. He didn't believe her father was even in Kankakee. They were fools, on a fool's errand. They had been fools to ever leave Tres Camarones. And they had joined all the other unwanted fools hiding in the long shadows of the United States. He had thought he was going to Beverly Hills, and here he was in Cow Pie Pradera. *Turdy-Birdies,* he thought.

Neoga. Mattoon. What kinds of names were these? Arcola.

He roused himself to say: "¿Arcola? Me arde la cola."

She laughed. "¡Ay, Tacho!"

He had told her his ass was burning.

Champaign. Rantoul. Freight rail lines ran along their left side the whole way. The sidetracked train cars looked to Nayeli like washed-up boats on the edge of a sea. Abandoned semitrailers stood at angles on the edges and berms of vast dead farms. The dark fields ran away from them until they vanished in the violent skies knotting up and relentlessly stalking toward them from Iowa and Nebraska.

Paxton. Onarga. Chebanse.

"¡Chingado!" Tacho cried. "¡Ya, pues! Where is this Kankakee, for God's sake? I'm through!"

"Soon, Tachito. You're doing great. Soon, you'll see."

And suddenly, they were crossing the Kankakee River.

"Look!" she yelled. "I told you! I told you! It's *beautiful!*"

"The Baluarte River back home," he sniffed, "is better than this."

Nayeli's father was near—she could feel him. He would be shocked to see her. He might be angry. But she knew him—knew his good heart. He would be so moved by her brave journey to find him, to save her home. His features would soften and his face would break into a smile, and he would embrace her.

Beyond the river, they saw the KANKAKEE turnoff on the right.

Tacho took in the sight in a swoon of fever. His ears burned. His eyes felt like two coals in his skull. He didn't trust what he was seeing. He didn't trust that he wasn't dreaming. He stopped at a stop sign and stared at the building in front of them.

"Is that there or not?" he muttered.

"Yes," she said. "It's a sign from heaven."

A statue of a huge hand on the roof of the building clutched a globe and held it up to the sky.

"We have been in God's hand the whole time." Nayeli smiled.

To Tacho, it looked like the poster for a monster movie at the Cine Pedro Infante.

He turned left.

"Get ready, morra," he said. "You're going to get what you asked for."

"I am ready!" she replied.

The minivan thumped as if Tacho were running over a hundred rabbits. They stared out the windows at sad East Kankakee. Old buildings and old motels. They saw an amazing little Victorian shed that had been some kind of ice cream parlor in its heyday and had now been turned into a Mexican taco stand. El Gallito.

"Menudo," Nayeli noted.

Tacho bit back on his rising bile.

They passed a carnicería.

"Meat!" she exclaimed, like an insane tour guide of trivial destinations. "And they sell fruit and vegetables. In Spanish! Kankakee has Mexicans! You see?"

"Oh, shut up," Tacho heard himself saying.

Suddenly, they were in a nice downtown. Red brick and a steely bright building. And out the other side. Strip malls. Gas stations. A building as pink as Tacho's Pepto. Farther out, they saw an upended bathtub half-buried in a yard and spray-painted silver. A statue of Jesus stood inside it, blessing the dog poo in the yard.

"Tijuana, USA," Tacho said.

They managed a U-turn, and they banged back through the nice part of town and limped to a motel near the meat market as the engine seemed to come undone and fall apart—great billows of acrid steam cloaked them completely from sight.

"Nayeli," Tacho said, "you have killed me."

They were in room 17, on the ground floor. The speeding Iowa rainstorm overtook them there and unzipped the sky. Great crashes of thunder shook the loose glass in the windows. The wind was ancient and cold. Tacho was so embarrassed by his diarrhea that he forced Nayeli to stand outside the motel room when he went to the toilet. She wore the fisherman's Steamboat sweatshirt and clutched herself, watching the muddy water run down the motel's drive and flood the street. Black men ran down the opposite sidewalk, grimly holding newspapers over their heads. Cars threw up fans of brown water, made desolate hissing noises on the wet blacktop. She could see houses behind the meat market. An orange plastic child's wagon lay on its side in the mud. She shivered.

When Tacho came off the toilet, he fell into bed and slept. He was hot—she wet a washcloth and put it on his forehead. He belched the odor of rotten eggs. She cracked the door to let in fresh storm air.

"I'm sorry," he said. "I let you down."

"No, you didn't!" she said. "Tachito! Here we are!"

"But I don't think...I think I need to stay in bed."

"That's all right. I should go find him alone."

"Really? You're not mad?"

But he was asleep again before she could reassure him.

In the lobby, she broke one of Tacho's bills and used the change to buy him a 7 Up from the machine. She bought herself a Dr Pepper and some peanut butter crackers. Not much of a supper, but better than nothing. The rain was still pelting the street. The girl behind the desk took a few minutes out of her Sudoku fix and explained to Nayeli that she could make long-distance phone calls from her room. "Dial nine first," she said.

Nayeli hurried along the side of the motel with her sodas.

Tacho was snoring.

Nayeli ate her crackers, drank her soda. She brewed some motel coffee in the little electric pot on the bathroom counter. She took out her father's postcard. Through it all, she had carried it, folded in half, in her back pocket. She opened it carefully, because it wanted to tear apart. The crease through the picture was white, and the paranoid old turkey now seemed to have a lightning bolt coming down beside it. Nayeli saw this as a prophecy. She wanted to ask Tacho: Is there not lightning striking right now? But she didn't wake him.

She took a shower. The shampoo came in a small foil envelope. She washed her underpants with the tiny soap bar under the steaming cascade of American water. It was different, she had noticed. Mexican water was weaker and had a distinct primordial scent. American water didn't feel, well, it didn't feel as *watery* to her as Mexican water.

Nayeli hung her panties on the towel rack and pulled on her other pair and the big sweatshirt and wrapped her head in a threadbare towel. Tacho had kicked off his blanket. She tucked him back in and kissed his forehead. He was awake enough to mutter, "I don't care what you do, you wench—I'm not having sex with you."

She hopped into her own bed and watched the flashes of lightning through the window. She pulled the phone toward her and hesitated. She had Irma's hotel number written on a piece of paper she had smoothed out beside her father's postcard.

"¿Bueno?" Irma said.

"¿Tía?"

"¿Sí?"

"Tía, it's Nayeli."

"Oh! My beautiful girl! How goes the quest?"

"Ay, Tía."

"No crying!"

"I'm not crying."

"That's my girl." A pause. "And how is my other little girl?"

"What other—you mean Tacho? That's mean."

"I'm just being funny."

"He is my hero."

Chastised, Irma sucked her teeth.

"How are things?" Nayeli asked.

"Oh, well. I have my problems, dear girl. Don't think it's all just fun and games."

"What's wrong?

"Well! It's Yolo. I swear. She says she's not going home with the rest of us."

"What!"

"The fool says she is going to stay in Los Yunaites with Matt."

Small rings of shock ran down Nayeli's entire spine.

"What does Matt say?" she gasped.

"Matt! Ha! He came creeping around here, and he confessed he doesn't want Yolo to stay!"

Nayeli jerked with the news.

"What—what did you tell him?"

"I told him to grow some balls and deal with it himself. It's hard enough being everybody else's aunt Irma. I'm not about to start being his!"

"I can't believe it, Tía."

"Your turn," Irma said. "Talk."

She waited to hear what Nayeli had to report.

"We are in KANKAKEE, ILLINOIS. Tacho is sick, so I'm going out alone to find my father."

"It's a great thing you have done, Nayeli."

"Is it?"

Irma was uncharacteristically pensive.

"Did you get the men?" Nayeli asked.

"Of course!"

"Good, Tía. I'm glad."

Tacho rolled over and mumbled, "Vieja fea." Nayeli didn't know if he was asleep or not. She smiled.

"There were many men," La Osa said.

"How many?"

"Seventy."

"What!"

"That was before we closed the doors." Irma chuckled. "Who knows how many we turned away."

"So you found all seven?"

"Well..." Irma turned away from the phone and said something. Nayeli heard the deeper tones of a man's voice but not the words. She stifled a scandalized laugh. *Chava Chavarín was in Irma's room!* "Well, anyway. We did not accept seventy men. We were, if you will recall, only looking for four more."

"Yes."

"So, after long consideration, we took twenty-seven."

Nayeli shouted, "What!"

"I have standards, you know!" Irma snapped. "By God, I wasn't going to take all seventy traitors back home!"

"Tía. Tía. We were only looking for seven. Total."

"Yes, well. Easy for you to say! I had all those men here, begging for mercy." Nayeli heard Irma light a cigarette and take a long pull. She coughed. "And all the while this fool Chavarín was falling for every hard-luck story! Chingado, you think *every* Mexican doesn't have a hard-luck story? If we had Yul Brynner, well all right, perhaps seven men could rid the town of bandidos. But with these weaklings? Twenty-seven of these cowards will barely do the job."

"But...how are we going to get twenty-seven men home?"

"I don't know, dear. That's your problem. I'm flying home with good old Ronald Colman here." Rustling. Giggles. Irma's love play.

It made Nayeli a little queasy. "That Brujo devil worshipper has a truck. Matt will let us use the minivan."

"We broke it."

Irma unleashed several of her time-tested epithets.

Nayeli reported on the journey and the breakdown.

"Well," Irma complained, "so much for that! Take a bus here, unless your good-for-nothing father drives you back. We'll round up something for the seven. The other twenty cabrones can find their own goddamned way to Tres Camarones! Show some mettle! Oh, by the way, I called my comadre Carmelita Tovar in Tecuala. She's flying up here next week to interview the rest of the seventy."

"Excuse me?"

"You started something, m'ija! I am trying to figure out how to organize the women to send expeditions to Chicago and Los Angeles. Drag some of these fools back where they belong." A male mumble in the background. "Yes, dear. Chava says I will become president of Mexico on a repatriation ticket!"

Nayeli grimaced: there was a long smooch.

They made up some chatter. Everyone was all right—Vampi was in love; Yolo was in love; Atómiko was still a complete, indefensible idiot (said fondly); Nayeli's mother was doing well and had recently screened a Godzilla film festival to great local acclaim.

"I am so tired," Nayeli finally confessed.

"Don't despair," Irma told her. "You changed the world."

"I did nothing, Tía."

"Look," Irma said. Nayeli heard her order Chava out of the room. Shuffling. Then: "Are you still there? Good. Look—you did something I could never do. You came here on a mission. Why do you think I allowed you to come? Eh? Why? Because you are the future. You had to be tested. And you passed."

Nayeli said, "I am not strong like you."

"Let me tell you something, Nayeli," Irma replied. "And I will deny ever having said this. You are stronger than I'll ever be. Yes, I am Irma! Yes, I am La Osa! Yes, I am the women's bowling champion of Sinaloa! But I am only that person in my village. Do you see?"

Nayeli was silent.

"I am a coward, Nayeli. I can't be a hero in the big world—it scares me. Exhausts me. I belong in Tres Camarones. They need Tía Irma to run things. But the rest of the world? Ay...Why do you think I needed you to be the warrior? Now, go get your father and kick his ass."

She hung up.

In the dark, Tacho said, "Nayeli? I want to go home."

She sat beside him and put the washcloth on his forehead.

"Tachito-Machito, mi flor," she cooed. "What about Hollywood? What about Beberly Hills?"

He shook his head under her hand.

"Sweetheart," he said. "People like us? We don't marry Johnny Depp."

She sat with him until he fell asleep.

Chapter Thirty-four

In the morning, Nayeli tucked Tacho in and put the Do Not Disturb sign on the knob. She wore her running shoes and the big sweatshirt. High orange-and-black clouds scuttled toward Indiana. She tucked her postcard back into her pocket. She was utterly on her own.

She walked down to El Gallito and tapped on the window.

"Hey," the guy inside said, "this is a drive-through. You'll get run over."

"Hola," she said.

"Quiubo," he replied, nodding once. "Want a taco?"

"I'm looking for my father," she said.

"Do you live here?"

"No, I came from Sinaloa."

"Ah." He stirred a pot of beans. Made her a burrito with cheese.

"What do I owe you?" she asked as he handed it out to her.

"One smile, Sinaloa."

She smiled like the sunrise.

"I am Nayeli."

"What's your jefito's name?"

"Pepe Cervantes."

"Don't know him."

"He came here a few years ago."

"I probably feed him. But I don't ask anybody their names. You know."

A car pulled up on the other side of the shack.

"I got work," he said. "Try the library."

"The library?"

"It's the big silver building downtown. They help everybody."

"But...I'm, we're..."

He laughed.

"This is Kankakee, morra! They like Mexicans here!"

She marched. Court Street was long and old. Behind her, the Marycrest Lanes bowling alley: she idly imagined La Osa decimating opponents there. City Housing Authority. Youth for Christ City Life. Aunt Martha's Youth Service Center. Trendz Beauty. King Middle School. She was shocked at how out of shape she was: her feet and legs hurt. Back home, she would have run this as a warm-up for a game.

"I am getting old," she said out loud.

When she got downtown, she approached the big silver monolith with caution. She followed the sidewalk down a hill and went to the lower doors of the library. She had never entered such a beautiful building before. Come to think of it, she had never been in a public library, either. A small group of Mexican kids sat on the bench outside, murmuring and laughing. She nodded to them and stepped through the glass doors.

So many books!

She stood there, looking around. Tables with computers. Elevators. A huge desk with white people to her right. She felt stupid and rural. She started to walk back out but was embarrassed to walk past the Mexican kids again. She went back in and sat on a soft chair and looked at the brightly lit room.

One of the white men behind the big counter saw her and went to a slender white woman and whispered in her ear. She looked up at Nayeli. She had short brownish hair and wore glasses. Nayeli liked the big hoops in her ears. Expecting a frown, Nayeli ducked her head. But the woman smiled when she looked back up. Nayeli smiled. The woman nodded her head and went back to her task.

Nayeli searched all the faces. She didn't recognize anybody. She wondered if she would know her father now if she saw him. Had he changed?

She sat down at the computer tables and clicked on the Internet. She started trolling. She Googled Tres Camarones.

"Do you need help?" a voice said.

Nayeli looked up. It was the smiling woman. Her name tag said: MARY-JO.

"¿Habla español?" Nayeli asked.

Mary-Jo laughed and held her fingers in the air, forming a li'l pinch.

"¡Muy poco!" she said.

Nayeli laughed.

"I look for my father," she said in English.

The young man from the desk walked by and said, "Miss Mary-Jo runs this city!" Mary-Jo waved him away. "You're in good hands," he called.

"Are you the . . . mayor?" Nayeli asked.

Mary-Jo laughed again, shook her head.

"My aunt is mayor," Nayeli explained, "in my town."

"Where's that?"

"Sinaloa."

Mary-Jo put a finger to her chin, thought.

"Come with me," she said.

Nayeli matched her brisk pace as they went behind the desk. She felt self-conscious, like everybody was watching her. But of course no one even looked.

Mary-Jo tapped on a chair back with her fingertips. Nayeli sat.

"We have some Sinaloans in town, I think. Working in the greenhouses. But most of your paisanos come from Guanajuato."

She grabbed a phone.

"Our sister city."

"Really?"

"Oh, yes."

Mary-Jo punched in some numbers.

"I'll call the police."

Nayeli started to jump up, but Mary-Jo took her wrist.

"Sit," she said. "Don't worry."

She smiled into the phone.

"Hi. It's me. Yeah, I always need something. Librarians never rest, didn't you know that? Can you run over here for a sec? I'll give you a cookie. Oh, good! Bye!" She smiled at Nayeli. "How about you?" she asked. "Would you like a cookie?"

Baffled, Nayeli accepted a vast sugar cookie and a pink napkin.

After a few minutes, a huge Mexican American detective walked in. He wore a suit, but Nayeli could see the cuffs on his belt. He had a badge on his jacket.

Mary-Jo said, "Nayeli's looking for her dad. From Sinaloa."

"Cervantes," Nayeli said. "Pepe."

"You come all the way from Sinaloa?" the cop asked.

"Excuse?" Nayeli asked.

"¿Viniste desde Sinaloa?"

"Sí."

He whistled.

"That's a long trip."

He got on Mary-Jo's phone and made several calls. Mary-Jo smiled at Nayeli. "I love Mexico," she said. "It's such a fascinating country!"

"Yes," Nayeli managed to say.

Mary-Jo patted her arm.

"Mexicanos," she said in accented Spanish, "son nuestros hermanos. En Kankakee—todos son bienvenidos." She beamed. So did Nayeli.

The cop dialed around for half an hour, jotting notes. He finally hung up the phone. Looked at his notebook.

"There's a gentleman," he said, "on the north end, around the corner from Donna's. Might be our man."

"Donna's is our pink building," Mary-Jo said. "It's quite a sight."

"Yes, I saw. Pepto-Bismol!"

The librarian and the cop burst out laughing.

He jotted down the address on a sticky note.

"Got a car?"

"No."

"Oh," Mary-Jo said. "I never went for lunch. Why don't I take her myself."

"Are you sure? I can take her."

"No, no. I'll be glad to do it."

"I don't mind."

"No, that's all right."

They were actually arguing about doing something nice for Nayeli. She loved KANKAKEE, ILLINOIS. It was the strangest place she had ever been.

It's not far," Mary-Jo said as they got into her car. "Just take a minute."

They pulled out of the lot and turned up the hill and beat it through the yellow light at the intersection.

"Our town," Mary-Jo said, "has seen some hard times. But it's a wonderful place. We're bringing it back."

They drove through the northern end of town, past the bathtub Jesus, to a small street near Donna's pink emporium.

"This is the street," Mary-Jo said. She slowed to make the turn, stopped at the stop sign.

"Is OK. I walk from here."

"Oh no, dear. I couldn't just drop you off."

"Yes, please. I must go. Sola. Yes? Is my father. Ha pasado mucho tiempo, y usted sabe que es difícil para mi."

Mary-Jo looked at her. She nodded. She gave Nayeli a small hug.

"Good luck," she said.

Nayeli got out.

"Gracias," she said, unable to say more.

Miss Mary-Jo waved her fingers and grinned and spun a quick U-turn and drove back into town. Nayeli stood and watched her go. She had the address in her hand. She breathed deeply and turned and started to walk.

She squinted at the doors of the little houses. Some of the people here had statues of geese in their yards, and they had dressed these geese in long skirts and bonnets, or in overalls. Nayeli didn't understand what the goose thing was all about. She apparently missed the address, too, because she ended up at a dead end. A barrier ran between two cottonwoods, and beyond it, a little green tractor sliced the mud of a field into curls of deep chocolate, as if God's own birthday cake were on the platter. Beyond the field, old highway 57 carried its endless stream of big trucks. Maybe she'd have a big black chocolate cake with her father when they celebrated.

She turned back and started walking the other way, watching for the number.

Was he there? Did he share a house with other men? Was he well? Surely he would laugh when he saw her. He would hurry to her and lift her in the air and spin around like he did when she was small. He would smell of Old Spice and his whiskers would prickle her face and she would cry, *¡Papá!*

What would she tell him? Where would she begin? With Irma's election? With Yul Brynner? She laughed out loud. *¡Ay, Tía Irma! Yul Brynner!* She put her hand over her mouth — she didn't want people thinking she was a madwoman. She snorted.

The trip, the Border Patrol, the dump... it had all been worth it. Just to take her father home. Just to see her mother's face. She bounced on her sore feet.

She passed the cross street and walked on. A big new pickup stopped behind her at the cross and made a left turn. She could hear the music beating from the cab as it drove up behind her then passed slowly. Some accordion banda music. Crazy norteño cowboy music.

The truck was a fat-bottom Dodge, electric blue. It had four wheels in back, and a bright silver toolbox in the bed. Twin aerials waved in the air. On one, the US flag, and on the other, the Mexican flag. Nayeli laughed again: in the darkened back window of the cab, there was a white cartoon of a bad boy peeing.

The big truck banged up into a driveway and shut down. The music snapped off. The door opened and a pudgy woman in yellow stretch pants crawled out of the passenger's side. She reached into the back — there were more seats back there. She unbuckled a toddler from a car seat and hefted him onto her hip. Nayeli could hear her voice but not what she was saying. She hurried, hoping to ask her if she knew Papá.

The driver got out on his side. He slammed the door and came around to the woman's side. He wore a straw cowboy hat and boots and tight jeans. Nayeli stopped where she was.

Don Pepe.

"¿Papá?" she murmured.

He had gotten fatter. His butt was round and his belly hung over his big belt buckle. He threw his arm around the woman and hugged her, turned her toward the house. He unlocked the door as Nayeli stared. He took off his hat and laughed at something the woman said and accepted a kiss on the mouth from her and smacked her bottom as she yelped and skipped inside. He briefly scanned the neighborhood—his eyes passed right over Nayeli—before stepping inside and slamming the door.

The street was silent. Not many birds at all, and the ones that were there weren't singing, just making desolate little cheeping noises. She could hear the tractor, of course. She could hear the engine of the big pickup truck ticking as it cooled.

And then, all she could hear was the sound of her soles and her breathing as she sprinted away.

Nayeli ran to the end of the block, to the barrier that ended the street. She jumped over it and ran out into the plowed field. The man on the tractor ignored her, as if he saw women in the rows every day. She shook, she gasped, she shouted as loud as she could.

"FATHER!" she wailed.

Over and over.

There were no words to begin to describe what she felt.

After an hour, she stepped back over the barrier. She walked down the street. She turned up Don Pepe's driveway. She could hear the baby inside, crying. She reached into her back pocket, withdrew the postcard. She smoothed it carefully. She tucked it under his windshield wiper. Nayeli walked away.

Chapter Thirty-five

———

The van was dead. They abandoned it in the parking lot. Miss Mary-Jo drove them to the Trailways station.

They pulled out of the lot and drove south, across the river.

"You would have never found the station," said Mary-Jo.

"Gracias," Nayeli replied.

A sign promised: TUESDAYS TACO NIGHT.

They beheld a small trailer park. A building offered SMOKED FISH. They drove toward the Economy Inn.

"What are you going to tell your mother?" Mary-Jo asked. "About your dad?"

"Nothing. He was gone."

WELCOME TO YOUR HOME ON THE ROAD.

"I am so sorry," Mary-Jo said.

SCHLITZ. THE CAPTAIN'S PUB. BUDWEISER.

"Here we are."

She followed them into the lobby. It doubled as the bus station.

Three men turned and stared. Ancient paneling. Cement steps. The smell of old men and old smoke and old breath.

"How do," the man at the counter said.

"Two," said Mary-Jo.

"Right. Where to?"

"Where are you going?" she asked.

"San Diego."

"Right-o."

They paid for the tickets.

On the television, CNN was showing a bleached and jumpy film of scores of Mexicans jumping over a fence and racing into Arizona. The three of them stood there, transfixed. The ticket seller turned and blushed. He snapped off the TV. He smiled at them in embarrassment. His teeth were brown and yellow.

Nayeli loved him.

The man said, "Sorry."

Tacho was studying the big route map on the wall. Their bus went right on down through Saint Louis. KC.

"Please," he said. "Not again."

The bus was coming. It rolled their way from the highway, made a sharp left into the lot. Pebbles and dirt clods crunched under its heavy tires. It groaned and hissed. The door opened. The driver got down, shook a leg, nodded to them.

"Folks!" he said. "Be right with you. Got to point Percy at the porcelain." He winked and strode into the lobby.

The wind was blowing.

Nayeli hugged Mary-Jo.

"Adios," she whispered.

The driver came back, took their tickets, and climbed aboard. Tacho flew up the steps and vanished into the bus. Nayeli followed. Mary-Jo stood in the cold wind, waving farewell.

The door closed. The bus burped and shuddered and rolled out of the lot. It turned right as the rain started to fall again. Mary-Jo ran to her car. When she looked back, the bus had vanished around the bend.

Chapter Thirty-six

Calexico.

Arnie Davis was back from San Diego, and his new uniform was roasting him. He was an agent, still, this week of yet another word-salad agency, the—what was it this time? The Customs and Border Enforcement, or the CBP or was it CPB? Whatevs, dawg. The government keeping itself busy.

He pulled his steaming shirt away from his chest. Not for the first time, he wondered why, if the guys invariably had to patrol in hot places, did the government give them forest green outfits?

Arnie didn't know what was worse, the Tijuana border canyons or this brutal stretch of I-8. Looking into tourists' cars at the roadblock. Boarding random buses, hunting for wets. Cripes. His knee was aching.

Definitely about time to cash in those chips and get to the Rockies and do some fishing.

He waved cars through. He grimaced. A Trailways bus was coming. He checked his forms, clicked the computer screen.

"Time to roust the good travelers, Bob," he said. His partner nodded. Why open your mouth to speak and lose more moisture to the burning air? He waved his hand, silently inviting Arnie to step right up and check that bus while he faded back into the shade and waited for a coed in a convertible to come along.

Arnie planted himself on the shoulder of the slow lane. Cones were set out, shunting traffic over. It was all pro forma. Dull as a factory job making left-handed widgets nine hours a day.

He flapped his hand up and down. The bus pulled over. He climbed aboard.

"Routine check," he told the riders. "How you doing?" to the driver.

"I'm good," the driver responded.

Arnie nodded to the college kid in the first row. A fat Mexican woman in the third row already had her green card out and held up. He took it and scanned it. "Ma'am," he said, handing it back.

Everybody on the bus needed a shower.

And then he got to the last row and beheld Nayeli and Tacho.

He stopped dead and stared.

"No way," he said.

"Is he calling you a buey?" Tacho whispered.

Nayeli looked up. She was too spent to smile. She was done.

"Hola," she said.

Arnie leaned on the seat back in front of her.

"What was your name?"

"Nayeli."

He shook his head.

"I'll be darned," he said. "Hey," he said to Tacho.

"Hey," Tacho said.

"You're Nayeli's Al Qaeda friend."

Tacho nodded. He weakly put out his wrists, awaiting the handcuffs.

Arnie looked around at all the heads studiously looking out the windows yet watching the events in the back of the bus.

"Small world, isn't it," said Arnie to Nayeli.

"We are in God's hands," she replied.

These kids were so bedraggled it was almost funny.

"OK," Arnie said.

He crooked his finger at them.

"Vámonos," he said.

Embarrassed, they trudged down the aisle, being stared at by the other travelers. The driver got their little bags out for them. He didn't make eye contact. They stood and watched the bus drive away.

Arnie opened his truck's rear gate.

"In," he said.

They climbed in.

He slammed it.

"Bob," he called over to the booth. "Two clients. Taking 'em in."

Bob nodded.

"Groovy," he said. He flashed Arnie a peace sign. Those migra agents. They were comical.

Arnie pulled onto the freeway. Turned up the AC.

"You OK back there?" he called.

"Sí."

He watched Nayeli in the rearview.

"Where's that smile of yours?" he said.

"Gone."

He drove a little farther.

"Weren't you looking for your father?" he said.

"Sí."

"What happened?"

"I found him."

"Oh."

The radio squawked.

"Not so good, huh?"

"Not so good."

Arnie pulled over. Put on his emergency blinkers.

"You told me a crazy story, I remember. You were going to smuggle wets back into Mex. Isn't that right?"

They both nodded.

"I don't see anybody," he said.

"In San Diego," Nayeli explained. "Twenty-seven."

"Bullshit!"

"Is true," Tacho said.

"No!"

Nayeli was so tired.

"Twenty-seven men waiting for me in San Diego. We go back to Sinaloa."

Arnie laughed.

He sat there looking out at the desert.

"You thirsty?" he asked.

"Oh, yes."

He got his thermal jug. He stepped out, slammed the door. Walked around. Opened the rear gate.

"Don't try anything stupid," he said.

He handed them the jug. They gulped the cold water.

"Gracias," they said.

Arnie sat in the open gate, one foot on the ground.

"Run this story by me one more time."

Nayeli started with Don Pepe. The bandidos. The election. The journey. (She left out the tunnel from her story.)

He kept shaking his head.

Finally, he said, "You're not lying, are you?"

"No."

"Is she lying to me?"

Tacho said, "No."

It was the darnedest thing Arnie had ever heard.

He hung his head and thought for a few minutes.

He sighed. Rubbed his face. They were never going to make it through the gauntlet. They'd be caught and reprocessed.

F-you money, he thought.

What could they do to him?

"I like you kids," he said. "I really do."

He slammed the gate shut. Went back to his seat, radioed in to the station. Tacho and Nayeli didn't understand the English or the migra codes. He eased back onto the freeway, pulled a U-turn, and drove them in the opposite direction. He got off the road and took them to a small house in a subdivision of Yuma.

He cooked them some eggs and tortillas.

Then, when night fell, he put them back in his truck, and he drove them west, never stopping until they hit San Diego.

Epilogue

The bad men had parked their trucks at the major corners of the village. Black Cherokees and Tahoes with dark windows. They simply sat, idling, throbbing with music. Grandmothers kept their daughters in their houses. Irma, home from the Yunaites, had to send Chava and García-García to Mazatlán for their own protection from the bandidos. But she promised the women of Tres Camarones that change would soon come.

Sensei Grey taught two new judo classes to those women who were sick of waiting for men to come.

The pigs and the donkeys spent their nights engineering daring escapes from their pens. Dogs and chickens refused to let the mornings be silent. Huge coconut crabs wandered into town from the estuaries and climbed the coconut palms to snip the cocos free. They dropped to the ground and split with a sound like a single horse's hoof on a cobble. The big crabs squatted over the brilliant white meat inside the broken shells and fed themselves with both claws, looking smug.

A Cherokee sat dark as night in front of La Mano Caída, but the morning rose in spite of it, and the day ignored it. Mockingbirds insulted crows from every phone line, and hummingbirds were indistinguishable from the immense black bees that trundled down from the slopes of El Yauco to plunder the red hibiscus and trumpet vines. The skiffs with bundles covered in blue tarps had begun to come ashore; sullen men who spared no friendly word to the women or the children loaded and unloaded flatbed trucks.

The day grew hot almost immediately.

Women were already making tortillas at the market. Women set out stacks of hard cheese and bowls of dripping-wet cheese. Women with blue tin pots came in from the outskirts to sell their fresh milk. Other women stood in line to buy two eggs, three potatoes, a bolillo roll or two, a small jar of marmalade. They remained silent. They kept their heads bowed. The only music came from the black SUVs.

Crazy Pepino was at work early. He rode his bike into the square as the sun rose every day. He swept the front steps of the Cine Pedro Infante. He cleaned the glass door with a squeegee. They were showing *Taras Bulba* and *The King and I* later that night. The window of a Tahoe rolled down, and a lit cigarette flew out and pinged off his head. Laughter.

When he was done with the theater, he rode his bike to La Mano Caída. It was locked tight. Pepino swept the porch. Checked the locks. Checked the windows.

When he was done, looking to make sure nobody was watching, he sneaked past the Cherokee with its gunmen in the street, and he swung around the side and climbed the building. He used the rainspout and the old water tank to get halfway up. From there, he could grab the roof and boost himself. He did this every morning, without fail.

He sat on the tin until it grew too hot to bear. He looked east. He watched through the trees. From the roof, he could see a small elbow of the road from the highway. The road to Mazatlán, where he had never been. It was all trees in that direction. All willows and pecans and mangos and hibiscus. Bamboo and banana and sugarcane.

Pepino liked it on the roof. He liked the breeze, except when it came from the river and stank of rot and mud. And he liked watching the wild parrots fly to the ruins of the church. He liked the butterflies and the occasional peek he caught through Yvette García's window of her unbearable hotness in her nightgown. The bandidos could not smack him or burn him with cigarettes up here.

But mostly, Pepino liked to watch the road.

Old women below scolded him: "Pepino, you maniac. Get off Tacho's roof!" But he was deeply into his mischief and ignored them. They gestured at the terrible Jeep, warning with their chin juts and their shrugs: *They will kill you.*

Those women were alarmed when they heard him shouting.

They hurried to the front of the shop and squinted up. Was he stung by a scorpion? A bee? Nobody knew. Why was he shouting? Wasps, some said—it had to be wasps. The doors of the Cherokee opened, and the bandidos peered up at him. They were just skinny punks with scrawny necks and bad expressions on their faces. They craned around, trying to see.

Pepino came to the edge of the roof and slapped the top of his own head.

"Pepino! Pepino!" the women cried. "Is it wasps? Are they stinging you?"

He jumped up and down. He yelled. He pointed east.

"Nayeli!" he yelled.

"What about Nayeli?"

"Nayeli!" He spun in a circle. "Nayeli and Tacho walking with a monkey!"

"What? What monkey?"

"Walking home. With a big monkey." He held his hands over his head. "With a big stick!"

The bandidos got out of their vehicle.

Pepino laughed and gestured down at them.

"Nayeli and Tacho," he warned, "brought an army!"

They all turned and looked at the spot where the road from the outside world passed through the dark woods and entered the village.

"Nayeli!" Pepino shouted. He pointed, he waved his arms in widening loops as if he were going to fly right off the roof. Voices came from the distance, small through the trees, and now Pepino looked like a mad conductor, bringing this choir forth.

They all heard a strange voice rising above the others. It called out:

"I am Atómiko!"

"The monkey talks!" Pepino shouted.

Now the women of Tres Camarones were smiling.

Acknowledgments

I first encountered the name Nayeli while doing relief work in the Tijuana garbage dump. It was the name of the daughter of my friend Negra. They had Tarascan roots in Michoacan, and to them Nayeli meant *flor de casa*. The flower of the household. The physical aspects of the fictional Nayeli reflect the real young woman. I hope she likes the book.

The banter and humor of the young women in this book owe a debt to our daughter Megan's circle of friends, once known as "the Sensational Seven"—some of whom were here often. As a dad, I found it deeply amusing to hear them worry, laugh, converse, and argue. I tried not to be a "creeper," as they say, but you can't help hearing things. Though none of them were models for the young women in my story, their energies were greatly with me as I wrote. Thanks especially to Elizabeth Biegalski, our cheerful neighbor. Other voices: Mariah Landeweer, Jamie Schertz, Emma DeGan.

As always, I owe a great debt to my friend Stewart O'Nan. When the writing life grows dark, you nudge me back onto the path. Constant reader, good critic, hardest-working man in show business.

Thanks to everyone at Little, Brown—especially Geoff Shandler.

ACKNOWLEDGMENTS

I feel that my books are duets with the best editor in the business: you make me better. A lot of the public life I have enjoyed these last few years is due to the superhuman efforts of Bonnie Hannah, publicist extraordinaire. Though Bonnie has moved on—it is the nature of the job—I know what she put into motion will carry us forward.

As always, thanks to the Sandra Dijkstra Agency. Sandy, Taryn, Elise, Elizabeth, Kelly, and everyone else in the Del Mar offices: gracias and love. Special thanks to Trinity Ray and the gang at APB. To Mike Cendejas at the Pleshette Agency: the master of the movies. You are a true friend. Thank you again, and I'll meet you at Barney's.

Although everyone in this novel is fictional, anyone with roots in or near Rosario, Sinaloa, will recognize names, personalities, locations, and addresses. Tres Camarones does not exist, which doesn't mean you can't find it. The Cine Pedro Infante does exist, but of course not in Tres Camarones. Aunt Irma is not really my own Aunt Irma, and I wish there were a real Atómiko. I went with a group of young women to Tacho's house late one night around Christmas Eve to see what kinds of women's dance shoes he had for sale. Just ask my brilliant translator and cousin from Tres Camarones, Enrique Hubbard Urrea—Mexican Consul General.

Miss Mary-Jo and the good people of Kankakee do exist, as does the welcoming atmosphere of the city. Its parameters are mine, since I wrote fiction, and the details are no doubt wrong. What is not wrong is the wonder that is Kankakee's library, and the hero of the city, Mary-Jo Johnston. (Not related to the fictional Matt Johnston.) May she rest in peace. This book is offered as a small token in her honor.

And Cinderella—everything, always.

About the Author

Luis Alberto Urrea was born in Tijuana, Mexico, to an American mother and a Mexican father. His bestselling novel *The Hummingbird's Daughter,* the result of twenty years of research and writing, is a fictionalized retelling of the life of Teresa Urrea, the "Saint of Cabora."

He is the recipient of a Lannan Literary Award, an American Book Award, a Western States Book Award, a Colorado Book Award, and the National Hispanic Cultural Center Literary Award, and he has been inducted into the Latino Literary Hall of Fame.

His nonfiction works include *The Devil's Highway,* which was a finalist for the 2005 Pulitzer Prize for general nonfiction; *Across the Wire,* winner of the Christopher Award; and *By the Lake of Sleeping Children.*

His poetry has been collected in *The Best American Poetry,* and a collection of his short fiction, *Six Kinds of Sky,* won the 2002 *ForeWord Magazine* Book of the Year Award, Editor's Choice for Fiction.

He teaches creative writing at the University of Illinois in Chicago.

BACK BAY · READERS' PICK

Reading Group Guide

Into the Beautiful North

a novel

Luis Alberto Urrea

Kankakee Gets Its Groove Back

by Luis Alberto Urrea

It seems the only time Chicagoans think of the small city of Kankakee fifty-five miles to the south is when the inevitable springtime storm warnings crawl across the bottom of our televisions. If a bad storm or tornado is coming, chances are pretty good that Kankakee is in its path. A few years ago, Kankakee was listed as one of the worst cities in America. David Letterman deepened the insult by shipping the city two prefabricated gazebos to elevate the livability factor.

When a Kankakee library board member, Mary Jo Johnston, recently invited me there to do a reading, she warned me to watch for wild turkeys on the highway. I expected twenty-five retired women in a quaint brick building. It took me three drive-bys to realize that the corporate tower in the center of town was the library and that more than 325 citizens of Kankakee were waiting inside.

This reception had little to do with me—and everything to do with Kankakee, the commercial engine of a county still reeling from an economic downturn. Kankakee is pulling itself back from the brink. And it all started with the library. The one thing that the people of Kankakee know is that to rebuild a suffering city, you first have to reconstruct its culture, its community.

Mayor Donald Green, sixty-three, has lived in Kankakee his entire life. But as Mayor Green started his thirteenth year in office last month, he did so in a town where 60 to 70 percent of the homes sold now are being bought by newcomers.

You could see that reflected in the audience at the library. There were the expected bright midwestern faces. But beside them were the faces of people who'd once lived in the Chicago projects and the towns of Guanajuato State in Mexico, who were now working in Kankakee's farms, nurseries, and restaurants.

When Mayor Green realized that the overwhelming majority of Kankakee's Hispanic residents (who account for about 10 percent of its population) hailed from Guanajuato, he took a delegation of community representatives down there to forge an alliance. By creating a "sister city" relationship, Mayor Green wanted his newest citizens to understand they have a role in determining Kankakee's future.

"My philosophy is you can take this community, revitalize it, make it financially solvent," he said. "You give it all back to the people of the community because they are the ones who have the power."

When Provena Health abandoned its headquarters in the seven-story Executive Center downtown in 2002, it was the community's idea to convert it into a library. Less than a year after the renovations started, the Kankakee Public Library moved from a dilapidated 105-year-old building into a sophisticated showplace that extended over three floors.

This new public library has become the cultural hub of the city, crucial to its downtown revitalization. A new bank and a satellite university campus have already been completed, and a park with a water fountain is on its way. (Mr. Letterman's gazebos are still in use.) "It all started with the library," Mayor Green said. "I can't tell you how proud that makes our community."

Our cities are scrambling to find fresh paradigms for a new America. Maybe, just maybe, the midwesterners, librarians, and Mexicans of Kankakee, Illinois, have found theirs.

This essay originally appeared in a somewhat different form in the *New York Times* on June 11, 2006. Reprinted with permission.

A conversation with Luis Alberto Urrea

What inspired you to write Into the Beautiful North?

Three things moved me to write the book: First, I was sick of immigration/border writing. It started to feel like it was all the same, making all the same points, by all the same writers. Second was my fascination with small-town life in both Mexico and the United States and the huge cultural changes going on in both places that I never see documented. And, finally, although it is a painful book in many ways, I wanted to write something that made me laugh out loud every day.

You were born in Tijuana but moved to California when you were four. How has your background influenced your writing and the different ways in which you've written about the U.S.-Mexican border?

Paradoxically, it makes me both an insider *and* an outsider. Many writers who write about the border are tourists. People from the border often resent these carpetbaggers who show up for a week or a month and then share their wisdom with the world. At the same time, it's useful for a writer to be a half step removed from the general current because we are observers. I feel that it gives me a fresh perspective on my country—both of them.

How did the experience of writing this fictional adventure differ from that of writing your nonfiction book The Devil's Highway? *Knowing what you know about the grim realities that illegal immigrants face, was it difficult to novelize—and even satirize—such truisms?*

My experience of this situation predates *The Devil's Highway* by a lifetime. Not only is my own history intimately involved with these issues, but I spent a substantial number of years doing relief work on the border and my first books were about places like the Tijuana garbage dump. What you need to remember about people is that they are complex and complete. The garbage pickers, the "illegal aliens," the border patrol agents, the missionaries are all funny people. The point is not *that* you are poor; the point is *how* you are poor. Everybody has a story.

Speaking of which, why did you decide to inject so much humor into the book?

Because I write funny books. I didn't inject humor into the book—that sounds like you're basting a turkey. The humor always, for me, rises from the story, the characters, and the milieu. It's just the way my soul works. I have often said in interviews that I write the funniest tragedies in town.

Is the idyllic—if off the beaten track—town of Tres Camarones based on an actual place?

Yes, it is. It's based on my father's hometown, a place as mythic to me as some of the villages in Latin American novels are to those authors. It existed all through my childhood as a myth and a tall tale, thus it bonded with my DNA.

John Sturges's film The Magnificent Seven *was one of the main catalysts for the epic journey of Nayeli, Yolo, and Vampi. Has a book or a movie ever influenced you in a similarly profound way?*

Absolutely. I'm a magpie picking up shiny objects to take back to the nest all day long. I write with the ghosts of 12 authors, 13 movie directors, 14 musicians, and Steve McQueen in the room.

The Magnificent Seven *was essentially a remake of Akira Kurosawa's masterpiece* Seven Samurai, *transporting the original's story from feudal Japan to the American frontier. In turn, you reset the story in contemporary North America. How specific is location to your books—that is, could someone "remake" them in a different setting and era?*

I think my books are pretty site-specific. Like much of the literature of the American West, it is imperative to my writing that place (landscape) be a main character in the story. Certainly in something like *The Hummingbird's Daughter,* the land itself is a mystical participant. I feel that in *The Devil's Highway* and *Into the Beautiful North* as well.

Aunt Irma and Atomiko are two of the most memorable characters in the novel: both are larger than life and possess stubborn ideologies that portray them as being tougher than they really are. What inspired you to include these personalities, and are they based upon anyone you know?

Atomiko is largely the product of my own sick mind. But if you go to the source, *Seven Samurai,* you know automatically who Atomiko is. He is Toshiro Mifune, the unwashed, unloved rogue Ronin warrior. But the personality traits are based on many scruffy, indomitable border rats, not least of which is my cousin Hugo, the family's notorious pistolero. Aunt Irma? Well, I have a terrifying Aunt Irma who is the retired women's bowling champ of Mexico...you figure it out!

Why Kankakee, Illinois?

I wrote a column for the *New York Times* about Kankakee, and the reception Nayeli and Tacho get in Kankakee should at least imply why Kankakee. It's a town that moved me and it's a population that inspired me and I always hopelessly, passionately, root for the underdog.

Questions and topics for discussion

1. *Into the Beautiful North* tells the story of a small group's successful mission to save their Mexican village in its bleakest hour. What are some of the other themes that Luis Alberto Urrea unpacks along the way?

2. Language and dialect play an integral role in the novel's style. Spanish words and phonetic spellings are laced throughout, and Spanglish and slang are used on both sides of the border. What does Urrea achieve by mixing language in this way? What does such usage say about the ability of language to bridge — or fail to bridge — cultural gaps?

3. *Into the Beautiful North* is divided into two parts — Sur and Norte. References to American pop culture abound in the first half as Nayeli and her friends speak of life across the border with unwavering certainty. Where do their ideas of America come from? How does the reality of their time in the U.S. compare to their initial ideas of it? Are they surprised or disappointed?

4. Nayeli tells García-García, "Perhaps it is time for a new kind of femininity?" What does she mean? Given the homage to *The Magnificent Seven* and *Seven Samurai* in the novel, how has Urrea played with gender stereotypes?

5. *Into the Beautiful North* examines physical and psychological borders. Urrea repeatedly shows that while the physical borders can be crossed, some that are culturally defined appear unbridgeable. What are those culturally defined differences, and do you think it's possible to eradicate such invisible borders?

6. After traveling thousands of miles in search of her father, Nayeli is unable to confront him. In your opinion, does she make the right decision to heed his words at this time — "all things must pass" — or should she have approached him?

7. What do you make of the overwhelming turnout produced by Aunt Irma's interviews? Why do so many men want to return to Mexico? Does this strike you as ironic?

8. Nayeli and her friends are inspired by the movie *The Magnificent Seven,* a remake of the Japanese film *Seven Samurai.* Both films climax with the showdown between good guys and bad guys, but Urrea ends his novel before such a clash. Why do you think he did so?

9. Were you surprised to find the Mexican characters so knowledgeable about American pop culture? If you were surprised, did it change how you think about Mexico?

10. Where did your family emigrate from? Did you recognize any parallels between your family's stories and *Into the Beautiful North?*

The Hummingbird's Daughter

A novel

"A powerful tale that satisfies the soul.... Opening the pages of *The Hummingbird's Daughter* is like being swept up in a whirlwind of description so sensuous that one tastes, feels, and hears the unfolding of events." —Rudolfo Anaya, *Los Angeles Times*

"This book is an astonishment, an intoxicating place in which to become lost.... The starry, meaty story makes you remember the pleasures of *One Hundred Years of Solitude*." —Karen Long, *Cleveland Plain Dealer*

"A luminous novel.... A book of surprises and savory treasures." —Joanne Omang, *Washington Post Book World*

"A sprawling, magical work.... *The Hummingbird's Daughter* constantly amazes and delights." —Larry McCaffery, *San Diego Union-Tribune*

"Wonders never cease in this novel, an extraordinary example of what can transpire when a remarkable story is granted to a truly gifted writer." —David Hiltbrand, *Philadelphia Inquirer*

"Magisterial.... Urrea's talents seem as vast as the high desert reaches of this stirring, stunning masterwork." —Lisa Shea, *Elle*

Amigoland

A novel by Oscar Casares

"By turns hilarious and heartbreaking, this story of two feisty, aging brothers and their bumpy road trip to the past is a delightful romp. Think *Sunshine Boys* go south of the border, but funnier, much funnier, and infinitely more poignant."

—Cristina Garcia, author of *Dreaming in Cuban* and *A Handbook to Luck*

Follow Me

A novel by Joanna Scott

"Joanna Scott has here fashioned a densely stitched crazy quilt of a story.... There's a lusciousness to all the excess, an egalitarian sensibility in keeping with the most quintessential aspects of American mythology."   —Leah Hager Cohen, *New York Times Book Review*

The Cradle

A novel by Patrick Somerville

"Nothing short of a surprising treat.... *The Cradle* is a lovely, finely wrought tale of unlikely redemption. In prose that floats so lightly as to seem effortless, Somerville takes the reader on unlikely journeys that result in unexpected consequences.... The final pages of the novel are surprisingly satisfying and right."

—Robin Vidimos, *Denver Post*

Back Bay Books
Available wherever paperbacks are sold